For my Beloved Sis.

Thank you to my comma warriors and beta readers:

Sherri Meyer, Stephanie Cunningham,
Kaila Duff, Karmen Vele,
Lydia Simone, Bibiane Lybæk,
Jennifer Swan, and Brittany VanLanen

Special thanks to Robyn Renee Rudock for Shara's court gown design.

QUEEN TAKES TRIUNE

THEIR VAMPIRE QUEEN BOOK 6

JOELY SUE BURKHART

Which Triune court is calling the last Isador queen to take her rightful seat?

There are three Aima courts: one dead, one full of monsters, and one with an empty seat that's ruled by the queen of Rome. While Shara Isador loves her monsters, she has no plan to unseat a Skolos queen. Nor does she wish to work side by side with Marne Ceresa on a daily basis.

Let alone the mysterious Dauphine, who might be closer than Shara ever suspected.

Shara might be a relative baby in Aima years, and she wasn't raised in a nest. She doesn't know the ancient houses or laws that bind the queens to the high courts. But there's one thing she knows beyond a shadow of a doubt.

What this queen takes, she loves, and what she loves, she keeps for all time.

Goddess help anyone who thinks to harm one of her own in order to sway her decision.

❈ Created with Vellum

1

SHARA

I held Guillaume while he vomited.

On his knees alongside the highway, he threw up so hard that I seriously worried about him. The last Templar knight heaved beneath my hands so hard I could hear things popping deep inside him. His bond crackled with tearing, searing pain.

Blood boiled up out of his stomach and sizzled on the ground. Some of the dried grass charred, but everything was frozen enough that it didn't actually catch on fire.

Vivian's blood was burning him from the inside out.

To gain access to Heliopolis, Guillaume, Mehen, and Rik had drunk from my fiery phoenix. As Ra's own daughter, she could access any of the portals throughout Cairo. She'd made that sacrifice willingly for me, despite a horrible past that made sharing blood with men difficult.

I'd never thought about what her blood would do to my headless knight—who had told me from the beginning that he could only drink queens' blood.

:I'm fine, my queen.: Even in his bond, his voice sounded strained and raw, his vocal chords blasted by flames. *:As soon as I get all of her blood out of me, I'll start to heal.:*

"It's kind of like eating a greasy chili dog," Daire said. I looked up at him, not sure what that had to do with anything. My warcat winked with an adorable dimple in his cheek. "It burns coming out, just like it burned going down."

Guillaume groaned out a laugh and wiped his lips with the back of his hand. "Terrible, but true."

I cupped his cheeks and dipped my bond through him. His esophagus and stomach were a ruined mess, like he'd chugged a couple of vats of acid. Tears burned my eyes. "Why didn't you remind me that you can't drink any blood but mine?"

He smiled and shook his head gently beneath my hands. "I *can* drink other blood, it's just not going to stay down and does nothing for my strength. I did what was necessary. The price was worth it."

Already his voice sounded better, though I could feel the pain radiating in his bond. My stoic knight had endured years of torture in a medieval prison. They'd even...

Guilt bubbled up in my stomach. I almost had to whirl away so I could throw up beside him.

They'd even chopped off his head.

So had I.

The horror of what I'd done to my beloved knight twisted my stomach. I buried my face against his throat and squeezed my arms around him. He'd gladly and willingly allowed me to kill him, even if that meant he couldn't come back.

Lying in my arms as I drained his blood and then reached for the guard's sword, G had fucking *smiled* at me.

Dying. If that was what it took for me to succeed in our plan.

"Always," he whispered, wrapping his arms around me.

My rat wriggled slightly against my midsection, a small reminder that I shouldn't squash her. Her favorite place to ride around with me was tucked inside my coat. A constant, warm little body. I'd already grown attached to her. She wasn't a pet exactly, nor a Blood, but holding her made me feel better. Usually.

I didn't know what to say to Guillaume. I could still feel the weight of that sword in my hand as it cut through his tendons and spine to cleanly decapitate him. I'd done it, even if that meant I killed him forever. I had no choice.

Not if I wanted to kill Ra.

Maybe a better queen would have allowed herself to be defeated to spare her Blood. It would have been the less selfish thing to do.

G seized my chin and jerked my face up to his. His eyes glittered dangerously in the moonlight. "You are the best and most honorable queen I have ever seen in all my centuries. If you had allowed yourself to be taken by Ra, then we *all* would have died. Hundreds of lives would have been at stake just between our Aima houses. There's no telling how many more Aima queens would have fallen to Ra with your power at his control, or what he'd do to the humans if he achieved his goal. He would have brought Heliopolis to our earthly plane and it would have been worse than hell on earth. You stopped that, as only you could."

It always surprised me where my Blood's lines were. Usually, none of them would touch me unless invited. Guillaume wouldn't even ask me to feed him, even though my blood would heal the internal burns quicker than he could heal himself. Yet now he squeezed my chin so hard that my face throbbed, because I had less than stellar thoughts about myself.

"Your life is all." Rik laid his palm on my shoulder, his grip just as firm as Guillaume's. "Whatever you need to do to stay alive is the right choice. Every single time."

"But I don't want to cross the line. What's to stop me from becoming another Marne Ceresa?"

Guillaume spat another mouthful of blood on the ground. "You could never be like her. Or Desideria for that matter. Love drives your actions, not ambition or greed for power. That's your strength, and why we love you so much, but it's also your weakness. Your only failing is the softness of your heart. A queen will at times need to act coldly and without compassion to protect her nest."

"I killed you," I whispered softly, shivering at the memory. I wasn't cold, but he tucked me closer to him and Rik dropped down behind me to press against my back.

Normally being sandwiched between two of my Blood was more than enough to turn my thoughts from worry or fear to something more carnal. But this time, my stomach still bubbled with guilt, my teeth chattered, and I felt...

Ashamed. And worse, afraid that I would let them down. That I would let *myself* down.

"Never," Rik retorted against my ear. "I have no doubt or fear in that regard, Shara."

He only rarely used my given name, and the soft, tender way he said it made my eyes fill with tears. Such steadfast love and devotion. They were the most honorable men I'd ever known.

Which made what I'd done to G that much worse. I'd put a massive dent in his shining armor. His own queen, whom he loved beyond a shadow of a doubt, had killed him. Used him. To win.

"The only way you could damage my honor is if you forced me to break my word. Even then, I would do it, Shara. I would break my most solemn oath for you. If that meant I could keep you alive, I would do it without hesitation."

"That's what I'm afraid of."

"A knight's honor is simple. His oath is given to his cause, and then he keeps that oath until his death. All the hundreds of years I lived and worked as a knight, I kept my oath. I kept my honor. But I was miserable. I lived in hell every single fucking day. Why was that, if I was so honorable?"

I blew out a sigh. "You swore an oath to Desideria and you kept it. She enslaved you with your honor."

Guillaume nodded solemnly, the lines deepening around his mouth and eyes, giving him a haggard look that I hadn't seen since he'd first come to me, starved and broken and nearly dead. "I would rather die in dishonor tomorrow in service to you, than keep my honor and live without you. You're my queen, Shara. Your actions go far beyond the simple concept of a knight's honor. It's my greatest honor to serve you, whatever task you set me to, and I will do it. Gladly. Without question."

I swallowed the lump in my throat. "What if I make a mistake? What if we die because of some stupid choice I make? That would wreck me."

"Then we die, and we count it an honor to die in service to you." Rik's voice vibrated with conviction. "You know this. Why do you question yourself now?"

I tucked my face against Guillaume's throat. The raw, ugly scar that looped around his neck pressed against my cheek. Maybe it was my imagination, but the scar felt thicker and rougher now.

Because I had dealt him a fresh wound in the same spot.

My voice broke. "Because *I* killed him. I didn't know if I could bring him back. That's awful, G. I'm so sorry. Please forgive me."

He nickered softly, a comforting low whicker from his hell horse. I'd never heard him make such a sound when in his human form. "There's nothing to forgive. You did exactly what you had to do to save us. I have one-hundred-percent confidence in you, my queen. I still do. I can only thank the goddesses that They allowed me to live so that I could see you take your rightful seat at the Triune."

I jolted against him and jerked my head up. "What?"

He stared back at me steadily. "You will be called to the Triune. We know it. Surely you know it too, which is one reason for your anxiety."

I dragged my gaze away, giving my mind a moment. I automatically flinched away from thinking about the Triune. Because of Marne Ceresa? Or because I was... scared? I didn't like it, but yeah, I was fucking terrified. We'd pulled over in the middle of nowhere south of Branson, Missouri. I wasn't sure if we'd even crossed into Arkansas yet. The hills were getting steeper, the trees closed in on the narrow black-top road. We were high enough that I could see a few lights in the distance, scattered few and far between. Lonely little cabins with the porch light still on. Waiting for someone to come home.

I tipped my head back and gazed at the night sky. Outside the city, it was dark enough that I could see millions of stars. It was a perfect, clear winter night. No moon. No clouds building on the horizon.

Yet I felt the coming storm.

Resentment stung. I'd already brought Keisha Skye to justice and ended Ra's reign of terror. We'd all suffered. I'd bled and bled and bled some more. Couldn't I have a fucking break before facing another challenge?

I didn't feel prepared for a Triune war. At all. I had a feeling it'd be the kind of fight where I'd be forced to smile and nod while pulling the knife out of my back.

"I don't want this battle," I finally whispered.

"I know." Rik kissed the top of my head. "I wish we could spare you from this fight, but your goddess has a purpose for you. She gave you immense power for a reason."

"And it wasn't just to kick Ra's ass," Daire added. "The Great One intends to bring the ancient houses to heel."

I looked up at him, usually my purring, joking Blood. It seemed so strange that he was the one who'd been gifted the most knowledge of the ancient Aima houses. As the youngest Blood, such diplomacy wasn't expected. But I'd already seen his gift at work. He'd known every single house and their background in New York, and his charm and ability to put defensive siblings at ease had worked wonders at bringing the former Skye siblings under my control.

I turned my head slightly and met Carys' gaze. Descended from the Welsh goddess of spring, Carys Tylluan had joined me in New York. She wasn't a strong queen—unless you counted a formidable ability to see numerical probabilities.

The kind of gift that a Triune candidate queen would value. Keisha Skye, the former queen of New York City, had seen value in such a gift. After seeing how Carys helped me confirm the most likely path to defeating Ra, I could too.

I started to stand, Guillaume and Rik automatically moving with me and lifting me to my feet. G started to back away, but I lifted my wrist toward him. "You should feed so that you heal quicker."

He caught my fingers in his and lightly pressed my wrist to his mouth, his lips caressing my skin. "I should decline and protest that I'm fine, but I can't find it in me to ever refuse to taste you when you're offering."

He bit me so gently that I barely felt the piercing of his fangs in the tender skin of my inner wrist. The stroke of his tongue tightened muscles deep inside me. It'd be ridiculously easy to let things escalate, but I'd rather get home to my manor house before indulging.

I focused determinedly on Carys's face and asked the hard question I'd been avoiding. "What's the probability that I'll be called to the Triune as they say?"

"One hundred percent." Her eyes gleamed with excitement at the prospect, though her bond weighed that ambition with sympathy. A much older queen who'd known what she was from birth, Carys had been raised in a nest and instructed in Aima ways from the beginning.

I'd expected her excitement. Her gift seemed tailor-made to assist in the political gambles of the biggest game of all. However, the sympathy made my stomach clench.

"I saw the likelihood in New York," she continued. "When you said you were going after Ra, I got chills down my spine and the hairs on my nape stood at attention. I still didn't know how you could be successful against him, but it didn't matter. I saw you taking a seat at a table with the crown on your head. I knew what it meant."

Her owl chirped and Carys nodded. "True."

"What?" I asked.

"I don't know *which* Triune is calling you, only that you will be called."

Guillaume licked my wrist and lifted his head, but he kept my hand in his, his fingers warm and strong. Rik had his palm in the small of my back, a steady, formidable force. My lifelines, holding me steady. Keeping me from freaking out. "I didn't know there was an opening on the Skolos court."

Carys cocked her head slightly. "There isn't. There are three queens on the Skolos Triune. One of them is related to your dragon."

Mehen stepped closer, a sneer twisting his lips. "A Gorgon still lives? How'd I miss one?"

I blinked, surprised at the bloodthirsty tone of his voice, though with hindsight, I shouldn't have been surprised in the slightest. Leviathan, king of the depths, had eaten so many Skye siblings in our fight that he'd been too miserably full to shift back to his human form. I couldn't begin to imagine how many people he'd killed over the centuries, even though he'd been locked in a prison outside of our world for most of those years.

I just hadn't expected that he'd have killed his own family.

He jerked his head to me, his eyes glittering like chips of emerald ice. "My own lovely mother exiled me from the nest the first time I shifted. I was seven years old. Not a single Gorgon nest would take me in. So yeah, I fucking destroyed them as soon as I grew enough in strength and age to accomplish the task."

Mehen was an Aima king, so he could shift into his dragon without a queen's blood to bring the gift alive inside him. They were notoriously dangerous to control. Guillaume had told me stories about a young king killing everyone in the nest accidentally.

My mighty dragon had gone back to do the deed on purpose.

He stood before me, eyes blazing with fury, his shoulders braced and wide, ready for a fight. His hands fisted at his sides. Outwardly, he was ready to tear me apart limb from limb.

Deep inside, all I could see was a dark-haired, green-eyed, skinny little boy, hugging his knees, huddled in a cave, cold and hungry and alone. Sobbing.

His pride kept him from ever admitting that he feared I would turn him away. He'd found acceptance in my nest, but deep inside him, the scared little boy still feared I'd abandon him, just like his mother. "You're *my* king now, and I will never allow you to leave."

His throat worked, his jaw clenching. He finally nodded but didn't attempt to say anything. I deliberately focused on Carys to give him time to pull himself together. "If the Skolos Triune is full, then what do you mean *which* Triune?"

"The third court is a possibility."

Originally, there'd been three courts of three queens, but the third court had died out ages ago according to Guillaume.

He nodded, confirming that memory. "But maybe Isis wants to revive that court."

"Was it Her court before it died out?"

Carys shook her head. "No single goddess controls a Triune. It's always been a trio, and to my knowledge, it's been at least ten generations since an Isis queen sat on any Triune."

Gina would know, of course, or I could check the legacy's journal. She and Frank had taken the jet on ahead to Eureka Springs, giving me time alone with my Blood.

Three queens. Could the dead Triune court be revived with me, Mayte, and Carys? Or Gwen? At least that way I wouldn't be stuck working with Marne Ceresa day in and day out...

Winnifred squawked and I didn't need to speak owl to hear the bird's snort of disgust in that sound.

Carys guffawed like I'd told the bawdiest joke she'd ever heard in her life. "I'm not strong enough," she wheezed out in between another round of laughter. "Nowhere near strong enough. Neither is Mayte, at least from what I can feel in your bond with her."

I crossed my arms, waiting for her amusement at my expense to calm down. I knew I was strong, but surely it wasn't that funny... "What about Gwen? Could she be on the Triune?"

"If she called all her Blood, maybe, but even the original Guinevere wasn't Triune." Carys wiped her eyes with a handkerchief. "Strength alone isn't always an indicator, though that's generally the first common item among Triune queens. And it's not common for sibling queens to sit together on the Triune. That implies an alliance beforehand that basically puts one goddess and Her line in control."

So if not any of my queen siblings, who else could the lost Triune intend to call? Leonie, maybe? She was the New Orleans queen, but I had no idea how strong she was. "I guess I still don't have a good understanding of my strength compared to any other queen. Maybe I need to see more queens in action first."

Involuntarily, I shuddered at the thought. Meeting Marne through the mirror had been bad enough. I didn't want to stand face-to-face with her so I could gain a better comparison of her strength to mine.

Carys stepped closer, and her owl suddenly hopped onto my shoulder. Surprised by the weight of the giant owl, I staggered a little, though G and Rik were quick to steady me. Her wings buffeted my face as her weight steadied. Then I felt the press of her talons on my shoulder. I had a feeling she was trying not to break my skin, which was why she kept fluttering her wings, keeping some of her weight off me.

"Winnie says a weak queen is like a sparrow on your shoulder," Carys said. "A strong queen is like her weight. Impressive, isn't she?"

Now that I had shifted my balance to accommodate the owl's weight, she stopped flapping her wings and settled on me even heavier. I turned my head, awed to see an owl so close. Her feathers were a snowy white mixed with gray and black. Even hunched down in a resting position on my shoulder, she was at least two feet tall.

"May I touch you, Winnifred?"

She made a low whirring sound that I took as acquiescence. Lightly, I stroked my fingertips over the soft, downy feathers of her chest. She tipped her head, inviting me to scratch beneath her chin.

"A Triune queen would be like Leviathan sitting on your shoulder," Carys said softly.

I gulped and met her gaze. When Mehen shifted into his dragon, he was massive. He'd easily clutched me in one big foot and had been too large to fit down the large hallway of my new tower once I'd eliminated Keisha Skye.

"A pebble to a mountain," Guillaume said softly. "And you, my queen, are the entire weight of the earth."

RIK

With all immediate outward threats conquered, I felt a shifting in the balance of the world and my queen's place in it. Shara Isador had faced every threat presented to her so far with courage and grace. I knew that she would face the Triune the same way despite her misgivings. A Triune call would be a gift from the goddess, and yes, the most dangerous threat she'd faced so far.

Power was a heady threat to everything she'd built.

As her alpha, I felt the rising pressure intensely. She would need us more than ever, even as our roles shifted. She still needed physical protection, but a queen of her power could protect herself much better than we could. Now, she would need us to lighten her load. To remind her to smile, and breathe, and enjoy the world she had wrought with her own blood.

I was a relatively young Blood and had never served a queen until Shara. Let alone a Triune queen. Luckily, I had a close second to assist me with the coming challenge.

Rightfully, Guillaume should be her alpha. He had the age and experience that I lacked. He'd served Desideria, who'd been the strongest and oldest queen on our Triune, for centuries. No easy feat.

:She has the alpha she needs.: Lightly, so as not to upset our queen, Guillaume whispered in my bond. *:Protect her back as always, but now protect her heart. The power and responsibilities of the Triune have a way of grinding down a queen's emotions until they forget who they are.:*

Pain in her bond jerked my awareness back to her. Not *her* pain, though she felt it acutely. I listened unobtrusively to her bond and felt her reaching toward her new queen sibling. Gwen Findabair had been a Skye sibling, but I hadn't known her during my short stint in Skye Tower. With Keisha Skye's demise, the tower now belonged to House Isador, and Shara had claimed Gwen as her sibling and left her in charge of New York City.

She was supposed to *help* Shara. Not cause her to feel pain or add another worry to her list.

I listened a moment to her bond, only to ensure that there

wasn't any immediate danger to my queen. Only a nightmare, though terrifyingly painful.

"Nevarre, I need my phone."

He brought it to her immediately and she called her sibling queen. "Gwen, are you alright?"

Guillaume caught my attention and shook his head imperceptibly. *:When she's Triune, you'll likely need to curb such eavesdropping.:*

Taken aback, I stiffened enough that Shara noticed despite her conversation with Gwen. She leaned against me, pressing her body to mine. A distraction, for sure, but also a show of easy affection that tightened my throat. *:What do you mean?:* I asked Guillaume softly, trying not to draw more attention to our discussion. *:I always listen to her bond. How else can I be sure she's well?:*

:A Triune queen will have a massive network of siblings to manage. You won't be able to listen to them all, even if she wants you to do so. But there will come a time when her business is not our business.:

:She is everything. Always.:

:Agreed, but don't be surprised if she doesn't include us in all her decisions. She shouldn't. Triune business is not our concern. Only her protection and health.:

I didn't like that idea. At all. I loved being a part of her life. I loved when she bounced ideas off us and asked for input. Though his advice made sense. I couldn't imagine Marne Ceresa discussing Triune aspects with her Blood.

Shara slapped the phone back into Nevarre's hand. "I am not like Marne Ceresa. You've said that many times before. Don't give me another reason to refuse such a call if it comes, because I won't change our relationship to sit on the Triune."

I wrapped both arms around her and curled my body around hers soothingly. I was so much bigger than her, a massive mountain of flesh and muscle. But she could topple me with a fingertip or a single thought. "There may come a time—"

"No," she retorted, her bond crackling with fire. "I won't keep secrets from you. From any of you, but especially my alpha."

Standing in the crisp midnight winter air with moonlight illuminating her face, she had never looked more formidable and regal. Her skin gleamed like cold marble, her eyes flashing like chips of obsidian. A queen, yes, but more...

Our goddess.

Guillaume dropped to one knee before her and took her hand, lifting her knuckles to his forehead. "Forgive me for upsetting you, my queen. I thought only to prepare your alpha for the trials ahead."

She softened immediately. Cupping his cheek, she rubbed her thumb over his lips. "As you told me, there's nothing to forgive, G. But I am not Desideria or Marne or any queen who's gone before and accepted such a call. If it comes down to loving my Blood as I always have and taking a seat on the Triune, I know exactly which one I'll choose."

Neither of us voiced the grim truth aloud.

The Triune would choose its queen.

Whether she wanted it or not.

2

SHARA

Home.

Every light was on in my manor house. Winston, Frank, and Gina waited for me on the front porch, bundled up in heavy coats and gloves but smiling.

My family.

I'd never had a homecoming like this before. Surrounded by loved ones, with a place of safety and warmth, eager for me to walk inside. I could feel the shimmering circle of energy as we drove through like a warm, tingling embrace. The land and house pulsed with excitement.

Because I was home. The nest was complete now.

Rik helped me off the motorcycle so I could join Gina, and because we were inside my blood circle, he didn't hesitate to leave my back for a minute to put away his bike. Engine rumbling, he rode on around the corner to park with the other Bloods' vehicles. It was quite the caravan, with everything from Xin's Ducati to Vivian's Hummer.

Nevarre, of course, had to land the helicopter in the field outside the grove.

Winston smiled as he bowed over my hand. "I believe we should add a helicopter pad to our list of to-dos, Your Majesty."

"The roof would be best," Gina said. "Though we'll need a structural engineer to go over everything carefully and make sure the foundation doesn't need stabilization first."

It made me snort with disbelief. Just a few months ago, I was cleaning hotel rooms anywhere I could find a job, moving from town to town. And now, I owned this incredible house and we were talking about adding a fucking helicopter pad. "And probably more garages. I don't know that they can fit all those vehicles into the one shed out back."

Gina gave me a quick hug. "Especially when you call more Blood."

I barely suppressed a sigh as we walked inside. I loved every single one of my Blood. Surely ten men and one woman were plenty for any queen's protection.

"I don't think I need to call any more," I finally said as I sat down in front of the fireplace. I wasn't cold, but I loved the flames. My gift of power sparked with joy, whispering to the dancing flames on the hearth. "Since Vivian joined me, I'm not tired like before. I've finally filled my reserves. I'm not that exhausted now, even after dealing with Ra."

Winston poured me a cup of tea and then quietly disappeared into the kitchen, though Gina sat with me. I eyed the stack of folders and notepads beside her chair and mentally sighed. Maybe I was more tired than I realized. Hopefully that stack could wait for the morning.

Carys plopped down beside her on the sofa with a heavy sigh. "You've filled the reserves you possess so far. That doesn't mean you can't have *more* reserves. A Triune queen—"

"Not again," I butted in with a scowl.

She humphed beneath her breath. "Stubborn fool."

Gina lifted her teacup to her mouth quickly, but I still saw the amusement on her lips. I scowled at her. "Not you too."

"A Triune queen will have upwards of one hundred Blood. Or more."

I set the cup on the side table a little too firmly, sloshing some of the hot tea on my hand. "Ow!"

Rik snapped to my side and lifted my hand to his mouth. I hadn't even heard him come inside. Lightly, he kissed the reddened skin and gave me a sultry look. "If you feed, I'm sure that small burn will heal quickly."

I swallowed the pool of drool that quickly accumulated in my mouth at the thought. Yeah, I'd love to feed. But upstairs. In bed.

Not here with Gina and Carys looking on.

I pulled my fingers away from his and unzipped my leather jacket. The rat popped upright, eyes bright and whiskers twitching at all the new smells. "We don't have any cats, do we?"

"None to my knowledge, Your Majesty," Gina replied. "Other than your Blood, at least."

I stroked my finger over the rat's head gently. "Go and explore, if you'd like."

Head cocked, she started to squeak out a complicated-sounding answer in rat-speak that I had no idea how to inter-pret. I wished she could communicate through our bond, but I'd only given her my blood, not taken hers in exchange. I'd come a long way from the scared human on the run who had no idea vampires existed, but I wasn't quite ready to chow down on rat blood. Not yet, at least.

"I don't recommend rat, my queen," Mehen muttered. "They taste like shit."

She clicked her teeth together and gave him a decidedly dirty look that I could decipher without a bond. Laughing softly, I stroked my hand down her back. She nuzzled my palm and then scampered off. Probably to get a bite to eat, if I had to guess.

"I had no idea rats were so affectionate and smart."

Rik swung his big thigh around behind me so he could sit with me between his legs. My favorite spot. "They are, but your blood certainly has much to do with her intelligence. Even a drop for a creature as small as she was quite a power rush."

Daire dropped down to curl around my legs. The rest of my Blood stood around the room. Even now, in a place of safety, they'd positioned themselves in defensive positions. Guillaume and Ezra stood at the door. Nevarre and Llewellyn stood at the windows. The rest of my Blood stood around us, relaxed, but on alert, their senses reaching out into the night.

Usually Rik sent them off on various duties, but tonight, he allowed them to stay close and position themselves as they wanted. I didn't need to ask why.

Dread tightened my throat. I didn't want anything to change. I didn't want to lose our closeness and the easy, loving bonds we all had. But they'd all heard or picked up on the discussion I'd had with Guillaume and Rik about the Triune. They knew what it meant even better than me.

I honestly had no idea how a queen should run a large nest. I'd never seen one bigger than Keisha Skye's, and I certainly didn't desire modeling anything I did after her.

But she'd had an eye on the Triune seat, and she'd surrounded herself with many Blood and siblings like Gwen and Carys to form her power base.

Now they were mine. House Zaniyah was mine, along with the surviving Skye siblings. I didn't have as many Blood as Keisha.

Yet.

So if more Blood were necessary from a power-base stand-point... Rik was going to allow my closest Blood every opportunity to enjoy this quiet time before the storm.

Before everything changed.

Llewellyn stepped closer and dropped to his knees before me to take my left hand in both of his. "Change is inevitable, but you're queen enough to control the change and adapt as you must."

I swallowed the lump in my throat. "I don't want to lose this."

"Then don't. Make that choice now to determine your priorities. There are ways to build a power base that don't require a huge nest and dozens of Blood. It may take longer, but if that's your priority, do it your way."

I nodded, though I wasn't comfortable with the idea yet. "What would my mother have done?"

He kissed my knuckles. "She wouldn't have come as far as you already have. She couldn't. She wasn't strong enough. But I know what she would tell you if she were here."

I did too. I heard her voice often in my dreams. Or on the distant breeze. In the whispering trees. A ghost that I couldn't quite see though I felt her always near. "She'd tell me that I'm Shara fucking Isador, and this queen takes what she wants and fucking keeps it."

Llewellyn's lips quirked. "Maybe not quite in those words, though the sentiment is spot on."

"I take it someone broached the Triune subject while you were on the road," Gina said.

I groaned and shot a dark look at her, though she merely arched a brow at me. "Let me guess. You've already got a file and a to-do list for that too."

She grinned and reached down to grab a black folder out of her satchel. "You know me so well. Actually, this is a list that Isador consiliari have been compiling for quite some time."

"Really? Like how long?"

She opened the folder on her lap and picked up the first page. "The original's stored in the vault, but this page is dated from the Egyptian twelfth dynasty, so it's well over four thousand years old."

"Um. Wow."

She handed the page to me. On the left was a copy of the original document, and on the right were notes and translations. And yeah, one of the first words that jumped out at me was *"Triune."* "You're telling me that Isador queens have been plotting to take a Triune seat for over four thousand years?"

"I'd be surprised if every major Aima house didn't have such a file on hand, even if their queens have never held a seat."

I handed the page back to her. "When was the last time an Isador queen sat on the Triune?"

"The lore passed down to me from Grandma Paula is that there's only ever been one Isador queen on the Triune, Renenet, and that was when the three Triunes were first formed. She ruled for a thousand years as daughters came and went, and when she finally retired, no Isador queen ever rose to her prominence again."

It finally dawned on me. They all thought I was going to do something that no other Isador queen had done in over four thousand years. Me.

"It's whispered that it was by choice," Gina continued. "Isador preferred to work quietly in the background and our house never lost prominence or power despite not sitting on the Triune. Evidently, our goddess has determined that now is the time for Isador to step forward and lead once again."

"Why now? Why me?"

"Only Isis knows."

A log popped in the fireplace, drawing my attention to the fire. Flames flickered against the dark stones, a soothing dance that mesmerized me. My magic stirred in response, crackling fire that seemed to want something. Flames reached toward me, licking hungrily at the grate. Maybe it was my imagination, but I'd learned not to discount anything that seemed magical.

As I stared at the flames, the tension in my stomach slowly started to uncoil.

"What am I supposed to do?" I silently asked the fire. *"What does She want?"*

The fire responded, crackling louder and flaring a moment, as if I'd thrown a balled-up piece of paper into the fire. As if I'd *fed* it. With my thoughts, fears, or doubts... Or all of the above.

"I'm scared. I don't know what to do. I knew how to handle Keisha Skye and even Ra. They deserved to die for their crimes. But the Triune is different. I'm not supposed to go in and kill everybody and bring them to justice. I have to work with them. These formidable, terrifyingly powerful queens..."

The fire flickered in sympathy, brilliant tongues of red and orange licking up the stone and flowing like a river over the small logs. Coals gleamed like rubies, pulling me deeper into the heart of the flame. Hotter here. Blue flames, flickering almost white. So beautiful. The fire didn't care about what it destroyed. It hungered. It burned. Even if it escaped the hearth and devoured my entire house, it didn't care.

Fire burned in me. My first gift. Is that what She wanted me to do? Scorch the earth and destroy the Triune?

An image filled my mind. I walked through a forest that felt familiar, as if I'd been there many times, but nothing looked the same. Large, hoary trees had been replaced by blackened, smoldering stumps and charred sticks against a cold winter sky. But as I walked, the sky took on a brighter hue and the air warmed. Brilliant green shoots poked up from the ash. New life would replace all that had been lost, though I still mourned for the ancient trees that had been consumed. What if my grove had to burn?

Even though it was only a vision, I flinched. Beneath my feet, I felt the earth groan in response. My grove's roots dug deeper, a thick, wide network that acted as sensors, while also supplying the trees with nutrients and water. My grove connected with the surrounding forest, tiny roots touching other trees, and more, further away. An interlaced network buried in the ground like super cables.

Even if a fire destroyed everything above, the roots were too deep to care. They'd send up new shoots. A few drops of my blood would bring the grove roaring back to life. The trees would go on, even the non-magical ones in the regular forest. New life would return, fueled by the dead wood and ash that enriched the soil.

Just as the Aima nests would go on if I burned my way through the Triune.

I blinked and the fireplace refocused in my mind. The vision faded away and I was aware of my Blood around me. Silently waiting on me to return.

I turned my head and met Gina's gaze. She picked up her pen, her eyes bright, her manner eager. Attentive. Ready to carry out my smallest command.

"I need to speak to Dr. Borcht again, at her convenience. It's not urgent but I'd like her to come here if possible." Gina's eyes narrowed with concern a moment, but she jotted the note and didn't question me. "Is there anything in that Triune folder about scorching the earth?"

Her eyes flared with surprise. "Not that I recall, but I'll look through all the notes and pull out any references to fire and... scorching."

I took a few sips of tea and then set the cup aside. "I think I'll head to bed then. We can continue this discussion tomorrow."

"Of course. Welcome home, Your Majesty."

I stood and gave her a hug. "Thank you for helping me make it such a wonderful home. All the improvements are looking great."

She kissed my cheek before releasing me. "My pleasure. Be sure to explore—there are several surprises already finished waiting for you to discover them."

"I can't wait. Is it too much to hope for a couple of months of quiet?"

She smiled. "Not at all. You may even get a few nice quiet years. Triune business moves very, very slowly."

Years? That would be fucking fantastic. Some of the dread loosened in my stomach. Deep down, I'd been afraid I'd have to go charging to Rome tomorrow. Or next week. Months or even years was definitely doable.

Goddess, let it be so.

3

LLEWELLYN

It'd only been a few days since my queen had freed me from decades of torture and taken me as her Blood, but those years trapped in Keisha Skye's nest seemed long distant. Shara's other Blood were easygoing and accommodating, because they only cared about one thing: our queen's happiness. As they should.

That she was happy to call her mother's former alpha to her side and embrace me as her own was a miracle I still couldn't quite believe. I had no expectations whatsoever. In fact, I'd be perfectly happy to occasionally stand close enough to her to catch the slightest whiff of her scent. Not even her blood—just the smooth, perfect expanse of her gleaming skin. That was enough.

So when she looked directly at me and said, "Llewellyn, with us tonight," I nearly expired on the spot. Even more shocking, she didn't request any of her other Blood and made no protest as Rik paired them for their duties and sent them out into the nest.

She looped her arm around Rik's massive biceps and headed upstairs. Following them, I listened intently to her bond, trying to anticipate her need and desire before she would be forced to ask. She could feed, definitely, but she wasn't ravenous with hunger. She could gladly fuck too, but again, that need felt secondary. She had something else on her mind. It wasn't a secret, exactly, though it felt private and heavy, so I didn't pry.

The tower bedroom was definitely fit for a powerful vampire queen. They'd found a huge bed that could easily accommodate even several big, bad Blood. The rounded stone walls felt like a foot thick, and while there were several windows, we were high enough to make it harder for thralls to get to her if her blood circle was ever compromised. The ceiling soared an extra story overhead, with thick antique rafters giving an old-world air. Fluffy pillows and bedding in white and fluttering sheers around the bed and windows gave the room a dreamy quality.

I shut the door softly behind me but remained in a guarding position near the door until my presence was requested.

"I'd like to soak in the tub awhile. I still feel gross after touching Ra, though I know it's all in my head."

Rik opened another door and steam billowed out. "Looks like Winston foresaw your desire for a long soak."

She sighed happily as she tugged her sweater over her head. "I love that man."

I watched her undress like a starving beggar on the street stands outside a restaurant, watching the patrons dine inside. Every Isador queen I'd known was gorgeous, but Shara took that beauty further. She was so breathtaking that it hurt to look at her. Her power made every inch of her shine with a soft, inner light, glowing as if she'd swallowed the moon.

A glorious hurt that I imprinted into my memory so I could pull this scene back up and remember every precious moment. The way her skin seemed to glimmer like raw silk. The long fall of inky black hair down her back. The spark of her eyes when she glanced over her shoulder at me. The quirk of her luscious lips.

"Are you going to stand at the door all night, or take a bath with me?"

"Whichever you desire, my queen," I rasped out, trying to keep my face smooth and relaxed, even though my gryphon shrieked with urgent glee at the thought of joining our queen for a bath. Even if all she wanted was someone to wash her hair.

She toed off her tennis shoes and shoved her jeans and panties down her thighs, bending down to work the denim off each foot. Staring at her ass, I swallowed hard and fisted my hands at my sides. She was my former queen's daughter. She'd already indicated reluctance at the thought of fucking a man who'd fucked both her mother and aunt. Though she had allowed me to join her before in New York, she'd been desperate. Her energy reserves had been extremely low, and she'd worked her way through all of us.

"I desire you to join me."

Her voice wound around me like warm velvet. I had my clothes ripped off before she could even straighten. When I scooped her up in my arms, she laughed and looped her arm around my neck.

"That's better."

"Your wish is my command, my queen."

I hesitated slightly as I neared Rik, who still stood at the bathroom door. Her silent, watchful alpha missed absolutely nothing. He was almost as tall as me, a feat since I was nearly seven feet tall, but he easily dwarfed me in sheer bulk and muscle. I'd never seen a man so heavily ripped, as if he pumped steroids and threw iron all day.

He was Shara's alpha. Not me. Never me.

I'd been her mother's alpha for centuries, and in hindsight, I'd been a relentless, unforgiving asshole. If a new Blood had dared touch a single strand of our queen's hair without my explicit permission, I would have ripped his head off. Literally.

I had the age and experience to challenge him for the alpha position. But we both knew I would never do so. A queen chose her alpha for very specific personal reasons. Rik was Shara Isador's alpha and always would be. I had no desire to interfere with their special bond, though I could only hope he'd allow me space enough to make my own bond with her.

I stared back steadily into his eyes, waiting for his reaction. I sensed a tightening in Shara's bond, a slight quiver of anxiety, but she released that tension quickly. I forgot that she'd only had Blood at all for a few months and knew nothing of our ways. That little reaction told me she'd once feared for Rik's safety, until she fully understood the crucial role her choice played in who led her Blood. Maybe Mehen had shaken her confidence early on. Leviathan was certainly a formidable beast, but nothing that her alpha couldn't handle with ease.

She said nothing to us, allowing Rik to handle whatever discipline he wished to hand out. As her alpha should.

His sudden grin made my eyebrows shoot upward with surprise. "Mehen? Really? Ask our queen how we handled the king of the depths when she first took him as Blood."

Released from his alpha stare, I looked into our queen's dark eyes glowing with heat. "We fucked him into submission."

I tightened my grip on her. "You can sign me up for that anytime."

SHARA

L lewellyn set me slowly into the hot water and I sighed with bliss. It wasn't the grotto with its incredible hot spring bubbling up out of the ground, but it was a close second. Even better, Winston had managed to find a tub that was large enough for both Rik and Llewellyn, with plenty of room to spare if I wanted another of the Blood to join me too.

Another time. I had some unfinished business to go over with my mother's former Blood.

"When I touched your memories in New York City, you said you had one for me alone."

Llewellyn's head cocked slightly, his eyes bright and keen as he slid into the tub with me. "I do. I have many memories of her that I'd love to share with you, but she had one message she encoded in my memory specifically for you."

I leaned up enough to catch Rik's hand and tugged him toward me. "You should see too."

He stepped in and slid behind me, drawing me back to lean against his chest. "If you wanted privacy for this message—"

"No. I have no secrets from my alpha."

He didn't reply, but I sensed a heaviness in him. The Triune talk had affected him, too. If my life changed, so did his. We'd have more Blood, siblings, and political agreements to work out. Eventually, I might be forced to consider taking Blood *not* of my own choosing and managing them all fell to my alpha.

I'd sworn to only take Blood that I loved. That oath still burned inside me, etched into my bones by my own will as queen. But such a promise might hurt me later. For instance, if I refused to take a Blood offered to me by Marne Ceresa…

The queen of Rome wouldn't take such an insult lightly. I couldn't remember who'd suggested it, but queens sometimes exchanged Blood as a sign of goodwill.

A furious flare of jealousy seared through me, making me

dig my nails into Rik's forearms. I would not give up one of *my* Blood. Ever. Especially to another queen.

I hadn't intended to feed so soon, but I'd broken his skin and blood welled from the small wounds. My strange nails sucked up those droplets of blood and hit my system with endorphins. I could taste him on my tongue. Hot smoking rock and iron, fresh from the forge. My mouth watered and I had to swallow or start drooling.

His chest rumbled against my back on a deep purr of satisfaction, and he tightened his arms around me.

Drawn by my rising hunger, Llewellyn glided closer. "The message is one of the last memories I have of her."

He hesitated, averting his face.

I reached up and cupped his cheek, turning his face back to me. His eyes were shadowed, and grim lines bracketed his mouth. "Forgive me, my queen, but at times, I hated you, even before she conceived you. I didn't want to lose her."

I flinched, my eyes filling with tears. "Having me killed her."

"I said pretty much the same thing to her, which lead to the message she left for you. Pull that memory from my mind so I may play it for you."

Keeping my hand on his face, I closed my eyes and focused on his bond. His gryphon welcomed me with a whirring purr. Feathers fluttered around me, filling my nose with his leathery scent. The still, deep river of his bond flowed around me, cluttered with his memories like fallen leaves and sticks floating downstream. They brushed against me, giving me a sense of his life. So many years, so many memories. The ones closest to me were dark and filled with pain. His years in the tower, tortured by House Skye. More years than I'd been alive.

I scanned further, awed as year after year of his life floated past. It still amazed me that Daire and Rik were considered young Aima. Llewellyn wasn't as old as Mehen but seeing the massive number of memories he carried made it easier to comprehend the length and breadth of his life. He'd seen so much. Wars no one remembered. Queendoms rising and falling, including House Isador under my mother's reign. And its inevitable fall with her death. No one knew I existed. Not for sure. They knew the Isador legacy hadn't passed to the Triune, but no one knew why. She'd died to keep my birth a complete secret.

One memory floated closer, drawn by my presence in Llewellyn's mind. I knew before it brushed against me that it would involve my mother. I sensed Esetta's spirit like a warm, soft glowing ember. She flowed over me, the memory bubbling up out of him.

His head tipped back, his eyes blazing red-gold as the memory projected out of him to play for me. A woman with long, shining black hair swept back in a messy yet elegant bun. Glittering eyes like black diamonds. High cheekbones and lush lips with a long, graceful neck that emphasized her regal bearing. Every ounce of her screamed queen.

Esetta Isador. My mother.

So clear and perfect in his memory that I swore I could reach out and touch her.

She smiled, but her eyes gleamed with a shimmer of tears. "You'll hate me before this is over."

I jerked back against Rik's chest as if she'd struck me. It took me a moment to remember that she wasn't speaking to me, but to Llewelyn. It was *his* memory, but I saw her so clearly, I felt the impact of her words.

"No. I hate *her*, this daughter you're determined to have. This daughter who'll kill you."

"Oh, Lew, don't think that way. She's not killing me. She doesn't even exist yet. I'm gladly sacrificing my life so that she might live."

"But why?" His voice crackled with agony, raw and brutal. I

could feel the pain radiating from the memory as if it were my own. "Why must we lose *you* for *her?*"

Her gaze softened to a dreamy distance. "I had a vision, a dream from Isis. She showed me two paths. Not just two ways that I might have a daughter of my own, but also what my child would be able to accomplish. On one path, I would see her born and raise her myself. House Isador would continue as we always have. Our queendom slowly diminishing, not in wealth, but in blood. She—we—would have a wonderful life, though all Aima houses would continue the slow decline into oblivion."

She paused, focusing back on Lew. On me, watching the vision so many years later.

"And the other path?"

"She would take not only House Isador, but also the Triune. She would rule the world, strengthened by immense power made possible by the greatest sacrifice a mother can make for her daughter. House Isador would soar in prominence, and she'd bring strong, vibrant Aima blood back to the world. We would have an immense impact on the future for generations to come, rather than slowly withering into nothing."

"So you chose fame over us," he replied flatly. Even in the memory, his heart weighed like a ton of cold iron.

She stared back steadily at him. Her chin rose incrementally, her eyes flashing. She didn't have to rebuke him.

He bowed his head and whispered, "Forgive me, my queen."

She lightly stroked her fingers over his bowed head, but he didn't look back up at her. I could feel her phantom fingers on my own head, and my heart twisted with yearning. The agonizing loss a child feels when she lost her mother very young and never knew her touch. Never felt her kisses at night as she was tucked into bed. Never felt her mother's arms wrapped around her.

"A queen must make hard choices for the house and the future of the world. Would I rather live in happiness with my beloved Blood and my daughter? Of course. You know my heart, Lew. The cost is high. So terribly high. But that's what makes this sacrifice all the greater. That's what will power my intention and magic into the life of my daughter. She'll be a force to be reckoned with. Even the Triune will tremble as she rises. And yes, it's with immense pride and joy that I know my sacrifice makes this possible. Not just for us, for House Isador, but for the Great One who will walk on this earth once more through Her chosen avatar."

She tipped Llewellyn's face back up to hers, and my heart clenched. Her face looked like it'd been carved from cold marble, and her eyes gleamed with the dark power of a goddess who could give life… or retribution.

"You know the plan I have set forth, Llewellyn Isador. But if you'd rather have peace, I will give it to you. You will never suffer what lies ahead, but neither will you live to serve another Isador queen."

It dawned on me that she meant death. She would kill her own Blood, the alpha she loved, to spare him the torture in House Skye.

He didn't hesitate, though I felt his gryphon shredding his heart with vicious talons. "I will always serve House Isador. I am ready and willing to carry out my queen's bidding, no matter what it is."

Her face softened, tragic pain in her eyes mixing with the sweetest, softest love. "Then this message is for my daughter, Shara Isador, the daughter yet to come. The Great One has dreamed of you for millennia. She has great hopes and plans for you, sweet child. She has waited with perfect patience for the right time and queen willing to sacrifice everything in order to give you life. For the right queen to give you shelter away from the courts so that you can determine your own path free of the rigid traditions Aima hold so dear. The very same traditions that have crippled us.

"Don't be afraid to break free of these traditions, Daughter. Isis wants you to tear down the walls and rebuild the courts in Her image. In *your* image. For Isis walks and breathes in you. Long live the greatest Aima queen yet to come and ever to be, Shara Isador."

"Long live House Isador," Llewellyn said, both in the memory and in the present.

"Long live Shara Isador, queen of my heart," Rik whispered against my ear.

4

RIK

S hara was the queen of my heart, but I had no doubt that she would also be queen of the world. She had the strength to bend anyone and anything to her will, whether it was the king of the depths who hated every Aima queen he'd ever met...

Or the queen of Rome.

But she wasn't ready to face that aspect of her personality yet. She didn't want those responsibilities, not that I blamed her at all. I certainly quailed beneath the mighty expectations of her future. Would I be alpha enough to help her? To keep her safe? Or would my love, and her love for me, for all of us, be a handicap?

As Guillaume had said earlier, her greatest strength was her capacity for love. I had no doubt that she'd burn the world down to save one of us. Any of us. All Marne Ceresa had to do was capture one of us and threaten to kill us, and I was dreadfully positive Shara would give her anything she demanded to protect us.

"I would." She turned her head back enough to look into my eyes, sliding more into my right arm so she could see my face. "I know my weakness all too well."

I stroked my thumb along the curve of her cheek, my heart swelling with so much love that my rib cage ached. "Everyone has a weakness, my queen. The trick will be using it to your advantage."

She smiled ruefully and shook her head. "I have no idea how to accomplish that, but it doesn't matter. I love you. I love you all. And what this queen loves, she keeps for all time. Coatlicue promised that we would all die together. If I lose one of you, then we all will walk in the afterlife together. No one will be left behind to grieve, and we're certainly not going to be easy to kill."

Llewellyn let out a soft grunt of derision. "Not by a long shot. Just remember one thing, my queen."

She turned back to him, cupping his cheek as he slid closer to us.

"There are worse punishments than death in this world. Much worse."

The stark pain in his eyes was a grim reminder to me of all that I stood to lose. Any Blood would be hard pressed to retain his sanity if he lost his queen suddenly, but an alpha who was so deeply tied to his queen...

How had Llewellyn retained his sanity after losing Esetta?

Shara whirled toward me so hard and fast that water sloshed over the edge. "Her name. You just said her name in your head."

"I've known her name awhile. I guess I never had cause to think of her directly."

The shining light in her eyes dimmed, which had not been my intention. "Because I killed you too, when I was the cobra queen. So you and Guillaume should both be able to say her name now. Can Nevarre? Since he was dead when he came to me?"

:I know that your mother's name was Esetta Isador, my queen,: Nevarre immediately said in her bond. *:I have heard her name in your bond many times, but I didn't wish to cause you pain.:*

I settled back against the edge of the tub and deliberately allowed my gaze to heat. "Kill me again, my queen. Though this time, kill me with pleasure."

SHARA

E setta. Her name echoed in my head, looping through my Blood bonds and amplified by Rik, Guillaume, and Nevarre's knowledge. They'd paid the ultimate price before, and I'd never have to doubt their readiness to do the exact same thing again. Any of my Blood would lay down their lives for me. Even if I took their life myself.

"Kill me next," Llewellyn said fervently. "Though I can almost hear her name without dying. I feel it in your bond. If you keep thinking and saying her name, I'm sure that you'll break the geas she laid."

Tears burned my eyes, but these were good tears. I'd be able to talk about her with someone. They'd be able to remember her. It'd make her more real to me too, though now that I'd seen her so clearly in Llewellyn's memory, her image was firmly implanted in my mind.

Rik smoothed his big palm down my back in a slow, easy glide that stirred my hunger. His eyes burned with heat. "Later."

It seemed like ages since I'd had his body stretched out beneath me. Since I'd been able to drop all my fears and concerns and just...

Fuck. Feed. And fuck some more.

In the safety of my nest, I could let down my guard. All of us could. Sure, some of my Blood would always be in guard mode even inside the nest, but the constant tension of danger loosened here. My nest was the safest place in the world. It would take a very unusual threat to breach my defenses, especially now that we'd added the grove and the birds.

I turned fully around to face him, straddling his lower stomach. Reveling in his strength, I ran my hands over the broad expanse of his chest and shoulders. Ripped muscle, hard and powerful beneath my hands, corded with tendons and sheer slabs of granite. Goddess. He was such a magnificent man.

He smoothed both palms up and down my back, his fingers massaging with just enough strength to make me melt. The perfect pressure in his hands. Reverence, but also power. Tenderness, but with the promise to blow my mind.

Letting my eyes flutter shut, I surrendered to the sweet pleasure humming through me. "Make love to me."

"Always." He didn't make an order to Llewellyn, even in the bond, but they both touched me. Held me. Hands glided over my skin. Soft kisses. The flick of a tongue. The faintest scrape of a fang over a vein.

My skin came alive with every soft touch, a rising symphony that lifted and carried me through a night sky. I didn't try to hold back or rush them along. I wanted to feel. Breathe. Revel in the hard stroke of muscle against me.

Rik slid into me with exquisitely slow, sweet torture. Cradling my ass in either hand, he effortlessly controlled how deeply he moved. A slow roll of his hips lifted me higher. Making me cry out. His dick rubbed inside me, and stars exploded behind my eyelids.

Shuddering, I came quietly. Gently. My breath caught in my throat, a ragged sigh escaping my lips. But nothing like the clawing, raging hunger that usually drove me. He stilled the slow rock so we could both feel the rhythmic clenching of my pussy. The flares of pleasure still trembling through me.

"So fucking beautiful," Llewellyn whispered against my ear. "I could watch you come all night, my queen."

Rik nudged up slightly and I groaned. "Just call me Shara tonight. I don't want to think about queens and Triunes right now."

Llewellyn growled softly and playfully bit my earlobe. "Shara."

I allowed my head to drop back against his shoulder, sinking deeper into the haze of peace and desire curling through me. Actually, I was floating, carried away on a gryphon's wings and cradled in a rock troll's palm.

The scent of blood made my stomach rumble, even though I wasn't physically hungry. Llewellyn's scent filled my nose. Leather and rich, warm sandalwood. His blood dripped down my back as he lowered his hand to smear a bloody path along my crack. He pushed into me, just as slowly as Rik had done, giving me all the time in the world to feel them. To think about their dicks gliding back and forth inside me, so close to each other. Filling me. Pushing me deeper into the water.

Wait, what? My mind jolted like I'd driven over a pothole. Water. I could hear the bubbling sound of the spring pushing up from the rocks and roots of my heart tree. Blood in the water. My head sinking beneath the surface. Light shimmered, but *below* me. That didn't make sense. Maybe I was turned around? But I looked up and I could make out the wavy image of the moon gleaming above me, bright and full, though distorted by the water.

"Shara?"

I blinked and focused on Rik's face. His brow was furrowed with concern, his grip tightening on my hips. Both Blood throbbed inside me, but they paused, waiting to be sure I was alright.

The image was gone, but I still felt the sensation of gliding through water. *Passing* through water. Of course. "I just had a waking dream."

"Your mother did that sometimes," Llewellyn said. "She often stared into the fire, like you did earlier, or floated on her back in water."

"For a moment, I swear your bond felt... stretched," Rik said. "Like you weren't here, even though I could touch you."

I combed my fingers through his hair and snuggled against his chest. "I don't think I was here. Remember the portal that Xochitl fell through in Mexico? I think there's one in my grotto."

Llewellyn pressed closer, covering my back so that I was completely surrounded by rock-hard muscle. Heaven on earth. "According to the old stories, any body of water can be turned into a portal for the right queen."

Rik's arms banded tighter around me, his voice dropping an octave. "As long as you take us with you."

Llewellyn pushed deeper, making me cry out. I gripped Rik's shoulders hard enough that I could taste his blood again.

I didn't tell him that I hadn't sensed him with me as I passed through the portal. Where would I need to go without my Blood?

5

MEHEN

I n all the many thousands of years in my life, there had never been anything as good as lying in my queen's bed. Even when a rat glared at me from her pillow with malevolent eyes.

Shara was goodness and light and joy, the purest love I had ever known. And I would kill untold numbers of people to keep her in my sights. Even if she never touched me again.

Even if all I was allowed to do was cradle her foot against my chest like she cuddled the fucking rat, I would do it. Reverently.

Luckily for me, for all of us, she wanted so much more.

Rik had sent the bird-cat out on patrol with Guillaume and Xin. The rest of us had stayed inside the house, hoping to be called to her bed. Even if all she wanted to do was sleep—sign me the fuck up.

I expected Daire to get the call to join her in bed, but not me. I wasn't known for my cuddling ability, not like the purring fur ball. He curled around her on one side and Rik laid on her other, leaving her feet to me. She was so soundly asleep that she didn't stir, even with Daire's purr shaking the bed.

I lost track of time, not sleeping exactly, but drifting.

Breathing in her scent and presence, reveling in the simple peace of holding my queen while she rested.

Hours passed. Distantly, I was aware of the sun rising.

Near noon, Shara woke up. One moment, she was deeply asleep, and the next, her bond hummed with rising power. She sat up, focused intently on her sibling bond.

Maybe I should have paid more attention, but I honestly didn't fucking care about the queen of Camelot. Not when my queen's silken skin beckoned. She was awake now, so I didn't have to be good.

I rubbed my face against her calf. One hand still held her foot, my thumb circling her sole, seeking out any painful pressure points that needed to be massaged. Her power washed over me in a crystal wave, making my scales shimmer.

Leviathan rose from the depths of my black soul. Eager. Hungry. Ready to chow down on our queen's blood and pleasure like the ravenous beast I was. The more she drew on her power, the harder the dragon rolled inside me.

I'd never been able to keep Leviathan contained. Even as a child, the dragon had roared out of me at will, a dangerous, uncontrollable monster that even my powerful queen mother had feared. Shara had tamed the beast, but she was distracted by whatever issue her sibling was dealing with.

Cackling with glee, Leviathan blasted my internal organs with hellfire.

I clutched Shara's leg, my face pressed hard to her skin, and breathed in her scent and power. I smelled her blood, which told me she couldn't afford any distractions right now. Some serious shit had to be going down for her to add blood to her power.

But the smell of Isis's lush oasis drew Leviathan harder to the surface. He swelled inside me, straining to be free so he could feast.

Sweat trickled down my forehead. My jaws ached with strain. But I held on, refusing to shift.

:Gwen's fighting a dragon,: Rik growled in my head. *:Can't you help her?:*

Why the fuck would I want to help any queen other than my own?

That was my first thought, because I've always been a selfish bastard. Gwen was Shara's sibling, and Shara was obviously trying to help her in some way. If Gwen was hurt or weakened, it would certainly affect my queen, and that would piss me off. Because Rik would climb into my ass and beat the shit out of me.

At least Leviathan stopped trying to surge out of me to ravish our queen. Instead, he focused on Shara's bond and this other dragon.

And yeah, I could see the hulking red beast on the other end of the sibling bond. The glint of malice in his eyes was all too familiar to Leviathan's own maniacal glare. My spine burned and popped as Leviathan's spiny ridge rose with aggression.

Dragons were territorial and rare, especially nowadays. I couldn't remember the last time I'd had a raging fight with another beast as big as me, and the dragon threatening Gwen was fucking huge. He'd definitely prove a challenge, and I couldn't fucking wait to rip his head off.

Despite our distance from New York City, I watched as Shara seized the other dragon's throat in a fist of power. Goddess help me, Leviathan almost rolled over on his back with pleasure at the thought of her grabbing him like that.

Gwen sagged beneath the surge of power flowing through her, but she was only a conduit for Shara Isador, last queen of Isis. She poured through the weaker queen like a massive bolt of lightning.

Leviathan crouched, eyes locked on the opposing dragon. Wings cocked. Ready.

The other man lifted his hand and a black cloud billowed up around him. The cloud had weight and substance that latched onto Shara like some kind of foul leech.

:Shara,: Rik bellowed in our bonds like crashing boulders. *:It may be poison.:*

She drew hard on her power, fire coalescing in her bond. *:I don't think it can hurt me, but hopefully Gwen is impervious to it.:*

I stared into the red dragon's eyes and read his glee. He *wanted* her to blast him, or at least try. He wanted her to drop all that impressive power into her attack.

A trap. It had to be. I'd seen plenty of dragons who breathed fumes, and this fucking mist wasn't poison. It sucked on her power, even as she built the inferno inside her bond.

Draining her. Feeding on her.

My teeth ached, every draconian instinct on full alert.

Before she could unload on him, I bit her calf. Hard. It was the only way I could think of to distract her long enough to break the trap. Still, I felt a massive dip in her bond. A drain that was sucking her down, just like the fucking portal in Mexico. I dug my teeth harder into her, breaking her skin and adding more blood. I would hold on like Tlacel had done.

Even if it broke every fucking bone in my body.

Daire slammed against me, adding his weight to my hold on her.

She dropped her power, releasing it back to the universe or wherever she drew from to work her magic. The black cloud snapped free and she metaphorically tumbled back to us, even though she'd never left this bed.

Limp and sweaty, she drew in a shaky breath. "What the fuck was that?"

I released the bite and licked at the marks I'd left in her skin. "A trap. He was feeding on you."

She took a deep, steadying breath. Her bond still spun crystal rainbows through me, but they were soft and muted.

"I'm a stupid, arrogant fool." She blew out a disgusted sigh and started to lift her arm back towards Rik but dropped her hand heavily to the bed. "Even my reserves feel thin. I would have burned through everything I had in another few seconds, and then he would've had me. He would've had us all. Fuck."

:Are you okay?: Gwen asked in our queen's head. *:What did Arthur do to you?:*

Ignoring her for the moment, Shara tugged on my bond, drawing me up in her arms so I could see her face. "After kicking Ra's ass, I thought I could defeat anything except possibly another queen. How did you know it was a trap?"

I shrugged. "He's a dragon. I read it in his eyes. He was too smug and sly to be facing a powerful queen like you. He fucking reveled in the fact that you were going to flatten him with everything you had, because that was exactly what he wanted."

She shuddered faintly, her fingers tracing my scales that never completely faded. Closing her eyes, she ran through the attack again, playing it in her head almost like a movie, making full use of Llewellyn's gift.

She paused the scene to study Arthur's face. The glint in his eyes and the faint curl of disdain on his lips were unmistakable. "He wasn't feeding on me. He was going to trap me. Look where the smoke is coming from. Can you make out what's on his hand?"

"Some kind of ring," Daire said. "Maybe a signet, but it's not the Pendragon crest. I can't make out the symbol."

She warned her sibling about the ring, and then focused back on me. "Thank you, my dragon."

Rik let out a grunt that sounded like a distant avalanche. "He didn't act as quickly as he should have, especially since we were fighting a dragon."

Displeasure burned like acid in the pit of my stomach, mixed with a heaping dose of arrogance. Though I deliberately kept my body relaxed, I couldn't help the heavy, sleepy look of the hungry dragon that started to peek through my features. Deliberately deceptive, the better to lure my victim closer.

Exactly as Arthur had glared at her.

"Enough," she said firmly, as much for me as for Rik. "He was fighting a dragon the entire time—his own. Containing Leviathan is no easy battle." She leaned up enough to kiss me, her luscious lips a beacon I would follow anywhere. "The king of the depths would have trashed the room and likely distracted me from dealing with Arthur. So you did well to keep him under control."

She entwined her arms around my neck, and I was lost. Trapped by nothing more than the glowing heat in her eyes. I settled against her, deliberately relaxing my muscles. This time, the sleepy-eyed dragon was ready to feast and fuck, not fight. "I don't want to destroy this big, beautiful bed."

Daire snickered and pushed his head closer to us both. "No shit. We'd have to go back to the bed that ate you."

Usually I didn't mind his teasing, catlike ways. In fact, most of the time I'd love nothing more than to stuff his smart mouth with my dick or fuck him for our queen's enjoyment.

But now, this very moment, I wanted something else. I couldn't even put it into words or dare to allow the thought to enter my mind. I couldn't possibly ask for such a thing.

Leviathan, king of the depths, did not *ask*. Let alone offer his belly in submission and bare his heart, even to his queen.

Shara settled back against her alpha and gave me a heavy-lidded, knowing look of her own. "Daire, could you go to the kitchen and let Winston know I'll be ready for lunch in about an hour? And take my rat with you. I'm sure she's hungry."

Without a word of complaint, he scooped up the little furball with red beady eyes, slipped out of bed, and padded out of the room to do her bidding.

We all knew that Winston would have her lunch ready at a moment's notice. The man had an uncanny sixth sense for guessing what our queen wanted or needed before she recognized the desire herself. A feat indeed since he didn't even have a bond with her.

She'd sent the scamp away.

For me.

Without making me feel like an asshole for even thinking that I should have our queen all to myself.

"I'm feeling a bit weak." She bit her lip, showing the glistening tip of her fangs. "I'm afraid I'll probably drain you nearly dry, my dragon."

I couldn't answer her. Not when every drop of blood in my body rushed to my already rock-hard dick.

My queen. All mine. Hungry and needy and looking up at me with those mysterious, endless midnight eyes.

Well, Rik was still here too, but I didn't give a fuck about her alpha. It'd take a bigger monster than me to pry him from our queen's side.

I dropped my head back, bowing my throat out in invitation.

She opened her thighs wider and reached between us to seize my dick. I almost blew my load without her fangs sinking into me.

"Oh, no, my dragon," she laughed softly. "You'll be inside me when you come."

SHARA

Some light flirting with Mehen was about all I could manage. I kept my face soft and hopefully relaxed, while deep inside, I mentally kicked myself.

I couldn't afford such mistakes. If I died, all of us would die, and I couldn't bear to have their deaths on my head.

Or worse, what if Arthur had managed to entrap me with that strange ring? I still felt thin and stretched inside, as if he'd managed to suck some deep, essential part of myself away. Certainly, he'd rocked my confidence.

I'd faced an ancient, powerful god and won. Never in a million years would I have thought an Aima king would rattle me. Not even the legendary Once and Future King. He was Gwen's problem to deal with—but she was my sibling and held New York City in my stead. If Arthur managed to trap or hurt her...

He would have a hold on me and my court too. A hold I might not be able to break.

Luckily, Mehen provided the perfect distraction.

I pulled him closer by his dick, but I didn't take him inside immediately. I squeezed him firmly, enjoying the way he throbbed and jerked in my hand. I rubbed the head of his cock against my clit, torturing us both. Hissing softly, he watched me with narrowed eyes that glittered like chips of emerald.

It was such a decadent, erotic thing to lie between Rik's massive thighs, his chest like slabs of granite against my head, while I enjoyed teasing another man. I could feel Rik's erection like a hard, thick piece of hammered steel against my left hip, where he'd tucked himself out of the way so I could lie against him comfortably. He'd gone from semi-hard to granite as soon as I'd touched the other man, though his bond was still tense.

He'd felt the drain of my power and energy as acutely as I had. Arthur Pendragon was going to be trouble, but I refused to worry about him any longer. Not with these two magnificent men in my bed, eager to refill the energy that I'd lost.

I dragged the head of Mehen's dick down the full length of my pussy, smearing him with the cream welling from my core. At least I wasn't bleeding any longer.

Another low hiss escaped as he curled his upper lip. "Fuck that shit. Blood is always better."

"Are you complaining?"

With a low snort, he thrust into my hand, angling his hips so he could slide between my folds, coating every inch of his dick with my juices. "You know I love to bitch, but I'll never mutter a single protest when it comes to anything in your bed. I'm up for anything and everything in that regard."

Heat pulsed in my core and I couldn't wait any longer.

Before I could drag his dick back down, he jerked out of my grasp and slid inside me on a long, heavy thrust that made me groan with relief. I didn't have to tell him what I wanted. I never needed to with any of my Blood. We were so tightly bonded that my slightest need echoed in their minds and hearts, making it easy for us to fully satisfy each other.

I'd felt his need to have me to himself, a thought he didn't dare acknowledge fully as one of several Blood to his queen. Even my alpha only rarely had me to himself. But I'd already decided to make sure I had more one-on-one time with each Blood. Mehen especially was a possessive dragon who loved to hoard his precious treasures. Including his queen.

This time, he didn't savage me like a hungry dragon. He moved lazily, a massive raptor circling high in the sky with only the barest flap of his wings to keep him aloft. I sank into the sensation, letting him carry me with him. Slow, steady, every thrust calculated to stir my need to a fevered pitch.

I rubbed my face between his pecs, inhaling his musky dragon. None of my Blood were as hairy as my bear, but Mehen's chest hairs prickled. I smoothed my palms along the curves of his shoulders, feeling the flow of muscle and tendon beneath my hands as he worked inside me. Down the long, lean line of his spine. Squeezed the full, rounded curves of his buttocks. Such a nice handful. I kneaded his ass, digging my nails into his skin.

He ground his hips against me, and a low growl rumbled his chest against my face. "Fucking perfect. Feed from my ass while I fuck you."

Laughter caught in my throat, turning to another groan. The head of his dick bumped up against my cervix in a pleasure-pain throb that cascaded through my body. My legs twitched, my hips automatically tipping up to take him even deeper. He pushed harder, pulsing and shifting inside me without lifting his weight. Pressure built inside me with no end in sight. I wanted to come. Needed to explode. But I couldn't quite push myself over that ledge.

He didn't give me any mercy or quarter, but inexorably pushed and ground on me. Making me writhe. Making me clutch his ass harder.

Finally, the tips of my nails punctured his skin. Rich, powerful, and ancient, his blood seeped into me, drowning me in sensation. I could taste his dragon on my tongue, hard, cool scales against my face, even though he hadn't shifted. Leathery wings wrapped around me, dragging me closer to his chest.

I had the sense of a deep, dark, secret cave. His dragon nest, where he kept his hoard. I expected mounds of jewels and gold, the traditional treasures that dragons supposedly kept, but his cave was barren. It wasn't his prison that he'd lived in for so long. When I'd freed him, I'd seen the piles of bones littered on the ground.

This place was special.

Secret.

His true hoard.

And the only thing that he hoarded…

Was me.

I came so hard that for a moment I worried that I'd shoved my wicked nails to the knuckles into his ass. His back bowed, straining against me. His ass flexed in my hands. In our bond, it felt like I'd shoved my hands up into his lower back. A giant fist burned against his spine, threatening to tear him apart.

I turned my head and sank my fangs into the firm muscle over his heart.

He exploded, bucking against me, a snarling, vicious dragon in full rut. I drank him down, fangs and nails locked in his body, a part of him as he was a part of me. Every drop of blood eased the stretched feeling inside, pulling me back and firming my power. My will.

I had faced the monster of my childhood, the queen of New York City, and the god of light, and won. Nothing could keep me weak or defeated for long, not with such magnificent Blood to fuel my desire and power. Love might be my biggest weakness, but it was also my greatest strength. I loved with the intensity of an off-the-scale hurricane and the fiery fury of Mount Vesuvius.

And I would kill to keep that love safe.

I loved Gwen like a sister, and I'd fight to the death to be sure any woman wasn't trapped into a loveless relationship with a man. She'd been fighting against her curse with Arthur for centuries and losing.

This time, the queen of Camelot had Isis's daughter on her side. The Once and Future King had met his match.

6

SHARA

Beneath the sweeping branches of my grove, green grass grew thick and lush. It might only be February, but winter had no hold on my nest.

I smiled at Nevarre and linked my arm with his. The rest of my Blood trailed behind, though Rik remained close on my heels. Gripping my hair, the rat sat on my shoulder, tucked up against my neck.

My raven Blood looked especially incredible today with the green-and-black plaid of his kilt draped over his shoulder and belted around his waist. With the old-fashioned fluttery linen shirt beneath, he looked like he'd walked off the set of *Outlander*. "Let's try this again."

We'd been on our way to the grove earlier, when we'd been interrupted by an unexpected visitor. My young adopted Isador heir, Xochitl Zaniyah, had discovered the secret passageway inside the dark hole marring the trunk of my heart tree that connected my nest to my sibling's. She'd popped out with her young friend, and then her mother and father had come to retrieve her.

Mayte had stayed for a most enjoyable interlude with me

and my phoenix at the grotto.

Already the confrontation with Arthur Pendragon seemed far in the past. A deep feeding with Mehen and Rik had settled the weakness I'd first felt. Enjoying a sensual feeding with my women had only increased my sense of pleasure and peace. I loved them all so very, very much. Just touching one of them made me feel better. Looking at them made my heart sing with joy. They gave me so much, selflessly offering their blood and their bodies, anything to make me happy. Just breathing the same air as my beloved Blood and sibling made me stronger.

Breathing the warm, spring-like air inside my grove, in the dead of winter... Magical.

The branches were so full of birds that I could barely see the leaves. Mostly large crows, but there were all kinds of birds, including a few emerald green and red quetzals from Zaniyah lands. The squawks and chirps stilled as I neared the heart tree.

Rose petals drifted down to the ground like fragrant droplets of blood. Blooms covered the thorny branches, filling the air with the fragrant perfume of rose and spicy musk. It reminded me of the incense that had burned in Isis's pyramid the first time I'd been called to visit Her.

Dozens of crows dropped from the branches to hop alongside me on the ground. One landed on Nevarre's shoulder, but none of them came to me. Head cocked, the crow made several soft guttural sounds not quite a caw, as if whispering to my Blood.

"She says the crow queen is sitting on her eggs, but she'll come to you at once if you desire," Nevarre explained. "Or she invites you to come to her nest."

I scanned the tree, involuntarily shivering a little as I remembered dying on its branches. Vicious thorns protruded from the limbs. One especially large thorn had staked me through the heart. I didn't immediately see a nest.

The crow fluttered down off Nevarre's shoulder to land on

the rocks lining the steamy grotto. She cawed louder, making sure I was watching, and then flew into the dark cave-like hole in the side of the trunk.

Interesting. I'd thought the crow queen had nested here inside my grove. Where had she gone, if all these other birds were here? I turned to Rik. "How many Blood do you think should go with us?"

"Depends on whether the rest can pass through if you're in danger. We carry your blood so I'm assuming you won't need to touch each of us to bring us through, but we won't know for sure until we test it. I'd recommend at least Nevarre and one other, my queen."

"Xin, would you like to go?"

My most quiet, reserved Blood immediately stepped closer, flashing a rare smile. "Surely you know if that's a ridiculous question, my queen. Of course. Should I go as the wolf?"

I didn't want to alarm the crow queen, especially if she was protecting her eggs, but I didn't know how crows in particular felt about wolves. "Not yet. Only if there's danger."

Rik gave orders to the rest of my Blood. "Guillaume, Mehen, be ready to come through immediately if she has need of you. The rest of you spread out and guard the perimeter of the grove. Nevarre, Xin, lead the way. I'll have our queen's back."

We made our way across the boulders and rocks that formed the edge of the grotto. Steam curled in the air, dampening my skin enough that strands of my hair stuck to my face. It also made the rocks slippery. Rik hovered close at my back, ready to grab me at the slightest slip, but I wasn't worried. Every inch of this place had been created for me, indirectly by me, or at least, by my magic gifted from the goddesses. I was descended from Isis, but this was Morrigan's grove. Even if I'd tried to leap to my death from the top of the tree onto the rocks below, I doubted it would work. I'd already died once to grow the magnificent old trees. The price had been paid. Gladly.

Nevarre glanced over at Xin, both of them at the edge of the dark hole. "Who gets to go first? Rock, paper, scissors?"

Xin shrugged. "You're the bird. You should go through first."

Nevarre shook his head with a wry grin. "I guess it doesn't matter since you're invisible anyway."

As his queen, I could still see Xin clearly. I wasn't sure if his gift would work on the crow queen or not, but it certainly wouldn't hurt. If even the god of light hadn't noticed the silent wolf padding along at my side as I'd neared the golden monstrosity of his throne in Heliopolis, then surely the bird wouldn't either.

"How does this work, my queen?" Nevarre asked.

I stepped closer so I could touch the smooth wood bared by the deep fissure in the heart tree's core. The trunk wasn't a solid cylinder like a normal tree, but instead was a twisted, braided clump of thick rose stems fused together to form the central trunk. I carefully touched the pad of my index finger to the dark wood lining the crack. The inner wood didn't have any thorns and was smooth, almost like it'd been sealed and polished.

Pressing my hand more firmly to the trunk, I merged my thoughts with the heart tree.

My blood still flowed through its limbs and deep into the soil. I could feel a heart beating, as if the tree was breathing, though I didn't sense a specific personality. It took me a moment to realize that was *my* heartbeat thumping through the trunk.

I powered the tree. My blood fueled its roses and the lovely grotto. Naturally it beat in time with my heart.

The other trees encircled me, creating a resonance like the sweet, clear chime of crystal bells. They protected me and the nest, just as my Blood did. Their network of roots stretched out into the surrounding woods, listening and searching for any threat. I could feel the animals living and sleeping in my trees. The squirrels tucked up in their fuzzy tails. Birds fluffed into balls in their nests, beaks tucked under their wings. Even a bobcat just a few miles away, cozy in a small cave above the river.

I turned my attention inward, focusing on the dark hole before me. I felt a deep echo inside, as if it wasn't just a hole in a normal-sized trunk, but a massive network of tunnels and passageways.

That word sparked something from my memory.

When I'd first gone to my mother's house in New York City, I'd found the secluded room where she'd birthed me. She'd written her last words to me on those walls, and there'd been something about passageways.

"'*Walk the ways cloaked in Shadow seeing all,*'" Nevarre whispered softly. "When you said Shadow, it resonated with my gift. That's why I remember."

I nodded, letting the thoughts flutter and swirl in my mind. There was something else. Something my father had said to me in the basement, the only time I'd ever seen or talked to him. "*The paths of death that lead to life.*" His deep voice whispered in my head from a great distance. "*The ways are open to you, Daughter.*"

The ways... through my tree? Or through the portal that I suspected lay in the steamy water of my grotto?

Or both?

There was only one way to find out. At least stepping into the tree didn't seem as dangerous as when Xochitl and I had almost fallen through the water portal to Huitzilopochtli's realm.

Besides, it couldn't be that hard to control the passageways if young Xochitl had managed to find her way to me. Though I had a feeling our goddesses were watching out for the young princess and would have blocked anything that might have been too dangerous for a child to face.

I listened a moment, letting the tree feel my purpose. I

wanted to go see the crow queen in her nest, wherever that was. Did I need to offer more blood to open the way? Or touch a secret pattern on the smooth wood? Or something even more mystical or arcane? I didn't feel moved to do any of those things. The tree seemed eager to have me inside, though perhaps that was merely my own quickening heartbeat. As I listened, I felt the sense of deep, endless passages firming to a single path. A small, round room carved like a bowl, though the entire chamber felt big enough to hold me and several Blood inside.

Intention. So much of my power depended on nothing more than my will to spark the magic, at least as long as I was willing to add blood to the mix if needed.

I gave a nod to Nevarre and he stepped into the gaping hole without hesitation. I should have been able to still see him. The trunk wasn't that big. But when he called back, his voice sounded much further away than even a few steps. "All clear."

Xin followed him, pausing partway inside to turn and offer me his hand. I took his fingers in mine and followed, watching him carefully. Rik's big palm was warm on the small of my back, a steady promise that he was there. Close.

Xin never wavered or seemed to disappear, but after a step or two, we were both inside a dark place that stretched high enough for Rik behind me, though Llewellyn might have to duck. I trailed my free hand along the wall, though it didn't feel like wood any longer. I couldn't quite place it. Cool, but not cold and damp. Smooth, but not as smooth as the wood had been. It didn't feel like rock and certainly wasn't crumbly like dirt. I inhaled deeply, trying to use my other senses to help pinpoint what we were walking through.

But my nose was no help. I couldn't smell rock or dirt or a hint of the forest or even the roses of the heart tree. The place seemed sterile. I strained to hear anything other than the scuffle of our shoes across the floor and my own heartbeat, but I couldn't sense anything else. Some light might help, but before I could call a small fireball to my hand, we stepped into the rounded room I'd sensed.

It did look like a large wooden bowl with steep, tall sides. A nest of sticks and twigs had been built in the center of the floor. The crow I'd made friends with sat on the nest, her wings outstretched slightly to completely cover her eggs, so I had no idea how many she'd laid.

It was lighter in the room than the tunnel had been, allowing me to study the details. Concentric rings in the floor flowed out from the nest, some thicker or lighter than others as if we were inside a giant tree.

My heart tree's diameter wasn't nearly this large.

I stepped over to the walls and ran my fingers over the smooth surface. It definitely felt like wood, hard and smooth as though a craftsman had sanded for days. I tipped my head back and found the source of light. A crack in the trunk at least twenty or thirty feet above allowed air and light to filter down into the chamber.

"Where are we?" I mused aloud. "It doesn't feel like we're in the grove any longer."

The crow queen chirped, drawing my attention back to her. I felt a tickle in my mind, almost like a small scratch. Or a knock. I nodded and she filled my mind with a picture of a huge tree from the outside as she flew around it. So tall that the top was shrouded in mist. A giant redwood, I thought, though I'd never seen a sequoia before.

She pulled me along in the vision, winging out over a sprawling forest. Mountains formed a formidable ridge on one side, and with her incredible eyesight, I could see the ocean in the distance. I'd never been to California, but it certainly looked like the coast.

In a matter of minutes, maybe a dozen steps, I'd traveled from Arkansas to California. Unbelievable.

:She's talking to you,: Nevarre said in our bond. *:That's new, isn't it?:*

It was. Before I'd resurrected Huitzilopochtli, she'd sent me a vision of stabbing herself on the heart tree's thorns. *:She bled on the heart tree—where my blood flows.:*

I could taste her on my tongue now. Black feathers fluttering against my cheek, the scent of forest and mountain air filling my nose. Similar to pine but not quite as pungent. If I were to guess, I'd say I was smelling my first sequoia.

This had been her home before she'd come to me.

How had she known to fly from California to Arkansas? The night Keisha Skye attacked my nest with ants, Nevarre had put out a call to all the birds in the area for assistance, but the crow wouldn't have had time to fly that far. She had to have already been close. I wasn't familiar with crow migration cycles, but I couldn't imagine a crow naturally flying so far from her home.

The crow queen's feathers rustled as she shifted on her eggs, drawing my attention back to her. :What's your name?:

She didn't give me a single word, but an image. A crow's wing, glistening with the soft light of a thousand stars. The night and darkness of her wing. Nightwing.

She chirped softly, but I felt an expectation from her. Hope. There was more to her name.

I felt her soaring high into the night sky, twirling and spiraling so the starlight flickered on her wings.

Nightwing Starlight.

Joy flooded my bond and she chirped again. In words, that was as close to her name as I could get.

I stepped closer to her nest and dropped down to sit cross-legged before her. "Thank you for sharing your name with me, Your Majesty."

She squawked and fluttered her wings, giving me an indignant look that made me smile.

"Nightwing. Is that better?"

She settled back down with a humph.

"I love your nest. Thank you for showing me your tree."

She preened, making a low coo as she fluffed up her chest feathers with her beak.

"I hear congratulations are in order."

She rose up enough to show me the speckled blue-green eggs beneath her. Something caught my attention and I leaned closer, trying to make out what it was. It took me a moment to recognize the bit of hair I'd given her. The strands were balled up beneath the eggs like a thin cushion. "Do you need more hair? That doesn't look like enough to keep them safe."

She shook her head and settled back on top of her eggs. An image of downy soft royal silk filled my mind, gleaming black like my hair, wrapped gently around her eggs. Evidently the few strands I'd given her were enough.

An image of hundreds of crows filled my mind, a steady stream of birds flying in and out of the heart tree. They each carried something, either in their beaks or grasped in their talons. At first, I thought they were bringing food to their queen, but as I watched, I realized they were tribute. Offerings. Shiny silver and other metals for the most part, but a few scraps and things I couldn't immediately identify either.

She made a different low-pitched call and several crows fluttered down from somewhere above us. Two of them held something in their beaks, and they laid the items down before me. I got the impression that they were male, maybe her mates. Or at least her guards, like my Blood.

I dropped my gaze to the items, trying to understand why she wanted me to see these. They didn't appear to be of much value. A scrap of baby-blue fabric, edges tattered and torn, and a piece of paper, wrinkled with faded ink that had bled out into an unreadable mess. It looked like it'd been rained on and dried in the sun several times.

I looked back at her, unsure what she wanted, but I didn't want to be rude. "Thank you."

She bobbed her head at the crow closest to me and he nudged the blue scrap toward me. I guess they wanted me to pick it up. I reached out and touched the tip of my finger to the scrap, and an image filled my mind.

A silken scarf wrapped around a woman's neck. It was a gorgeous scarf, light and soft with an old-gold fringe. It seemed very expensive and old, like a treasured antique. It was her favorite item in her extensive wardrobe, the kind of accessory that always made her feel beautiful and special. Just by touching the scrap, I could feel the wave of pleasure and fondness welling up inside her each time she wore it.

I had no idea who she was, but she felt like me. Another vampire queen.

I picked up the scrap and closed my fingers around it, trying to gain a better sense of its owner. A better connection. Nothing changed, even with the scrap wrapped completely in my hand.

Maybe a little of my blood would help.

Carefully, I punctured my left palm with my right index finger. Blood welled on my skin, flooding me with heightened senses. Every color seemed more vivid. I could feel the gentle breeze outside the tree, even through the thick, stout walls of the chamber. My bonds gleamed in my mind, not stretched or strained despite the distance from the rest of my Blood. In fact, they felt so close that I could smell their individual scents.

Even more, I could suddenly see the passageway we'd traveled through, and the rest of the complex network that led from my heart tree to all over the world. For a moment, my mind rebelled. It couldn't grasp the directions or distances, because they were impossible. The paths lay on top of one another but went to different places. It was like trying to picture four or five dimensions at once, rather than a normal three-dimensional space.

I had no idea how the passageways worked exactly, only that I was pretty sure I could get to anyplace in the world in a matter of seconds.

Pushing the impossible pathways out of my head, I focused on the scrap in my hand. With my blood scenting the air, I could almost see the woman who owned the scarf. Her hair was short and very curly. Her face young, as if she was only in her mid-twenties, though I sensed weight to her, as if she was very old. Warm brown eyes. A wide, generous mouth with laugh lines.

I saw her walking down a street wearing the scarf. Details were faint, though. I had an impression of dark, old buildings. It all felt old-world with cobblestones and bricks stained by many years.

I set the scrap back down on the floor and took a deep breath to clear the image away. Then I picked up the piece of water stained paper. Immediately, I could tell it was *her* paper. The same woman. She'd written the words herself, sitting at an old-fashioned writing desk in front of a large window. I could hear the scratch of the fountain pen's nib on thick, elegant stationery. Violet ink in a gorgeous hand. But I couldn't read the words. They looked foreign. French, maybe.

I touched Guillaume's bond and shared the image of the writing with him. :*Is this French? Can you read it?*:

Several long moments went by and he didn't answer, though I felt his rising intensity in my head. He could see the paper and understood it perfectly. As he read it…

His bond weighed heavier in my head and took on a sharp, deadly edge like his favorite sword.

:*What is it?*: I asked. :*What's wrong?*:

:*The signature,*: he finally replied.

At the bottom of the page, only a swirling D was written in calligraphy with thick, elegant swipes like the first letter in a medieval manuscript.

:*Desideria? Was this hers?*:

:No. I'd recognize her handwriting anywhere, and this is too delicate for her. She would have signed her full name and her stationery always bore her house name at the top. This paper only has a seal, but it's one I recognize well.:

At the top of the page was a blue-and-red fish.

:Not a fish. A dolphin.: He waited for my reaction, but I could only mentally shake my head. I had no idea why a dolphin would be significant. *:The royal seal of the Dauphine.:*

Oh crap. The other elusive Triune queen, who hadn't been seen in years.

:Try centuries,: Guillaume said grimly. *:We know she's still alive, but no one knows where her nest is. She disappeared well before the French Revolution, but I don't have an exact date. Gina would be able to find out.:*

:What does the letter say?:

:She's writing to a contact in Quebec, likely a sibling though she keeps it very vague in case the letter is intercepted. She says a sighting has been made in the United States. Focus activity toward the south while she works northward.:

I still didn't know why he was so concerned. This didn't sound that bad. A sighting of what?

:You.: His voice rumbled with the strident neigh of his hell horse. *:This letter is dated just before Christmas.:*

Before I'd "come out" so to speak as the Isador queen. Rik and Daire had found me a week before Christmas just miles away from here. I'd had no idea what I was until they'd come to me and saved me from the thralls that had surrounded me.

My mind raced frantically. I'd been so focused on Marne Ceresa this entire time, but maybe the Dauphine had always been closer. Marne hadn't known about me until after New Year's, when I'd made Mayte my sibling and returned to Eureka Springs. She might have suspected what I was when she saw the footage from Christmas Eve, when I'd taken Leviathan, but she'd sent Byrnes to me with a message when I returned from Mexico. *:Does it say where the sighting happened?:*

:Kansas City. When would she have seen you there, before Christmas? Before I came to you?:

The window between Rik and Daire becoming my Blood, and then Guillaume, was very short. Just days. *:Other than the incident with the saleslady and when Ra attacked through the portal, I can't think of anything.:*

:I was there for those attacks. This would have had to be before. I believe I would have been able to sense her presence, though she's very good at masking even her servants. Rik wouldn't have known what to look for. Can you think of anytime you felt uneasy for no reason?:

:The bar,: Rik growled in my head. *:Remember? You didn't want to go down the dark hallway to the restroom, but I couldn't sense anything amiss.:*

We'd gone shopping, and then I'd danced with Daire. Rik had been so grumpy and uneasy. I'd just barely started my period, and we'd all assumed that was why he'd been so tense. That was partly why he'd had such a hard time that day, but maybe he'd sensed something else that he couldn't recognize.

:It's very likely,: Guillaume said. *:Little is known about the Dauphine, but she's rumored to have servants acting as her eyes and ears in the world that are basically mindless shells. As such, they're nearly impossible to track. I never saw one myself, but Desideria was all-too familiar with her Triune sister's tricks.:*

Goosebumps flared down my arms and my fangs throbbed with urgency, as if I needed to feed and feed and feed, gaining power to defend myself against this threat. I couldn't believe the Dauphine had been that close to me. Before I'd even known how to protect myself. Before I'd gained enough Blood to do anything at all.

I must have been a few steps from... death? Or being forced into becoming her sibling queen? Who knew what the mysterious Triune queen had intended if she'd found me basically defenseless. Though I wasn't naive enough to assume she'd had only goodwill and friendly intentions on her mind.

I focused on the crow queen. *:Do you know where this letter was found?:*

Her head cocked, her bright eyes locked on me. A sort of invitation, I thought. I slipped into her mind like I'd done with my rat so I could see through her eyes.

No, not her eyes. It was another crow. A male. But she could see through his eyes, which gave *me* the power to see too. Ramifications flickered briefly in the back of my mind, ideas and ways I could use this gift. If she could see through all her subjects' eyes, and I could see through hers...

I basically had a massive spy network all across the United States.

She cawed softly in my head and sent me several visions in rapid succession. Stonehenge. Steep cliffs and brilliant green fields with low rock walls. More fields of long lines of short trees with green fruit. Olives, I thought. The savannah with its baking, dry heat. A deep humid jungle.

Places from all over the world. Not just the United States.

Awed, I asked, *:Can you see all birds? Or just crows?:*

She showed me an image of a crow on a branch, chirping and talking to a snowy owl. A bright-colored parrot. A small brown starling.

So she couldn't see through other birds' eyes... but her kin could talk to them.

Amazing.

She pulled me back to the young male crow. He sat on an iron railing several stories above the ground. A narrow alley lay below, paved in uneven cobblestones. The house across the alley was a large, sprawling three-story building with pinky-peach stucco. Dark green shutters and trim lined the rows of windows. A fountain bubbled in a tree-shaded courtyard that faced the crow's vantage point. Probably the rear of the building, I thought. Another two-story building ran perpendicular to the other, with a swimming pool in between them.

As he watched, an unassuming beige sedan slowly drove up the alleyway and parked directly beneath where the crow watched. A man got out of the car and walked across the paved courtyard to the back building. He didn't approach the double doors but walked along the shorter building toward the last window on the end. A hand stretched out with several envelopes and packages. Without slowing his step, the man took them as he passed, and then looped back toward the car.

He opened the driver's door but paused a moment to flip through the stack. It looked like mail, but through the crow's eyes, I didn't see any stamps. This mail wasn't meant for any regular post office. I tried to identify any unique features, but he wore a baseball cap pulled down over his eyes that shaded his face. He didn't have a beard and wore jeans and a plain T-shirt. Even the cap was a basic run-of-the-mill faded red hat without any insignia or logo.

He could be anyone, from anywhere, and I'd never recognize him.

The young crow crouched, wings poised. Another crow swooped down from the roof of the building across the street and snatched at the baseball cap. The man cursed and flung his hands up around his head, batting at the crow.

While the young male quietly swooped down and snagged the envelope that had fallen onto the top of the car.

He swept up on silent wings, weaving his way through old brick buildings. I scanned the area through his eyes, trying to identify the city. The air was humid and smelled of a river or lake. Rather swampy.

Iron railings and balconies dotted most of the older buildings. We flew over an old gnarled tree drooping beneath the weight of moss clinging to its branches. The south. But where?

Even though this had happened months ago, it seemed as

though the young bird felt my urgency. Or maybe he'd been taught to always look around and note his location anytime he found something of use to his queen. He took a leisurely loop across the large, sprawling city. In the distance, I could see water and ships. Even a few steam paddle ships moving up and down the river that dumped into the bay.

Not the bay. The gulf. New Orleans. I was sure of it.

I broke contact with the crow queen and looked up at Rik. "Didn't you say that Leonie Delafosse is the queen of New Orleans?"

He nodded. "As far as I know, yes."

"Have you met her? Any of you?" I asked aloud, though I knew each of my Blood could hear the thought in our bonds.

:No,: they each replied.

A queen no one had ever met. And the enigmatic Triune queen was in New Orleans. "Could she actually *be* the Dauphine? G, would you recognize her if Gina can get us a picture of her?"

:It wouldn't do any good,: Guillaume responded. :The Dauphine was rumored to be able to easily change her appearance. That's how she's been able to live undiscovered for so long.:

The more I heard about this queen, the more I was kicking myself that I hadn't been digging for information about her before now. I touched Gina's bond. :I need all the information you can find about the Dauphine and Leonie Delafosse.:

Focusing on the crow queen, I inclined my head to her. "Thank you, Nightwing Starlight. Your family has been most helpful to me."

She chirped softly and rustled her wings, settling deeper on her eggs. An image of war filled my mind. Clanging swords, exploding guns, flash and fire and death. Carnage.

Clearly a warning that the Dauphine was not a queen to fuck with.

Steel hardened my tone. :Neither am I.:

7

SHARA

As soon as we stepped outside my heart tree, the rat leaped off my shoulder and lightly raced along the prickly limb, looking for the perfect thorn.

She was so small, and most of the thorns on the heart tree were at least as thick as my thumb. A massive spike had stabbed through my back, impaled my heart, and protruded from my chest. I didn't want my little friend to hurt herself that badly.

I lost sight of her, but I felt the moment she picked her thorn. Her blood sank into the heart tree.

Into me.

Soft fur brushed my face, her tiny paws pressed to my neck, even though she wasn't on my shoulder any longer. Curiosity had always burned inside her, driving her to explore. Flashes filled my mind of endless pathways. Narrow, tiny holes where she'd barely been able to squeeze through. Subway tunnels. Sewage. Plumbing. She'd explored—and mapped—them all.

She scampered back down to the limb just above my head. Whiskers twitching, she squeaked.

:Penelope.:

I heard her name as clear as a bell in my head. Nodding, I smiled up at her. *:Thank you, Penelope. I'm so glad you decided to leave your home behind and come live with me instead.:*

Blood dotted her chest. I reached up, both hands cupped to catch her, but she squeaked rapidly, backing away. *:Queen. Servant.:*

Sighing, I lowered my arms. *:I would gladly heal you.:*

Her whiskers twitched and she dropped down to the ground.

I gasped. It had to be at least a six-foot drop. Her legs were like little sticks.

A sound echoed in her bond, suspiciously like laughter.

"I think she's laughing at me," I said aloud. Clearly, she'd felt a demonstration of her resiliency had been in order.

Her tail flicked up in agreement, and then she darted away.

:Wait! Where are you going?:

Images snapped through my mind quickly. Night. Day. Night. Day. Night. Day.

Okay. She intended to be gone for at least several days. Determined not to worry about her, I turned back to my waiting Blood. "I wonder where she's off to in such a hurry."

Daire snorted. "She's off to get laid."

Mehen heaved out a long-suffering groan. "You'll have every inch of the nest covered in rat piss and bird shit by this time next year."

Several crows swept down from their limbs and dive-bombed my dragon, slapping him with their wings and cawing furiously while he tried to bat them away.

"I'll bring food every single day for a year to the first one who shits on him," Daire yelled, laughing so hard he could hardly get the words out.

Throwing his head back, Mehen roared with dragon fury at the birds and they finally flew back up into the trees. "Fucking nuisance." He sneered at Daire, brushing off both of his shoulders. "No bird crap, either."

Nevarre huffed out a laugh. "That's because they don't like you."

"No shit," Mehen snarled. "The feeling's mutual."

"You're not really going to crap on me in this challenge, are you?" Daire asked, only half joking. "Though I hope we are friends. Just not *that* good of friends. No offense."

We'd been inside the crow queen's nest for so long that I was afraid that it might be too dark for the entertainment Nevarre had promised me. It was late afternoon, and the weak winter sunlight would only last another hour at most. Lightly, I squeezed his hand. "Is it too late in the day? We can always wait until tomorrow."

"Not at all, my queen." He lifted my hand to his mouth and lightly kissed my knuckles. "Besides, your warcat has been challenged. My honor won't wait another day for satisfaction, though I assure you, I have no intention of shitting on him. Or even asking the birds to shit on him."

It seemed like ages ago when Daire had made the nevermore joke. We'd been sitting in the limousine before heading into Skye Tower to face Keshia Skye. An entire history book of action had happened since then, even if it'd only been barely a week.

Nevarre had challenged Daire to meet him on the green. Whatever that meant. I couldn't wait to find out.

Evidently the twins were in on at least some of the details of the challenge. Itztli had spread out a blanket on the ground in a sunny spot inside the circle of my grove. Tlacel had brought a picnic basket. If I knew Winston, it was packed with all kinds of sumptuous snacks. My stomach immediately growled, so Rik hustled me over and set me down on the blanket, while Tlacel started loading me a plate.

Nevarre came to stand before me, waiting until I looked up at him. He grinned and tossed his incredible hair back over his shoulder. I couldn't believe how long his hair had gotten. It hung down to almost mid-thigh. "For your entertainment, my queen, I've challenged Daire Isador to meet me on the green. Do you accept my challenge, warcat?"

Never one to miss out on some mischief, Daire sauntered up to stand with him. He flashed a grin, making the dimple dance in his cheek. His tawny hair had grown out considerably since he'd come to me. All of my Blood had started growing out their hair, though they'd all have some catching up to do with Vivian, who held the record for the longest. "I have no idea what the fuck this is about, but yeah. I'm always up for a good challenge."

Nevarre lifted his chin, signaling Ezra and Llewellyn to come closer. They each carried a massive log on their shoulders. Holy crap. They had to be at least twenty or thirty feet long and as thick as one of Rik's mighty thighs.

My burly bear grunted with disgust, swiping at the sweat glistening on his forehead. "It's already too fucking hot to be lugging giant logs around. Thank goddess you didn't want to do this in the middle of summer."

"It's not that bad," Llewellyn said mildly. His face and tone didn't show strain, though in our bond, I felt the immense weight of the log pressing against his shoulder. He could barely hook his hand over the top to steady it in the cradle of his arm.

Daire was one of my shortest Blood, barely taller than me. The log was almost three times his height. And while he was stronger than any human, he surely wasn't as powerful as Ezra or Llewellyn. Ezra's thick barrel chest and wide shoulders were struggling to contain the log, and Llewellyn was significantly older than either of them, making him stronger. Yet even he was feeling the strain of holding such a large log.

Daire snorted. "You've got to be shitting me. A caber toss? Really?"

"It's the best way to settle a friendly challenge," Nevarre replied.

Daire started toward Ezra's log, but suddenly changed direction. Breaking into a run, he called back over his shoulder. "I'll be right back!"

"You fucking son of a bitch!" Ezra growled. "You'd better hurry or you can try tossing me first."

Oh boy, I could all too easily imagine how a toss between Ezra and Daire would go. Laughing, I settled back against Rik's big body. This was going to be even more fun than I'd thought.

Tlacel handed me a small plate absolutely loaded with goodies. Fried chicken, potato salad, brisket, and potato wedges, plus food under the chicken leg that I couldn't even see. The plate was heavy enough that I set it down on Rik's thigh. "Thank you, Tlacel. This looks incredible."

Rik reached around me to pick up the chicken leg. He tore into it like a caveman, startling another laugh out of me. He was always so particular about making sure I ate enough, that I was actually shocked that he ate before me. Not that I cared in the slightest.

"Grab our queen a breast or chicken strips," he said in between bites. "She doesn't like dark meat."

He was right, though I couldn't remember ever telling him or eating fried chicken with him before. His bond simmered with smug amusement. :*No one knows your stomach as well as I do.*:

:*No one knows any part of me better than you do,*: I retorted back playfully.

:*A-fucking-men.*:

Tlacel handed me a deliciously crisp chicken strip that made my mouth water just looking at it. I took a bite and moaned. Winston had seasoned it beautifully, with enough cayenne pepper to make my tongue happy. I normally didn't eat a ton of spicy food, but I definitely loved flavorful chicken.

Daire came racing back across the lawn and I almost choked on the bite in my mouth when I snorted. Rik thumped me on the back, making sure I could breathe.

With a towel wrapped around his waist—and absolutely nothing else—Daire slid to a stop beside Nevarre. "I don't have a kilt, but I'm going to show off my legs as much as him, or it's not a fair competition."

Nevarre scowled at him and popped his hips enough to make the kilt flare up dangerously high. "It's not my legs I intend to show her, but I assure you there's no competition in that regard."

"Jealous?" Daire planted his fists on his hips and deliberately waggled his groin at the other man. No one was surprised that the towel was tented. I'm pretty sure the guys walked around with a hard-on ninety-percent of the time.

:Try one hundred percent of the time,: Mehen muttered.

"Hardly." Nevarre pulled the long tail of his plaid free from the belt at his waist so he could drag his shirt over his head. He deliberately tossed it in Daire's face. "Though we'll go chest-to-chest as well as kilt-to-kilt."

Daire's purr rumbled the ground, sending a delicious thrum through my body. "Mmmmm, smells good, bird brain, but not as good as me."

"Yeah? Do you care to make this challenge even more interesting?"

He winked at Nevarre and gave me a saucy grin. "Yeah. Because she's going to bite me first."

Nevarre shook his head, making his long hair glisten and dance around his shoulders. "It's a bet, cat. The first one she sinks fangs into is the winner."

I wheezed for breath, trying to stop laughing. "Stop making me laugh so I can eat."

Ezra growled. "Are you lousy motherfuckers ever going to take this fucking log off my shoulder?"

"Fuck yeah." Daire stepped closer, eyeing the log like he actually thought he could lift it. He shot a wide-eyed look over his shoulder at me and pouted. "You actually think I can't throw it?"

"It's at least three times taller than you," Rik reminded him. "Even I'd have a hard time managing something that long and heavy without transforming to my rock troll."

"And I've been standing here holding the fucking caber like a goddess-damned ijit." For all Ezra's complaining, I didn't actually feel any strain in his bond, at least nothing that suggested he was struggling to hold the massive log.

:He just likes to complain,: Mehen assured me.

:Like some other people we know,: Llewellyn added, earning a very disgusted dragon glare.

"At least let me go first to show you how it's done," Nevarre said.

Daire nodded grudgingly, so Nevarre took position in front of Llewellyn. "All right, let's position the thinner end down at the ground. It's easier to get my hands underneath it."

The two Blood eased the thick log down to the ground with the narrow end braced in the grass. Nevarre slowly bent down, shifting the log inch by inch onto his shoulder, while he eased his fingers underneath the cut edge of the log.

Oh. My. Hot. Kilt. Alert.

As he bent down, the kilt rode up. And up. Giving me a good, long look at the backs of his hamstrings. I'd never really thought about hamstrings being sexy, but I couldn't look away as the lines of sinew and muscle worked beneath his skin. He wasn't a thick, bulky man, but lifting that caber onto his shoulder made everything he had bulge. Deliciously.

My mouth was watering, and it had absolutely nothing to do with fried chicken.

With a deep grunt, he pushed his knees straight and began

walking rapidly across the grass, picking up speed. Until he heaved the log straight up, every muscle straining.

With an extra kilt flip that showed me he definitely wasn't wearing anything underneath.

I was too entranced to notice how far the log sailed or how many times it flipped, but by the whoops and cheers from the rest of my Blood, it must have been a good throw.

He sauntered back, grinning and sweaty and so damned delectable that I tugged on his bond, willing him to come straight to me. Which he did, much to Daire's chagrin.

As the other Blood approached me, Daire hurried to get the log shifted onto his shoulder with Ezra's help. "Not fair, Nevermore. You have to at least wait until I've made my toss and have the same chance to flash her."

Staggering beneath the weight of the giant caber, he started a precarious trek across the grass.

But not before Ezra yanked the towel off his hips.

So Daire made his first-ever caber toss stark naked. Luckily, he didn't rip off half his skin from the rough bark of the log. We were all laughing too much at the sight of his shiny white ass staggering across the knoll to see if his log even flipped all the way over or not.

Even Vivian was laughing so hard that she'd bent over, gasping and holding her stomach.

Nonchalant despite—or rather, knowing him, because of—his complete nudity, Daire strolled up toward the picnic blanket like he wore the finest, most expensive suit in the world. Though he was definitely breathing hard, and the log had scraped a raw patch on his shoulder. "Not bad," he wheezed. "If I do. Say so. Myself."

I collapsed back against Rik with another round of giggles.

Nevarre waited until some of my mirth quieted, and then he crossed his arms over his chest. Nose in the air, he managed to sound like a highland laird. "Such flagrant disrespect of our time-honored traditions earns you a disqualification."

Daire snorted. "Bullshit. You're just mad I found a way to show up completely naked to a kilt contest."

"This was never a kilt contest." Nevarre loosened the plaid wrapped around his hips. His hair had fallen across his shoulder and clung to his dampened cheek and neck. He peeked through that black silk to make sure I was looking at him.

Eyes smoldering, he held my gaze and dropped the kilt. I heard the plaid fall gently to the ground.

I'm not going to look. I'm not. I've seen his cock before. Don't be ridiculous. You don't have to look.

I swallowed hard. And looked.

NEVARRE

I would die a thousand deaths if only my queen would look at me with such hunger again.

Her gaze locked on my cock, and yeah, I felt the surge of lust in her bond. But she wanted so much more from me. When a queen fucked her Blood, he went eagerly, no doubt about it. We lived to serve and could only hope to be given the chance to touch and please her, when she had so many others just as eager to take their turn in her bed.

Most queens didn't have a preference for a specific Blood. We were protection. Guards. Food when she hungered. Sex when she desired it. But that was it.

Shara Isador wasn't like that in the slightest.

I'd served a queen before who had held my bond and feasted

on my blood and body both, but she'd never owned the slightest part of my heart. For Shara, I'd cut my heart out of my chest and feed it to her bite by bite with my own hands.

I wasn't a big man in any of the usual ways a queen might measure her Blood. But she looked at me like *I* was the gift. Like I mattered. Even if I was one in eleven, or twenty, or one hundred. She'd always look at me exactly the same way.

As if she'd just been served her favorite dessert.

She leisurely dragged her gaze back up to mine, and I loved the way she allowed herself to enjoy every inch of the journey. "Turn around," she ordered softly, her luscious lips curving in a sensual, knowing smile. "I want to see all of you. You too, Daire."

I did as she asked, not even trying to hide my smirk at the other Blood's sound of disgust. I had him beat in this department, and he knew it.

I might not have the biggest dick, the most muscles, or even the longest hair, but I had the fullest, roundest ass of the bunch.

She didn't say anything, but I felt the burning imprint of her stare on my skin. Her fangs pulsed and throbbed with the beat of her heart, and I knew I'd won the bet with Daire.

"No fair," he grumped, giving my shoulder a friendly shove.

"Your ass gets tapped all the time," I replied. "It's about time someone else gets some recognition."

I'd deliberately stepped close enough to the edge of the blanket that she could touch me if she wished. I felt the whisper of her breath across my skin as she leaned closer. Her fingertips traced the bare skin at the top of my boots and lingered in the hollows behind my knees. Her light, soft touch made me quiver with urgency. My heartbeat thudded so hard in my skull that if she spoke, I didn't hear.

She leaned closer, her hair tickling the backs of my thighs. Her fingers traced the dome of my right kneecap and inched up with agonizing slowness to massage my quad.

I'd fantasized about her touching me like this. But I'd never dreamed my queen would tenderly rub her cheek against my ass. My queen should never humble herself like this. I should be on *my* knees worshipping her.

Voice shaking, I started to turn toward her. "My queen should never be on her knees."

She wrapped her fingers around my dick, freezing me in place before I could fully face her. "Don't be ridiculous. I have you right where I want you."

Ever so slowly, she glided her fingers up and down my aching cock, making me tremble against her. Her lips pressed to my ass, trailing soft kisses across my hip and cheek. Across the small of my back. Down to the other side, pausing long enough for her tongue to swirl across my spine. While her fingers glided lazily over me.

I couldn't seem to catch my breath. My chest heaved harder now than when I'd lifted the caber onto my shoulder. Blood pounded in my veins, flooding my groin. Eager to satisfy my queen's hunger.

She licked and kissed my ass until I panted and shook in her grasp. Flames boiled my blood, pressure rising until it felt like the top of my head would explode. Or maybe that was just because I arched back so far, offering myself to her. Silently begging. Pleading.

I didn't want to come so much as I wanted to feel her fangs inside me. Though her bite would certainly push me over the edge.

My raven strained, wings beating frantically as if trying to tear out of my skin.

I felt the first sweet pain as the tips of her fangs began to penetrate me. Time stilled, letting me feel each delicious moment as she slipped inside me. My queen. Marking me. Feeding on me. Goddess, I could die again this very moment with joy, though I'd never want to cause Shara to feel a single moment of grief.

Exquisite sensation rolled through me as the cutting tips of her brutal fangs sank into me. She tightened her arms around my jerking hips, her fingers locked around my cock as it spurted with release. But my pleasure came from feeling *her* enjoyment in our bond.

She loved holding my ass firmly in her jaws, her fangs deep in my flesh. It was as close as she could get to fucking my ass without figuring out how to strap on Vivian's phoenix, if that would even work.

:*Would you even want that?:* Shara whispered in my head. Her emotions were so tangled with mine that it took me a moment to sort through what she was feeling and thinking. Shock first, that I would even suggest such a thing. But then curiosity. And yeah, interest. A lot of interest.

:*In a heartbeat. Fuck me any way you want, my queen. I'll love every second of it.:*

I'd never touched Vivian's mind out of respect for her and what she'd gone through in her father's house. She didn't like men to touch her—so surely she wouldn't care to have any of us pawing through her memories either.

She blazed into my mind like a red-hot searing poker. :*Smoak would do anything for our queen, as would I. But more, he'd fucking love giving her a new way to fuck you.:*

Quivering, I sank down to the ground as the last spurt pumped out of my spent cock. Shara caught my shoulders, cradling my head on her lap. I looked up at her, aching with so much love that I couldn't speak. I couldn't thank her appropriately. I couldn't convey how much she meant to me. To us all. To have a queen who cared about us at all...

Let alone loved us enough to give us our heart's desires, no matter what we needed.

Her tongue flicked out to catch a droplet of my blood sliding down her bottom lip.

And goddess help me, my cock went rock hard all over again.

"Alright, you motherfuckers," Mehen growled, raising his voice as if he was arguing with someone, though I hadn't picked up on any disagreements or ribbing going on. Granted, I'd been greatly distracted, and the grouchy dragon didn't need much irritation to cast his ire about like the primordial monster he was. "Who the fuck is going to challenge *me* to a caber toss?"

"Me," Ezra bellowed, shoving his way through the twins and Xin to get to the log Daire had tossed. "As long as the winner gets a bite on the ass, I'm in."

Daire sidled closer, trying to slip between me and Rik. But I was as immovable as the rock troll in that regard. "And the loser?"

"The loser can watch from the sidelines," I retorted, surprising even myself with the harshness to my tone.

Goddess damn me for a fool, but I didn't want to share. Not this time.

Guilt tightened my throat and I didn't dare look into her face to see her reaction. It wasn't a Blood's place to demand or ask for anything. Especially in our queen's bed.

I thought Rik would reprimand me, but he didn't even give me an alpha thump in the bond. Maybe because there was no need. I'd never challenge his authority. It wasn't in me.

I started to sit up so I could gather my dignity and my kilt to slink back into the shadows, but I couldn't get up. My head was pinned, my hair tangled on something. I reached down to find the snag and found my queen's hand fisted in my hair.

"Were you thinking about going somewhere?" She'd never used that tone of voice with me before, a sort of silky, luscious menace that curled my toes and made my dick throb at the same time.

I jerked my gaze up to hers, rolling my head so I could see, even though it pulled my hair enough to make my eyes water. "No, my queen."

"Good. Because I've got half a mind to ask Smoak to give me some assistance now."

I relaxed back onto her lap, my tension melting away. "Now would be fucking perfect, my queen."

8

SHARA

I normally didn't mind Daire's antics, but this time was Nevarre's turn with me. It wasn't such a big deal when Daire wanted to join me with one of the bigger, more dominant Blood, because the more the merrier in that regard. They enjoyed forcing him into submission, and I enjoyed watching it. But Nevarre was too quiet and reserved to stand up and make demands for himself. He'd already assumed that I'd welcome another man, rather than finishing what we'd already started. And normally, maybe I would have. With so many Blood in their prime, they all wanted time with me, and while I did have an immense hunger, and had worked my way through them all in a single night...

It hadn't been one at a time. It was much easier to fuck all eleven of them in groups of two or more.

I pushed on Daire's bond, mentally giving him the equivalent of a friendly slap on the butt while shoving him away too.

"This is Nevarre's time."

Still rumbling with that deep bass purr, Daire acquiesced, but he put an extra sashay in his step as he backed away.

I touched Vivian's bond. *:You said Smoak would be willing to assist me?:*

Her bond crackled with the rising phoenix. *:Without question. He'll always do as you wish, because he serves the same as I do. But in this? He'll fucking revel in your pleasure, my queen.:*

The phoenix slipped through Vivian's bond and slid into me on a wave of fiery warmth that made sweat glisten on my skin. Burning myrrh and cinnamon filled my nose. My own gift of fire flared brighter, and the phoenix danced and writhed in those cascading flames. Power rose, baking my internal organs and heating my bones to an uncomfortable level.

The phoenix screeched, bathing me in golden flames.

I concentrated on banking the fires swirling inside me. *:Don't burn me to a crisp.:*

The phoenix settled with a sheepish flicker of flames. He didn't communicate in sentences or words, exactly, though I got the impression of contriteness. Along with *sweet, hot fire.*

Mehen snorted. *:Join the club, asshole.:*

Vivian snarled at him. He gave her a lazy, heavy-lidded dragon stare. Though he didn't say a word, I felt Leviathan crouched inside him, tail lashing. Ezra was still bellowing for him to dragon-up and grab a log. Daire purred like a thunderstorm, trying to snag my attention.

While Smoak took the opportunity of my distraction to wallow in my gift again. My face burned like I'd fallen into a furnace. *:Rik.:*

"Daire, Itztli, Tlacel, Llewellyn, and Mehen: go check our queen's borders. Xin, Ezra, and Guillaume, keep the others busy and give us some privacy. Go!"

With a scowl, Vivian stepped closer. It took me a moment to realize she wasn't glaring at me, but at her phoenix. *:Smoak! Behave yourself or she'll never trust you to help her again.:*

The phoenix flared one more time and then quieted to a rippling lake of fire. I took some deep, calming breaths, waiting for my senses to adjust to the strangeness of having him inside me.

All of my Blood could shift into another creature, but their gifts didn't have separate personalities. Leviathan probably came the closest to actually being an individual separate from Mehen, likely because of the thousands of years he'd been imprisoned in his dragon form. But even when he was the dragon, he still felt like Mehen.

Smoak felt like an entirely different entity from Vivian. For one thing, he was male, and she was distinctly female. She preferred women—and would probably cut off the first man's head *and* dick who even thought about touching her—but she was still feminine. She loved the female body and reveled in my pleasure as much as my men. She knew exactly what it felt like when someone sucked on my clit, because she'd experienced it too.

Simmering inside me, Smoak was a mythical creature of liquid fire who had one thought only—getting his dick inside someone. Anyone. Male, female, he didn't care, but he definitely identified as male. Yet there was a fluid sense of Vivian inside him too. A kinship, or sisterhood. A deeper understanding of what it felt like to be female.

:*When I was born, Smoak was both male and female for many years,:* Vivian said in our bond. :*It was only when I began having sexual experiences that he started to identify more strongly as male. At first...:* Her bond weighed heavily in my mind, and I sensed old, shadowed hollow spots of pain. :*After what they did to me, I hated him for choosing to be male. Sometimes I still forget and refer to the phoenix as she, and there is a female aspect within Smoak. But he's primarily male and has a male's urges.:*

"It feels like you have a fever," Nevarre whispered, rubbing his mouth against my thigh.

I wrapped another length of his incredible hair around my

fist and tugged his head up so I could see his eyes. I didn't try to be gentle.

His eyes gleamed like obsidian pools beneath a full moon, full of deep, dark secrets waiting to be explored.

Smoak swelled inside me, and for a moment, I feared my skin would actually tear under the force of his flames. My skin felt too tight. Too hot. But then he flared out of my body, casting flames down my arms. I could feel him hovering over my back, his wings shimmering over my shoulders.

Flames danced up and down my arms. My eyes felt too hot and bright, but otherwise, I didn't feel burned or hurt.

Nevarre dragged his fingers through the flames dancing down my arm, and I could feel it, even though he didn't touch my skin. He touched the phoenix's essence, his fire. Smoak's flames didn't scorch our skin, but he made me feel what he felt. Through Vivian's bond, he was connected to me. A part of me.

Ignoring my hold on his hair, Nevarre nudged his head closer to my pussy. Though that word didn't feel right at the moment. Not with Smoak inside me. He knew and appreciated that sex organ, but he wasn't interested in taking Nevarre inside us.

He burned to be balls deep in Nevarre.

Heat pulsed through my groin and settled against my spine like a burning fireball. It burned and throbbed hard enough that I groaned. Holy fuck. Aching pressure expanded inside me. Desperate need, like if I didn't sink into Nevarre this very moment, I'd die in horrible agony.

He tugged against my hold. "Let me be the first to touch you like this."

I didn't even realize I'd closed my eyes. Blinking furiously, I pried my eyes open and looked down at him. He'd wriggled closer to the juncture between my thighs. His face was illuminated with flickering flames, and his eyes were locked on a shining red-gold rod.

Oh. Shit.

My dick. Or rather, Smoak's. But it felt like mine. I could feel the heat crackling inside it. Coiling pressure, building every second toward detonation. Molten fire simmered in my nonexistent balls, desperate for release.

I'd never dreamed it would feel like this. So... real.

My fingers loosened enough for Nevarre to lean up and swallow down the fiery cock that jutted up from my groin. I gasped, choked, and gasped again. Unable to breathe. Unable to think. I could feel the heat of his mouth. The press of his tongue. The slight scrape of his teeth. Through my bond with him, I could feel the searing heat of phoenix flesh in his mouth. The taste of smoldering cinnamon on his tongue.

The thought of coming and feeling this pressure exploding out into his mouth nearly made me spurt like Mount Vesuvius. I wanted to come like a man. I wanted to feel spurt after spurt sizzling on his tongue.

But I wanted to feel what it felt like to fuck his ass more.

I hauled his head up and made him look me in the eyes. His pupils were almost completely black. He was so zoned out that he'd let me do anything.

Lust thundered inside me, and for a moment...

I was terrified.

I didn't want to hurt him. I didn't want to take him thoughtlessly and fuck him like a mindless bull in rut. Nevarre didn't deserve that. No one did. But I didn't trust my judgment in this moment, not with Smoak's sizzling glee driving my own lust to a dangerous peak.

Rik rumbled soothingly in my mind, calming my turmoil immediately. :*That you're worried about your judgement only shows exactly how in control and mindful you are. Nevarre is fine, but I'll monitor him for you, my queen. You can trust me to put a stop to it if I have reason to fear for his safety or wellbeing.*:

:*And I will call Smoak back if he's out of control,*: Vivian added.

:But I assure you that in all my years of carrying him inside me, we've never hurt our partner beyond anything they enjoyed and desired.:

"Please," Nevarre rasped, drawing my attention back to the soft, fuzzy look in his eyes. The kind of look that Daire got after Mehen wrestled him into submission. Or how Mayte had looked at Vivian, her hair tangled in my Blood's fist, when we'd fucked at the grotto. Nevarre looked at me like I was his entire world. He'd stop breathing if I told him to.

A dark thrill of power rushed through me, along with the heavy weight of responsibility. Respect. And yeah, a sense of humbleness and awe.

He trusted me so much that he'd given up complete control to me. His life was in my hands to do with as I pleased. I would treasure that trust like I would shelter and guard a baby bird that had fallen from its nest to land at my feet.

"Fuck me, my queen."

NEVARRE

I'd never felt like this before. Soaring through the sky—even though I hadn't shifted to my raven. Free and weightless—but also bound and heavy. The more force Shara exerted to control my body, the more I seemed to soar.

And the more all the sharp, hard edges inside me softened.

Most days, I felt more like a pretty glass trinket than Morrigan's Shadow. I'd tasted the cold grave before, and though Shara had breathed life back into my body, sometimes my mind returned to that dark stillness. I could and did function like normal, but deep down, I couldn't forget that I'd been dead. I'd failed.

Inevitably, I would fail again.

So I felt... brittle. Like a raven hand-carved from a chunk of obsidian. If someone pushed me off the shelf, even accidentally, I'd shatter into a million pieces.

When my queen touched me, she warmed that cold, thin glass back toward life and light rather than death and emptiness. Even if she simply held my hand or smiled at me, I could feel her love sinking into me.

She used my hair to turn me around and shoved me in the back, pushing me down on my stomach. I was clumsy and slow, as if my body was drugged, even though my mind shot rapid-fire images at me so quickly that I barely had time to register them.

My beautiful queen, lit with fiery wings. Spicy plumes of smoke curled around her. Her eyes flickering with wildfire.

I couldn't see her with my own eyes, but through our shared bonds, I saw her lithe, feminine body riding me. Controlling me. And I'd never seen anything more perfect in my life.

She let out a high-pitched shriek in our bond that my raven recognized as an exultant mating call. Pressing against my back, she wrapped her arms around me, holding me as she fought to control the phoenix.

I didn't want her to slow down or deny herself. I wanted it all. Her lust, but especially her urgency and force. I wanted— needed—her to take me. Use me. As she saw fit.

If she didn't... I didn't think I would ever fully recover. I'd just crack apart, wings and heart irrevocably broken.

Even our bond crackled with flames. :*I don't know how much is me, and how much is Smoak.*:

:*It doesn't matter. I want this. I want everything.*:

Yet she hesitated, and a fine, thin crack splintered through me.

I had been used before by my former queen, and ultimately discarded when I failed to be of any further use to her. When we lost Morrigan's Grove, Elspeth didn't need a Morrigan Blood any longer. I had no power left. I'd failed our goddess.

But I had been more than her Blood. On paper, we had been man and wife, so she could access the deed and title to our house's lands when my mother passed.

I'd known I was a tool, a path toward increasing Elspeth's power base and her stature as queen. Mother had arranged the marriage, and I'd gone through with it willingly. It was a business transaction among houses. Nothing more.

When we lost the grove that my house had nurtured for generations, it hurt. Terribly.

But not as badly as feeling my wife dissolve my bond and walk away.

I didn't mind being used. I'd liked having a purpose. But I fucking hated being discarded afterwards like a piece of useless rubbish.

The thought of Shara using me for any purpose, but especially for her pleasure, made my heart soar like never before. But if I fell from this height...

There wouldn't be much left but a few sharp splinters of black glass to remind her that I'd ever been hers.

Pain seared through my scalp, jerking my gloomy thoughts away from my unfortunate failures of the past. My scalp burned as she wrapped another length of my hair around her fist. Leaning hard on her forearm, she pinned my head beneath her.

I could smell the rich loam of the grove, bursting with life and power. Mother Earth did Her best to renew the seasonal lifecycles, but without mankind's care and nurture, the earth was failing. Polluted and poisoned. Drained and raped of resources. Left to rot beneath an unforgiving sun.

Like my mother's grove, destroyed by men and machinery. Irreplaceable trees uprooted and stacked like refuse to be senselessly burned.

This earth smelled of Her power, fed by my queen's blood. My fangs throbbed gently like a sad goodbye.

I tried to focus on her, but my mind floated like a cloud. Not in bliss this time. Ironic. This time I wanted nothing more in the world than to be used roughly, and my queen could not bring herself to crack me open for fear of hurting me.

I tried to tell her it was alright. I understood. I loved her so much. Too much, perhaps.

Shara's voice snapped and crackled like roaring flames devoured her from the inside out. "Do you know what heat does to shards of glass?"

I couldn't answer her. I was too far gone.

Her fangs plunged into the meaty muscle of my shoulder, slamming me back into my body. I convulsed beneath her, my seed spilling onto the eager ground. Wave after wave of fire roared through me.

No. That was my queen's fiery dick as she pushed into me.

My body resisted, making her pant and shove harder against me. The angle wasn't right, not with her mouth locked to the punctures so she could feed. Her hunger pummeled my senses like furious giant wings, beating me into glorious submission.

Yes, my queen. Use me. Take everything. Break me.

She released my shoulder long enough to rise up and work deeper into my ass. She filled me, inch by inch, staking claim on my body. Possessing me.

Pushing away all my failures of the past. Those memories curled like delicate paper as she blasted another wave of heat through me. The cracks and brittle spots that had been barely holding me together gave way, splintering beneath her force.

I cracked open and fell apart. The years of my life blasted away in the furnace of my queen's desire.

Her fire melted all those sharp, useless pieces into a red-hot core of something new. Something so bright that I couldn't look at it. It hurt. Burned. Deep inside. So hot. All the dark memories and old hurts charred, seared away by her heat. The blackened bits flaked away, leaving only a pure, bright glow.

So she could reshape me like a master craftswoman using a torch to blow molten glass into a fantastical new shape of possibilities.

Her climax sent a searing wave through me. I was drowning in cinnamon and myrrh, boiling in a lake of fire hot enough to char the meat off my bones. She screamed with release and swept me away. Up and up, carrying me on burning wings. We flew together on silent wings, ever higher. Through thin, cold air, and beyond to an endless black velvet sky sprinkled with diamonds, so we could crash into the blazing sun itself.

Slowly, I came back to earth. My queen's hair in my face. Her mouth still on my shoulder, licking the blood from my skin. She probed the punctures with her tongue, drawing the last of the blood from the small wounds. With a low, soft sound, she curled around me. On me. Inside me.

And I never wanted to leave. I never wanted to get up. Not if she had to slide away and leave me empty once more.

Her dick pulsed faintly inside me. A promise that she could and would fuck me again.

I couldn't fucking wait.

She slipped down from my back to cuddle against my side, drawing a soft cry of protest from my lips that I couldn't suppress entirely. "Are you sure? I didn't hurt you?"

Rolling to face her, I stared into her eyes as her bond flowed through me like thick, raw honey, searching for any doubt or injury.

She saw everything. She always had. And she still wanted me to be her Blood. I wasn't worthy of such a queen, not after my failures. "I loved every bloody moment."

I heard Daire's purr a moment before he padded up and dropped down across my legs and Shara's. No one cuddled like the warcat, and our queen definitely loved his purr. But I couldn't help but feel as though he was intruding. His charming grin and easy manner were easy to like. Unlike my quiet ways. The darker mood that often hung over me like a cloud that I couldn't shake. The fear that any moment, our queen would recall that I'd been dead. She'd take back the life she'd breathed into me and I'd... Go back to the cold, silent grave? Or wander the earth like a mindless thrall.

"How are your tail feathers feeling, huh, Nevarre?" Daire grinned, batting his eyes at Shara. "I'd loved to be tapped by that phoenix anytime, anyplace."

Shaking her head, Shara combed her fingers through his tousled hair. "Weren't you supposed to be on guard duty?"

"I was. But there's nothing for miles and miles. Please, my queen?"

I didn't protest or plead for her to deny him. It wasn't my place. I wanted to get up and quietly withdraw, but I knew my hair was tangled beneath her. Besides, I didn't want to give the warcat the satisfaction of a retreat.

"Maybe later," she told him, focusing on me. "When you were dead, what was it like? Or is it too painful to talk about?"

I shook my head. "I don't remember much, honestly. I remember the crash. The pain in my wing as I tried to shift. Brigid was bleeding, but she was still alive. Even trapped in the wreckage, she was more worried about me than herself."

Lifting my wrist, I showed my queen the simple bracelet I wore. "She tied this on my broken wing and told me never to take it off."

Shara fingered the bracelet. It wasn't much to look at, just a simple braided cord of natural jute and a faded blue wool, a bit frayed and stained. Some of those old brown marks were likely remnants of Brigid's blood, as she fumbled to make the knot even though her fingers were slippery with blood gushing from her forehead. She'd barely been able to see, but she'd still smiled at me.

"There's power in it," Shara whispered. "Her intent is still bound to it. Bound to you. Her magic kept you bound to this plane until I could call you. If she were still alive, she would still have command over you. Perhaps even enough strength to force you to do her bidding over mine. I could try and break you free from her will, but it might kill you."

"She'd never do such a thing," I whispered hoarsely, my eyes burning even after all these years. *Ah, Brigid, my sweet lass.* "Her last words were, 'Wait. Wait for her.' She knew. Somehow. She always knew."

"How long ago was the accident? A year? Several?"

I shook my head ruefully. "I have no idea. I've never had a good sense of time. I slept for a while, but I was occasionally aware enough to realize that I was trapped. It was cold and dark and quiet. Sometimes I heard whispering, but no matter how hard I strained, I couldn't make out the words or who it was. Then one night I was awake and fully aware. I was needed. Urgently. I leaped into the air and flew straight to you."

Shara kissed the knotted string and then pressed her lips to my pulse beating so strongly in my wrist. "I'm grateful that she was able to save you, though I hate the thought of you lying trapped somewhere, waiting for me to call you."

Closing my eyes, I kissed the top of her head and breathed in her scent. "I'd wait however long it took to be here, now, with you."

9

SHARA

D r. Mala Borcht set her typewriter bag on the table beside me and then fucking curtseyed like I was the queen of England. "Your Majesty, how may I be of service?"

"First of all, you can forget all the formalities," I said tartly. "Please, sit. Would you like some coffee?"

Smiling, she took the seat between me and Gina. "Coffee would be great."

I hadn't seen her since Christmas Eve, when we'd gone to Venezuela to free Leviathan. That was the last time I'd asked for the doctor to accompany me on one of my dangerous adventures, because I'd realized something on that trip. She was an incredible doctor, but if I was injured, there wasn't anything she could do to help me, other than tell me exactly what was wrong.

I had the power to heal myself, in minutes versus days or weeks with conventional medicine. When the mighty dragon had broken my arm, I hadn't needed a cast. I'd needed his blood.

But I still did need her medical expertise, especially when it came to my Aima parentage. There was so much about being a queen that I'd learned, but no one had explained one very important thing that I needed to understand.

Daire set a cup of black coffee in front of her and added a little more to my cup to warm it. Gina offered a plate of blueberry muffins still warm from the oven. I took another one, even though I'd already had two this morning.

Rik didn't say anything, though I felt his intensity. His bond glowed hotter, like he'd started using bellows to heat up a forge. He passed through me, using his bond to search through my body like a spotlight.

I knew exactly what he was searching for, and there was no need. I had a lot of questions, but I was pretty fucking sure I'd know if I was pregnant.

:Just checking,: he whispered in my head soothingly. *:I'd know too.:*

"I have some biology questions," I said aloud. "Should we wait until you've finished eating?"

Dr. Borcht laughed softly. "Not at all. I could eat my lunch while watching a dissection. What questions do you have, Your Majesty?"

"Shara," I said firmly. She was friends with Gina, and I trusted her implicitly, but some of the humans close to me were very determined to stick to formalities. Winston would probably never call me Shara, but I hoped that she would. It just made it easier for me to talk to her about such personal things. "Since Rik and Daire found me before Christmas, my periods have gotten worse each time."

"Worse in duration? Or volume and symptoms?"

"All of the above. I'm almost afraid that eventually I'll just bleed all the time."

"You have been under a great deal of stress lately. That can affect your hormone levels."

I sipped my coffee and picked at the muffin, taking a small bite off with my fingers. "I did need the extra power boost to go after Keisha Skye, and then I went straight after Ra too. I was hoping to have a few quiet months or even years here at my nest, but I don't know how long I'll have before I have to deal with the Triune. I don't want my periods to get so bad that I'm constantly miserable before we discuss my options. Plus..."

I blew out a sigh. If I were a human woman banging ten guys, I couldn't imagine *not* being pregnant at this point. "I need to know how Aima queens get pregnant. I need to understand my cycle better before something happens accidentally."

Dr. Borcht shook her head. "I can say with a high degree of confidence that an accidental pregnancy will be nearly impossible. Aima queens don't conceive the same way that humans do. But let's go back to your concern with heavy periods first. There are some medications we can try that might help with the severity. Some medications work better than others on your kind, and I don't think anyone has tried hormonal therapy before. There just hasn't been a need. Aima queens don't generally come into heat any longer."

"See, that's one thing I don't understand. Am I 'in heat,' like breeding? Or is it part of a normal menstrual cycle?"

"I'll need to do some regular bloodwork to be sure, so I can analyze your hormonal levels every week. The one set of bloodwork we took several months ago isn't enough to establish what a normal cycle is for you. But I can certainly hypothesize..."

I nodded. "Please."

"Very well. What I think is happening with your longer and more severe periods is that your body is trying harder to conceive each month. It's nature's way of telling you that you're fertile and in your prime. You have powerful, virile Blood at your disposal. Biologically, this is the prime time for you to conceive, and so your Aima biology is trying to make your body as inviting as possible, both for your alpha's sexual interest and for carrying your offspring."

I frowned, picking at the muffin to find only the blueberries. "I won't be forced into anything. Not even by my own body."

"Don't think of it that way necessarily. It's not a negative thing. You will still choose whether or not to take advantage of the situation. It's just your body's way of signaling its readiness, even eagerness, to carry the next Isador queen."

"You're not the one constantly bleeding and dealing with higher tensions among my Blood because of it. Or feeling exhausted and wrung out from bleeding so much. Not to mention the cramps and generally feeling lousy." Grimacing at my grumpy tone, I tried to lighten my mood. "Sorry, I'm not trying to be bitchy. I know it's supposedly a miraculous thing for an Aima queen to be able to breed nowadays. I'll have a child someday, but I won't be forced into having a child before I'm ready. I'm sick of bleeding heavily day after day."

"I understand completely. Let's try some medications to see if we can calm your hormones down a bit. I'll do weekly blood tests so we have a good baseline of where you are, and then we can start after your next period. It may take some experimentation, but I'm sure we can at least lessen the severity of your symptoms."

Smiling with relief, I nodded. "Sure, that makes sense. Thank you. I was afraid you'd be appalled or refuse to even consider anything that might slow down my periods, since I'm assuming that's basically Aima contraception."

I was surprised when her face hardened, her eyes glinting with sudden determination. "A woman's body is hers to do with as she pleases, whether she be Aima or human. No one's going to force you to procreate, Your Majesty, least of all your personal doctor. I'm here to serve you and you alone. If you wish to use contraception of any kind, I will do everything in my power to make sure we find an appropriate solution that works with your body to achieve your goal."

She smiled and lightened her tone. "Besides, no one's done any research in this area, so I'm intrigued by the possibilities."

Gina leaned closer, keeping her voice low. "We should talk

about *how* to conceive, just so you know how it's done. When you're ready, of course."

I whispered back, "Is it a secret?"

Dr. Borcht chuckled, shaking her head. "Not at all. I think she's just trying to spare poor Winston the gory details."

Winston called out from the kitchen. "Don't mind me, I've heard it all. You forget that I served the queen who managed to conceive our current queen in secret after hundreds of years of failure."

I could only imagine how much Winston had overheard over the years, especially now with my Blood and our sexual activities. It wasn't like I ever tried to be quiet, and there was always excessive evidence left on the sheets. Both blood and semen. Sometimes I remembered to call the fluids to me to increase my power, but often times I didn't. I was just too busy running off to my next battle, or excited to go for a walk in my grove, or to take a leisurely soak in the grotto.

For fuck's sake, I'd had group sex out in the open twice yesterday alone. If Winston had happened to look out the window, he'd have seen me ravaging Nevarre on the grass.

Groaning softly, I covered my mouth. My cheeks burned with embarrassment, hotter than when Smoak had been inside me.

Which made Daire snicker. Rik dropped an arm around me and pulled me close.

Ezra bellowed from the kitchen. "Sign me up to be ravaged next."

"Fuck that shit," Mehen retorted. "You still owe me a caber toss first."

Nevarre strode around the table with a slow, arrogant pace meant to draw my attention to him. He flipped his hair over his shoulder and managed to give his hips enough of a shake to send the kilt flapping up a bit, giving me a tempting glimpse of the rounded curve of his ass. If his hair got longer every day, I was starting to suspect that his kilt got shorter. "Ravage me any time, my queen. I'm ready and eager to serve."

I couldn't be even moderately annoyed. Even though my cheeks burned hotter, which made all my Blood laugh more too. I waggled my finger at him, and he sidled up between me and Dr. Borcht. I hooked my arm around his waist and pulled him into the curve of my body, the same way Rik was holding me.

"Winston, I hope to goddess you weren't looking out the window yesterday," I said, trailing my fingers up beneath Nevarre's kilt. I just couldn't help myself.

Winston came over to clear away the muffin I'd demolished, along with the other dirty dishes. "Not to worry, Your Majesty. I learned that lesson long ago. Your mother loved to have garden parties before she closed the London house."

Llewellyn snorted. "That's a nice way of saying she was famous for her outdoor orgies. She loved to fuck beneath a full moon."

Oh dear. Poor Winston.

Daire's purr dropped another octave. "When's the next full moon?"

"Five days," Xin replied before Gina could look up the moon cycle on her phone. "Wolves know."

I could only imagine how gorgeous my silvery wolf would be in the full moonlight dancing across the snow. "Will you howl for me?"

"Of course. I'll see if I can draw the pack in to sing too."

I blinked, wondering if I'd misunderstood him. "The pack? You mean there's wolves in Arkansas?"

He shrugged. "There are now. I've seen their sign."

"Where?" Ezra demanded. "I've not seen any wolf tracks."

Xin gave him a cool look that could have frosted over Smoak's fiery breath. "Then you've not gone out as far as I have into the surrounding woods. I assure you there are wolves in the forest. Real wolves, not Aima shifters. I haven't spoken with them, but they left signs for me. Wolf song may draw them closer, and I can learn why they're here."

"So we're all agreed that our queen should host a garden party in five nights?" Daire asked.

"Aye," "yes," and "fuck, yeah!" echoed around the room, making me roll my eyes. As if anyone would expect any other answer.

"Focus, boys," Gina broke in with a firm voice, though her eyes sparkled with mischief. "We're supposed to be talking about Aima conception, not planning a garden party."

"It could be the same thing," Llewellyn muttered.

I gave him a pointed, arched-brow look and then firmly ignored him. "So how do queens conceive?"

"It's two parts," Dr. Borcht replied. She held up a finger. "First, her body must be ripe. She must be breeding. As you've learned, few queens breed any longer, which has drastically affected Aima numbers. I'd guess there's fewer than twenty thousand Aima still living in a nest and actively serving a queen, and likely only a couple of hundred queens at most who're powerful enough to support a nest. As more and more nests dissolve, Aima have spread throughout the world and integrated into human society, though they may still carry enough Aima blood to sense your magic."

"And the second?" I asked.

She held up another finger. "Sacrifice."

Surprised, I looked from her to Gina, who nodded solemnly in confirmation.

I'd never thought of my mother's death as a sacrifice, but that was exactly what she'd done. She'd killed herself.

For me.

Would I be required to sacrifice myself to continue the Isador line?

RIK

I squeezed my queen so hard that I felt her ribs creak against mine, while every muscle in my body rebelled.

"Never." I tried to soften the harshness of my voice, but the rock troll rumbled through me, giving me too much volume. "You won't need to give your life to have an heir. Don't even consider such a thing."

"He's right," Gina added quickly. "Your mother's sacrifice was an extreme case. Back in the old days, when conceiving a child was easier, a queen would generally only offer her own blood in a ritual sacrifice to her goddess. Or perhaps make a special item using her gifts. When the basic rituals failed to result in conception, it was only then that queens began trying more desperate and drastic sacrifices."

Dr. Borcht nodded. "Especially after Keisha Skye sacrificed her alpha's life to conceive. I can't begin to estimate how many alphas willingly sacrificed their lives for their queens to no avail."

Shara shuddered and pressed her face more fully against my chest. "I would never sacrifice one of my Blood, let alone Rik. I don't care if I never have a child and the Isador name dies with me."

I didn't say anything. I didn't have to. She knew full well that I'd lay my life down for her in a heartbeat. If she wanted a child and that was the only way to ensure it…

"No." Jerking her face up so she could glare at me, she retorted as roughly as I had spoken just moments before. "I refuse to even consider it."

"Neither of you are going to have to die," Gina said firmly. "I'm sure of it. That's why your mother did what she did, so that you could bring back the magic and power without facing such a sacrifice. Ask Mayte what she sacrificed to have Xochitl. She and her god are still alive and well."

I felt Shara reach out to her sibling queen. *:Mayte, Gina's telling me about Aima conception. What can you tell me about your ritual with Coatlicue? Did she require a great sacrifice from you?:*

:Not at all,: Mayte replied. *:I went to my favorite temple a few miles outside my nest and made my usual sacrifice. Just my blood and prayers, asking for Her guidance and blessing. Tepeyollotl joined with me on the peak of the pyramid and by morning... I knew that I carried Xochitl. Your mother was right. Tepeyollotl's blood was powerful enough to rejuvenate my line and give us the magic we needed to conceive.:*

She hesitated a moment, and I felt her rising excitement in our queen's bond. *:Are you thinking about conceiving an heir? With Rik? Or will you find your own god?:*

I practically ground my teeth to dust, but I said nothing. If Shara had to call a god to have a child, then call a god she would. I'd find him and drag him to her if I must. Fuck, I'd throttle him into submission, the same as I'd done to Mehen. My queen would have everything she ever wanted, even if that meant a god powerful enough to give her an Isador heir.

:No,: Shara replied. *:I only wanted to know how it's done. I'm not ready for a child. In fact, I asked my doctor to give me something to help control my periods a bit. They've been pretty miserable lately.:*

I felt Mayte's wistful disappointment in the bond, but she didn't press Shara or question her decision. *:Oh, no, I'm sorry, my queen. I hope the doctor can help. If you have any questions later, I'm happy to help you in any way. When you're ready, of course.:*

"She says that she made her usual sacrifice," Shara said aloud. "Tepeyollotl was enough to give her Xochitl."

Gina glanced at me a bit warily. "Will you go after a god too? When it's time?"

"I don't know. I don't think so. No, I think my problem will be wishing that I could have a child with several of my Blood."

She snagged my right hand and pressed her lips to my knuckles. "Of course I'd love to have a child with Rik. But can you imagine a baby dragon growing up with us? Or a tiny horse galloping around? Or a wolf? I wouldn't want to leave anyone out, but I'm also not eager to have a dozen or more children."

"Intention," Dr. Borcht said suddenly, her gaze distant as if she was running a complex experiment in her head.

"How?" Shara asked. "You mean..."

Her mind buzzed with ideas, and for the first time, I felt a strange pang in her heart. A yearning mixed with growing hope. She held not one baby, but two. No, three.

Of course, it would be three. We Aima loved our threes.

"You set the intention." Dr. Borcht focused on her, eyes shining with excitement. "In your ritual with your goddess, you begin the spell, or the magic, that enables conception. I don't see why you couldn't choose multiple Blood to help conceive your child."

"Children," Shara clarified softly. "Gina, are there any precedents for a queen having twins or triplets?"

"Oh, my. Well, I'm sure there are, but it would have been thousands of years ago, before we lost the power to conceive. I can look through the archives if you'd like."

Shara interlaced her fingers with mine. "No. There's no need."

The soft yearning pulsed again in her heart and then eased. It wasn't yet time.

I pressed a kiss to her knuckles, the same as she'd done to me. I didn't need to say anything.

She knew.

My queen would receive exactly what she desired. I would make it so or die trying.

10

SHARA

I waved goodbye to Dr. Borcht as her car pulled away. She'd drawn enough of my blood to make Rik jealous. Hopefully she could prescribe something to help before my next period started.

"I've gathered the information you requested," Gina said as I turned back to go inside. "Well, at least as much as I could find. There's not much."

"I guess that's not surprising, given that the Dauphine's so good at hiding." I started to go back toward the kitchen, but I hadn't seen any of Gina's folders in there. We might be more comfortable in front of the fire anyway. There'd be room for all of us, including Carys.

I frowned, trying to remember when I'd last seen her. The night we arrived, but not yesterday for sure. I'd actually forgotten about her.

Oops. I wasn't used to having house guests, and with all our private festivities going on yesterday... Hopefully she hadn't heard or seen more than she cared to know, either. "Has anyone seen Carys this morning?"

I could have used her bond, but I liked having all my sibling bonds quiet and masked in my head. In New York City, I'd gained nine more siblings counting Gwen and Carys, and if I listened to them all in my head, I'd go nuts. I even kept Mayte's bond muted, though I did reach out for her more often than the others. We each needed our privacy and alone time with our families. I didn't care to have my life spilling over into hers or vice versa, especially when it came to private moments with our Blood.

"I saw her in the library," Daire said.

"WHAT?!" Mehen exploded into action, slamming doors and crashing into the wall as he skidded around the corner in a flat-out run.

I raced after him. I didn't know what the problem was—only that I had the feeling we were headed toward dragon detonation. Opening Carys' bond, I warned her, *:Mehen's pissed and headed your way.:*

She didn't respond or even acknowledge me, which was also troubling. I pushed deeper, eavesdropping more into her mind. She sat on the floor surrounded by piles and stacks of books, happily reading.

The library door slammed against the wall with a resounding crash. "Get your filthy hands off my books!"

Carys looked up mildly, glasses perched on her nose. Winnifred flapped with alarm from her nap in front of the cold fireplace to crash around the exposed beams. She rained feathers down on us. Hopefully, no bird shit.

"Your Majesty, you have such an incredible library," Carys gushed in that baby-coo voice she usually only saved for her owl. "I found a gorgeous copy of Shakespeare's *Comedies, Histories, and Tragedies*, as well as a first collected set of *Poems*. The value of these two books alone is probably as much as you paid for this falling-down manor."

Mehen stalked a slow circle around the oblivious woman, his eyes glittering with pure murder. "Yes. Right beside the first edition Dumas and *The Workes of Geoffrey Chaucer.* Books I have claimed for the purpose of reading to our queen as she wishes."

"Oh, pish posh," Carys retorted. "If she wants to hear some bawdy jokes, all she has to do is listen to this horny bunch of fools."

"You crusty botch of nature! You have no idea what our queen enjoys. How dare you come into *her* library and lay hands on her *treasures* without at least asking? The gall!"

Of course. Dragons always had a hoard. Evidently, Mehen considered this library to be part of his most prized, secret collection. No wonder he was so upset to see Carys going through the books.

"You're a tedious bore. Books can't be locked up behind glass and beheld from afar. They're meant to be held and stroked, fondled as you gently turn each and every page to read the next wondrous passage."

Daire snickered. "Sounds like you should take a few of these books up to your room for some private time, Carys. Or maybe get yourself a couple of Blood of your own."

She sniffed with disdain, and I felt a strange sensation in my sibling bond with her. A pop, as if someone had opened a bottle of champagne.

Daire yelped and clamped a hand on his butt cheek. "Ouch! No fair! My ass is strictly off limits."

She snorted and rolled her eyes. "Yeah, right, tell that to half the men in this room."

Still clutching his buttock like she'd struck him with an arrow, Daire limped about the room. "Hey, I resemble that remark. Not that it's any of your business."

"She does have a point," I said. "I'd rather—"

Mehen whirled around to stalk toward me. Head lowered, eyes blazing with fury, nostrils flaring wide with each breath, fury pumping in his veins. Oh, my sexy, wicked dragon. "You can't possibly mean to let her touch these priceless artifacts. They're mine. I claimed them for you."

His dragon reasoning made perfect sense to him, even though I owned the nest itself. "Can't you share?"

His eyes bulged with fury as if I'd called him a sniveling pussy. Hands fisted, his shoulders corded with strain, he opened his mouth. Shut it. His throat worked, as if he was trying to think of something to say that wouldn't offend me as his queen.

I allowed my eyes to smolder as I stepped closer to him. Heat rolled off him and I could feel the tension singing in his muscles. He ached for a fight. He burned to protect his hoard. It was his instinct, as basic and necessary for him as breathing.

I simply had to turn his mind to other equally compelling instincts.

I laid my palm on his chest, enjoying the way he hauled in every breath like he'd just run a marathon. "I loved listening to you read in a French accent. Maybe you saw another book we could read? Something... sexier?"

"I'm listening," he rasped out. "What did you have in mind?"

Uh... I had no idea. Mom had homeschooled me before her death. After that, I was on my own and always on the run. I'd enjoyed reading when I was a teenager, but I couldn't worry about carrying a bunch of books with me.

A modern romance wouldn't hold Mehen's interest for long. He needed something elegant, interesting, old-fashioned...yet erotic as hell. Something that would hold his interest, even if Carys was touching his Shakespeares.

"I don't know if you'd be interested," Carys drawled. "But I did see a copy of *Les Liaisons Dangereuses* on that shelf behind you. Third row up on the right."

Ezra retorted, "What does that mean, for us cretins in the back?"

"*Dangerous Liaisons*," Carys replied with a smug smile. "I think that may intrigue our queen."

I wasn't familiar with the book, but Carys said, *:You're welcome,:* in our bond, so I was pretty sure it would check all of Mehen's boxes. Playfully walking my fingers across his pecs, I asked, "Would you read it for me? Please?"

He bent down enough to hook his arm beneath my butt and swooped me up against him. Striding furiously across the floor, he scanned the shelves and snagged the much-loved tattered copy of the aforementioned book, as well as another. He let out a low grunt of satisfaction. "The Marquis de Sade too. This ought to be fun."

"Not so fast, dragon." Ezra came closer to look over the shelves. "We all ought to be able to pick out a book to read to her."

Mehen let out a derisive snort that rattled his chest against mine. "The bear can read? Color me shocked. No fairytales, Goldilocks."

"Shut the fuck up, lizard breath." Ezra stretched up and snagged one book off the shelf. "Ah. This will be good."

Mehen glanced at the book in his hands with a sneer twisting his lips. "You can not only read, but you can read in German? Now this I have to see. I can't imagine our queen enjoying guttural mumbling as much as musical French, although that's the perfect book for you."

"What?" Daire asked, popping his head around Ezra's back to see. "*Das Parfum?*"

"*Gesundheit,*" Mehen practically chortled. "Smelly fucker."

Though his mirth quickly changed to a groan when I nipped his earlobe. "Anyone else who wants to pick out a book to read to me, grab one and let's head upstairs."

There was a stampede toward the shelves, though Mehen headed for the stairs, determined to be the first to read to me.

Leaving Carys to enjoy his hoard. At least for now.

11

SHARA

I lost at least three days in the bedroom while my Blood read to me. Not that I was complaining in the slightest.

This was what I'd sacrificed so much to gain. All the pain and worry and danger faded away beneath their sing-song voices and pure enjoyment in the literature they'd selected for me. Everyone took a turn while we puppy-piled in my bed. The bed was definitely huge, but with twelve people…

Some stacking was involved to get everyone close.

Even Vivian joined the pile, which warmed my heart. When she'd first come to me in New York, she'd been as prickly as Mehen and Ezra combined. But my guys made every effort to ensure that no one touched her inappropriately or made her uncomfortable in any way, so she gradually relaxed.

She trusted us. That touched me more than I could say.

I rested the entire time, feasting on the simple joy of having them close and touching like this. Their scents and the sensual heat from their bodies. Their laughter and banter when someone tried to act out a scene or switch to a new character voice for fun. I didn't have to feed on their blood to feel my power and strength welling like the Fountain of Youth.

Though, yeah, I did feed. A lot. Sex and blood and more sex. Again, not that a single one of them complained.

But I did have work to do. I had no idea how long Marne Ceresa might give me before she made her move, but I knew one thing for certain. She was playing the game. Hard. And she'd probably already moved her pieces into place on the board without me having a clue.

If that wasn't enough to give me insomnia, then I had to face the fact that the Dauphine was even closer. Guillaume was more worried about her than Marne, which told me exactly what we were up against. My Templar knight had served the most powerful Triune queen of the three. If he was worried...

I was a fucking nervous wreck.

I hoped Gina had found out more information with the extra days. Maybe there was something in the Isador folders that would help me piece together a plan of action.

I didn't want to carve out more territory or claim more power. I didn't want a showdown with the most powerful queens in the world. All I wanted was more of this. My Blood. Peace. Laughter.

If I had to kill to protect it...

So be it.

I couldn't wait any longer to come up with a strategy.

Just in case Carys was still fondling Mehen's beloved books, I asked Gina to meet me in the main living room. There were plenty of chairs, leather sofas, and large casual pillows cast about on the floor to make lounging comfortable, and it was close to the kitchen so we didn't have far to go for snacks.

Overnight, we'd had nearly eight inches of wet, heavy snow that made me glad for the cheery fireplace. With Rik's big body blazing heat against my back, a cozy fire on the hearth, and a cup of hot cocoa, I faced the mountain of folders Gina had gathered.

"First, I thought we'd zip through a few administrative items, if you don't mind."

I nodded. "Of course."

"Have you made a decision about whether to keep Kevin as your second consiliarius? If so, we ought to get the appropriate paperwork signed as soon as possible."

I snickered. "Vampire non-disclosure agreements?"

Gina wasn't amused. "Absolutely. We need to lock him into silence before we let him any further into your house's business. He's been absolutely professional and competent as far as I know, but I thought the same with Madeline. You may also want to consider giving him a tiny amount of your blood to bind him to you, if he's willing."

Madeline had been Keisha Skye's consiliarius. I'd actually been a few minutes away from making her my second under Gina, when we discovered that she'd been contaminated by the god of light. Her demise had not been pretty.

Kevin Bloom seemed to be a great replacement. He was young, bright, and extremely talented despite his age. He also had an eidetic memory, which could spell bad things for House Isador if he was going to betray me.

I touched Carys' bond, and when she didn't respond right away, I gave her a harder knock. I respected her privacy and would never use my sibling bond with her to force her into anything, but when I called upon her, I fucking expected a response.

:What?: She retorted.

I did the mental equivalent of raising my eyebrows in the bond, waiting to respond to her.

:My queen,: she added in a more civil tone, focusing more fully on me. *:Did you know that you've got an incredible first-edition set of J. R. R. Tolkien's books including The Hobbit? I can't believe the previous owner didn't auction some of these treasures off, especially if*

they needed money. You could practically buy the entire state without ever touching the Isador legacy.:

:I didn't inquire about the previous owner's history. I need to know what the probability is that Kevin will betray me if I make him my second consiliarius.:

:My gift doesn't work that way. I need to see him and you together to make that kind of calculation. That's why I insisted on accompanying you. I can't do you any good if I'm not physically present.:

I wanted to snipe back, "that would have been nice to know," but it wouldn't gain me anything, though it might make me feel better. *:Duly noted. Thank you for categorizing the library.:*

My gratitude fell to the wayside. She was already lost in the books again. Mentally sighing, I touched Gwen's bond. I'd been avoiding her the last few days to give her plenty of time to claim her Blood. After thousands of years, Guinevere was at last reunited with Lancelot. I sure wasn't going to interfere in that reunion anytime soon, let alone risk peeking into her mind at the most inopportune moment.

:My queen,: Gwen replied at once, much more civilly than Carys had done. *:I've been hoping you'd reach out so I could discuss a proposition with you. But your question first, of course, my queen.:*

:What do you think of Kevin? Is he trustworthy enough to become my official second consiliarius?:

:I'd recommend him without question,: Gwen replied. *:He helped me face Arthur with great courage, despite only being human. I'd trust him with anything.:*

It could still be a trap. The man was Byrne's grandson after all, who just happened to be Marne Ceresa's American consiliarius. *:Good to know, thank you. What did you want to talk about?:*

:I have an issue that I need to deal with.: She hesitated, taking a deep, slow breath before continuing. *:I need to leave your tower temporarily to retrieve another of my Blood.:*

Her bond trembled with emotion, though she wasn't afraid.

She was pissed. I had a feeling that retrieving this Blood of hers was going to be quite the battle that had been a few thousand years in the making. *:Of course. Let me do some checking with Gina and my Blood to see if I should come back to New York while you're gone, or if the nest will be alright unguarded temporarily. When do you need to leave?:*

:Well, soon, but there's a wrinkle that I don't know how to resolve. I need to leave the nest without Elaine Shalott knowing. I don't want her to see me coming. If she knows, she'll be too prepared, and I'm afraid you'll be finding another queen to hold New York City for you.:

Gwen had warned me that she already carried a blood bond with this other queen. In fact, Elaine had used that bond to prevent Gwen from ever claiming her own Blood. Even more despicable, Elaine had done so because she intended to bond Gwen's alpha to herself.

Luckily for Gwen, I was the stronger queen, and I was able to free her from that old oath. However, she did still carry Elaine's blood. If she wasn't as respectful of her sibling's privacy as I was, then Elaine could easily pinpoint Gwen's location. If she was strong enough, maybe even Gwen's thoughts or intentions.

Not good, for either of us.

My mind raced. The more I thought about Gwen and her need, the more my blood seemed to spark in my veins. There had been a trick that I'd planned to try before we went to Skye Tower last month that might help us. *:If I pull her blood out of you, would she still be able to track your location?:*

Gwen's bond jumped around in my head like a flaming kangaroo. *:What? How? I don't know. I don't think anyone knows. I don't think it's possible.:*

:It was only a test, but I was able to pull Keisha's blood out of a sample of Rik's blood before we came to New York. If I can do that on a larger scale and pull all of Elaine's blood out of you, then surely she won't have any way to monitor your location.:

:If you think it's possible, I'm willing to try. Though I'm sure she'll have eyes posted at all the major airports and ports just to be safe.:

My grove whispered in my head. *Nest. Tree. Guard.*

Along with the whisper, I felt a physical connection to that distant blood circle in New York City. I didn't know if a tree could grow in the darkness of the tower's basement, but evidently Morrigan's grove had an idea.

My lips quirked. *:I think I can get around that too. Hire a team to open up the concrete floor in the basement. I'll need to be able to reach into the soil. Say at least a six-foot square, though larger is okay.:*

:Immediately, my queen. When will you plan to arrive?:

Gwen was too polite to demand my presence at once, though if it were one of my Blood trapped somewhere, I'd be pretty damned impatient myself. *:I have something planned for the full moon, but could come the day after.:*

:Thank you, my queen. That gives me time to prepare.: I had a feeling that Gwen was the kind of person who could keep her face and voice completely modulated no matter what kind of shit was going down. However, her bond told me that she was crying happy, hopeful tears inside. *:All will be ready for you.:*

:Did you learn anything more about where Arthur's ring came from?:

:Not yet. The only person who may know is my aunt, but she's fully under House Shalott's control now. If I can sneak into England without Elaine knowing, then there are a few places I can search for answers.:

I pulled back from her bond and focused on Gina. "Two things. Gwen says Kevin is absolutely trustworthy, and she needs my help in New York for a day or two. I'd like to head there the day after we have the full moon garden party."

Gina pulled out her phone and started to send out the many texts to get another trip planned. "Will you want to stay at the tower or your mother's house?"

"Mother's, without question."

"Magnum will be thrilled to have you back so soon. Alright, that's taken care of."

"So what did you find out about Leonie Delafosse?"

Gina handed me a disturbingly thin folder. "As you can see, not much. House Delafosse came to New Orleans in the early 1700s from a minor French house. They are loosely allied with House Valois, which is descended from the Dauphine. But most minor houses are allied to larger houses, or they're swallowed up. Either they die out, or they get absorbed by the larger house and lose their own name."

"Valois." I turned to Daire. "Where did I hear that before?"

"Rosalind Valois," he replied immediately. "She was allied with Keisha and also her lover."

Oh yeah. She actually had her consiliarius reach out to me as soon as Keisha was gone to claim I was now her sibling by default. When I told her I'd be happy to accept her bond as *my* sibling, she suddenly wasn't interested. "Is Rosalind related by blood to Leonie?"

"Not that I could find, at least in the last two thousand years. All queens are related if you go back far enough."

I frowned, letting the details bounce around in my mind. Something was bothering me, but I couldn't put my finger on it. "Rosalind and Keisha. Did they care for each other? Like me and Mayte?"

"They were lovers, but I don't know how much they truly loved each other," Rik said. "I always had the impression that it was more convenience than any emotional attachment."

"So they were just allies," I said slowly. "Didn't you once say that they argued over which one was stronger?"

"Most queens keep the sibling contracts confidential, but it's clear to the outside Aima courts which queen is subordinate. It was never clear in the case of their houses which served the other."

I turned to Guillaume, waiting a moment as he stepped closer from his guarding position near the door. "When we talked about the Triune the other night, you made it sound like the call would come whether I wanted it or not."

He nodded solemnly. "The call will come. I'm sure of it, my queen."

"Then why was Keisha trying so hard to get on the Triune, if in the end, she wouldn't have had any say in the matter?"

He shrugged. "I don't believe she would have ever received a Triune call, no matter how many allies she had. But some queens believe if they grow their power base and prove themselves worthy, that the goddesses will call them to the Triune."

"God helps those who help themselves," Rik added. "Or in this case, goddesses."

"I don't know that's necessarily true," Gina replied slowly. "Name one Triune queen who *earned* her way to the table by making allies."

"Exactly," Guillaume said. "That's why I don't believe Keisha would have ever been Triune. I have to believe that the goddesses would never have wanted such a queen to sit at their table and make decisions for our courts, no matter how strong she made herself. You can't kill and torture your way to the Triune."

"Marne Ceresa is Triune. So was Desideria, and she certainly tortured you."

He nodded. "She did. She also exterminated countless queens' nests when they failed to ally with her. But that was *after* she was Triune."

I blew out a sigh. My stomach was a roiling pit of acid just talking about the Triune and the possibility that I would be called. Especially if all that power was what had made Desideria into the kind of queen who'd kill hundreds of people and torture her own Blood.

Guillaume went down on one knee before me and took my

hand in his. "I don't care how much power you gain. You are not the kind of queen who'll ever be content slaughtering people for your own amusement."

I swallowed hard, searching his eyes. "But I have killed many people already, or they're dead because of me. Keisha. Her Blood. Ra. Madeline. That saleslady in Kansas City. How many more will I add to my list? Especially if Marne tries to hurt any of you in order to get to me. I'll fucking kill her, G. Just thinking about it makes me so angry..."

Fire licked at my veins, making the fine hairs on my nape quiver. My power rose, eager to be used. Ready to defend my Blood and nest, even if that meant death. I could almost feel Smoak hovering over my back again, screeching in glee as I bathed the world in flames.

"Good," Guillaume growled, squeezing my fingers hard enough that I blinked away the fire threatening to blast through me and focused on him. "Blast those fuckers who stand in the way of what your goddess set you to do. Anyone who threatens you should die. Anyone who thinks to sway your hand by using one of us against you should die. We need a queen who's ready and willing to kill to defend her court."

"Use us," Mehen added, his words more of a hiss as Leviathan perked up inside him. If there was going to be killing, the dragon was more than ready to feast.

"Isis gave you monsters for a reason," Llewellyn reminded me. His eyes were bright and eager, the gryphon ready to tear my enemies to shreds. "And remember why..." He paused, his shoulders tight. The cords in his throat standing out in stark relief. "She..." He shook and swallowed hard, trying to break the geas that kept him from uttering my mother's name. "She hid you for a reason. She sacrificed her life for a reason. So you could grow up free of the normal court in the shadow of Triune rule."

"As strong as you are..." Guillaume nodded slowly. "They

wouldn't have allowed you to live without swearing to one of them. That's exactly why Desideria used me to exterminate nests. If a queen was strong enough, she joined Desideria or died. There was no in between. Marne seems to be cut from the very same cloth. I don't know enough about the Dauphine, but I would hazard a guess that she'd do the same."

"I was used to kill the young before they could mature." Xin spoke softly, but even Guillaume twitched, his right hand automatically sliding toward his hip where he must have a weapon stashed. "Even Wu Tien child queens were eliminated if they were considered a threat and weren't tightly bound to the ruling queen of the clan. They would have killed you in the cradle, my queen."

Chilled, I rubbed my arms briskly, trying to dispel the sense of foreboding. Rik wrapped his arms around me, sheltering me deeper in his embrace. Chin on my shoulder, he held every inch of me against the solid protection of his body.

"You know..." Gina stared off into space. Deep in thought, she tapped her nails on the arm of the chair. "Why didn't Keisha Skye ever go after Leonie? Or did she, and it was kept a secret? But why?" She focused on me, and I could almost see the wheels turning in her head. "Isn't that strange? The most powerful queen in America, at that time, at least, was content to allow a stray queen to rule her court without interference. When she laid a geas on Zaniyah's blood circle forty years ago and waited like a giant spider to take Mayte into her house."

"We weren't high enough in House Skye to know much." Daire shifted closer to me and draped one arm over my knees. "But I never heard of any talks or treaties with House Delafosse. We knew Leonie existed, but Keisha never said a word about her."

Rik's chest rumbled against the back of my head. "Meanwhile, Keisha was sending out small teams like us, hoping to snag a young queen to her house."

"Exactly." Gina snagged a laptop out of her bag and opened it on her lap. "Let me check the postings and see if anything was ever made formal."

I combed my fingers through Daire's hair, and he nuzzled my hip, pressing more of his body against me. "Postings?"

"Anytime the Triune wants to make an announcement, the message is posted so that all Aima can read it. Any sibling agreement is announced through formal Triune channels, or it's not considered a legally binding agreement. There could still be a private blood agreement between the queens, but if there was a dispute, they couldn't come to the Triune for assistance if it wasn't announced. Back in the old days, the announcement would have been posted at the crossroads or taverns, with a sort of magical flare that would draw attention to it."

"Did you post the formal announcements when I claimed Zaniyah?"

Gina lifted her gaze to mine, her brow furrowed. "Yes, I did so automatically. I'm sorry, my queen. I should have made the process clear to you in case you didn't want any Triune attention brought to you."

I smiled, shaking my head. "No, don't apologize for doing a great job. I'm trusting you to handle all of the Triune law since I don't have a clue. I want my relationship with Zaniyah to be public, so she has recourse if anything happens to me. Gwen and Carys too."

Relieved, Gina quirked her lips. "And the other queens you bonded in New York City?"

I rolled my eyes. "Them too, though honestly I can't even remember their names at this point." Gina returned to scanning her computer screen, her fingers moving quickly as she flipped through several pages. I had to admit that I was intrigued. When I thought of ancient thousand-year-old vampire queens, I never imagined they'd communicate through websites or email or whatever it was that Gina was referencing.

"It's actually a database, and…" she muttered something beneath her breath and frowned at the screen. "Absolutely nothing is coming back for House Delafosse other than the original recognition of their blood ties to House Valois. That's extremely odd. Wait. Oh, fuck."

I jerked upright, ready to grab Guillaume's sword myself at her exclamation. I don't think I'd ever heard Gina curse before. "What?"

"I never noticed it before, but guess who created the Triune database?" Wide-eyed, Gina picked up her phone. "A certain Kevin Bloom. Let me call him and see if he still has access to the back-end data. Maybe there's some kind of security in place that's keeping me from finding the information we need."

She dialed his number and flipped on speaker phone so I could hear.

Kevin answered on the first ring. "Ms. Talbott, how can I help you?"

"I'm here with our queen—"

"Your Majesty, how can I be of service?"

I could tell from his high-pitched voice that he was excited. Had Gwen hinted to him that I was going to call and ask him to be my second consiliarius?

:No,: she retorted in my head, surprising me. I didn't realize she was still connected to me. *:I'd never do such a thing.:* Then she added hastily, *:I'm sorry for eavesdropping, Your Majesty. I wasn't sure if you'd need anything else, and you didn't shut down my bond.:*

Anxiety tightened my bond with her. She truly worried that I'd be angry that she'd been on the other end of the line, listening in, even though it was my fault for forgetting to hang up. *:Thanks for staying available, Gwen. We're trying to track down some information and need Kevin's assistance.* He sounded like a kid getting ready to open his birthday presents, so I assumed he might already know.:

She laughed softly. *:He's always that excited.:*

"I have an important question to ask you, and Gina also needs some information to help me to pinpoint a theory." I caught Gina's gaze, and she nodded, telling me to go first. "Kevin, I'd like to make a formal offer for you to become my second consiliarius, on one condition."

"Yes?" His voice trembled. Gwen sent me an image of the young man clutching his phone in a fierce grip, his eyes wide.

"Would you be willing to take a small amount of my blood? This would allow me access to—"

"Yes," he blurted. "Yes. It's an honor. I'd be delighted, my queen."

Shaking my head slightly, I continued the warning despite his agreement. "It would give me access to your mind and location. I try very hard to be respectful of Gina's privacy, but I've been grateful for the ability to find her and send her a silent communication."

"Most of the older queens require it from all their human servants," he replied. "Consiliari even more so. I totally understand and would have suggested it if you hadn't asked. Grandad certainly carries Marne Ceresa's blood, and she uses it often to keep him apprised of her orders despite the distance between them."

"If you're sure—"

"One-hundred percent," he said again immediately.

"Then I'm coming to New York in a few days to assist Gwen, and we can formalize everything at that time."

"Yes, yes, that'd be fine. Hold on a second, Your Majesty."

Something muffled the phone, but I could still hear his enthusiastic whoop. Gwen sent me another image of Kevin hopping and dancing around the room, grinning from ear to ear.

"Pardon me, Your Majesty." He managed to sound much more subdued when he returned to the phone. "I look forward to serving you in any way possible."

"I'll send over an example contract for you to take a look at," Gina said.

"And I'd like you to write up any specific requests you have," I told him firmly. "You've seen the other sibling contracts we negotiated so you know what kind of fairness I expect."

"Of course, my queen. How else can I be of assistance?"

"I'm trying to find information on a certain queen and any sibling arrangements she or her house has made in the last few centuries. I'm not having any luck, and I noticed that you were the database creator. Can you—"

"Already pulling up the back-end data," he replied. "Just a sec... Okay, shoot. What's the name?"

"Leonie Delafosse."

"I can tell you without even searching that there's nothing, but I'll try... Yep. No matches, other than the original connection to House Valois through some distant queen. I couldn't read the original ledger when I input the data into the tables."

Gina let out a soft whistle. "Wait, you actually looked at all the old documents and put everything in manually? Yourself?"

"Yes. It actually didn't take that long, even though it spanned several thousand years. There just aren't that many queens left to worry about, and before Desideria Modron's reign of terror, queens lived for basically forever and alliances didn't change that often."

Certainty burned inside me, a growing resonance that told me I was right. "So Keisha Skye never lodged any kind of sibling agreement with Leonie Delafosse, even though Keisha was setting herself up to be *the* American queen. Even though Keisha wanted to make herself powerful enough to sway the goddesses into giving her a Triune seat. There has to be a reason that everyone left Leonie alone, even Keisha."

"Maybe she just wasn't that powerful..." Daire lifted his head from my lap. "Scratch that. Keisha had plenty of siblings who weren't that powerful. We all knew about Leonie, but I couldn't tell you anything about her, other than she's in New Orleans."

"Vampires were good for business," Rik said slowly. "That's all I can remember Keisha saying about Leonie. What business? Keisha didn't give a fuck about any of her many businesses she owned. All she cared about was bringing more queens under her power."

"It's her," I whispered. "The Dauphine. It has to be. She's powerful enough to make everyone look the other way. Fuck, she's basically hiding in plain sight, and no one ever thinks twice about an insignificant queen in New Orleans. How old is she? What are her powers? How big is her court?"

I looked around at my Blood and watched them shake their heads, shrug, or frown, trying to remember anything.

"A geas. She's put a geas on everyone, the same as my mother. Only we can evidently talk about her, but only as an insignificant queen that no one cares about. She had to have done something to Keisha that made her look the other way. Some kind of nudge or secret agreement. Are there any other logs that we can search that aren't official Triune logs? Like the visitor logs, or even phone records. Did Madeline ever call Leonie's consiliarius? Did Keisha ever travel to New Orleans, or did Leonie ever go to New York?"

"I'll look through everything Madeline Skye left in her office," Kevin said immediately. "She kept meticulous records, so there could be some minor note or reference, even if no formal agreement was ever made. I'll let you know what I find."

"Great, thanks, Kevin. Hopefully you'll know something by my visit."

"I'll get to work immediately, my queen."

Gina disconnected the phone, but I still felt Gwen hovering quietly and unobtrusively in my mind. Before I could ask, she replied, :*I never saw Leonie at the tower, or heard Keisha mention her. But I wasn't one of Keisha's friends or trusted confidantes. I prob-*

ably wouldn't have known her even if Leonie stayed in the tower.
Would you like for me to ask some of our other siblings?:
:No.: I spoke the rest aloud so Gina and my Blood could hear too. "Let's come at this from a different angle. Search the archives for any obscure or ancient ties of my other New York City siblings to House Valois instead of House Delafosse. I know one of the queens was basically a spy for Marne Ceresa, so it's likely that the Dauphine has a contact inside the tower as well. Maybe even a queen who doesn't have a clue that she's working for anyone other than a minor New Orleans queen. So don't ask anyone else anything. Let's see what Kevin can dig up and go from there."

Gwen pulled back from our bond and I allowed it to close. I still couldn't shake the uncomfortable sensation that we were missing something. "Who is Leonie's consiliarius?"

Frowning, Gina ran through her phone contacts. "I actually don't know. I'll have to look it up."

"Another vampire database?"

She snorted and dialed another number. "I wish. Try a good old-fashioned phone book. Angela, I need the consiliari contact reference book. It's in my desk in the Kansas City office. Yeah. Sounds good, thanks."

She hung up. "Angela's on her way. I hope you don't mind, Nevarre, but we thought we'd use the helicopter for this kind of last-minute trip back and forth. It's easier to get the helicopter up than the jet, especially since the nearest airport big enough to accommodate it is in Harrison."

My raven Blood stepped closer. "Do you need a pilot?"

Eyebrow arched, Gina gave me a slightly wary look. "Would you mind? I wouldn't dare send one of your Blood away on even a short mission without your approval. Otherwise, I'll just hire someone from Harrison to make the trip for us in our helicopter."

My gut instinct was to seize a handful of Nevarre's hair in

one hand and his kilt in the other. Other than the coordinated attack on Heliopolis, I'd never been parted from any of my Blood. Of course, they often were "away" on guard duty, but they were always close enough to return to me in minutes. Nevarre was a powerful son of Morrigan who'd been alive hundreds of years. Surely he could survive a short helicopter trip to Kansas City and back. I refused to even think about the car accident that had killed him and his druid witch years ago. That had been Ra's doing, and I'd handled the god of light.

Besides, Nevarre *wanted* to go. Desperately. Not to be away from me for even a heartbeat—but to do some small service for me. Something only he could do. To my knowledge, none of the other Blood could fly a helicopter or airplane.

"There's no need to wait for a subpar substitute when you have a pilot here," I finally said grudgingly. Though I did snag his hand and pull him down into a kiss. *:How long will you be gone?:*

:Only a few hours, my queen. I'll be in constant contact.:

:Fly safely, my Shadow.:

:Always, my queen.:

12

EZRA

F ucking guard duty. Paired with the motherfucking dragon yet again. Rik had to be laughing his ass off every time he sent me out with Mehen. At least this time, he'd also sent Guillaume with us. The horse had no patience for the dragon either. Luckily, Mehen was fairly sated and satisfied. His belly wasn't stuffed full of the meat of our queen's enemies, but he'd had his fill of her blood, sex, and reading for days. I honestly couldn't say which he'd relished more.

Fat and sassy, he'd shifted to his dragon and made a slow circle above us. He was too lazy to walk with us. Thank goddess the knight was content to just walk and look. It was a fucking waste of time anyway. Our queen had killed a fucking god. I couldn't see how much of anything would ever intimidate or scare her now.

I drifted off a bit from the other Blood. My skin felt itchy, and yeah, I was grumpy. Even more than usual.

I stopped beneath one of the giant trees and leaned back against the bark. I breathed in the silence and the sense of reverence. Walking the grove was like visiting an ancient cathedral or standing inside Stonehenge, not that I'd ever been. I could feel the breath of the goddess on the wind and almost hear Her voice.

My grizzly growled mournfully. The woods had always called to me, stirring a deep yearning that had made me a loner most of my life.

The crisp winter air, the soft snow underfoot, the trees so still and silent that I could almost hear the gentle plop of each snowflake. Once upon a time, drinking in this stillness would have soothed me like nothing else in this world.

Now...

I couldn't stand the quiet. I didn't want to be alone.

No. Fuck me. I was fucking terrified.

I tried to remember what my life had been like before.

The solitude of the forest. No guard duty. No bitching dragon. No alpha.

Oh, Rik was a fine enough alpha. I'd seen plenty worse for sure.

But it still galled. Not that he told me *what* to do, but that I did it without question. Even dumb shit like guard duty on a nest full of watchful birds and sentient trees, powered by a queen strong enough she might as well be her goddess. That irritation was there, and sometimes it gnawed at me like a burr under Guillaume's saddle. I wasn't the kind of Blood who bent my head to anyone but our queen. Rik knew that and he didn't take advantage of his position.

But still. It galled.

Or, at least, it'd used to. Before.

But I didn't want to think about that.

I found myself staring out at the snowy woods and wishing to goddess I could forget the past few months. Back then, I'd been alone, and I hadn't fucking cared. I could find a nice cozy hole somewhere alone and sleep the winter away. Maybe even the whole fucking year.

Guillaume joined me beneath the branches, and the griz

thought really hard about biting his head off. He'd grow it back. No fucking loss.

"You would leave our queen?"

"Nobody said anything about leaving. I know my duty."

"I don't stay here for duty, my friend."

I didn't look at him, but I felt my lip curl up with disdain. "I'm not your *friend,* knight."

Unperturbed, Guillaume squatted down and dug around in the leaves and debris from the tree with one of his knives. I hadn't even seen him pull it out. "Warriors-at-arms, then. We've certainly seen some shit in the last few months. More than I've seen in the last two hundred years combined."

I grunted in agreement. We'd barely spent a month in Shara's nest together, and even that was broken up by trips to New York and Egypt. She was definitely in high demand, and if he was right...

And de Payne was always fucking right.

Then Shara was about to get a million times busier with Triune business.

Not a life I'd ever imagined for myself. Yet the thought of losing it all almost made me blubber like a baby.

"I still remember the first time they cut off my head," Guillaume said in a soft, almost wistful voice completely at odds with the words themselves. "I'd seen plenty of death and torture before, and yeah, I'd dealt a great deal of suffering myself. I knew my duty and I did it well. I didn't question my oath, honor, or service. I took my orders and executed them. That's what a de Payne did. Without question."

I wasn't sure what his point was, but I couldn't remember the knight ever telling this story before.

G wiped the blade clean on his sleeve and then stroked his fingers over the steel lovingly. "In all those years of dealing death with my knightly honor, I had contemplated what the end of my own life would be like. It was a sort of escape from the horrors of war. A future blessing that I held sacred in my mind. When the bloody faces and screaming mouths followed me into sleep, I'd awake, drenched in sweat, and I'd think, someday, I'll die. I'll die in honor and it'll all be over. It'll all be worth it. I'll be free. Aima are damned hard to kill, so I knew it would be many centuries if I were lucky. Yet I still had that hope of a peaceful death. That would be my reward for lifetimes of blood and pain."

He glanced up at me and smiled, a grim twist of his lips. "And then I found the true horror of my existence. Because I could not die. I was trapped in an infinite war, bound by my honor. First to my house, and then to Desideria, and she used me well. Too well. I refused to count the number of lives that met their end on my blades, because it was always a grim reminder that they had what I could never have."

I still had no fucking clue why he was telling me this. I didn't know what he wanted from me, and words had never been my strong suit.

Griz paced inside me, whuffing nervously with every step. The bear had gotten me out of some serious shit before. If he was worried...

I pushed up from the tree trunk and headed for the next tree. Maybe G would take the hint and leave me the fuck alone.

"What did the demon child show you in her blood circle?"

Hairs all over my body shot up with alarm, zinging with warning. Just like they'd done when I'd stepped into that foul trap in the dark basement.

Jaws clenched so hard my teeth ached, I fought back the foulness threatening to bubble up. I reached for griz, desperate for the bear's take-no-shit attitude. But he'd retreated at the first hint of that memory. Leaving me alone in the cold, dark circle with a demon.

Fuck me sideways, but I could still hear her creepy child-like laughter as she made me whimper and scream.

"I don't think Rik will mind me telling you that he saw me taking his place as alpha. Over and over. All the ways he could fail to protect our queen. All the ways I'd gleefully make him watch and suffer until I killed him. Tanza pulled up the worst possible thing that could happen to him and made him live it in her circle so she could feed on his pain and horror. That kind of torture leaves a permanent mark on a person."

My shoulders shook. My hands ached, my fingers drawn up into fists so tight my nails were cutting my palms, even without the bear's claws. Worse, though, was that raw, zinging feeling in my skin. That sense of impending doom crawling through my nerves.

Guillaume placed his palm on my back and my skin tried to jump off my bones and fucking dance a jig. "Shara purged you of the demon's blood, but she can't take away the memory. If you allow it to fester..."

"I'm fine," I managed to say somewhere between a growl and a whimper.

The knight wasn't fooled. "Sure, sure, you're fine. Big tough man like you doesn't need anybody to talk to. You don't need anyone to watch your six or sharpen your swords or take a turn at the watch. You always liked being alone in the woods."

A sound tore out of my throat that shamed me to my core. It made my knees tremble. Drenched in sweat, I fought to plug that tiny leak, but the fucking knight didn't have any mercy.

"That's it," he whispered, gripping my shirt. Pinning me in place. "She gave you exactly what you used to love. The solitude of the forest. No people. No politics. No queen. No alpha. No smartass warcat or arrogant dragon. Just you, with the thing you used to love the most destroyed forever."

My heart pounded so hard that I thought my rib cage would crack. I couldn't say anything. It hurt too fucking bad.

All my life, I'd loved being alone. That was who I was, and I'd taken pride in being the outsider. The loner that no one cared about. The forgotten one. It'd allowed me to make my mark on the fringes, listening in where no one expected, because I kept to myself and didn't play sides.

I'd never loved anyone until Daire. Losing that young scamp decades ago had taught me a very painful lesson. I'd gained him again for a time, but then lost him to Rik. I'd told myself it was no big deal. I was fine. Shit happened.

But I'd come cross-country on foot over a thousand miles to find him when I suspected he was in trouble. Only to find that I was the one in trouble.

Shara fucking Isador trapped me with her delicious blood and her toe-curling power.

In Tanza's circle, I'd learned exactly what it meant to serve such a queen.

Losing Daire had hardened my heart and honed me into the axe-wielding wild man I was now. Losing my queen...

I'd never dreamed such horror and pain could exist.

Even now, I felt the absolute soul-wrenching agony of watching her eyes narrow with suspicion when she looked at me. Tanza had contaminated me, and she'd whispered in my head that I'd never be free of her. My queen would look at me and always wonder if she'd gotten all of that black, foul taint out of me. There would be a kernel of doubt in her eyes. And that kernel would sprout.

I would bitch one time too many, or pick a fight that I shouldn't, or refuse one of my alpha's bullshit orders. Something would crack her confidence in me, and she'd wonder.

She'd remember the demon crawling and rotting in my soul.

I'd live every day dreading that look of doubt. Watching the blackness spread, not in myself, but in my queen. For that was the horror Tanza gave me. Not the taint inside me—but the stain on my bond with my beautiful queen. That blot of black ink would spread throughout our bond, destroying her trust and love, until one day, she would send me away.

I'd lose her.

I'd lose the shining, soft look in her eyes. The smoldering taste of her blood. The fierce rush of her pleasure blasting through our bond. Her courageous stand against anything and anyone who threatened me. The threat would come from inside her, and there was nothing I could do to stop it.

Until she was gone.

A tear trickled down my cheek and I wanted to die. If Guillaume had still held the knife in his hand, I would have plunged it into my heart over and over. I would rather die now than suffer one second of my queen's doubt. To lose this paradise of having not just her, but Daire and all the other Blood too.

I couldn't be alone again.

Not now.

Not ever.

Guillaume gripped my shoulder hard, squeezing like he thought I was going to fall apart. But it was the motherfucking dragon who destroyed the last of my reserves.

"You fucking moron," Mehen growled, giving me a good shake. "She won't ever let you go."

I threw my head back and bellowed with agony. Fear. Despair.

My bear roared and clawed, adding to my pain.

Her bond flared inside me, a beacon to the wild animal tearing me up. *:Ezra. You're my bear and always will be.:*

:I can't.: I panted in our bond, a shivering, sobbing wreck. *:I can't lose you.:*

:Come to me. Come to me now.:

<hr />

SHARA

Oh Ezra. My poor bear.

I couldn't bear his pain and fear.

He came to me, crashing through the undergrowth, careless and desperate to reach his goal as quickly as possible. The mighty grizzly was king of the forest and feared nothing.

Except losing me.

He didn't even hesitate at the door but rushed headlong to fall to his knees before me. Burying his head against my stomach, he wrapped his arms around my waist. I held him, running my hands over his broad shoulders. I combed his thick, curly hair with my fingers.

Daire joined us, pressing close to the big man's solid bulk and letting out his rumbling purr. Ezra's shoulders quivered beneath my hands, his back heaving with frantic breaths. But slowly, he started to settle against me.

My first instinct was to quickly scan his body and search for any lingering taint, but I feared that would only alarm him. It was too similar to the nightmares that Tanza had planted in him. I didn't doubt his commitment to me. I certainly didn't doubt my ability to heal. I'd already scanned him thoroughly and fed him heavily with my blood. To do so again, with that memory hovering in his mind, would damage him even more, perhaps irrevocably.

I didn't say anything. He knew how much I loved him. That was what hurt him so badly. He had to accept the fact that I wouldn't send him away, even if I suspected he was contaminated. I could argue and swear the truth to him, and he wouldn't believe it. He had to *feel* it. He had to know it. For himself.

So I held him, murmuring nonsense to him in a soft, gentle voice as I smoothed my hands in circles over his body. Daire did the same, pressing against Ezra's back, cuddling against him the way only a purring warcat could do, even in his human form.

Slowly, Ezra's breathing steadied and he eased against me. No longer shaking and troubled, but at peace. When his shaggy head finally lifted and his dark eyes met mine, I smiled and reached up to gently tug on his beard. "There's my grizzly."

He swallowed hard. "My queen."

I leaned in close, so our noses almost touched. I could smell the spicy cinnamon of his fur, mixed with spruce and sweet tobacco. Holding his gaze, I willed him to believe me with every fiber of my being. "I will never abandon you, and I will never make you leave."

His eyes were so sad, dark and wet like pools in a secret oasis. "You cannot save us all."

My face hardened and my power sparked, casting specks of glitter into the air around us. "Watch me."

"My queen," Nevarre said, drawing my attention to him. He hesitated at the door, holding what looked to be an old phone book in his hand. "I'm sorry for interrupting. I return with the information your consiliarius required."

Smiling, I draped my arm over Ezra's shoulders and pulled him with me as I leaned back against Rik. When Nevarre had first left, I'd touched his bond constantly, reassuring myself even though it wasn't necessary. I'd just liked feeling him in my mind while he was away. I wouldn't say I'd gotten used to his absence, but I had at least adjusted to it. "I'm so glad you're back."

"That was quicker than I expected." Gina gave him a teasing wink and then accepted the phone book. She immediately started thumbing through the pages. "Is the helicopter still in one piece?"

Nevarre winked back at her. "More or less."

I turned my head aside offering my neck to Ezra. "Feed, my bear. Let my blood draw you closer and soothe your weary beast."

I didn't have to tell him twice. In seconds, his fangs penetrated my skin with a searing sting that quickly faded to sensual enjoyment. Goddess, I loved to feel my blood flowing into them. Every swallow brought us closer, entwining our souls so tightly I couldn't tell where I began and Ezra ended.

I was inside him, as surely as I'd been inside Nevarre. I didn't need a blazing phoenix dick to claim him.

He grunted against my throat. *:Claim me any way that you'd like, my queen, though I admit that I'm not too sure about lighting up my asshole with flames.:*

I couldn't help but laugh.

:My tail feathers were completely unsinged,: Nevarre said in our bond, making me laugh harder.

"Well, I guess it's time to head to the table for dinner." Gina tossed the book on the coffee table and smiled brightly at me. "Hungry, my queen?"

"Wait," I said slowly. "What just happened?"

Her head tipped slightly, her brow furrowing. "Nothing, yet. Aren't you hungry? Winston said he'd wait for Nevarre to return before he'd serve."

I shifted forward, disentangling myself from Ezra so I could stand. Rik pushed to his feet, holding me against him. His hand spanned my stomach, ready to yank me up and get me to safety. I could feel his senses straining, searching for anything amiss. We weren't under attack. Nothing unexpected approached the nest. Mehen and Guillaume were still out in the grove and saw nothing to report.

Yet something was very, very wrong.

"You just sent Nevarre on a three-hour flight to Kansas City and back to retrieve that book. But you're not going to tell me what you found?"

"Oh, that?" Gina glanced at the consiliari phone book and shrugged. "It's nice to have on hand as more sibling requests come in. Thank you for sending Nevarre to get it."

Carefully, I touched her bond. She was confused by my reaction, but otherwise, she seemed fine. Her mind wasn't frozen or clouded. I didn't sense any stray entity or magic affecting her. "I asked you to contact Leonie Delafosse's consiliarius. You said we needed the book. Was she not in there?"

"Who?"

:She's been spelled,: I warned my Blood silently so as not to alarm her. *:Nevarre, did you feel anything strange when you touched that book?:*

:Nothing, my queen. She had it open, though. Could the spell have been written on one of the pages?:

"Leonie. Remember? She's in New Orleans. I wanted to talk to her, but you didn't know her consiliarius' name."

"Oh, that's right." Gina laughed self-consciously, her cheeks darkening with embarrassment. Hands trembling, she picked up the book and started flipping through it.

I stepped closer, Rik glued to my back. My blood scented the air until it seemed to hum with power. I gathered my will into magical chains and nets, ready to seize anything that might crawl out of that book.

"Here it is." She ran her finger over the paper and hesitated, staring at the page. I felt a sinking sensation in her bond, and she raised her gaze back to mine. "What was I looking for? I'm so sorry, my queen. I can't remember."

"It's alright. I was just curious. Why don't you hand me the book? I'll look it up myself."

"Of course." She stretched out her hands, the book open, but I didn't take it right away. I didn't even look at the pages. Not yet.

I had to be absolutely sure that whatever trap lay hidden in those pages, I could break it. Luckily, I already had plenty of my best weapon at the ready.

I swiped my index finger through the blood trickling down my throat and stretched out my hand toward the book.

Immediately, I sensed the flare of magic on the page. It was small, and certainly insignificant if I wasn't looking for it. My blood amplified the signature, letting me see the tendrils of a delicate, intricate spell written on the page, almost as if the magic was in the ink itself.

"Can you turn it around for me so I can read it?"

Gina did as I asked, and the tug grew stronger. Out of the corner of my eye, I could see the spell spinning slightly on the upper left-hand corner. Exactly where my gaze would automatically fall in order to begin reading. It definitely wasn't an accident that was the location of the spell.

I focused on the opposite page. The first house name listed at the top was Edda. So we were definitely in the right part of the book. Out of the corner of my eye, I watched the tendrils of magic reaching for me. It felt like a wide, slow tidal whirlpool, gently seeking across the sandy beach. Inviting me to play, even though I knew there were vicious riptides hidden just below the surface.

Without looking at the spell demanding my attention, I swept my bloody finger over the paper.

The spinning whirlpool dissipated like fog.

"What was that?" Gina's voice shook. "A spell?"

"Yes." I focused on the left-hand page. A small rune was written in the upper corner. It seemed familiar... but also strange. It stirred the delicate hairs on my nape with dread, even though I didn't know what it meant. "It's safe now. Does anyone recognize that symbol?"

Guillaume and Mehen had returned at the first hint of danger, the rest of my Blood in a circle around us.

Mehen let out a dragon hiss. "Sigil, not symbol. It was crafted with a very specific intention that only the maker would know as she wrote it."

"Agreed." Guillaume glided his finger in the air over the symbol, tracing the swirls and harsh lines. "It's made from certain letters, but each letter's broken into pieces, which makes it impossible to understand unless you're the maker."

The sigil almost looked like an S on its side with a rocking-chair base. An umbrella handle popped up toward the right corner, with a triangle and hook at the end.

"It was some kind of forget-me spell," I mused aloud. "Almost like the geas my mother used to make everyone forget her. But this one only activated when Gina saw it. Does every consiliarius book have that symbol in it, then? Or only ours? How did we get it?"

"They're printed by the Triune." Gina turned the book back around and glared at the symbol. "I can see it now, but I swear, when I looked at the page before, I didn't see anything remarkable. In fact, I can't even remember *what* I saw, only that it wasn't important."

"House Delafosse is on that page," I said softly. "Can you read the consiliarius's name now?"

"Wrenna Jade."

Mehen grunted. "That's not a name. It doesn't *ring* like a name. It means something else. What's the Dauphine's given name?"

"Jeanne," Daire replied immediately.

Gina rushed over to her purse and dug around for an ink pen. Slowly walking back toward us, she crossed off the letters one by one. "Okay, the letters left are W, R, A, and D."

My magic pulsed in my blood, the letters pounding through me like a gong. "Ward. Ward Jeanne."

Guillaume and Mehen looked at each other and said, "Fuck."

13

SHARA

Shaken, I leaned against Rik, soaking in his heat and strength. Sure, we'd figured it out before the spell had gotten me too, but it'd been close. Too close. If I hadn't been bleeding, would I have noticed? Even if I'd realized that Gina had forgotten to look up the name, I would have taken the book and looked at it too, falling prey to the exact same sigil.

"That's how she stays hidden," Guillaume said. "She uses sigils to hide in plain sight. Has anyone ever talked to Leonie or her consiliarius in person? I'm guessing the answer is no. People know of Leonie, but in reality, have never talked to her."

Gina paced back and forth, her heels ringing smartly on the wooden floor. "It's all too fucking smart. Aima queens and their consiliari will follow strict protocols when contacting an unknown queen. Which means consulting the book to find her consiliarius. Only the rune wipes the desire to find her out of their mind and they move on, never realizing the truth."

"How many other pages have that same kind of ward?" I dabbed more blood on my finger. "We ought to scan every page to be safe."

Gina shook her head. "Actually, I don't think that will be

necessary. The books are regularly updated by the Triune. Well, regularly as far as Aima are concerned. I believe this book was sent to me about twenty years ago, so she's been Leonie Delafosse at least that long. I don't know that she'd need to ward any other names, though I guess it's possible."

I frowned. Another coincidence that this new book had been sent out shortly after my birth? Fucking hell.

"Let's scan to be safe. It wouldn't surprise me to find that she has a couple of different aliases set up. She'd want a new identity to assume if anything happened to Leonie."

We spent a few minutes flipping through the book, while I held my finger over the pages, searching for anything unexpected or strange. We didn't find any other sigils.

"That doesn't mean that all of these names are real," Gina said. "I recognize many of them and have spoken or interacted with most of them over the years, but there are still plenty of names that I don't know. They could be her previous aliases, just waiting for her to need them again. All we know for sure is that her current alias is Leonie Delafosse."

"So what now?" I paced back and forth before the fireplace, letting ideas bounce around my head. "We know who she is."

"More than that," Guillaume replied, shaking his head. "You are the *only* queen to know who she is. After she's hidden herself for hundreds of years, you know her secret name, and you know how she wards herself."

"The question, then, is what do we want to do with this information?" My blood hummed and sparked with excitement. "Do you really think that Marne Ceresa doesn't know that Leonie is really the Dauphine?"

"Guaranteed," Gina replied grimly. "While they're both on the Triune, they're not exactly friendly. There's been bad blood brewing between them for centuries, and Desideria capitalized on their animosity to bring more and more courts under her control."

"What happened to make the Dauphine disappear like that?"

Guillaume grunted. "No one knows but her. I can tell you that the Dauphine came to Desideria, either for help or with some kind of a proposition, and Desideria laughed in her face. Literally. I don't know the details, and whatever happened after that died with Desideria."

"So Marne might not even know why the Dauphine went into hiding."

Gina winced slightly. "I don't know that 'into hiding' is the best way to describe what she did. She's not hiding. She's using her power to mask herself from the world. Hiding in plain sight, but not out of fear. She didn't withdraw or run from something. She's still a very powerful Triune queen with countless threads and allies throughout the Aima courts. We may not know or see her but trust me, we all know she's out there. If a call came for an audience with her, we'd go. Immediately. Just like we would if Marne requested your presence. Any Aima queens would heed such a call."

"Your mother did," Guillaume said.

I whirled to face him. "She did?"

"She was the cobra queen who envenomed me and ulti-mately killed Desideria. She came as called to House Modron. I wasn't privy to why Desideria requested her presence, but I do remember Esetta Isador coming to court."

A jolt rocked through me every time I heard my mother's name spoken aloud. I glanced at Gina, her brow furrowed, a questioning look in her eyes. She couldn't remember or say my mother's name. Yet. Goddess let her not know for many, many years if it meant her death.

I'd forgotten that he'd once died the same way as Rik. He'd known what was happening to Rik, because he'd already lived it.

Guilt and regret surged inside of me. I hated remembering what I'd done to him.

He dropped a hand on my shoulder and squeezed lightly. "Carrying your venom has come in handy. I have no regrets." I leaned back against him. My rock, solid and unshakeable. "If Marne and the Dauphine are in some feud that no one but them knows the details of, then maybe I can use that. I'm sure Marne would be willing to pay a pretty penny to gain this kind of information. Not only do we know the Dauphine's alias, but also how she hides. Not that I'd care to pass that little tidbit on to Marne. Her mirror magic's already freaky enough."

Daire snickered. "I'd love to use that mirror magic to see the look on the Dauphine's face when she realizes you know who she is."

Ezra cuffed him in the back of the head. "Yeah, sure, throw some gasoline on the hornet's nest. It'll be great fun fucking running away from an angry horde."

"Maybe there's a way to let her know I know her secret identity, but also hopefully indicate my intentions."

"What are your intentions?" Gina asked, her brown eyes sparking with interest.

"I want allies, especially allies that could help us against Marne if need be. Who better to reach out to with a peace offering than her bitter rival?"

Guillaume nodded slowly. "It might work, though there'll be hell to pay when Marne finds out."

"I can't trust either of them. They're both the kind of queens who'll smile at you and admire your dress, but then dump a bucket of foul pig blood all over you when you least expect it."

"Well, you're not fucking Carrie," Ezra grumbled. "You'll blast these bitches to kingdom come first."

"I can't blast them if I'm supposed to work with them." I rolled my eyes. "Though blasting would certainly be the easiest solution."

"No blasting." Laughing, Gina shook her head. "If you want to let her know that you've bypassed her ward, but you also are following the Aima protocols, then I recommend we reach out to her consiliarius, just as you intended to do from the beginning. Then I can work with her to convey your desire to meet."

I nodded slowly. "That tells her we broke the sigil but are still politely reaching out to her. Yeah, I like that."

Lips quirked, Gina picked up her phone. "Are you ready to kick the hornet's nest?"

"Go for it."

14

SHARA

I sat back down, nestling into the heat of Rik's body with Daire against my knees, while Gina made the call. She put it on speakerphone so I could hear everything. It rang five times before the call was picked up.

"Hello?" A female voice said.

"Good afternoon, this is Gina Isador calling on behalf of Shara Isador, who would like to arrange a meeting with Her Majesty Leonie Delafosse."

There was a long pause, enough that Daire wriggled against my legs with impatient glee.

"I see," the woman finally replied. "How may I help you?"

I couldn't help but note that the woman didn't state her name.

"My queen is newly risen to her house after being lost for several years. She's reaching out to all the queens in the Americas hoping to make alliances. Naturally House Delafosse came to mind."

"Naturally." Her voice dripped with sarcasm.

Gina looked at me and shook her head slightly. Our initial

plan wasn't working. For whatever reason, this presumed consiliarius wasn't buying our alliance story, even though that was exactly what we intended.

"From what I hear, your new queen isn't making alliances, but rather taking siblings."

If Leonie Delafosse was really just a minor queen holding court in New Orleans, then that would be a completely valid concern. I didn't blame her if she was afraid that I'd use the alliance excuse to force her into a sibling relationship.

If she were actually a minor queen.

And if I were the kind of queen who'd force anybody to give me their blood and support.

"Who is it?" A different voice spoke, soft and feminine and very southern belle.

Holding Gina's gaze, I asked, :*Probably Leonie?*:

She nodded.

The call was muffled a few moments, as if we'd been put on hold or someone had covered up the microphone. Then the second woman spoke again.

"My, my, a new, sweet young queen. Are you as strong as they say you are, sugar?"

I bristled but didn't say anything right away. Her tone gritted with fake sugary sweetness. I'd worked in Alabama before, so I knew the *"bless your heart"* tone. Which was basically the polite way to say, *"go fuck yourself,"* or *"what a fucking moron,"* or rarely, it might actually be sincere, which made it all the more deadly a phrase to use.

"I guess that depends on who you ask," I finally said. I didn't want to make an enemy of yet another formidable queen, but I wasn't going to be walked on, either.

"Keisha Skye didn't have a chance to ask."

I kept my voice even and calm, though sparks flared in my blood. "She shouldn't have fucked with my Blood."

Leonie laughed, a high, sweet trill that was actually quite musical. "So fierce and protective. You're the queen of New York City now. What do you want with me?"

While she hadn't acknowledged the broken sigil that pointed to her secret identity, it glared like a neon elephant in the room between us. She had to know that I knew, but she continued to pretend to be nothing more than a minor queen enjoying the vampire-friendly city of New Orleans. So I'd play along.

"I'm reaching out to all the queens I know of, especially the ones who're close. I'd like to form as many alliances as possible."

"House Delafosse won't be consumed by Isador."

"I didn't consume House Zaniyah. I don't know all the ins and outs of Aima politics yet, but we don't have to be siblings. I just want to know I have friends when Marne Ceresa comes calling on her mirror again."

"She's given you a mirror?" Her tone sharpened, her pitch higher, as if she were trying to convey fear. But I couldn't see the Dauphine ever being afraid, even of the queen of Rome. She was a very good actress, but I had the feeling that if I could have seen her face, her lips would have been twisted in disgust rather than true fear. "That's a horse of another color, then."

"I buried it in salt and locked it away, but yeah." I heaved out a sigh, trying to put on as good a show as she was. "I wish I could toss it into the deepest part of the ocean."

"It wouldn't do you any good." Her voice sounded distant, as if she was deep in thought. "I understand why you're so eager to gain allies against House Ceresa, but I don't believe I can help you. House Delafosse has taken great pains to remain neutral, which is one of the reasons Keisha Skye was content to leave me alone. Let me discuss your situation with my consiliarius and she'll reach out to yours once I've come to a decision."

"Thank you, Leonie."

"You're welcome, Shara."

The call ended. I looked from Gina to Guillaume, Mehen, and Daire, my most politically savvy Blood. "What do you think?"

Gina dropped down into her chair and grabbed a tissue from her bag to mop her face. "You did extremely well if that truly was the Dauphine. I know it must be her, but it's so strange. She never once indicated that she was anyone but a minor queen. Are we sure it's her?"

"It has to be," I said.

Guillaume grunted in agreement. "She's good at hiding in plain sight. That's her gift. That's exactly why she hasn't been discovered in so long. Naturally she'll keep up the illusion as long as possible."

"The real question is what the fuck is she going to do now that we know?" Mehen shook his head. "It won't be good, I can tell you that. She did seem interested in Marne's mirror, though."

"Is that a good or bad thing?" I asked.

Ezra let out a disgusted humph. "No way to fucking know."

Guillaume nodded in agreement. "My sentiments exactly. Something tells me that—"

Mehen broke in. "Don't use another one of your tired horse or barn metaphors, knight."

Guillaume gave us one of his rare grins. "Something tells me that a dragon would rather die than give up the hoard no matter how shitty it is. Is that better?"

Mehen slapped him on the back. "Fucking A."

Gina met my gaze, a smile twitching her lips. "So, what do we do now?"

"Is she actually a dragon?"

Guillaume shrugged. "Nobody knows."

"Well, I don't care to sit around and wait to be dragon chow, but didn't someone promise me a full-moon wolf howl?"

Xin materialized beside me, making Gina let out a startled little gasp. "The wolves are ready to sing for you tonight, my queen."

15

XIN

I loved being the silent, invisible threat. My true nature had always been that of a lone wolf. A ghost barely seen, drifting away into the forest. So faint and silent that I might have been a figment of imagination. I had never regretted my gifts and embraced them wholeheartedly.

But I had to admit that when my queen saw me—truly saw me—that she rocked my soul like nothing else in this entire world.

Being able to do one small thing to make her smile... fucking priceless.

I only wished I'd been able to call a few hundred wolves to sing for her. The pack I'd scented hadn't claimed this territory as their own, but we were too far south for any other wolves to be nearby. I'd been surprised to find any true wolves in the area at all, and I wasn't sure that they'd join me in wolf song, though the instinct was strong.

Wolves loved to sing to the full moon. I loved my queen. I would pour every ounce of that love into my howls and hoped they joined in.

She walked beside me, her fingers gripping my ruff.

Showing his trust in me, Rik walked behind us, allowing me to be the closest Blood to our queen's person in case of attack. Granted, we were on her property and inside her blood circle, but I appreciated his gesture. Rik wasn't an alpha that feared losing his place or focused on gaining status. Our queen's well-being and happiness were the only prize he sought.

In the center of the grove, I paused and sat back on my haunches. She tipped her head back and stared up at the gleaming moon. Opal moonbeams danced on her skin, illuminating the face of our goddess. I couldn't help but howl with joy, lifting praises to the goddesses who'd formed such a miracle in flesh and blood.

Come, my brothers. Come see the goddess who walks on this earth and allows me to sit at her feet.

"Oh, Xin," she whispered, stroking my fur. "That's so beautiful."

She dropped down to her knees in front of me and pressed her cheek to my chest. Arms around my neck, she listened to me howl like I was the fucking Vienna Symphony.

The wolves came, drawn not by my howl, but by the hypnotic pull of my queen's pleasure.

They crept from the woods one by one to sit at the edge of the blood circle. Six wolves in all, each as large as me. Their mournful cries blended with mine, telling a sad tale of their journey.

"What is it?" She whispered, lifting her face from my fur. "What do they say?"

:Their king is looking for his sister. She's been imprisoned somewhere, taken from their home.:

:Like an Aima king? I thought you said the wolves weren't like us.:

:They aren't, but the king isn't here. Wild wolves don't have kings, so it's likely that he's an Aima king.:

She turned her head and stared off into the forest. I could

feel her senses flowing through the trees like a gentle spring wind, seeking anything amiss. Anyone who didn't belong.

I met the largest wolf's gaze outside the circle and read the thousands of tiny details in her posture to decipher the truth. :He's hiding from you, my queen.:

:Me in particular?:

:All queens.:

:Then he is likely an Aima king.: She didn't call her power forth, and her will continued to flow gently over the landscape. In our bond, I watched as she found deer, dogs, even a distant bobcat. But no wolf king.

She pulled back her attention and focused on the wolves outside the circle. Most of them had lain down around us, but the largest female still sat opposite me, watching intently. Ears perked, her tension was clear to me. She was ready to flee at the first sign of trouble.

"Tell your king that he's safe from me," Shara said to the wolf. "I don't feel him nearby, so he's not meant to be my Blood."

The female whined softly and looked at me. She curled her tail around her haunches and dipped her nose. Shock. They didn't know if my queen's words were truthful.

I kept my head up, shoulders wide and proud, eyes bright and unclouded by any indecision. I would trust my queen with my life. They could take her word for what it was. A promise that their king would be safe.

Shara smiled softly, tipping her head back once more to bathe in the moonlight. "I don't take what's not mine, and your king isn't mine. I would know it."

The female wolf looked back over her shoulder and whined again. Several moments went by, and I thought he wouldn't show himself. Honestly, I couldn't blame him. I wouldn't have believed a queen like Shara existed either, at least until I found her, and she claimed my bond as her own.

One moment, there was nothing but trees and bushes outside the circle. Then suddenly, he was there. He didn't step out of a hiding spot or straighten from a crouch but appeared to unfold from dark shadows that curled around him. He was a massive black wolf with amber eyes that glinted with a sharp, cutting edge that bordered on madness.

The look of a rabid dog who'd sooner bite than ever allow himself to be captured.

Shadows flowed around his legs, and though he stood tall, with ears perked, I had a feeling he'd disappear in a heartbeat if Shara attempted to control him.

"Good evening, wolf king." Shara inclined her head politely and kept a hand on my shoulders. "I'm Shara Isador, last daughter of Isis, and this is my wolf Blood, Wu Tien Xin."

"Eivind Ironheart." The black wolf's words were distorted by his beast's growls but still understandable.

Sensing my awe filtering through our bond, she asked, :*Who is he?*:

:*Ironheart's descended from Fenrir, the great Nordic wolf who'll start Ragnarök, the end of the world. Supposedly Fenrir is descended from Loki himself.*:

:*And Fenrir's sister?*:

:*She's descended from Hel, the queen of the underworld.*:

"How can I help you, Eivind?"

He blinked, the only outward display of his surprise. "House Isador offers assistance?"

"Yes, of course," Shara replied. "Your pack indicated that you're looking for your sister. What happened to her?"

"She's been taken. I don't know who would dare such a thing, but she's gone. Not even I can find a hint of her scent anywhere."

Shara stepped closer to the blood circle, keeping her hand on me. The other wolf tensed, the hair rising along his ruff and down his spine. Like the fucking queen she was, she completely ignored him and sat down before him, completely unafraid.

I sat on my haunches beside her, casually at ease—but ready to leap on the other wolf and rip his throat out at the first sign of danger.

"What's her name?"

"Helayna Ironheart."

"Did she have Blood of her own yet?"

"No. She was only sixteen years old when she was taken."

Shara's eyes narrowed, her bond radiating with fury. "Did Ra take her? I know he was taking young queens to Heliopolis. We searched thoroughly, though, and we never found any hostages."

"A thing of darkness took her."

I felt the twinge of pain in her bond, even a bit of doubt. Our queen ruled all things dark, what most would consider monstrous. She'd embraced her darker aspect for the most part, but she didn't like the idea that a creature of darkness could have taken this young queen.

She reached out into the night, searching for the dark power she'd inherited from her father, Typhon, god of monsters. With the full moon so bright in the sky, the dark tendrils of violet power had withdrawn deep into the earth.

Blowing out a sigh, she focused on the wolf king. "I'll try again when I can tap the darkness. If she's held somewhere where the sun doesn't shine, I will find her. I promise. What does she look like?"

His head tipped, a flash of white fang warning of his mistrust. "Why would you help me, Isador?"

Moonlight hung about her head like a glowing nimbus, but shadows thickened across her back and shoulders. Her jaguar's wings fluttered softly, even as a dark shadow rose up over her head and arched protectively over her, shielding her from the moon.

A red diamond glittered on the shadow cobra's hood.

"Because I can, wolf king. I won't stand by in silence while another woman is abused or threatened in any way."

He snarled, his words garbled. "So you can take her for yourself."

Shara looked back at him steadily, though her shadowed cobra hissed and swayed above her head. "As the Great One is my witness, I will never take what isn't mine to love. So you remain free, wolf king, as will your sister."

"House Isador never lies." Rik's deep rumble rolled though the ground. He didn't make any threats either, but I could feel the heavy promise of crushing rock in our bond. "What this queen takes, she loves, and she keeps for all time. I pity you for not feeling one moment of the love she gives us."

Ignoring the other wolf's ire, I lay down and curled around my queen, dropping my head in her lap. She stroked my head and scratched my ears, completely at ease.

When we made no other show of force, Eivind calmed his snarls and sat back on his haunches. I sensed the silent communication passing among the pack, but I didn't try to eavesdrop. Not with my queen's fingers in my fur.

Finally, the wolf king spoke once more. "She looks like me."

Shara's head cocked, a smile twitching on her lips. "A ferocious black wolf?"

The wolf king straightened, shadows unfurling about him as the wolf disintegrated. A tall man with long, reddish hair and beard stared back at her with the same glowing amber eyes as his wolf. He stood like a king, the proud lines of his face proclaiming his lineage from Loki. "Though her eyes are ice blue."

"Trapped in darkness," Shara whispered, staring out into the night. "Did she wear a locket? Something silver?"

The wolf king charged closer, slamming up against the blood circle. It cast fiery sparks around him, but held, denying him entrance. "You've seen her? Where?"

"I'm not sure, but I have seen a queen locked in darkness. My crows have her necklace. Can you describe it?"

"It wasn't a locket, but a circular pendant with two heads meeting. One represented Fenrir, and the other Jörmungandr, the world serpent. His body was twisted around the tree in the middle. The runes for Hel were scattered in the leaves."

Shara touched the crow queen's bond and gently prodded her awake. *:Can you locate a silver necklace that has a wolf, serpent, and tree on it? I've seen it before, when I was in New York.:*

In the distance, I heard the sleepy caws as the crow queen roused her soldiers to do our queen's bidding. Within minutes, one of the large birds dropped down before our queen with a silver chain held in its mouth.

"Thank you," Shara said as she took the necklace from the crow. He bobbed his head and then hopped up to sit on her shoulder. The crow queen swept down to land on her other shoulder.

"Huginn and Muninn," Eivind whispered hoarsely. He dropped to his knees. "Forgive me, Queen of Isador. I had no idea."

:I don't know much about Norse mythology, but I guess two ravens are significant,: Shara said in our bonds.

:Thought and Memory,: Mehen replied. *:They were Odin's ravens who brought him information from all over the world.:*

Studying the pendant, she reached up with her other hand and stroked her fingertips along the crow queen's sleek breast. The bird cooed softly and nestled deeper against Shara's neck, so that her hair fell over the bird like a blanket. "This does look Nordic to me, but I'm no expert."

She held the pendant up so Eivind could see it. "Is this your sister's necklace?"

"Yes. Great One, please help her. I'll submit to you at once if you promise to find and release her."

"As I said before, you're not mine to take, wolf king. Though

I'll do what I can to help you find your sister." She dropped her left wrist down closer to my head. "Xin, will you draw my blood, please?"

There were a dozen ways she could have drawn her blood, yet she gave me the honor. Whining softly, I licked the delicate skin of her wrist and then carefully applied pressure with my canines to make neat punctures. The scent of her blood was like a sword thrust into my gut, slicing me in half. Her power rose in a cascading fountain of glistening diamonds and rubies, shining in the moonlight.

She focused on the pendant in her right hand. "I see her," she whispered in a dream-like voice. "Deep. Dark. Forgotten. Her hair is bound in one long braid that hangs down her back, tied in a red cord. She hates it tied up like that. It's against her nature. He... controls her. With that braid."

"Who?" Eivind growled. His pack howled and milled around him, adding to the clamor of rage pounding through him. "Who dares to hurt her?"

"She bleeds," Shara whispered, her voice catching on a sob. "She hurts. Silently. She bleeds for him. He needs it."

"WHO?"

In our bond, I could see the young woman in our queen's mind. Her slender back, bare, sprinkled with freckles. The simple braid. And black, clawed hands clutching her tighter. Drawing her blood.

:Could you find this place?: She asked me.

My wolf nose could follow my queen into Ra's hellacious city, and had found Xochitl, hidden away in the Zaniyah house to protect her. Perhaps I could find this woman for my queen.

I focused on her image, allowing my queen's bond to guide me deeper to this hidden place. I could smell the woman's blood. Apples. Warm, spiced apples, as if sliced and baked into a pie. A hint of fur and leather too. My wolf strained harder, whuffing loudly to draw as much of her scent as possible.

Something else was there with her. Something that smelled like scales and snake, with a thick musk of poison. Coils slithered around her, squeezing her tighter. Making her cry out. Shadowed fangs struck at me like a roaring freight train.

My eyes jerked open and I stared up at my queen. *:Snake.:*

Nodding, she raised her attention to the waiting wolf king. "A snake holds your sister against her will."

His shoulders quivered, and the gleaming golden light in his eyes died. His head fell forward, his long hair falling forward to shield his face from our prying eyes. "I know where she is."

"Where?" Shara asked softly.

"Jörmungandr took her," he replied, his voice flat. "So she's in the deepest, coldest, darkest place in the nine worlds."

"I'm sorry. I don't know where that is, or how to reach her."

His once regal features were haggard, his eyes dark with grief. "No one can reach her. She's in Hvergelmir, at the root of Yggdrasil. No mortal can reach her, even an Aima queen descended from the Great One."

"Why would Jörmungandr take her?"

His eyes hardened like amber diamonds as his wolf flowed back up to swallow his human form. "I don't know, but I intend to find out."

As he sank into swirling shadows, he released a mournful howl. His pack howled around him, their song of rage tugging on me until I rose up and howled too.

They turned and faded back into the forest one by one, still pausing occasionally to howl at the moon. The pack instinct was strong. My wolf wanted to join them, racing silently through endless forests, nose to the ground while we hunted for the missing queen who smelled like warm spiced apples.

But *my* queen smelled ever so much better.

Night-blooming jasmine and desert sands. Hot, thick blood, the taste burning on my tongue. I dropped my nose and focused on her. She smiled, though the twinge of sadness in her eyes made me pull my tail tight.

"For a moment, I thought you'd leave me."

:Never, my queen.:

She raised her bleeding wrist toward me, but I resisted the equally-compelling urge to lick that warm trail of blood from her skin. If she thought I would ever abandon her, then I didn't deserve such a reward.

"Drink, my wolf, and know that I love you."

SHARA

Sadness lingered, even though my ghostly silver wolf lowered his muzzle to my wrist. I couldn't shake the image of the young woman trapped in darkness. I still held her necklace in my hand, so perhaps that explained the connection I felt.

I allowed the pendant to slide off my palm. As the silver chain slithered to the ground, I saw again the dark scales tightening around her. The stench of the snake was still thick in my nose. I'd smelled Mehen's scales before and it hadn't bothered me.

"Because I'm not a fucking bag of festering poison," my dragon retorted.

"What do you know of Jörmungandr?"

Mehen came closer and dropped down beside me. "He's another bound monster whose release is supposed to bring about the end of the world."

The crow queen chirped and sent me an image of her cozy, warm nest.

"Of course, Nightwing. Thank you for coming to help me

with the wolf king. You can take the necklace back with you until we find its owner."

The other crow hopped down from my shoulder to snag the silver chain and the crows flew back toward the heart tree. "What else do you know about his legend? How did he become imprisoned?"

"Odin threw him the fuck away into the deepest part of the ocean," Mehen replied. "When Jörmungandr is finally freed, he'll drip poison and blood into the oceans and destroy the world."

"Ragnarök," Rik added as he dropped down behind me. He wrapped his arms around me, and I instantly felt better. Less sad and hopeless, and more solid. How could I ever feel uncertain when I had solid rock at my back? "The great battle where the world is destroyed and many of the Norse gods are killed. I know a bit about it since I'm descended from giants, though my line is Germanic not Nordic."

"Forgive me, my queen." Xin looked up at me, no longer his ghostly wolf, though his eyes were haunted. "The wolf song was supposed to bring you joy, not sadden you."

I hooked my arm around his neck and drew him closer. "I loved it. For a moment, though, I felt you gliding away from me. Not physically, but mentally. Like you were already gone with the pack."

"The pack instinct is strong," he admitted, pressing his forehead to mine. "But not stronger than my love for you, my queen."

Ignoring the other man, Mehen leaned in and playfully nipped my shoulder. "How about we get this garden party started?"

I raised an eyebrow at him, though a smile quirked my lips. "What did you have in mind?"

"An orgy beneath the full moon." He gripped the material of

my dress in his teeth and gave it a tug. "Duh." Rik thumped him in the bond, and he grudgingly added, "My queen."

Though this wasn't a formal affair by any means, I'd selected a gauzy silver gown that made me think of the full moon. I'd wanted to look the part of a garden party, even if it was just us. Besides, I was starting to like having nice clothes for a change. Especially when I put on something pretty, and then saw the heat glowing in my Bloods' eyes when they looked at me.

This dress had simple but elegant lines, falling from an empire waist with a hi-lo hem so I didn't have any issues stepping on the gown in the front, but the train was long enough to drag behind me. The small cap sleeves continued the look of an historic gown.

Though no lady would have gone out in a mostly transparent dress. Certainly not without anything else on beneath it.

Mehen tugged harder on the material and something popped. I narrowed a hard look on him. "I like this dress. It probably cost a fortune."

"I like it too." His eyes glittered in the moonlight, spinning green fire. "But I'd like it better if I could shred it off of you with my teeth."

"Why should you get the fucking honor of ripping our queen's dress off?" Ezra growled, stepping closer despite the look of malice that Mehen shot him. Xin let out a low, rattling snarl as the other man neared. "I've got teeth too, motherfucker."

"All of us have teeth, you idiots." Guillaume's voice rang in the night like a general ordering his troops to war. Usually he was the seasoned voice of reason, but tonight he strode into the fray and actually cracked Mehen's and Ezra's heads together so hard that I winced.

"Nobody cares about *your* teeth, plow horse," Mehen retorted back, completely unfazed.

Ezra even managed a sneer at him. "I'd love to see you try to get her dress off with hooves instead of claws."

Mehen snorted. "Me too."

I stood and planted my hands on my hips, glaring at each of them. "What the fuck is wrong with you guys? You never bicker like this. Well, you don't, G."

My Templar knight drew himself up and squared his shoulders. "Fucking full moon madness, my queen. My apologies."

I looked around at my Blood one by one. They'd all crept closer to me, subtly pushing at each other and jostling for position, though only Xin, Mehen, Ezra, and Rik were close enough for me to touch. "We've had full moons before."

"Sure," G replied tersely. "But we've never been outside *beneath* the full moon, other than Christmas Eve."

"And you know how that fucking went," Mehen added.

Yeah. I sure did.

I reached up behind me and slowly lowered the zipper of my gown. The metallic sound was loud, broken only by my Bloods' heaving breathing. Slipping from my body, the gown puddled on the ground at my feet.

"Mother of Goddesses," Mehen whispered, his voice reverent.

"Amen," Ezra said.

Even Rik, my steady, constant alpha looked like his rock troll had piledrived him into the ground.

I shook my hair back off my shoulders. "Who's first?"

16

SHARA

I expected a mad scramble toward me. Some grabbing, slinging me around, and some frantic, hard fucking. Sign me the fuck up for that.

I didn't expect them to turn on each other.

Mehen seized Ezra and sank his fangs into the man's arm hard enough my bear roared with fury. He promptly twisted around and swiped his hand across my dragon's neck. Partially shifted, his claws shredded Mehen's throat open.

Not to be outdone, Xin shifted fully to his wolf, clamped powerful jaws on the back of Ezra's neck, and shook him like a rag doll.

My mouth fell open with horror. They'd never fought each other like this. Like they were seriously going to kill each other.

Teeth. Claws. Fur. The thick, raw scent of blood.

The smell of them was thick in the air. Feral and rank and so fucking hot I couldn't focus enough to draw my power and command them to cease their fights.

It was too fucking incredible. Horrible, but compelling. I couldn't look away as they rolled and clawed and tore each other to shreds.

For me.

Daire had his teeth buried in Llewellyn's shoulder and hung on his back, while my gryphon wrestled the twins. My Templar knight had drawn his heaviest sword and traded blows with Vivian, who held slender, curved blades in each hand.

I met Rik's smoldering gaze, and if I'd had panties on, they would have disintegrated in that glowing forge of lust.

Bulging arms crossed over his chest, he stood with shoulders impossibly wide, ignoring the squabbles around him. None of them dared touch my alpha, or so I thought.

As he reached for me, something silver flashed behind him. A metal tip protruded from his stomach. He let out a low grunt of pain. But he ignored the blade sticking out of his stomach and bent down to press his lips to mine.

"Rik," I gasped against his mouth, my fingers seeking out the wound to test how bad it was.

He captured my hand in his and lifted my bloody fingers up toward my lips. "No worries, my queen. We bleed for you."

The blade disappeared a moment, only to slam back into him hard enough he arched against me.

With a disgusted growl, he reached behind him and dragged Guillaume around by his throat. Even with a meaty arm clamped around his neck, G still plunged the blade into my alpha again.

Rik did nothing to stop him. Ignoring the blade completely, he smeared his blood on my lips. "Why would I stop him from giving you every drop of blood in my body?"

"But he's stabbing you."

Rik tightened his arm around Guillaume's throat. My Templar knight's face started to turn beet red. He couldn't breathe, but he didn't do anything to try and free himself either, even as Rik wrestled him down to the ground in front of him.

Guillaume lay against his chest, between Rik's thighs, like I normally sat, though Rik didn't ever strangle me into that position. Blood coated them both, dripping down to the ground. Mesmerized, I couldn't tear my gaze away.

"Come, my queen. Stab yourself on something more useful than the knight's blade in my ribs."

Gulp. I didn't know when they'd had time to remove their clothes, but now I couldn't stop staring at Guillaume's massive erection.

Rik jammed his fangs into G's shoulder, making him buck his hips up in invitation. He didn't drink my knight's blood but pulled back so blood spurted down Guillaume's chest.

So much fucking blood. My fangs throbbed in my mouth but didn't descend. There wasn't any need, not with my Blood ripping each other open for me. I straddled Guillaume's hips and started to slowly impale myself while I licked the rivulets of blood from his skin. I couldn't take him inside quickly. He was just too big. I had to work my hips, gliding him deeper inch by inch. Torturing us both with exquisite pleasure.

Their mingled blood flamed through me. I pushed harder against him, forcing him deeper, making us both groan, though his came out choked. His face was almost purple, but Rik didn't give him any quarter. Neither did my knight. He crossed his arm over his chest so he could plunge the blade backwards hard again, sinking deep into Rik's shoulder.

I'd never seen injuries bleed like this. His blood sprayed up violently, as if he'd been shot or a major artery had been severed, though Rik didn't seem to be in any significant pain or danger. His eyes still smoldered, heavy-lidded and dark as he watched me ride the other man. His lips slanted in a sensual, knowing curve of wicked satisfaction.

I smeared my fingers in the blood coating Guillaume's chest, reveling in the velvety sensation of liquid power flowing over my skin.

Suddenly, I wanted to roll and wallow on them. Until every inch of me was covered in their blood.

"You heard our queen's desire," Rik growled.

One of them dropped down behind me. I didn't know which. I didn't care. They were mine. All of them. Their blood mine to call.

Even if that meant wearing it like a crimson second skin.

Hot, sweet blood cascaded over my shoulder and down my breasts, bringing with it the scent of fur crisped with frost. Xin, my silent, ghostly wolf. He bled on me so heavily I was afraid that he'd slit his own throat. More blood, this time scented with cinnamon and bear. My hair was sticky and heavy. Blood on my face. Pouring down my throat.

While I rode Guillaume to oblivion.

Beyond words. I could only feel. Feel every wondrous inch of their bodies against me. Hot muscle. Steel cocks. Hands and mouths. Fangs puncturing my skin. All of them.

They fed on me.

While I fed on their rising lust and the ocean of their blood.

Drifting on a red sea of pleasure, I found the lost, trapped queen again. I wrapped my arms around her, trying to warm her icy skin.

"I will find you," I promised her softly.

"I'll be dead before you do."

She felt so real against me, shivering and miserable and scared. As my wolf had sensed earlier, her skin smelled like warm apple pie. Was I really here? Or was it only a blood-drunk vision? Did it matter?

"Taste my blood. It'll strengthen you and help me find you."

"I can't," she whispered. "He'll only find you and drag you here too. Then who'll save us?"

"Where is here? Who is he? How long have you been here?"

"I don't know. I only know that he's so powerful that even the gods fear him."

Ragnarök, the end of the world. Evidently I needed to read up on my Norse mythology. Hopefully there was a book in the library.

I turned my senses outward, searching for anything I could use to pinpoint our location.

Darkness. Complete and utter darkness. It enfolded me in eager arms, thick, dark violet power begging to be used. I just had to figure out the *best* way to use it. I could tear down the thick walls I sensed around us, but what else would that allow in? Something worse than the creature who'd taken her? I didn't dare expose my presence until I knew how to bring her back to her brother. Eivind had hinted she wasn't even in our world any longer.

Her voice broke on a sob. "I'm so alone."

I opened my mouth to insist that I wouldn't abandon her, when I felt something in the darkness stirring at her words. Thick shadows swirled closer, but I didn't sense danger. It— they—wanted to be used. By her, not me.

My dark power slithered in my mind like black silk heated by my Bloods' bodies, carrying me their intention. *We. Come.*

To her *call.*

"You're not alone," I whispered against her ear. "Call them. Your Blood wait in the darkness."

"My Blood? Here?"

My body weighed heavier, dragging me down as if I slipped down the side of a cliff. I saw her face peering down over the edge, her hand reaching down toward me. Her stunning blue eyes shining in the darkness.

"They will come," I mumbled, trying to hold on to the vision.

"Who, my queen?" Rik asked, gathering me closer.

"I saw her." My head lolled to the side, my muscles limp and unresponsive. Though I could feel his arms around me. He carried me. Somewhere. The garden party must have ended.

My Blood. Wounded and bleeding. They probably needed

me to heal them. I fumbled around inside my head, trying to call forth my power.

"Shhh," Rik murmured, setting me slowly into scalding hot water that told me immediately where we were. "All is well."

My grotto. Goddess above, it felt so good. I wanted to close my eyes and sink beneath the surface, drifting into darkness. Maybe I would find her again.

"No one needs healing, my queen. Your pleasure and blood already did that work for you. Just rest."

"But she needs help. She needs her Blood."

"Then they will answer her call, as I answered yours."

Floating in the water with his arms around me, I stared up at the moon shining low in the sky. Gloriously bright, so close that I swore I could reach up and touch it.

"*Call me,*" something whispered.

Rik didn't turn his head or ask me who had spoken. Maybe he didn't hear it.

It took all my strength to roll my head toward the voice I'd heard. Water. Dark and swirling. Around...

I blinked. Surely I was hallucinating.

A tentacle rose from the water long enough for me to see it and acknowledge it for what it was. Then the dark creature sank back down into the water.

My grotto wasn't that deep or large, but that tentacle had been... Huge.

"Rik," I whispered, searching the water. "Are your feet touching the bottom?"

"Of course." His big palm slid up beneath my hair, supporting my neck. "Did you see something? Was it the lost queen's Blood?"

My eyelids drooped. I nestled my face against his throat and breathed in his scent. Smoking hot rocks. Sparks from a forge. Red-hot iron.

"Monster." My words slurred as sleep claimed me. "Mine."

His chuckle rumbled through his chest, rocking me deeper into sleep. "Well, you are the queen of monsters. I look forward to seeing this new Blood you call, my queen."

17

SHARA

I t was already evening before we arrived in New York City the next day. I'd slept heavily, barely even stirring as Rik carried me from the grotto to bed. I thought I'd dream of the other queen, or at least the tentacled monster I'd glimpsed, but if I dreamed at all, I'd forgotten.

As soon as I awakened, I'd searched outward for any sign of either of them, but I couldn't feel them anywhere. If the male voice I'd heard in the grotto belonged to a future Blood, then he was beyond this world or so far away that I couldn't sense him. I wasn't sure how he'd been able to reveal himself to me, but I had to hope that I'd be able to find him when it was time.

Because one thing I'd learned long ago: if the goddess sent me a Blood, it was for a very good reason. I would need this new monster. Desperately. Or She wouldn't have sent him to me.

I'd left Carys at home. She'd barely been able to look up from the stacks of books around her. If I'd torn her away from that library, she'd have been even grumpier than usual.

Gwen had arranged for an incredible meal in the tower. The food was just as good as anything Winston had ever made for me, though definitely high-end 'citified' food. Everything was carefully plated and artistically arranged like a Michelin five-star restaurant. It was fantastic, but I'd honestly rather eat Winston's family-style food any day.

Gina and Kevin sat with us, though at the opposite end of the table. Their heads were close, their voices low, as they caught up on consiliari business. I trusted Gina to fill me in on only what I needed to know.

Though Gwen sat apparently at ease while we ate, chatting about how things were going here in the tower, her Blood were another story. She'd introduced them to me immediately, and though they'd never actually served as knights in the Middle Ages, I could still see the legendary warriors that Lancelot, Bors, and Mordred must have been. They hovered around her, refusing to sit and eat with their queen, leaping at any chance to fill her glass or fetch the smallest crumb for her.

Her alpha, Lancelot, stood at her back, both hands on her shoulders. They'd all dressed formally in black suits, but he stood in a stiff guarding position, his steely blue eyes missing nothing.

"I still can't believe I'm in the presence of Guinevere's and Sir Lancelot's descendants," I said. "Though I wish you'd sit down and dine with us."

"And I can't believe that I'm in the presence of Sir Guil-laume de Payne." Lancelot gave him a salute, his fist over his heart. "I might be Lancelot reborn, but you were actually a Templar knight. Even in my time, you were already legendary."

Guillaume flicked his wrist and a knife slid down into his hand. He saluted Lancelot with it the same way, hand over heart, but he kissed the blade before re-sheathing it. "It would have been an honor to ride with you."

Gwen must have prodded her alpha in the bond, because his face reddened and he quickly added, "In the presence of the

Great One's last daughter, naturally we stand to show our respect."

I snorted and picked up my wine glass. "I don't require such nonsense. In fact, it makes me very uncomfortable when people start bowing and scraping. I'm just Shara, and I don't want or need any formalities."

Gwen picked up the wine bottle, poured more of the rich, dark wine into my glass, and then topped hers off as well. "Our queen deserves the absolute best from us. Without you, I wouldn't be here with my Blood at all. You helped us accomplish what our lines haven't been able to do for generations."

"So now it's time to defeat Arthur once and for all."

Gwen gave me a tight, hard smile, her eyes glittering like sharp shards of glass. "The once and future king has always been my curse. But with your help, I can hopefully end his reign of terror for good. It won't be easy, though."

"Who's the other Blood that you need to go after?"

"Merlin. He's been trapped in Avalon since before the original Arthur's death."

"The wizard?" My eyes widened and I laughed sheepishly. "Are wizards actually real? I mean, I never thought vampires were real either, so I don't know."

"He did have great power," Gwen replied. "Which was exactly why Arthur had him trapped."

"We don't know for sure that Arthur did it," Lance added. "It's likely, but it could have also been *her*."

"Elaine Shalott." Gwen practically spat the other queen's name. "Some of the legends say that it was the Lady of the Lake who lured Merlin into a cave or tower and locked him up, so that Arthur could be defeated. Though I despise her, I don't think it would have been Merlin she chose to lock up if she had that ability. She definitely would have tried to trap Lance—and herself, of course—in Avalon far from me."

"Is she the Lady of the Lake?" When one of us said Elaine,

Lance visibly blanched, so I made a note to avoid saying her name again if possible.

"Not directly." Gwen sighed and sipped her wine, her brow furrowed. "The legends are mixed up and vague. Sometimes she's called Nimue or Vivienne, with several different variations and spellings, so no one's really sure. The Lady of the Lake is credited with giving Arthur the sword and even raising the original Lancelot. *She* did neither of those things. The original writers of the Arthurian stories were men, and humans at that. Who knows what all they got wrong or just ignored?"

The Blood with the wicked skulls inked on the backs of his hands drawled, "She'd fucking love to be associated with the Lady of the Lake. Much better than the truth."

"What is the truth?" I asked.

"She's much more likely to trap and rape me than ever give a damn about Excalibur or Merlin," Lance said in a flat, dead voice that still managed to quiver ever so slightly.

Gwen reached up and placed her right hand over his left that was still on her shoulder. At her touch, the tension straining in him eased. "Even in the legends, she bespelled Lancelot so that he thought she was Guinevere. Some even have her bearing his child. If she could get him away from me, she'd do it in any way possible, whether that meant murder or betrayal. She has no sense of honor or even a modicum of understanding of what's right and what's terribly wrong. She's always been obsessed with him and will do anything to have him."

He squeezed Gwen's shoulder, and I could feel the silent promise passing between them. He would rather die than serve Elaine again in any way, while Gwen swore to never let him go. In fact, the hard coldness in her eyes as she met my gaze told me she'd do anything to protect him. Anything at all.

I set my glass down and pushed away from the table to stand. "I think it's time we work some New York City magic."

Gwen leapt to her feet, ever the polite hostess—but relieved that I wasn't going to make her wait any longer. "What do you need, my queen?"

I tipped my head, letting ideas bubble up in my mind one by one. I needed something to hold the blood I pulled out of Gwen, at least temporarily. I certainly didn't want to ingest Elaine's blood—I just wanted to separate it from Gwen's. Finally, I smiled and picked up my glass. I saluted her and then drained the bit of wine still remaining. "Nothing but a blade and this cup. Let's go somewhere quiet and comfortable to give this a whirl."

In a few minutes, Gwen had us both seated in chairs before an elegant fireplace with a flickering gas-blue flame. My chair was big enough for Rik to sit behind me as we preferred. She sat alone, but Lance stood at her back, with her other Blood at each hand. It was only a wing-back chair, but looking at her, I could see the medieval Queen Guinevere staring back at me.

She wasn't beautiful exactly, though she was very pretty. Her brown hair was swept back in a classic chignon. She also preferred classic clothing, if the fifties swing dress was any indication. White with large red cherries almost like polka dots. It was unusual but suited her perfectly.

It was her face that arrested attention. Her nose and chin were a touch too sharp, but her generous lips and the crinkles around her mouth and eyes promised smiles and good humor, despite the long curse that had haunted her family's house. Her eyes gleamed with the kind of innate pride and power that comes from knowing you're descended from an ancient royal house like Camelot. She might have been forced to live without her Blood at Elaine's whim, but she'd always known what she was.

A queen. Not just a vampire queen, but the kind of queen that even humans still remembered and told stories about.

I reached out, palm up, and she leaned forward to slip her

hand into mine. It was a bit of strain, but before I could ask, her Blood lifted her chair to scoot her closer.

"Rik, if you could hold the glass for me..."

"Of course, my queen." He positioned the glass beneath our clasped hands.

I turned her wrist slightly, balancing her hand on the edge of the cup with one of my silver nails pressed lightly to her skin. "Do you recall how much of her blood you drank?"

Gwen grimaced. "Very little. Only a few swallows—just enough to formalize the sibling agreement. But it was enough to give her control over me."

I released her hand a moment so I could puncture my own wrist with the tip of my nail, though my blood did not flow. At her soft gasp, I smiled. "I've been using a trick to hold and capture my blood when I'm on my period, so I don't leave my blood everywhere. It's just not safe."

Closing my eyes, I settled back against Rik and breathed deeply. "First, I'm going to scan through my blood and see if I've picked up any of her blood from you. Since you're my sibling, and you're hers, it's possible I may already have a drop or two of Shalott blood inside me."

I didn't open my eyes, but I felt Guillaume's disagreement in our bond. "G, what are you thinking?"

"Forgive me, my queen, but I doubt that you'll find any other queen's blood in yours. You're the superior queen. You take what you need and assimilate it for your power stores. Your blood is yours. Our blood is yours. Your siblings' blood. Because you're our queen."

I nodded slowly. "That makes sense. But I'm going to look to be sure."

It was almost like healing myself, though I didn't have any injuries. I allowed my consciousness to slide through my body, searching for anything out of sorts. Anything that didn't belong.

That wasn't me. Then I focused more specifically on my blood. Magic shimmered through me, eager and ready to be used. I'd fed heavily from my Blood last night, but I couldn't begin to sort out Rik's blood from G's. Daire's from Mehen's. As my knight had said, it was all mine. There wasn't anything that I could separate from myself because I commanded it all.

Blowing out a sigh, I opened my eyes and gave Guillaume a wry smile. "You're right. I couldn't find anything that wasn't me. I guess my blood truly has absorbed all of you to the point that I can't separate it out."

He inclined his head, his lips twitching. "Old age is occasionally useful for something."

"Then why hasn't my blood in Gwen already taken over any other queen's blood in her body?"

"It may have," he admitted. "You're strong enough that even a few drops may be plenty to break another queen's hold completely. But the volume of your blood in hers is likely not enough to completely assimilate the Shalott queen's blood that still resides in her."

"Instead of trying to separate out that blood, would it be better to just destroy it with mine?"

"If I may, my queen?" Lance asked. I met his gaze and nodded. "If *she* has any sense of our queen's location, then it may be best to allow her to think that we're still here in New York City, rather than attacking on her own turf. That would be impossible if you completely destroy any traces of her in my queen."

"In that case, it'd be best to separate out the blood—so she thinks Gwen's still here." I pressed my nail back to Gwen's wrist and punctured her skin but used my magic to hold the blood inside her body, rather than allowing it to flow out.

My power rose, cascading through my body like a million fireflies. I sent one of those sparks into Gwen, searching through her body for anything that didn't belong. Anything that wasn't hers... or mine. I could definitely feel small bits of foreign blood in her, almost like grit. I didn't try to touch each piece and burn it out—I'd be here all day.

Instead, I called it out.

This blood is mine to command. Repel any contaminants. Push them out.

Her magic flared, answering my command. Her eyes widened with surprise, but she didn't resist me. With my eyes closed, I could see the shining brightness of her power sweeping through her veins, pushing the grit outward to the small hole I'd made in her wrist.

The White Enchantress had grown in power significantly from when I'd first met her. With the blood of Lancelot, Bors, and Mordred at her command, Gwen was definitely stronger than Mayte. I still wasn't that skilled at evaluating a queen's magic level, but I was pretty sure Gwen was even stronger than Keisha Skye had been, despite all her efforts to solidify her power base through any means necessary to gain a Triune seat.

House Camelot shone like a beacon once more with Gwen's Blood at her side. If she could free Merlin too... We'd make a formidable team.

Tingling pressure at my magical plug in her wrist made me open my eyes so I could watch as the foreign blood welled up at the small wound. My power allowed the grit to slide through and spill into the waiting cup. But not a drop of Gwen's natural blood fell through.

"Amazing," Gina breathed. "I've never seen anything like this done, by any queen. Ever."

Lance breathed deeply and made a low, choked sound as he turned his face away. "It's *her*. Definitely. I can fucking smell her."

Gwen smiled at me, a bright, fierce show of teeth that made the hairs on my nape rise. "I'm finally free of her. Thank you, my queen. Camelot is forever in your service."

We waited a few more moments to make sure I had pulled all that remained of House Shalott out of Gwen. It was only a thin layer of blood in the cup. Maybe a mouthful at most, but she'd been young when Elaine had taken her as a sibling. Despite her cruelty in keeping Gwen from her Blood for hundreds of years, Elaine's blood looked much like any other. A reminder that any of us were capable of such misdeeds. Even me.

:*Never,*: Rik growled in our bond. :*I don't believe that for a second.*:

He handed the glass to me, and I held it up to the light, watching the swirl of red against the crystal. To keep it from drying out, I sealed it with my power, holding it fresh and wet and red in the glass. Hopefully Elaine would believe her former sibling was still here in the tower.

Looking at her blood, I could almost feel a connection to her. A compulsion to read her location and try to understand her motivations. I loved Rik more than life itself. I'd do anything to protect him. Yes, even kill, in a heartbeat. But if he belonged to another queen...

Isis had sent him to me for a reason. The Great One would never have sent me a Blood that loved another queen. I knew that wholeheartedly. I wasn't sure which goddess had founded Shalott's line, but somewhere, somehow, something had gone wrong with Elaine. She'd fallen in love with a Blood never meant to be hers.

But I resisted the urge to seek out her secrets. I didn't want to give her any indication that Gwen was up to something, or that I had any reason to search Elaine out.

I handed the glass to Gwen. She held it as carefully as she'd grasp a deadly poisonous snake. "Do you think we need to put a guard on it?"

"G, what do you think? Could she use this blood to spy on us or anything else? I don't want any nasty surprises."

"Anything's possible, my queen."

I frowned at the glass, my mind racing. "Let's take it to the basement with us. I can use the darkness to bind it, and I'll add my blood too. That should be enough to make sure she can't cause any mischief."

Gwen stood as I did. "What exactly are you planning to do in the basement, my queen?"

Grinning, I entwined my arm with hers. "We're growing a tree."

ITZTLI

A tree. My queen was going to grow another tree. *Great Mother, I beg to be her sacrifice once again.*

Rik broke us up into teams, one to go ahead and my group to follow after in the small service elevator. This was her tower, but he'd never take her safety for granted, especially with several hundred siblings living here.

My brother talked with the other queen's Blood as we took the elevator down. I didn't pay attention to their conversation, even though Tlacel seemed animated and talked at length. He was normally the quiet, soft-spoken one, so it was unusual for him to connect with a stranger so easily.

I couldn't focus on what they said. All I could think about was the thick limbs shooting up out of the ground, binding me for her willing sacrifice.

My heart pumping in her hand.

Dark need rose from the depths where I kept it chained and hidden from everyone except my queen. If she didn't need me for this tree, then I could only pray that she'd be able to send the monster back into the basement prison of my soul.

Sweat trickled down my chest and my nostrils flared with

each heavy breath. Eager to draw in the scent of my queen. My prey—who, in turn, made me her conquest with a simple look. The thick, unrelenting darkness of the subterranean levels only heightened the monster's senses. I could smell the lingering stench of fear and pain in this place. The many lives that had been lost to the demon child who'd been hidden here.

Pain. Torture. Death.

My domain.

Another of Gwen's Blood came to stand by me. I hadn't caught his name, only that he wasn't her alpha. We were the last group of Blood to arrive, so the others already stood circled around the queens. Every muscle in my body demanded that I shove my way through the Blood between us so I could fall at my queen's feet. But she hadn't called me. She hadn't indicated that she even needed such a sacrifice this time.

"I sense the hunger for pain in you," the other Blood said in a low voice pitched only for my ears.

I didn't try to hide it. "Yes."

"The same need lives in me."

I glanced at his face, trying to remember his name. He had a thick scar across his forehead and from the tats on his hands, I assumed his arms and chest were likely covered in ink too.

The same as me.

I liked the pain of a needle or thin blade sinking into my flesh, though it was only an appetizer. It kept the edge off, though a simple tattoo couldn't satisfy the Flayed One's need for pain.

"Which of your brethren satisfy the darkness for you so that you can touch your queen without violence?"

"None," I answered slowly. "She—"

"Itztli," Shara called softly.

My name rang like a gong, echoing with the might of a cannon blast. My black dog bayed with a booming voice, announcing the coming hunt. I smiled so widely that my face hurt, but I didn't give a damn what the man thought of me. "Yes, my queen."

The other Blood made way for me so I could step closer to her. A small ball of fire hung above her head, slowly spinning as it cast sparkling rubies over her face. Thick shadows clung to her gown, swirling and writhing with ecstasy at her presence. She was Typhon's daughter, the god of monsters and all things of darkness.

Here, where the sun never shone, things of the dark reveled that their mistress had come.

Unsheathing my obsidian blade, I dropped to my knees and bent low, laying the knife at her feet. "Use me as you see fit, my queen."

Her fingers stroked over my hair and across my cheek to my chin, tipping my face up to hers. So tender and gentle—a heart-rending pain to bear. I didn't want her to have to hurt me, or worse, to allow me to hurt her. But staring into her shining eyes, I couldn't hide the monster inside me.

She gripped my chin firmer, letting the tips of her nails dig into my skin. "Do you feel it?" Her voice a soft, husky whisper, she let her head fall back a moment, her body swaying slightly. "The darkness plays a midnight sonata for us. There's something inside you that calls to the shadows here. Something new."

I was already a huge black dog with a taste for pain. I shuddered to think about what new thing might crawl out of me, especially here, in the demon child's deadly playground.

She released my face, making me jerk my attention back to her. "I don't think we need your heart this time, or your pain. We need mine."

I swallowed hard. My nape prickled and I didn't have to turn around to know that Rik was staring hard at me. I could feel his grim gaze like a jackhammer thumping my shoulders. Alpha would skin me alive if I harmed one hair on her head. Sadly, there was a large part of the monster that wanted to do exactly that, just to feel the overwhelming bliss of so much pain shredding my nerves like razor blades.

Ignoring her alpha's silent warning, she stepped closer to the fresh hole in the ground. I smelled her blood first. The incredible instant blast of a million complex scents all hitting my nose at the same time. Desert sands, cool water, night blooming flowers. A summer evening, the air warm and thick and lush with the scent of her need, as if she'd parted her thighs and allowed her desire to flavor the night. All laced with the rich, spicy scent of copper.

My mouth watered. My fangs descended. My hair spiked, rising like an aggressive dog's ruff. I didn't shift, but I felt the massive black dog braced, ready to pounce.

Shadows curled around her, a black swirling tidal pool that came eagerly to lap the smallest drop of our queen's blood.

She drew her silvered nail down her left wrist all the way to her elbow, providing a liberal offering of blood to splatter on the exposed ground and the eager shadows. Her blood glowed against the darkness, streams of shining magma spending across an obsidian landscape. Glowing molten rock, so bright and beautiful that my eyes watered.

I refused to look away. Or move a muscle. Even though I was slobbering at the mouth like a rabid dog.

She held her arm out over the dirt, letting her blood soak the ground. "Let's see what kind of tree grows from blood in complete darkness."

At first, the shadows were too thick to see anything. The ground groaned beneath our feet, making the stories of concrete and steel above us shift. I didn't spare a glance up or around at the man-made walls. The tower had withstood the tsunami of power released from the blood circle that our queen had dropped around the building without even stepping it out. I was pretty sure it could handle a tree growing in the basement.

I hadn't seen her grow the grove in Arkansas, though I felt

her memory in the bond. She'd died on the heart tree that grew over the grotto. She'd only taken out my heart and then put it back inside its cavity. I never died—my heart had continued to beat eagerly in her hand. So death wasn't *required* for her to grow a grove tree.

However, as the first limbs appeared, an icy chill trickled down my spine. Bone-white and thin, the branches quivered as they strained to reach her. I'd gotten used to the sentient trees in the grove, but this new sprout seemed... off.

Maybe it was the corpse-like branches that looked more like bleached bones than wood. Or the eerie, low moan that my dog's sensitive ears picked up. Like a distant, mournful winter wind, the wood groaned as it reached for her.

She smeared her blood on the smooth white wood, and red buds sprouted. Small flowers unfurled to dangle from the thin limb like living droplets of blood.

But only the limb that she'd touched.

She turned and held out her other hand to me. "The tree would like more of my blood."

Rooted to the spot, I didn't move a muscle. There were a million ways she could give the tree her blood and none of them involved me.

Certainly, none of those ways involved me raking claws down her arms and back while she rode me. Or me gripping her delicate throat in my jaws.

The dog her power had given me growled and slobbered, more monstrous than ever. A twisted hulking beast that barely even resembled a normal four-legged hound any longer. My mind flashed to the glittering black eyes of the demon child, cackling in the darkness. Had Tanza possessed me somehow? A remnant of her spirit contaminating me?

Shara said there was something in the darkness that called to me.

Sweat dripped down my forehead as I fought to contain the darkness rising inside me.

Without saying another word, my queen reached up to her shoulders and easily swiped the spaghetti straps down her arms. The gown slipped down her body to disappear in the shadows.

And I was lost.

SHARA

Goosebumps flared across my arms and not from the chill in the air. Thick velvety shadows caressed my bare skin, suddenly engulfing me in an embrace of darkness that stole my breath.

I stood in a flash flood of dark power that rushed and crashed through the underground tunnels. The currents swirled and pushed against me, dumping power through me that had nothing to do with the blood dripping from my wrist. This was the kind of power that I'd never have to bleed before touching.

The power of endless night and absolute darkness. My father's realm, and now mine.

I'd been born in darkness like this. It knew me, enveloping me in enthusiastic power surges that overloaded my system. Too many sensations. Too much information. Millions of bits of data rushing at me with the speed of a supersonic jet, dumping into my brain at once. I couldn't make sense of anything.

I lost my footing, swept away into chaotic riptides and endless chasms beneath the earth. I couldn't breathe. Think. For all the power filling me, I didn't know how to save myself and pull my mind back from the brink.

Strong arms seized me. Crushed me against a stone-hard

chest. I clung to that body like a drowning woman lost at sea. I fought through the tastes of New York City and the multitude of humans living above to focus on the man. The dog. I could feel his black fur beneath my hands. His powerful jaws locked onto my nape and he lifted me, cradling me like a baby kitten in his vicious teeth. He dragged me back to the shore. Away from the tumbling darkness swallowing me up. Something hard pressed against my cheek. Smooth, sleek wood.

The tree. Finally, my mind refocused on my surroundings. I wasn't lost in an underground sea at all. Darkness still crashed around us like turbulent waves, but the tree anchored me. It gave me something to hang on to. It needed me, as much as I needed it.

Hot breath panted against my ear. "It needs your blood."

Yes, I remembered now. It took all my effort to peel back the overwhelming curtain of darkness to focus on the tree against me. The trunk had widened enough for me to wrap my arms around it, gripping branches on the other side for leverage. My bare toes dug into the soil, moistened with my blood.

Itztli pressed against my back, a solid, heavy heat. I closed my eyes, bracing my cheek against the sleek wood, and breathed him in. As dark as the silky shadows flowing around me, heavy with desperate need. Aching with love.

"What do you need, my Blood?" I thought I spoke aloud, but I honestly wasn't sure, not with the streams of power flooding me.

"Pain," he replied hoarsely. "As much as it shames me."

I could taste his regret in the shadows twining around our legs. And yes, his fear. He didn't want to be evil like Tanza. "Never regret a need our goddesses gave you. Embrace it. Revel in it. As I revel in you."

"I'd rather Rik put me down like a rabid dog than ever hurt you." His voice broke, and in our bond, I heard the desperate howl of his beast. Usually a massive black dog, his monster had changed here in the darkness. I couldn't make out his shape, though it was still a black creature of the night.

This creature had sharp claws too. Although Itztli held me carefully against him, he didn't expect me to surge to the side, deliberately scraping my hip on his lengthening nails.

Thick shadows lapped at my torn flesh eagerly, making me shudder. Not with pain or dread, but ecstasy. Velvet slid over my skin, sensuous and dark and tempting. It wanted my blood as much as the tree did, and I didn't mind the pain. Not at all. In fact, the stinging burn in my skin intensified my senses. I could smell his homeland, the lush jungles, ripe fruits, and rich, dark cocoa that flavored his blood. The sleek black fur of his beast. Even the obsidian blade smelled sharp and cold with the bite of blood along its edge.

The bond gave me access to his heart and mind, but here in the darkness, the shadows heightened that connection. I could taste his scent on my tongue. I breathed in the darkness of his need like a knife-thrust to the gut. His blood flavored the air. He'd gnashed his lips open, trying to contain the beast roiling inside him.

And yes, my darkness liked that very much indeed.

If we'd been moon-mad last night, now I was drunk on shadows. High on darkness. I needed so much more. *We* needed. We needed it all.

A grim, dark hurricane powerful enough to level the entire city crested inside me.

More. Blood. Pain.

I ground my buttocks against him, surprised to feel fabric against my skin. In my head and in the bond, he was a lithe dark creature of the night. He certainly wasn't clothed.

As I moved between him and the tree, something sharp jabbed me in the ribs hard enough to draw blood. The trunk shuddered beneath my cheek and the sharp tip of the limb pressed harder. Another stuck my opposite thigh. It wasn't the

piercing agony of the heart tree that I'd grown in the nest. Not
with Itztli's heat against my back. No, this was ever so much
better than suffering on those thorns.

"I want you inside me." I gasped as the limb dragged down
my side, scoring my rib cage with its thin, razor-sharp tip.
"Fuck me on this tree, as I fucked you on Zaniyah's. Let me give
the darkness some pleasure with the pain, not just the hopeless
torture it endured during Tanza's reign in this room."

Despite my words, he still hesitated. Such an honorable,
loyal man, very much like his black dog. Only it wasn't the loyal,
faithful hound that I felt inside him any longer.

I sank deeper into his bond, down to the secret place inside
him where he tried to keep his darker need buried. His monster
blinked at me, large, liquid eyes like spilled ink, shining despite
the lack of light.

:There's always light in me now,: Itztli growled, his words
garbled by the rising beast. :Because you're inside me.:

I smiled at the creature and slowly turned my back, peeking
over my shoulder with heavy-lidded, sultry eyes. I reached up
and pulled my hair aside, baring my throat and the curve of my
shoulder.

Something large surged up out of him. Claws seized me, his
fangs buried in my shoulder. Not to feed—but to hold me in
place. To pin me against him, like a jaguar would pin his mate
for breeding. Only I didn't think this was a jaguar. My winged
cat didn't answer this creature's call. I couldn't hear the sound it
made, but I could feel the vibrations against me, rumbling
through me like Daire's purrs.

He surged into me, shoving me hard against the tree. More
branches poked and stabbed me, but the pain was distant. He
felt too good, a beast unleashed with a voracious hunger. So
often my Blood tried to handle me gently, afraid to fuck me too
hard. Like I might break.

Fuck that shit.

Fuck it *hard*.

He gripped the front of my throat in one hand, his thick arm locked around me. His other hand hauled my hips back so he could slam deeper. He thrust so hard that I would have groaned if I had any breath left. Everything tilted crazily, like I'd fallen, though I could still feel the tree against me.

His claws dug deep into my skin, adding more blood for the sacrifice.

I floated, wrapped in black silk and fur, shadows and blood. I'd never fully understood a submissive's mindset, even though I shared such a deep bond with Daire. It just wasn't in me to surrender. To give up and allow another to control me completely.

If I'd given up and surrendered, I would have died a long time ago. And even though I loved Daire absolutely without question, I'd never really gotten it. Until now.

Pain and pleasure carried me deeper. Higher. I felt the sensation of claws and branches tearing my skin. I knew it hurt, but here in this safe darkness, wrapped in Itztli's arms, it was like adding a shot of whiskey to my coffee. Salt to my caramel.

I just felt. So. Fucking. Good.

Nothing else mattered. I could simply exist here. I could float on the tree and know that it was in the goddess's hands. In Itztli's hands. My body was a vessel tonight, and that was perfectly okay. Because only I could carry his need like this, and not break. I could accept his beast without reservation. Fur, claws, fangs, wings and all.

Yes, wings. I felt something fluttering above us more substantial than the velvety shadows wrapped around me. My dog had sprouted wings, though I still didn't know exactly what he was now.

His jaws clamped harder on my shoulder, his teeth and fangs grinding on bone. More pain, sharper now. An extra shot of espresso to add kick and depth to my pleasure. Because I was climaxing. I had been for a while as I drifted. I tightened my muscles, squeezing his dick harder, my pussy hungry for more. I didn't want him to stop. I didn't want it to end. I didn't want him to ever slide free and leave me empty.

Tightening his grip on my throat, I felt his sudden realization. He could tear my throat out. Easily. His big hand and vicious claws would make quick work of the deed. And yeah, there was a part of his monster that wanted to see the violent spray of my blood gushing from a torn throat. Even the tree shuddered beneath me, horrified and yet haunted with longing for such a feast.

I wasn't afraid. I could heal it. I could bear it. If he needed it.

His silent call sang through me again, a deep bellow that made my bones resonate like a deep bass drum. His cock throbbed inside me, adding to the vibration. I climaxed again, or harder. Longer. I wasn't sure. I couldn't remember what it felt like not to come. Not to feel pleasure liquifying my muscles. Not to feel the hot throb of release.

My feast had only just begun.

I drank him in through my skin, everywhere we touched. His pleasure. His sweat and come. His emotion. His relief that he hadn't ripped out my throat. His lingering horror that I would have allowed it, confident in my ability to heal whatever he did to me. His heart thudded against my back, reminding me of the other tree we'd grown together. How I'd grasped his bare, bleeding heart in my hand and felt the pulse of his life against my palm. I could have killed him then, the same as he could have killed me now.

This need we shared was dark. Yes. Pain-filled and bloody and so fucking delicious. I could only hope that we needed to grow a tree every month.

He groaned against my ear, making my lips curve. A human sound, not a beast's roar. He moved on top of me, trying to shift the bulk of his weight off me, though I didn't mind. "Are you alright, my queen? Have I injured you? Alpha!"

I groaned too—with regret as his dick slid out of me. "I'm fine," I mumbled, trying to open my eyes. It was so fucking dark. Had the small fire ball I'd set for light gone out? Why couldn't I see?

Gentle hands swept over my face and I realized hair covered my eyes. Mine. His. A sweaty, tangled mess. All the Blood had started growing their hair out, first to compete with Nevarre, and then with Vivian, who had the most beautiful fiery red hair I'd ever seen. Itztli's was more of a mohawk, with the sides of his head shaved close to his skull. But the top and back were still long, and he usually wore stiffened spikes in a showy ridge down his head.

A hand cupped my cheek. Rik's. I'd know his touch anywhere. "What a beautiful tree you've grown, my queen."

I smiled and blinked until my eyes focused on him. But his head was lower than me. I started to sit up, wincing as tender skin pulled and bruises throbbed.

"Heal yourself, and then I'll help you down."

Heal? I looked down at my chest and winced again. I was covered in blood and scratches. Some were from Itztli's claws and others were from the tree.

Itztli drew in a shaking breath. "Goddess. Forgive me. Take every drop of blood in my body, my queen."

I shifted closer to him and gave him as stern a frown as I could muster when I was still buzzed with pleasure. "I don't need your blood to heal. I'm fine." I closed my eyes and concentrated intently, willing my flesh to heal and the bleeding to stop. A few moments of uncomfortable tingling as my skin knit back together and I was as good as new. "See?"

Rik lifted his arms, and I finally realized we were up in the tree. I'd been leaning against it in the beginning, but evidently, we'd somehow ended up on top of its branches. It wasn't as tall as the heart tree in Arkansas, thankfully, so no one had to climb up to bring me down.

Cradling me in his arms, he ran his bond through me, looking for any lingering injuries. I didn't mind, even though I'd told him I was fine. Sometimes it was nice to be taken care of— even when I didn't need it.

"Gorgeous," Gwen breathed out a sigh of awe as she stared at the tree. "I can see exactly where you were lying. The flowers grew in the shape of your body, as if you'd stretched out on top of a tree to take a nap."

Only then did I remember that she and her Blood had just watched me and Itztli fuck on top of a tree. And I was still naked. Her Blood didn't ogle me like human men probably would have, but it still made me blush.

I'd have been furious if one of my Blood was naked in front of her or another queen. Absolutely livid. They were mine. MINE.

Yet here I was completely naked in front of three strange men and my Blood didn't even care.

"Oh, trust me, we care." Daire grinned as he handed me my discarded dress. "But they'll never be yours like we are, and you're our queen. If you want to march stark naked down Broadway, then so be it."

I wriggled in Rik's arms, silently telling him I wanted him to put me down. He did so, though I felt the reluctance in his bond. He still worried for me, and yeah, he was a little jealous too. Well, that wasn't the right word. He didn't begrudge my time with Itztli at all. He just wished I'd do the same with him.

I blew a puff of air against my tangled hair, lifting it out of my eyes. "Anytime, alpha. Anytime."

I started to pull the dress back over my head and froze. My head rang, my ears screeching with a vicious alarm. My heart pounded so hard that my ribs hurt. That sound. Goddess. Tangled up in the material, I finally got my hands clamped over my ears, but that didn't help. The fire alarms weren't shrilling here in the tower. This was an internal alarm.

My nest. My trees.

INTRUDER. MURDER. DEATH. COME NOW.

"Shara!" Gina sobbed, threading her way through everyone to reach me, her phone clutched to her ear. "Your nest is under attack. Frank's been hurt. Winston..." She hauled in a tremulous breath. "He's afraid Frank might be dead."

I didn't wait for the dress to settle around my body. Whirling back to the tree, I dove through the dark hole that I knew would be waiting.

I'm coming!

19

SHARA

I felt Rik's fury in the bond, but I didn't care. I couldn't wait for him to send a few Blood ahead of me, not when Frank and Winston were in danger. They were my family.

Goddess, please keep them safe!

They were human. They wouldn't stand a chance against anything strong enough to actually attack my nest. It was supposed to be fucking impenetrable.

After a few steps inside the tree's portal, I saw the opening ahead that would let me out at the grotto. I tore both wrists open, dripping blood as I ran. I readied every attack and defense that I could think of in my head. A shield. Fiery ropes to bind. My jaguar's teeth and claws. No. My cobra's poison. But what if the creature attacking had wings?

The wyvern? Though it wouldn't be agile on the ground.

Still in my human form until I could decide the best attack shape to take, I raced out of the heart tree and scrambled up the slick boulders that formed the edges of the grotto. I probably should have ducked down and scanned for the attackers first, but all I could think about was getting to Frank and healing him before it was too late.

Could I resurrect a human? My jaws ached, holding back a scream of rage. I couldn't fucking believe that someone would sneak into my nest. My human friends were defenseless without me here, and that hurt most of all.

I hesitated a moment, frantically scanning the surroundings. Everything looked different. The large oak tree that had been the closest to the heart tree was gone. No stump, no chopped-up limbs or remains. Just gone. I whirled, trying to find the rest of the grove, but other than the heart tree...

My grove was gone.

Biting back another cry, I reached inside myself for my grove. I could still feel the ancient trees' fury and the shrill alarm screeching through my connection with them. The intruder hadn't been able to destroy them, but I had no idea what had happened.

Panting, I ran around toward the front of the house. Most likely, Frank had been at the guard station near the gate.

"Shara!" Winston yelled to draw my attention to him on the porch. I could only stare. He held some kind of huge gun that looked completely out of place against his double-breasted suit coat. "There! In the trees!"

A new clump of trees stood just inside my blood circle. My fucking grove had *moved*? I shouldn't be surprised. These trees had been destroyed in Nevarre's nest and I'd regrown them with my blood in a matter of hours. And they talked to me. Of course they could also move to attack any threats.

The flap and rustle of wings rushed overhead as Leviathan led the charge from the air. My dragon swooped low over the trees and sent me what he saw. Frank, on the ground. Not moving. A woman stood over him. She glared up at the great beast's belly as he flew overhead, and my heart stopped.

Mom.

It was her face. I recognized the blue dress she wore, though it was tattered now. She'd called it lapis blue. Before I'd known our heritage through Isis, I'd thought it was a weird way to say turquoise. We'd playfully argued about it for years.

Of course, she would have been buried in her favorite dress.

Leviathan circled back and swept lower. *:This was your mother? But how?:*

I ran toward the grove, my mind reeling. *:Not my mother, but the woman who raised me. My aunt, though I always called her Mom. Selena. She died in Kansas City.:*

The trees' limbs had woven together, making a thick barrier to pin the intruder, though they allowed me to pass without a single poke. Once through, I stumbled to a halt as she turned to face me.

"Shara Delaney Dalton."

It was Mom's voice. The one she used when I was in trouble. Only she would have ever called me Dalton, after Dad, the human she'd loved. My middle name had been his choice, supposedly his mother's name. Was Delaney my real middle name? Or had that been a farce that she'd made up when she'd claimed to be my mother?

"Just look at you," she continued in that same tone that made my shoulders automatically hunch with shame.

It was like all the years had been stripped away and I was an awkward teenager again. My dress was barely on, one strap completely torn. I was covered in blood. My hair a mess. Barefoot.

"You reek of sex and blood. I guess you are your mother's daughter after all."

That jerked my head up. I squared my shoulders and tipped my chin higher, shaking my hair back from my face. "Something you neglected to tell me about, right, *Mom?*"

She smiled and it wasn't her looking back at me. Mom had never looked at me with such disdain. She'd loved me. She'd given up her life for me. Literally dying, trying to buy me some time to escape from the monster who hunted us.

It was her body, though. Now I could see the awful wound stitched together on her neck. Greyson had ripped her throat out. Locked in the basement, I'd been forced to watch her die. I couldn't save her.

The dress was definitely her favorite one, and she wore the necklace Alan had given her the last Christmas he'd been alive. Inside the heart locket, I'd see a picture of the three of us. It was the last time I could remember being truly happy as a child.

Her skin had a ghastly bluish tinge. This close, I could see streaks of dirt on her face. The tattered dress was faded and also streaked with dirt. She lifted her hand to tuck a strand of hair behind her ear—a normal gesture I could remember her doing a million times. But I noticed the torn, broken fingernails on her hand.

As if she'd dug her way out of the grave and then walked all the way to Arkansas on foot.

Rik slipped an arm around me and tucked me back against him. The rest of my Blood surrounded the grove. Some in the air, but all of them shifted to their beasts. Ready to protect me.

But this threat was already dead.

"Oh, goddess," Gina whispered, her voice breaking.

"Is it really her?" I asked softly.

"It looks like her. She left instructions that if she died, she was to be buried in that dress beside her husband, Alan Dalton."

"How did you return so quickly?" Mom smiled, but it was a mean, nasty twist of her lips that I'd never seen on her face before. "I had such grand plans, Shara. I wanted this homecoming to be extra special. But these cursed trees put up quite a fight, and I certainly didn't expect you to return—" she kicked Frank's crumpled body on the ground "—before I had my fun."

I fought the urge to look down at Frank and see if he was still alive. I didn't want her to hurt him more, or to try and use him as a bargaining chip.

:Aima should never be buried like humans.: Guillaume's bond

196	JOELY SUE BURKHART

cut as sharply as his Templar sword. *:This atrocity is why. Someone has animated her corpse.:*

:Marne?:

His hell horse blew out a rattling snort and pawed the ground. *:It could be, though I've never heard of her having such power.:*

"Do you like my special gift to you, Shara?" Mom's corpse asked, making me shudder.

"How did you cross into my nest? You never shared blood with me. I had no idea what we even were until after your death."

"A valuable perk to being dead." She shrugged. "A *goule* can pass through any blood circle."

That word echoed in my head. *Goule* sounded like something Mehen would have read to me.

In French.

Which meant...

:The Dauphine.: Mehen snarled in our bond.

My stomach sank. I'd been so confident. So sure of my strength and power. I'd handled Ra. I'd figured out how the Dauphine was hiding. I'd learned how to play the Triune games.

Shifting pieces on a chess board while smiling and nodding and plotting the next dozen moves ahead. I'd been playing the game perfectly, setting one queen against another.

Now Frank had paid the price for my arrogance.

"There's something quite horrific about dead loved ones returning with a message, don't you think?" Mom kicked Frank's body again. "In the land of swamps and gators, I learned a little voodoo of my own. Leave House Delafosse alone, Shara. We have no interest in any dealings with Isador. Forget you ever called my consiliarius. Forget her name. And I won't be forced to pay you such a visit again."

I bit the inside of my cheek, holding back my reaction.

Keeping my face smooth. My mouth shut. Even though my mind raced.

She was still sticking to the House Delafosse cover. Meaning... what? Did she think we'd stumbled across the fake Wrenna Jade name and number by accident?

Could she honestly be so confident in her ability to hide that she didn't realize that I knew the truth?

Or did she think this little scare would be enough to buy my silence?

"Or next time..." She leered at me, smiling widely. "I'll be forced to find your real mother's corpse to bear my message."

:Never,: Llewellyn retorted in our bond. *:She would have made sure to destroy her body, so nothing like this could ever happen.:*

Mom's body crumpled to the ground. Gina started forward, but I grabbed her arm, holding her back until it was safe. She was just as human as Frank. If I lost her...

Neither body moved. A soft sob escaped Gina's lips. I hadn't realized that she was so close to Mom. She'd made it sound like they'd rarely had contact at Mom's request. I focused on her bond, and her fear and worry tightened my throat. She wasn't upset about Mom, who'd been dead for over five years.

She was crying for Frank. I hadn't realized how much she'd come to care for him. They'd made the trip from Kansas City together, giving me time with my Blood on the road. Had she fallen in love with him then? Or earlier? How could I have been so self-absorbed to not notice my closest friend falling in love?

I stepped forward, Rik moving with me, a solid rock at my back. Daire's warcat and Xin's wolf approached the two bodies on the ground.

:He's still alive.: Xin grabbed a mouthful of Frank's shirt and dragged him toward me. Daire crouched by Mom's body, ready to leap on her if she moved again.

I sank down to my knees as Xin dragged Frank closer. I could smell his blood now, and something else that was foul.

Dead and rotten.

I swallowed hard, willing my stomach to toughen up. I had a feeling that smell came from Mom. I couldn't look at her. Not yet. I wasn't sure what I was going to do about her.

Frank's shirt was torn open, wet with dark fluids. Gina gagged at the smell but smoothed his hair off his brow. "It's alright now. Our queen's here."

"Sorry." His eye fluttered open and he gasped softly with pain. "Tried to stop her."

"Shhh." Gina cupped his cheek, leaning down over him. "There was nothing you could have done to stop her."

I focused on the small amount of my blood he'd taken back in Kansas City. He still carried my power inside him, enough for me to scan his body. His pulse was weak, his heart beating unevenly and much too rapidly. His skin was damp with clammy sweat, and I could feel the heat flaring off his chest. The sickly-sweet smell of infection and decaying flesh rose from the jagged wound.

Dribbling blood all over his chest, I focused my power on him. I could feel something inside him. Worming deeper through his body, spreading foulness like a cancer.

I sent my power pulsing through him, my blood going on the defensive. I touched the black rot spreading through him, driving it back toward the wound. Pushing the contamination out of him.

It had spread quickly, destroying tissue. I couldn't imagine how much pain he'd endured, waiting on me to show up.

Guillaume laid a hand on my shoulder. "Too much of your blood is just as dangerous for him, my queen."

My fury had made my blood seep faster from the wounds on my wrist. I'd bled so much that blood dripped from Frank's chest and down onto the ground. I swiped my fingers in the blood pooled on his skin, pleased to see the deep slash had already closed.

I scanned through his body again, a quick swipe to ensure nothing tainted remained inside him. His fever was down, his pain gone, and he reached up to lightly touch Gina's cheek.

Mom croaked, her voice rattling like sticks covered in sandpaper. Calling me, trying to say my name.

Dread roiled in my stomach, but I stood and walked toward her. Though I reached back silently and Rik's big hand engulfed mine.

She lay on her back, arms and legs bent at unnatural angles as if a child had been playing with a doll and tossed her on the ground. The smell of decay was thick in the air, making Daire wrinkle his warcat's nose. Now that I was close, I could see that some of the streaks I'd thought were dirt were actually rotted places in her skin. She was starting to look like a television mummy.

Tears thickened my throat, but I made myself smile. "Hi, Mom."

She tried to lift her hand, but her arm flopped helplessly at her side. I reached down with my free hand and wrapped my fingers around hers. Brittle and thin, her fingers didn't feel real, and she couldn't squeeze them around mine.

Her eyes were dried and shriveled but still conveyed a deep, abject horror. Her mouth opened, her throat working desperately, but she couldn't get the words out. Her throat wouldn't work.

I squeezed her hand and pressed a kiss to her dry knuckles. "I know, Mom. It's my turn to take care of you, okay?"

Gently pulling my hand free from Rik's, I held my bleeding arm over her body, letting my blood splash on the faded lapis blue she'd loved so much.

:Her spirit is trapped inside the body,: Guillaume warned. *:What's been done to her is an abomination.:*

I swallowed my tears, determined not to worry or frighten

her more than she already was. *:I know. Her eyes look back at me now, not the Dauphine's.:*

I needed to destroy her body so she could never be turned into a walking corpse again, but I couldn't bear to burn her alive. She was still inside the rotted body, fully aware of what was happening to her, even though she couldn't control the zombie she'd become without the Dauphine's will.

I'd only dealt with one other mummy before, though I'd brought Huitzilopochtli *back* to life, rather than trying to free his soul. I closed my eyes and forced myself to look at her body through my power. The stench and rot were amplified in my heightened senses. I could see the dead, shriveled cells. All the trauma of death. Even after five years, the violence of her murder still echoed in her body. The pain as her former alpha had torn open her throat. His desperation burning like madness in his eyes as he devoured her. All he'd wanted was to be her Blood again.

But she had no power left to give him. Only her life.

I stared up at him through her eyes and read the subtle compulsion that had twisted him. He'd definitely turned himself into a thrall, a monster, by killing humans once his queen had died. But someone else had whispered poisoned secrets to him. Someone had sent him out after his lost queen and her daughter who wasn't actually hers. They'd told him lies, enraging his madness until he was their perfectly obsessed hunter.

I remembered the night I'd killed him. He'd told me that my father was Leviathan. He'd told me that name on purpose.

Someone had given him that name, hoping that he'd share it with me.

So maybe a desperate, lonely young woman in search of the father she'd never known would seek out the monster known to have killed queens for at least a thousand years.

I'd destroyed Greyson before I ever knew about the Dauphine, but I had to wonder if she was the one behind his corruption. Even then, she'd been close to finding me. She'd already been here in America, sending out her careful feelers looking for me. She'd known to look in Kansas City—likely because of Greyson, who'd been able to sniff out his former queen's existence even without her power.

I'd sensed the spy in the dark hallway at the bar. How many other invisible watchers did she have? How many were here in Eureka Springs? She'd known that I'd left the nest, but she'd been surprised that I'd returned so quickly. She hadn't known about my grove. She'd been trapped by the trees, and now she knew that I could instantly travel from New York to my nest. Maybe not how, yet—but that it was possible.

She'd deliberately sent Mom to me, trapped in this rotting body, with her warning.

I pushed away the memory of Greyson tearing out her throat. Another memory fluttered up at me. Waking in darkness. Forced to claw and dig her way out of a six-foot-deep hole. Compelled to stagger across Missouri to find me in the hills of Arkansas.

Knowing that she was dead. Feeling the rotted corpse imprisoning her soul.

Someone I loved—so that it would hurt all the more.

Other than the monsters that had hunted me all my life, I'd never really hated anyone before. But I hated Jeanne Dauphine for this. I burned with a cold, icy rage.

Fire had been my gift from the beginning, but this emotion was a blistering blizzard that would obliterate everything in its path.

I reached deeper into Mom's corpse, past the paper-thin skin and sharp, dry bones of her rib cage. In the center of her body, I felt a faint stirring. A hint of feathers and movement, though it was bound tightly, trapped against bone and dried sinew. I grasped the caged thing with my power and pulled it out of her.

Opening my eyes, I saw a hawk sitting on her chest, holding

her locket in its beak. It was larger than my crow queen, but not a massive bird of prey. Dark brown feathers covered her body, and her head was darker, almost black. She opened her wings, though she didn't fly away yet, giving me a glimpse of the stripes of lighter colors on the undersides of her wings. I'd seen something like that before, but it took me a moment to place it.

On the legacy box, there was an image of Isis with Her horned crown and red disk, one arm lifted up with a cup in Her hand. On either side of Her, outstretched wings reached from side to side on the box's top.

Wings like these—with dark and light striped chevrons.

The hawk's head tipped sideways, and she dropped the locket into my lap. She chirped several times. I didn't need to have my crow queen or Nevarre's raven translate for me. *I'll always love you.*

Then she sprang up into the sky, gone on silent wings.

Picking up the locket as I stood, I stepped back from Mom's body. Tears streaked my cheeks, but I managed to smile. Her spirit was gone, freed from the hell that the Dauphine had put her through. Now only one thing remained to ensure she couldn't do it again.

The blood I'd dripped on Mom exploded into flames, quickly blasting through the dried flesh. I watched her burn, making sure there wasn't anything left that the Dauphine could ever use.

I lifted my head, not surprised to find that my trees had silently gone. I hadn't heard them move back to their positions around the heart tree. Clouds covered the moon and the temps had warmed enough that most of the snow had melted. It wasn't quite time for new life to start sprouting, but a tender young plant shot up out of the ground, fed by Mom's ashes and my blood.

Turning back toward the house, I didn't wait to see what

new tree would grow there. I already knew it would be beautiful. As beautiful as Selena Isador Dalton had been.

"Shara!" Gina called.

I glanced back over my shoulder but didn't pause my step. She had her arm around Frank's waist, supporting him, though he didn't need her help to stand after I'd healed him. The tender look he gave her warmed the frigid hurricane of snow blowing in me but didn't dispel the coming storm. "I'm so happy for you and Frank. I'm sorry I didn't notice before."

Her eyes shone as brightly as the moon. "What are you going to do now? What do you need?"

I kept walking toward the house so rapidly that even Rik had to hurry his step to keep up with me. "I need the mirror."

Itztli rushed past us so quickly he was a blur, but I still made out his black leathery wings. His new shape was a giant bat. *:At once, my queen.:*

Gina gasped, and both she and Frank started running after me. "Marne Ceresa's mirror?"

"The very one." I smiled grimly at Winston as I climbed the front steps. "That's a very nice gun you have there, Winston. It goes so nicely with your bowtie."

He inclined his head, tucking the hefty gun against his chest. "At your service, my queen."

Pausing on the top step, I arched a brow at him. I'd been in a hurry earlier, but I definitely hadn't missed him calling me by my given name. "Already back to formalities?"

His lips twitched as he opened the door for me. "It appears so, though I'm sure I'll slip once more if the nest ever comes under attack again."

My rage had cooled slightly, from a punishing blizzard to only a killing frost of ice. I smiled, even though my face felt brittle. "How about I go on the offensive this time?"

He shoved the gun back over his shoulder, letting it dangle

down his back by a strap, and headed for the kitchen. "Then I should put on a pot of tea, Shara, my queen."

20

MEHEN

It took all my self-control not to blast the entire fucking world with dragonfire.

Fuck them all.

Fuck the queens who plotted and schemed to hunt Shara down and kill her before she could ever find us. Fuck especially the Dauphine, who'd fucking hurt my queen.

Hurt her like I'd never felt before.

I'd been betrayed. I'd been hurt. My own fucking mother had exiled me. I'd lain in a festering prison locked away from the world for centuries with only the occasional rat snack and power-hungry queen to devour. Yet I'd never hurt as badly as I fucking did right now.

Fucking evil queen. I'd drag the Dauphine to my prison and bind her there in my place. Only I'd go there occasionally—just so I could eat off one of her body parts. A queen that old would live a long time. I could feast on her for eons.

And it still wouldn't be enough to punish her for what she'd done to Shara.

My fucking queen. Fucking *crying*.

"Fuck that shit," Ezra muttered under his breath as he

shrugged on yet another fugly flannel shirt. We'd all started stashing spare clothing around the nest so we could easily dress after shifting if Gina or another queen was present. "Mother-fucking zombie queen's gotta pay."

For once, I was in complete agreement with the grizzly. Normally I wouldn't bother with clothes after an attack—hoping for another bloody orgy with our queen to help her recover. But this time even our queen's heavenly body couldn't lure Leviathan into subsiding completely.

"Oh, she will," Shara replied, her lips curved in a grim smile that made my hackles rise with glee. "Nevarre, would you pick me out a new outfit?" He started up the stairs immediately, taking steps three at a time. She called after him, "Something comfortable and casual. Gina, let's set up the war room in front of the fireplace. I want Gwen, Kevin, and whoever else needs to be a part of this discussion online if they're available."

:We're always available for you, my queen,: Gwen replied in Shara's head.

Itztli charged down the stairs as quickly as Nevarre had gone up. He held the mirror under his arm, still wrapped in heavy black velvet. I could smell the coffee grounds it'd been buried in. When the Triune queen of Rome sent you a gift, it was wise to treat it like a fucking Trojan horse.

"Keep the cover on for now," Shara said. "Hopefully she can't eavesdrop as long as the mirror isn't activated, but everyone keep that in mind."

Gina flipped on two new television screens on the wall, revealing Gwen and Kevin on one screen and two of her assistants on the other. "I'm so glad we had these installed. Can everyone hear?"

"Loud and clear," Gwen replied. "Technology is cooperating today."

Nevarre returned with clothing, so Shara stepped off to the side behind the couch and quickly dressed in worn, soft jeans and a black hoodie with the Isador logo on it. She arched a brow at him but slipped it over her head. "Isn't wearing my own logo presumptuous? I don't want Marne to think I'm trying to sell something."

"It was the softest sweatshirt I could find. Besides, it'd only be presumptuous if we *all* showed up in her court wearing matching Isador shirts, though I think it'd be fucking hilarious."

She started to head back to the main group, but Nevarre reached out and lightly rubbed his thumb against some flecks of blood that had dried on her chin.

"Oh, yeah. Thanks for the reminder." She wrapped her arms around his neck and leaned into him.

That was the only warning we had before a fucking bomb detonated inside her.

Her power hummed in my bones like I'd been struck by lightning. She called her blood to return to her. Since every drop of blood in my body belonged to her, it felt like my skin was going to dissolve to make way for all the power surging toward her.

Thumps and growls and screeches filled the room as our beasts roared to life at her call.

The king of the deep swelled inside me with a fierce bellow of exhilaration. I would have shifted and demolished this entire fucking house without her quick command.

:No dragons in the house.:

Quivering, I endured Leviathan's thrashing and howling for what seemed like an eternity. When I finally managed to blink and focus on the room, the rest of her Blood were still fighting their own beasts. Ezra was even furrier and thicker than usual, though Vivian only had a sheen of sweat on her skin from her phoenix's glowing nimbus.

"Fucking hell." Ezra pulled the tattered shirt off and threw it on the floor in disgust. "That was one of my favorites too."

"I can't tell any difference." Daire snickered. "It already looked like a rag."

"Sorry, everyone." Shaking her head, Shara laughed softly. "I forgot to warn you, and I guess I bled more than I expected tonight."

Guillaume let out a grunt that still sounded more horse than man, though he hadn't shifted that I could tell. "Or you're just that much more fucking powerful when you're pissed."

"Could be," she said lightly. As if her bond wasn't still a raging thunder-blizzard threatening to bury New Orleans neck-deep in snow.

Rik was still so hulking big that the chair creaked and groaned as he sat down and drew her in between his thighs. Gina adjusted a small camera focused on her so that the telecommuters could still see her.

"The nest was attacked tonight," Shara began. "By the Dauphine."

Kevin's mouth fell open and the two assistants on the other screen gasped. But no one questioned her. If our queen said it was the mysterious Triune queen, then it was so.

"I'm sorry I left New York so unexpectedly. We didn't have time to swear you in, Kevin. But I'd like to do so before Gwen takes care of her business so that you can manage the tower in her absence. If you don't mind some woo-woo travel, I'll explain to Gwen how the tree works. You'll need to know anyway so you can make your plans."

The young man grinned. "I'm always up for some woo-woo travel, my queen. I'll gladly come to you as you wish."

"If you carry my blood, you can use the portal inside the tree to travel to me or anywhere in the world, as long as there's a portal on the other end. I'm not one-hundred percent sure how that works yet. They've always been trees for me, but they may be something else for you, Gwen."

"Do I need to draw blood first?" she asked.

"No. Just set your intention. You carry my blood, so it should work. When you're ready, try it out and bring Kevin through to Eureka Springs. You'll need to touch him to bring him through."

"We'll try now."

They both disappeared from their screen, so Gina turned it off. "Angela, pull up everything we know about both New Orleans and Rome."

"The queens or only the cities?"

"Both. I'd like maps of known Aima holdings in both cities."

"How about travel plans and flight times?" The other assistant asked.

"Not yet," Gina replied. "I'm going to turn your screen off for now but stay close. I'll call you back when more of our queen's plans are ready to execute."

I couldn't remember the assistant's name, and the tedious details bored me. Leviathan still rolled inside me, riled up and ready for action. He wanted to feast. Too bad I couldn't just shift and fly south. I'd level Delafosse's entire city in a matter of minutes and fill my belly at the same time.

"In the old days, that might have worked," Guillaume said beside me. "I would have gone in and exterminated the entire nest. Xin could slip in and simply kill the queen and be done. Our queen doesn't work that way."

I grunted sourly as Leviathan heaved a giant plume of disgusted smoke. "More's the pity."

"Why not put your dragon to better use?"

I arched a brow at him. "You have a suggestion?"

"There's another dragon in this world who's caused our queen some trouble. See if your beast can figure out where he is."

The knight had a point. Once upon a time, there'd been thousands of dragons, both wild and Aima shifters. That might sound like a lot, but dragons had always been in the minority as far as shifters went. Only phoenixes, gryphons, and sphinxes were rarer.

Dragons had always been able to sense once another. It made it easier to avoid territory disputes and preserve our kind as long as possible. Millennia later, I'd thought it likely I was the only dragon left in the world. However, the bastard king was still out there somewhere.

He, too, had hurt my queen. Granted, not as badly as the Dauphine, but he'd still shaken her confidence and drained her power.

"My queen?" I paused, waiting a moment for her to turn to me. "I have an idea that requires my dragon."

"Of course, go. I'll call you if I need you."

I loved that she didn't question me. She didn't doubt me. She wasn't suspicious that I'd try to escape or betray her in any way.

"Take Vivian with you," Rik ordered. "Always stay in pairs in case we come under attack again."

Thank goddess he didn't send the bear or the knight with me. I didn't know much about the fiery phoenix yet, but she didn't seem to be the kind who'd bitch and moan like Ezra.

She stepped in front of our queen and bowed low, arms crossed over her chest. She wore two short swords crossed on her back, both within easy reach. "My queen."

As she straightened, Shara reached out and seized her thick braid. Her hair seemed alive with fire, crackling with color and energy even in a tight coil. Shara tugged her close and kissed her. "Don't be afraid to singe his hide if he's too hard to handle."

Straightening, Vivian shot me a confident look that made me grin. A very toothy smile of a hungry dragon. "He won't be too hard to handle."

I headed outside, not waiting to see if she followed. As soon as we were far enough away from the house that my wings wouldn't accidentally take off the roof, I stripped off the sweatpants I'd just pulled on and stuffed them up in the lower branches of the gnarled oak.

Without saying a word, Vivian propped her swords against the tree's trunk and tugged her tank top over her head. At the very same moment, Gwen's group stepped out of the heart tree a couple of hundred yards away. She held Kevin's hand in her right, and her alpha's in her left, bringing them through the portal by our queen's blood that hummed inside her.

Before they could see me, I shifted to Leviathan. I was too close to Vivian, so I almost knocked her down.

"Watch it, fuckface," she retorted, shoving my tail away.

:Hurry up and fucking shift.:

"Why?"

:She doesn't like other queens to see us naked.:

Vivian snorted as she worked skin-tight leather pants down her legs. She had long fucking legs. It took forever.

Gwen and the other men came closer. Fucking moron. I lifted a wing to cover Vivian's pertinent parts.

"Welcome to House Isador." Teeth gritted, Vivian tried to push my wing out of her face. "Our queen's waiting for you."

Watching our strange tug-of-war, Gwen's lips quirked. "Thank you."

"That's a nice wing you've got there," Lancelot drawled.

Kevin just stared at us with wide-eyed awe. Surely he'd seen plenty of Blood shifted before—but maybe not a dragon.

"My wings are made of sunfire, thank you very much," Vivian snarled.

I could feel the rising heat of her phoenix, but the obstinate woman was determined to prove that she could handle me. Even if I was only trying to help her avoid angering our queen.

Two could play this game, and I was centuries older than her. I dropped my wing, letting her have the victory.

But before she could celebrate, I sat on her.

All several thousand pounds of dragon flesh. Plopped on top of her without a care.

I bared my teeth at our guests and allowed smoke to puff out as I chuckled. Though it came out more ferocious than simple amusement.

The human looked like he'd messed his fucking pants, but the former knight threw his head back and roared with laughter.

His queen gazed up at him, her eyes wide, shining in the starlight with a soft glow. Evidently Lancelot du Lac hadn't laughed so freely in a very long time.

The phoenix blasted me with enough flame to melt down the Statue of Liberty into a puddle of bronze, but dragonhide couldn't care less about fire. Even sunfire from House Helios.

Still laughing, the knight tucked his queen close and they headed on up to the house. The human followed along behind, though he kept looking back over his shoulder at us. Probably to make sure I wasn't going to sneak up and eat him. He'd make a tasty little snack, but I doubted my queen would be pleased if she lost yet another consiliarius before she could swear him in as Gina's backup.

Once they were finally gone, I unfurled my wings and leaped into the sky. I didn't pause to wait for the phoenix. She'd fucking follow or not. I didn't fucking care. She could explain to Rik why she chose to disobey his order to accompany me.

The blood circle tingled along my hide as I exited the nest. For this to work, I had to be outside our queen's protections. To avoid any unwanted attention, I flew higher, well into the thick clouds blanketing the sky. The air tasted like snow. One last hurrah before spring broke winter's hold on the earth.

I loved flying, especially up high like this. So still and quiet. Nothing to impede my flight. Nothing to stop me from simply flying off into the east to meet the rising sun.

Except my queen.

Yeah, once the thought of being bound to a queen had pissed me the fuck off. I'd killed plenty of other queens just to be sure that they couldn't trap me into service. Shara had broken down my prison walls and dragged me snarling and snapping into her world. Prepared to be chained and enslaved, I found that this queen had conquered me with one thing only.

Her love.

Even this high up, I felt her bond. Not a tether to drag me back to her service—but a shining highway that would always lead me home. The light in the darkness. The warm candle in the window.

The fierce as fuck queen who'd find her way into Heliopolis or Rome or wherever the fuck we needed her, because she would always be sure her loved ones were safe.

To be one of those she counted as precious...

I'd kill anyone and anything who thought to harm her.

I spread my wings out to cup the maximum amount of air and drifted in a slow downward spiral. Centering myself, I reached deep into my chest cavity. Below my black heart. Underneath my bitter liver. To the very base of my spine and the root of my massive body. On a human, it'd be the root chakra. For me, it was where I stored my dragon dick, curled up like a python inside me.

I hadn't mated as a dragon in... Mentally, I flinched away from that raw, burning memory. Fucking that dragon had ended with me cursed, locked in a prison outside this world. I'd fucking learned my lesson all too well.

I didn't need to unfurl the dick to make this work, though I'd seen plenty of males using the call as a way to showcase their mighty cock to interested females. The only female I was interested in already appreciated my human-sized cock. Vivian sure wouldn't give a damn, and I sure as fuck wouldn't want her gossiping to the others about it.

Closing my eyes, I blocked out my sense of the phoenix. Of

course, she'd followed me. We might be badass fucking Blood in our own right, but none of us wanted to be on the rock troll's bad side. I didn't care to see how many bones he'd break in my body before he'd allow Shara to heal me. He'd been tough on Daire when I'd first joined the group, and he fucking loved the little furball shit and had spent years with him before Shara called them. I wouldn't stand a fucking chance of earning a single drop of mercy. He still hadn't fully forgiven me for breaking Shara's arm when she'd freed me from the prison.

I cracked my jaws open, hauling in as much air as my lungs could hold. Then as I exhaled, I shoved power through my root chakra. My scales itched at the vibration rolling through the air, but it wasn't an audible sound.

:*What the fuck was that?*: Vivian asked.

:*Dragon sonar.*:

I felt the vibration rolling through the air, racing across the United States. Out over the oceans. North to the icecap. South across jungles and desert and mountains to the other ice cap. But the pulse faded before it touched Europe or Asia.

Fucking hell. I was seriously out of practice.

But one thing I knew already. Arthur's dragon wasn't anywhere in North or South America, nor was he flying over one of the oceans bordering either continent. I would have felt a ping as my vibration rolled across the miles.

The tingle on my scales warned me that Shara's blood circle was close. I shifted my wings slightly, widening my flight path so I didn't cross over into the nest. I sucked in several deep breaths, gaping my jaws open wider. I needed more air. More power. I had to fucking wrap the globe in sonar if I was going to nail the bastard. And so help me goddess, I was going to fucking pin Arthur's hide to the motherfucking wall once I found him.

He was an Aima king—but so the fuck was I. And I guaranteed I had at least a thousand more years of hatred than him, burning in the pit of my stomach to fuel my rage.

I filled the bellows of my lungs, panting in air until my chest ached. Then some more. Shara needed to know where the bastard was hiding. I'd never searched the entire earth before, but I knew it could be done. It had to be possible. There was at least one other dragon still living in this world and I would find him.

I thrust power through my root chakra again, sending a deep, sonorous pulse out into the night. I pushed until I was lightheaded. Until every molecule of air in my body was depleted and I started to sink like a stone through the winter air. All my will. All my love.

Not for me. But for Shara.

She needed this. She needed me.

The phoenix nudged me, a hot pulse of fire to remind me to breathe again and catch some wind beneath my wings before I cratered the earth. I'd sunk beneath the cloud bank, but I didn't try to pull back up to my previous altitude. If this pulse didn't find Arthur out in the world somewhere, then I'd have to crawl back to Shara and admit defeat.

I strained to feel the slightest echo. Underground. Thousands of feet up. Over mountains. My pulse shot across the oceans and vibrated across Europe and Asia. Racing around the globe. Fading… But almost there. Almost meeting.

One ping lit up as my echo faded away. Then, shockingly, another.

Two dragons. Together. Either in Western Asia or the Middle East—I couldn't tell for sure. Turkey, maybe? Even before I'd been imprisoned, there'd only been a handful of dragons left. One of them had to be Arthur, and—

An answering pulse ripped through me. Higher, lighter than my deep soundless bass. It tore into my dragon hide and shoved pokers deep into my brain. Searing endless pain.

I tumbled toward the earth, struck by a metaphysical arrow

that had been directed straight at me. My dragon senses shrilled wildly, overloaded by the other dragon's sonar.

Her sonar.

The one who'd imprisoned me.

:Tiamat!: I managed to scream through our queen's bond. Hopefully the old fart could tell her where that meant Arthur was hiding.

Then I braced for impact.

VIVIAN

Catching a massive falling dragon wasn't high on my bucket list. Especially after the bastard had fucking sat on me. Humiliating me in front of our queen's guests.

Shara's bond surged with worry. *:Mehen!:*

Mentally, I rolled my eyes, but I answered back. *:I've got him.:*

Smoak dove beneath the tumbling dragon and then surged up against him, slowing his descent to a controlled dive rather than a reckless crash. We both still hit the ground.

Hard.

The bastard on top of me. Again.

Gnashing my teeth so that sparks danced around me, I finally shoved the senseless dragon off me.

:Is he injured?: Shara asked. *:Does he need healing?:*

I scanned him from head to fucking toe and didn't see a single mark on him. *:He's not bleeding and nothing seems broken. The answering pulse seems to have knocked him out.:*

The glow of her bond shone through his hide as if she'd turned on a giant spotlight inside his gullet. I hoped he fucking choked on it.

His tail twitched. His wings shifted, rustling across the ground.

:He's coming around,: I told Shara. *:I'll get him back to the nest as soon as he can shift.:*

:I'm sending Llewellyn to help, in case you need to fly him back.: The intensity of her bond lightened, and the glow faded from inside him. I shifted around so I could lean back against him. While we waited, I'd at least have a fucking backrest. After all, he'd used me for a chair.

:What happened?: He finally asked, his words slow and heavy.

:You passed out and fell out of the sky, fuckface.:

He lifted his head slightly and then lowered it with an oomph, smoke curling from his nostrils. *:Hurts.:*

I'd promised our queen that I'd take care of him. Grudgingly, I used her bond to check inside him, just to see how bad his pain was.

Surprisingly bad. It felt like he'd swallowed a large grenade full of glass shards that had suddenly gone off inside him. He wasn't actually bleeding, and his organs were fine, but his internal sensors were frazzled like a fried circuit board.

Lightly, I said, "Dragon sonar hurts like a bitch, huh?"

He blew out several plumes of smoke. A dragon chuckle. *:That was more like a nuclear bomb's EMP. Totally wiped me out.:*

We sat in silence a few moments, waiting on the other Blood to arrive. We'd flown further from the nest than I'd thought. Mountainous hills rolled across the countryside, carpeted in trees. We'd come down on a fairly flat plateau, providing a good view of the land surrounding our queen's nest.

In fact, I could see the light down in the valley miles away, overlooking the river. She glowed. Not just the lights from her manor house, but the warm, soft glow of her power.

:About earlier.: He heaved out a heavy sigh, his lips curling as if he'd eaten something foul that even a carrion bird wouldn't touch. *:I'm sorry.:*

My eyes widened, and I kept my face averted so he couldn't see the shock on my face. I could count the number of sincere apologies I'd heard from a man on one hand. Easily. Because it was never. Let alone an apology from someone like this arrogant asshole. :*Our queen asked us not to be naked in front of other queens, and there one stood. The only thing I could think to do was cover you up. Since she welcomed you with Mayte, maybe it wouldn't have been a big deal. She'd skin us males alive before she'd ever let us touch another queen. Not that we would ever want to.*:

I couldn't remember him ever saying so many words to anyone—especially without a fuck or two thrown in—and in an apology, no less.

He didn't make excuses or jokes. He didn't bitch and moan about me being different or female. Despite being an obnoxious jerk, he actually knew how to apologize without making it seem like it was my fault in the first place.

Maybe that's why the tiniest crack in my heart opened and allowed a tidbit of my past to slip out. "In Heliopolis, we weren't ever allowed to be nude. The sun god's priests all had weird hang-ups about women's nudity being the root of all evil. Fuck, I can remember taking baths with a robe on to cover up and hide my perfectly natural body from the males. Not that it kept Ra from raping and brutalizing any woman he wished to have. Nothing stopped him. After I left Heliopolis, I realized the truth. The clothing and nudity rules were just another way to control us. So I vowed to never cover my body out of shame again."

Maybe something inside him really had been injured. Because the dragon's heart cracked open and let me have a secret too. :*I found Arthur, but he's with Tiamat, the Mother of All Dragons. Even better, She's the one who cursed me and fucking locked me up all those centuries ago.*:

:*Why did She do that?*:

His lips pulled away from his teeth, but he didn't make a

sound, so I wasn't sure if it was a snarl or a draconian grin. *:Because I fucked Her daughter instead of Her.:*

I humphed out a disgusted breath and pushed to my feet as the gryphon neared. I thought Mehen was trying to be sincere, but in the end, he was just another asshole making a poor excuse of a joke at a female's expense.

:No, really.: He lifted his head and shifted his clawed feet beneath him. *:It was a breeding thing. She's desperate to sire more dragons before we all die out, and I was young and stupid and arrogant.:*

:More arrogant than now?: Llewellyn asked as he landed beside the dragon. *:I find that difficult to believe.:*

:I was an unbearably large asshole the size of the Titanic and just as doomed to destroy myself. I thumbed my nose at the Mother of All Dragons and snuck off with Her wild-born dragon daughter. Goddess, she was a fighter. She practically gutted me, and that was just her idea of foreplay.:

The gryphon clicked his beak. *:I've heard a wild dragon will kill a male who isn't strong enough to force her into submission.:*

:Fucking truth. Tangling with her almost killed me, but then again, that's what I wanted.:

I blinked, surprised again at the nugget of truth slipping out of Mehen's mouth. Maybe he really was severely injured.

He cautiously stretched out his wings and lifted them, testing the complex muscular system across both shoulders to be sure he hadn't damaged anything in the fall. *:When Tiamat cursed me to live as a dragon imprisoned beyond this world until a queen could free me, She told me She was saving my life, not destroying me as I deserved. I didn't understand what She meant until Shara was the one to free me.:*

I clenched my jaws, suddenly overwhelmed with a raw flood of emotion that almost brought me to tears.

Even after I'd been allowed to leave the hellacious sun

palace, I was still doomed to death and destruction. Just like Mehen.

I'd been sent out into the world to kill as many queens as possible by letting them have a taste of my fiery blood. Queens had died in my arms, burned from the inside out by my blood until they were piles of sooty ash. I'd been free... but also enslaved as surely as Mehen's dragon had been trapped.

Until Shara had sipped my blood and conquered the fires burning in my veins.

:*She freed me too,*: Llewellyn whispered fervently. :*She freed us all.*:

Rather than agreeing with him—and probably bursting into messy tears, which I did not do, ever—I embraced Smoak's form and sent a red-hot glowing poker jab into Mehen's ribs. :*Can you fly, fuckface?*:

He snapped at my flank, though I easily side-stepped his wicked teeth. :*To Rome and back, firecrotch.*:

21

SHARA

R elieved that Mehen was apparently unharmed and headed back to me, I concentrated on my guests.

I hadn't thought much about formalities when I'd asked Gwen to bring Kevin to me. I hadn't even warned Winston that another queen was joining me. Gracious as always, he quickly returned to the kitchen and grabbed another cup, though he lightly chided me. "If I'd known you were expecting guests, I would have used the finest china, my queen."

"This is perfect, Winston. Thank you. This is Gwen Camelot, her alpha Lance Camelot, and my soon-to-be second consiliarius, Kevin Bloom. I can't remember if I formally introduced you before. Everyone, this is my very dear friend and Isador butler, Timothy Winston."

Gwen had started to lift the cup to her lips, but she quickly set the cup down. A sound escaped her lips, almost like a hiccup. Lance immediately leaned down to offer her comfort, gently patting her shoulder.

She was fucking crying.

Oh goddess. Had I made a horrible faux pas? She'd been introduced to me as Gwen Findabair, but surely now that she'd claimed her Blood and taken her rightful place as queen of her house...

I checked her bond and breathed a small sigh of relief. She was overwhelmed with joy and gratitude. Not furious or embarrassed that I'd gotten her name wrong.

Winston handed her a napkin and she lightly dabbed her eyes. "I'm so sorry, my queen. It's just the first time I've ever heard my house name used like that. Camelot has been dead for so long that I feared my house would only be a distant memory."

"Camelot lives once more in you, and I'm honored to call you my sibling." I turned my attention to Kevin, who waited not-so-patiently off to the side. As soon as I looked at him, he snapped to my side. "Are you sure—"

"Yes," he said quickly, grinning. "I'm sure. I've wanted nothing else, even though Grandad tried to scare me off at a young age."

"How did he try to scare you off?"

Kevin chuckled, shaking his head. "He took me to the office when I was six, determined to bore me to death with all the menial recordkeeping tasks the job requires. He showed me a simple spreadsheet and gave me a stack of receipts to enter. He told me later that he expected me to sneak outside to play or to start drawing on the receipts. Something a normal kid would do. Instead, when he came back, I'd entered all the receipts and color-coded them by categories I'd made up."

"How old were you when you created the new Triune sibling database?" Gina asked.

"Eighteen."

"Amazing," Gina replied. "And Marne Ceresa isn't going to be furious at us for taking you away from her house?"

"Not at all. Grandad set the expectation for me a long time ago that I was to find my own house to serve. That's how I ended up at House Skye."

I'd torn both wrists open deeply not even an hour ago, but

the delicate skin was smooth and unblemished. Even the heart tree's thorn that had gone through my heart hadn't left a scar.

I punctured my right wrist with the tip of my nail and offered my hand to him.

Kevin dropped to his knees as he took my hand in shaking fingers. "I swear my life to you, Your Majesty, Shara Isador, last daughter of Isis. I will gladly serve your house and yours alone in any way that you direct. I will protect your legacy and house with my life and every skill the goddesses granted me."

Smiling, I nodded, and he dipped his head down to my blood.

Power flowed through me, bubbling up like a pure, sweet spring from the depths of the earth. My bonds shimmered, the scent of my blood stirring my Bloods' beasts.

Purring, Daire pressed against my left knee. "Long live Shara fucking Isador."

"Long live our queen," Rik murmured against my ear.

As Kevin swallowed my blood, I sank deeper into him, infusing him with power. His mind was like a formidable computer, lightning fast and so incredibly organized. Maybe it was the anecdote he'd told me earlier about color-coding the spreadsheet that flavored my impressions, but his brain seemed to naturally group things into unique segments that at first glance didn't make sense.

It was as if Carys had re-shelved the library by the color of the books' spines rather than their genre, title, or author. You'd never dedicate a shelf just to red books, regardless of what they were about. But that was exactly how Kevin's mind worked.

I touched one section and found memories of his childhood, but there were holes in those memories, sometimes years apart. A section right beside it also had memories of his childhood. It took me a moment to figure out that these memories were organized by location.

All the memories of his Grandad's office were here. These

other memories were somewhere else. I flickered through them, watching just enough of each one to pinpoint where they took place.

It was only when I saw a familiar face that I realized these memories were all from a surprisingly simple yet elegant cottage.

In Rome.

Marne Ceresa stood with her back to a young Kevin, maybe ten or twelve years old. She was humming softly and wore a light cotton dress that made me think of spring. Sunlight poured in through the window where she worked, illuminating her blonde hair in a halo uncomfortably similar to Ra's golden glow.

"*Don't ever forget where you came from,*" she said as she turned, holding a wet soapy dish in her hand.

The queen of Rome. Doing dishes. It was so unexpected that my eyes popped open. Dazed, Kevin had straightened, his pupils dilated and dark. "Whoa. I think I can smell color now."

"It's amazing, isn't it?" Gina laid a small lap desk between us on my knees and offered me a pen.

I took the pen but didn't sign the papers yet. The old-fashioned fountain pen had a nice heft to it. "What did you ask for?"

He shrugged self-consciously. "The standard starting salary and an apartment in the tower, if that's not too much."

I didn't have to ask Gina to know that she'd made some adjustments after Kevin's requests. "House Isador doesn't do anything *standard.*"

"Oh. Well. That's fine. I'll gladly accept—"

"Kevin," I broke in, giving him a stern look that made his mouth fall open with surprise. "I'm very disappointed."

He gulped. "You are? I'm so sorry, my queen. I shouldn't have asked—"

I picked up the page Gina had deliberately put on top. "Only one hundred thousand dollars a year? For your services? Don't you realize that Gina's going to work you at least two hundred thousand dollars' worth?"

"Uh—"

"And you asked for a studio apartment. We don't have any studios in the tower, do we, Gwen?"

She coughed slightly, her lips twitching. "None that are currently open, my queen."

"So naturally we gave you the apartment just beneath Gwen's penthouse. You need to be close to her as we go forward."

For being an especially bright young man, he could only stare at me stupidly. "But. My queen. That's... Impossible. That apartment is... is..."

"The entire floor, I know." I signed the page with a flourish and offered the pen to him.

He stared at me like I'd suddenly turned into the cobra queen and spit numbing venom in his eyes.

"There was one very interesting item in his request, my queen," Gina said. "I don't know that you saw it."

"Well, it's too late now. I've already signed it." He still stared at me, stunned, so I had to tease him. Just a little. "Unless you want me to tear this page up before the contract can be completed..."

He snatched the pen from my fingers and quickly signed the page, like he really thought I'd change my mind.

Gina gathered the papers. "I'll fax these to the Triune office now."

"In Rome?" I asked.

"The main Triune office is actually in New York City, though they also have offices in London and Amsterdam."

"Wait, what? The whole time we were in New York City, the Triune was actually there?"

"Neither Triune queen is *physically* there and it's not a nest, but yes. These offices are manned by a team of trusted people from each Triune's house and handle all Triune business for the queens." Arching a brow at me, she grinned. "I'm sure that you can guess who's in the New York City office."

"Byrnes."

"Keisha Skye often complained that the Triune offices were in her city, but she had no access to them," Gwen added.

Kevin grimaced. "Grandad prefers the west coast, but he does spend the majority of the year in the Triune's New York City office, unless he's traveling on Ceresa business."

"Wow. I guess next time I'm in town I should see if he'd like to go to lunch."

Kevin's mouth hung open and it took him several tries to get the words out. "You'd... do... that?"

"Only if you'd go too. Don't we need to maintain good relationships between our consiliari?" I gave a subtle tug on Itztli's bond, and he immediately stepped forward to lay the wrapped mirror on my lap. "I have to make a quick call, but I don't know how long it'll be before she picks up."

Bracing myself, I slipped the black velvet away from the mirror. I half expected to see Marne staring back at me, but the surface reflected my image back, just like a normal mirror. My wrist was still bleeding slightly, so I turned my arm over the glass and allowed a drop to plop onto the surface.

Instantly, the glass smoked over. Goosebumps flared down my arms and I shivered as power pulsed through the mirror so hard it vibrated on my thighs.

Gina's phone rang. She looked down at the number and then raised her gaze to mine, a wry smile on her lips. "That was fast." She answered the call, putting it on speaker. "This is Gina Isador."

"Good evening, Gina. This is Byrnes Ceresa calling on official Triune business. House Isador is summoned to appear in court."

Gina's voice didn't change as she replied, "Of course."

Though in her bond, I felt both terror and excitement. She'd never been to Triune court before, though evidently Grandma Paula had gone with my mother before. "Where should we appear?"

"Her Majesty Marne Ceresa summons Her Majesty Shara Isador to appear in her Rome court in the next eight hours."

Fury shot through Gina's bond, but she again kept her emotions hidden. Eight fucking hours? That was an impossible timeline without some significant power and effort on the queen's part. Unless you had a magical tree at your disposal, as I did. "I will convey the summons to my queen."

"Thank you, Gina." He hesitated a moment, and then asked, "If it's not too presumptuous, could you tell me if House Isador has intentions to make an offer to my grandson?"

Gina looked at Kevin, eyebrows raised in silent question. He stepped closer to the phone. "They have made an offer, Grandad, and I accepted it just a few moments ago. I now serve House Isador as consiliarius."

Byrnes didn't say anything for several moments. Long enough for a bead of sweat to slowly slide down Kevin's forehead.

Gina was still pissed. In my new bond with Kevin, I felt the tension shimmering inside him. The urge of a young man to earn his admired and respected grandfather's approval, but also a fierce desire to forge his own way and damn the consequences.

I could only imagine what Byrnes was thinking. If Marne Ceresa intended to wipe out my house or teach us a lesson in some way, then now his grandson was tangled up in that punishment. If she intended to kill us all…

Well. She'd find that House Isador was a very resilient target. She could try to swallow me—and find a very big monster stuck in her craw. My only regret was accidentally pitting a grandson against his grandfather in a bloody war.

"Very good," Byrnes finally said, his voice soft and almost…
choked.

Goddess. Marne must really intend us all harm. Eyes
narrowed, I clenched my jaws. Power roared inside me. Begging
to be used.

Murderous fury pulsed in my Blood as *they* begged to be
used. Could Xin actually find a way to slip inside Marne Ceresa's nest and assassinate her?

:Absolutely.: His wolf howled with fierce exultation in his
bond. *:Without question. Use me, my queen. It's an honor to kill in
your service.:*

"I'm so proud, Kevin," Byrnes finally said. "Thank you, Your
Majesty, for giving him a place in your house. I know he'll do
excellent work for you."

Kevin's eyes welled with tears. "Thanks, Grandad."

"Take care of yourself, young man. I still expect to see you
for lunch next week. If your duties allow it, of course."

"Of course," he whispered, swallowing hard.

"Well, then." Byrnes cleared his throat. "Goddess speed your
journey to court, House Isador."

Gina disconnected the call and her shoulders drooped.
"Goddess."

Kevin plopped into the nearest chair and mopped his forehead with a handkerchief. "Well. At least Marne doesn't intend
to kill us all, right? Or Grandad wouldn't remind me of our
lunch appointment."

I breathed deeply and concentrated on relaxing. I sank
against Rik, dropping my head back against his chest. Daire
curled his arms around my leg and rubbed his chin on my thigh,
his purr steady and comforting. My other three Blood quietly
returned while I was dealing with Byrnes. I checked
Mehen's bond, searching for anything that needed to be healed.

He still felt tender and raw deep inside. Not injuries, exactly, but my blood would do him some good. Pulling on his bond, I lifted my arm to him in silent invitation.

Dropping down before me, he wedged himself in between my thighs, forcing me to open my knees more. Daire refused to relinquish his place but grudgingly made room for the dragon too.

Mehen kissed my wrist but didn't sink his fangs into my skin. He leaned heavier against me and pressed his face over my breasts.

My dragon didn't want to feed. He wanted comfort.

I wrapped my arms around him and stroked my fingers over his bare shoulders. He'd pulled on his jeans but hadn't bothered with a shirt. Rubbing my fingers over his head and down his neck, I soothed him until he was ready to tell me what he'd found.

When he finally spoke, he didn't lift his head from my chest. "Arthur's with Tiamat."

"Who's that?" Gwen asked, her voice sharp. Not with jealousy—but with the bloodthirsty determination to add a new name to our list of enemies.

"The Mother of All Dragons, a Mesopotamian goddess."

I'd picked up on enough of his conversation with Vivian earlier to know that Tiamat was the one who'd imprisoned him millennia ago. "I won't let Her have you."

He tightened his arms around my waist, leaning harder against me. "She's a goddess and has been alive since the dawn of time."

"And you're *my* dragon now."

Finally, he lifted his head and gave me a sultry, knowing look, his eyes glittering like molten emeralds. "I know you won't let Her have me. I just wanted to hear it. Besides, She's too busy fucking Arthur to sire a new generation of dragons to worry about me."

"How long will She keep him do you think?" Gwen asked slowly.

Mehen snorted. "Only a few years, if he's lucky, unless he was smart and managed to bargain with Her beforehand. She won't let him escape until She has what She wants, and She's not going to be happy with a single egg. She'll have a whole clutch to fertilize."

Gwen and Lance shared a long, silent look. When she finally turned her head to meet my gaze, I almost felt sorry for Elaine Shalott.

Almost.

"Then by your leave, my queen, I'm going to prepare for a trip to the UK."

Smiling, I offered her my hand, and when she took it, I tugged her down for a quick hug. "Go and free your Blood."

She searched my face. "I can wait until after your appearance at court if you're worried."

"Not at all. You've already waited centuries to have Merlin. I won't be the cause of any more delay. This is between me and Marne, just as your problem is between you and *her*. Hopefully Arthur will be otherwise occupied and you won't have to deal with him at the same time, but call on me if you need help. Mayte and I will be with you in an instant."

Kevin stepped closer and bowed formally. "My queen, thank you for accepting me into your service."

"I trust you to mind the tower while Gwen is gone."

"Of course. Hopefully Grandad will still speak to me after your trip to Rome."

I grinned, shaking my head. "I'm not making any guarantees."

22

SHARA

Having friends stop by was great and all, but I still breathed a sigh of relief when everyone was gone. The mirror had gone back to clear while we talked to Byrnes. Evidently, Marne Ceresa had answered my call through her consiliarius and had no intention of using the mirror.

Mehen hissed beneath his breath as Carys strode into the room.

Holding a book, she looked around the room as if slightly befuddled. Pushed her glasses up on her nose. Sniffed with disgust at Mehen.

Then her gaze fell on the mirror in my lap. "What the ever-loving *fuck* are you doing? Are you mad?"

My eyebrows arched at her tone. To make matters worse, Mehen vibrated with menace, his dragon incensed by her attitude. It certainly didn't help that she held one of *his* books.

"I meant to have a little chat with Marne Ceresa, but—"

Carys slammed the book down on the side table closest to my chair, startling Winnifred, who appeared to be asleep on her shoulder. "And you didn't think to tell me?"

"Honestly… no. I forgot that you were even here." I started to wrap the mirror back in its velvet covering. "I never see you, unless I hunt you down, and when I ask you something in the bond, you're... difficult."

"Stop." Quivering with rage, she glared at me. Mouth pinched, hands fisted, ready to rip me a new asshole. "I'm the one who's difficult? When I'm forced to deal with a wet-behind-the-ears slip of a girl who doesn't even have the fucking brains in her head to wipe her blood off a mirror charmed by Marne fucking Ceresa?"

If I hadn't made the rule about dragons in the house, I'd be tempted to let Leviathan teach her some fucking manners. I didn't expect stuffy protocols. I hated all the bowing and curtseying and "Your Majesties." But I damned well would be treated with a modicum of respect in my own fucking house.

But then it dawned on me, once my pride got out of the way. She was abso-fucking-lutely right.

The mirror. I'd bled on it. I'd activated it. And yeah, I'd been ready to send it back upstairs with Itztli without a care in the world. Confident in the salt and coffee grounds and complete darkness to hold the queen of Rome at bay.

When I'd fucking left the front door to my house wide open.

"You're right," I said softly. "Daire, would you mind cleaning the mirror?"

Immediately, he dropped to my feet and swiped his tongue over the surface. Purring, he lifted his head. "Mmmm, I like some salty coffee with your blood, my queen."

I wrapped the mirror in velvet and lifted it up for Itztli, but he dropped at my feet and pressed his forehead against my knees. "Forgive me, my queen. I should have reminded you to cleanse the mirror as alpha directed when you first received it."

One by one, the rest of my Blood did the same, bending knee and ducking their heads.

We'd all forgotten, despite Tepeyollotl's warning.

"You're right, Winnifred," Carys muttered. "Exactly like herding cats."

Daire's purr rumbled louder. "Excuse me, you rude old bat, but I'm the only cat here. No offense, Itztli."

"None taken." He lifted his head and took the mirror from me. "Though bats aren't rude. She's much more like Mehen in that regard."

"I ate bats too," Mehen warned, snapping his teeth. "Just another kind of rodent."

I sighed and looked at the book she'd brought to me. *The Prose Edda.* I flipped through a few pages, enough to figure out that it was Norse mythology. She'd picked up on my sudden interest in Ragnarök and tried to do something nice.

Though goddess, I wished she wasn't so damned prickly.

"I'm sorry, Your Majesty," Carys said gruffly. "I shouldn't have insulted you, and I have mostly abandoned you to your own devices since you brought me here. I don't know what it is, but I can't seem to leave your library. It's like there's something there that I *have* to find. It's important. What's happened that you felt the need to reach out to Marne Ceresa?"

"Oh, nothing much. Let's see, I broke the Dauphine's sigil that wards her secret identity, grew a portal tree in the basement of Isador Tower, rushed home to find the nest under attack by a zombie that used to be my Mom, cremated Mom's body so it can't happen again, and decided to strike back at the Dauphine by telling Marne where she's hiding. But instead, as soon as I activated the mirror, Byrnes called Gina and summoned us to court."

Winnifred flapped her wings and Carys stared at me, aghast.

Feeling a bit better, I managed a smile. "So, care to go to Rome with me? We have eight hours to get there."

"She can't attend with you," Gina said. "The summons is for House Isador only."

"But she's my sibling queen now."

Carys wilted. She actually looked disappointed that she wasn't getting to go to Rome. To fucking court, called before Marne Ceresa for goddess only knew what reason. "If Byrnes didn't list me by name, then I'm not allowed to attend. Hellfire and damnation. I would've enjoyed seeing you kick Marne's ass."

That easily, she made me forget our earlier argument. She didn't doubt that I'd survive this mess. Her only regret was that she wouldn't get to see it for herself.

Gina flipped on the second television screen. "Angela, Marissa, are you still there?"

Her two assistants immediately sat down in front of the camera.

"Yes, we're here," Angela said. "I got your text that you're required to be in Rome in eight hours. How the fuck are you supposed to pull that off? Oops, sorry for my language, Your Majesty. Even the newest jet can't make it to Rome from New York in that timeframe, and you'd still need to get here too."

"Don't fucking worry about it." I smiled, keeping my voice light. "I won't need the jet. Gina, did Alice finish the formal presentation gown?"

Alice Wong was a clothing designer I'd met in Dallas. I loved her gowns so much that we'd basically paid her an obscene amount of money to create as many beautiful and fantastic gowns as possible in her unique design. I hadn't seen sketches, but I knew whatever she designed would be incredible.

Gina nodded. "It arrived while we were in Cairo, though I haven't taken the time to unpack it yet and see what she sent."

"I'm assuming the Blood should all wear their tuxes?"

"Absolutely," Guillaume answered before Gina could.

"Fuck me," Ezra muttered.

"Alright, let's get ready to rumble. Everybody get dressed." The Blood started upstairs, all except Rik and Nevarre. Rik, because he couldn't get up until I did, and Nevarre, because he'd somehow become my personal dresser.

"I'm headed back to the library, my queen," Carys announced. Loudly, so Mehen would hear, even though he'd left the room.

I felt him shoot a murderous glare in our direction, but Guillaume and Llewellyn both took an arm and kept dragging him upstairs. "What's the probability that we all return from this trip alive and well?"

She grimaced, shaking her head as she headed for the door. "You're already pissed at me. Just know the odds are stacked against you, but that's never stopped you before. When I find what you need, I'll send it to you in the bond. Goddess let me find it soon enough to help."

Gina waited until the room had quieted, then she gave her assistants a somber look. "All contingencies are in place. Kevin is returning to the tower now. Gwen has business of her own to resolve. I expect you two to help him in any way if something happens to me."

I leaped up and grabbed her shoulders, whirling her around to face me. "Why wouldn't you return with me?"

She smiled calmly as her hands settled on my shoulders. "It's been my greatest honor to serve you, my queen."

Tears burned my eyes. "What aren't you telling me?"

"Queens are too precious in this day and age for the Triune to risk losing your bloodline. So if there's any punishment the Triune metes out to our house, it usually falls to the first consiliarius to satisfy that judgement. That's why I needed to be sure you had another consiliarius lined up before we ever had to go to court."

Oh goddess. My throat ached and I clutched her too hard. I felt my nails digging into her shoulders, hurting her through her clothing. I couldn't risk drawing her blood and drinking her

accidentally, but I didn't want to let her go, either. "Why didn't
you tell me? What can I do to protect you?"

Smiling, she patted me gently. "You rule as queen. That's
what you do to protect us all. I'm confident that we'll come out
of this unscathed, but if Marne Ceresa is determined to exact
some retribution on our house before we're allowed to leave, I'll
pay that debt gladly."

"No. Absolutely not."

"If it comes down to it, you must." I opened my mouth to
retort, but she gave me a firm shake. "From a purely legal angle,
if the Triune orders that all of Isador must die except for you,
then that's what happens. We are all subject to the Triune's will."

"That's ridiculous. She's only one queen. She doesn't speak
for the goddesses."

"She does, or she wouldn't be Triune."

I shook my head desperately. "I don't believe it. Desideria
killed entire nests, and she was Triune. Are you saying that was
the goddesses' will?"

"Unfortunately, yes," Gina replied. "Until her death, which
was also at the goddesses' will. It might have taken decades or
even centuries for Their will to come to fruition, but we have to
believe that in the end, Their will triumphs. The Great One
willed you into existence. She willed you to defeat Keisha Skye.
I believe She wills you to handle the Triune as well, but how
that unfolds, I can't say. None of us can. But I am ready and
willing to serve, not just you, but Her as well. If my life is
required, so be it."

"But…" My voice broke. I couldn't begin to think about
losing her.

I'd lost so much already. My mother at my birth. The parents
who raised me. Gina had been with me on this journey since the
beginning, and I hadn't even known it. I'd never even known of
her existence until Rik and Daire found me, but she'd been
searching for me, fighting for me, my entire life.

I trusted her. Implicitly. I loved her dearly. My friend. My closest advisor. I relied on her for everything.

Goddess. Please. I can't lose her.

Gina kissed my cheek. "I don't expect Marne to execute any of us. That's not her style. She'd much rather watch us squirm and suffer for decades under her thumb. But you know I have to have a plan in case the worst does happen. Everything's taken care of. Just in case."

I kissed her cheek back and then threw my arms around her, hauling her into a bear hug. "Just in case. But I swear, Gina..."

She laughed tearfully. "I know. Me too."

"Promise me something," I said as I loosened my fierce grip on her. I pulled back enough to look her in the eye. "When we come home, all of us, alive and well, you and Frank will invite me to the wedding or handfasting or whatever future you decide to have together."

"Oh." Her cheeks pinkened, her eyes glowing with a soft light that made my heart hurt. In a good way. "I wasn't sure... I mean, we're both in service to you. I didn't want to complicate that."

It was my turn to give her a firm shake. "Don't be ridiculous. Complicate the fuck out of it. Marry him if you'd like. Have some kids with him. I know you love him, and I couldn't be happier for the two of you."

She laughed, shaking her head. "I'm too old for kids, but I'll consider something more permanent. If I have your blessing."

"Wholeheartedly. You both deserve all the happiness in the world. Besides, if I'm to ever to have daughters myself, they'll need a Talbott to help manage their legacy."

Her eyebrows arched. "Daughters, as in plural?"

I took Rik's hand in one of mine and Nevarre's in the other. "I think I'll be like Tiamat in that regard. I'd better have a whole clutch of eggs when the time comes, because I've certainly got a lot of mates more than eager to help me."

Gina's lips quirked as she looked from one Blood to the other. "Usually only the alpha sires a queen's heirs."

Rik picked me up, tossing me over his shoulder playfully. "Our queen does what she wants, and if she wants more than one baby daddy, then by goddess, that's what she'll get."

From upstairs, I heard a lot of voices yelling at the same time, but I made out Mehen's voice above the others. "Dragon baby daddy says fucking amen!"

23

SHARA

I wasn't surprised that Alice had outdone herself. My Triune court gown started with a deceptively simple sheath of gossamer white silk so thin and light that you could see the outlines of my thighs and the dark circles of my areolae. The back was mostly open with only thin straps to hold it up. The bottom was hemmed with delicate white lace and pearls.

The next layer made tears fill my eyes. I hadn't thought to tell her about Mom's favorite dress, but this material was a gorgeous lapis blue silk. Probably an easy guess with my heritage, but I loved it just the same. It went on top like a super long vest with a tight-fitting bodice that hugged my curves down to my waist. The skirt flared out and split like tulip petals, framing the white sheath underneath and giving tantalizing glimpses of my legs as I moved.

A puffy blood-red skirt attached around my waist with a heavy golden belt in a deep V that pointed to my womb. The airy material billowed around me like a princess skirt and trailed behind in an eight-foot-long train edged with millions of tiny seed pearls and golden beads.

The whole ensemble was topped with a heavy crimson cape

that latched around my throat in a golden filigree necklace. As Gina placed Isis's grand horned crown on my head, I stared at myself in the mirror, comparing what I saw now to the scared young girl I'd been just a few months ago.

Alone. On the run. Afraid to sleep. Not enough to eat. Nowhere to call home. No one to even talk to, let alone love.

Now, I was surrounded by loved ones. I had my Blood, Gina, my sibling queens, Winston, Frank, and Kevin, plus Angela and Marissa and countless other people silently working in the background to keep the Isador legacy grinding along smoothly.

I owned properties all over the world, but my home was here, where I'd started this journey toward a golden crown and a gorgeous dress. With an appointment to meet one of the most powerful queens in the world in the most dangerous chess game of my life.

I couldn't help but laugh softly to myself.

"What?" Gina asked, standing behind me and adjusting my upswept hair around the crown.

"I don't even know how to play chess."

She grinned and stepped back, making a twirling motion with her finger. "You could have fooled me."

I turned carefully on ridiculously delicate gold, strappy heels so high that I'd break my neck for sure if I tripped. "Do I look as scared as I feel?"

Eyes shining with pride, Gina ducked her head and lowered herself before me in a deep, formal curtsey. "Your Majesty, you look absolutely breathtaking."

I heaved a sigh and patted my hips. "No pockets. How am I supposed to carry my knife?"

Rik stepped closer, holding my pitifully small pocketknife. He knew better than to say I didn't need a weapon, or that he was my weapon. I loved him without question, and I had plenty of magic and power to devastate the world with fire and goddess only knew what else.

But I felt better with something physical to protect myself. Just in case.

"I think we can find a place for you to wear it." His voice rumbled through me, making my nipples harden against the silken material.

He picked up the end of the cape, sliding his fingers up inside until his lips curved in a slow smile. He slipped my knife inside the small, slim pocket, lifting the inside of the cape to show me.

Gina laughed softly. "When a queen says she wants pockets in all her gowns, then a designer worth her salt will surely find a way to conceal said pocket. Especially when she wants to keep selling her expensive and lovely gowns to that queen."

I trailed my fingertips up Rik's impressive forearm. He'd rolled the sleeves of his white dress shirt up to his elbows, and though he wore the black pants of his suit, he wasn't even carrying the tuxedo jacket. The shirt strained across his chest and shoulders, and I had to seriously wonder how he'd even gotten into the pants. The tortured material outlined every.

Incredible.

Inch.

Thick muscle corded beneath my fingers and something popped.

A button flew off the shirt and went sailing over my head to ting against the wall.

Daire laughed so hard that he half collapsed against Mehen, who certainly didn't mind. "Goddess help us when the zipper gives way."

"Shut the fuck up," Rik retorted, though without any real heat. "I already ripped the shoulder seam of the jacket. Sorry, my queen. Your alpha will have to be informally dressed for this occasion until I can get measured again."

"Don't fucking bother," Daire chortled. "You'll just keep getting bigger. Might as well rip off the arms and slit the thighs.

You'll look like the Incredible Hulk running around in tattered pants."

I looked around at my Blood as they gathered near. Mehen was perfectly lickable in a long-tailed tuxedo. Nevarre's kilt was tempting as always. Vivian wore an elegant suit with skin-tight tuxedo pants and a short bolero-style jacket. Xin, an elegant black-silk tunic embroidered with silver wolves and moons. Gina's black tea-length skirt and jacket were topped off with elbow-length black gloves and a snappy wide-brimmed hat.

With a chill, I realized they all looked like they were going to a high-society funeral.

"Maybe we are," Guillaume said in the agreeable, fatalistic voice of a Templar knight who'd seen it all and lived to tell about it. Even if he lost his head in the process a time or two. "Though it'll be hers, not ours."

"Fucking A." Ezra jerked at the black silk tie hanging loose around his throat. "Can someone fucking tie this for me before I strangle myself?"

"Here, let me." Llewellyn stepped over and tied the black silk with a flourish.

Ezra started to turn away and cursed. "You fucking rat-tailed bastard. You tied my beard in it!"

"Maybe you should trim it," Llewellyn replied in a light, helpful voice.

Snarling, Ezra jerked the tie off and slung it across the room. "If the alpha doesn't even have to wear the strait jacket, then surely the grizzly can get away without the tie."

"Be my guest." I raised my voice over the rest of my Bloods' laughter. "I want you to be as comfortable as possible, though I admit that seeing you all dressed up makes me want to strip you down to your skin and show you exactly how much I love you. Each of you."

Their laughter died and they crowded around me, dropping to their knees in a circle around me. I touched each one of them.

A kiss here, a stroke there, a soft touch. They leaned in, pressing shoulder to shoulder to get as close to me as possible.

My Blood. Such honor and dedication and loyalty. "I couldn't ask for any better friends, lovers, and guards. I love you. All of you. No matter what, we're coming home and I'm going to remind you each of exactly how much I love you all over again."

Gina dabbed at her eyes. "Not to rush you, my queen, but we only have an hour left in our deadline."

I straightened, tipping my chin up beneath the heavy weight of the crown on my head. "Do you know where in Rome we're supposed to go? How much time will we need to get there once we're actually in the city?"

She grimaced. "I have no idea, but I have a feeling that Marne Ceresa will know exactly where we are once we arrive."

"I wouldn't be surprised if she has cars waiting for us," Guillaume said. "Even though we don't know where we're going, she must have an idea of how you'll arrive, or she wouldn't have set such a short deadline."

"Unless she wanted us to deliberately fail." I shrugged, pushing away that doubt. "Well, let's go. Who's been to Rome before?"

"Are you fucking kidding?" Ezra grumbled. "Who in their right mind would step into the Triune queen's city voluntarily?"

We headed downstairs, and Winston stood waiting at the door. He took my hand in his and bent low to kiss my knuckles. "Your Majesty, safe journey."

"Thank you, Winston." When he straightened, I leaned up on my tip toes and kissed his cheek. "Hopefully you won't have any excitement while I'm gone."

"No worries," he said cheerfully, tilting his head toward the corner. "I'm prepared this time."

The huge gun he'd been carrying was stashed against the wall.

Mehen was right—it was snowing again. Huge, wet flakes had already covered the ground. Rik swept me up in his arms and strode toward the heart tree. He didn't pause but ducked inside the black hole.

Trusting me to guide us straight to Rome.

24

SHARA

I closed my eyes as Rik carried me to the biggest battle of my life. I didn't think or worry or plot out an attack. It was too late to change anything now. My feet had been set on this path before my birth.

Great One, please guide me. Strengthen me. Shield me when needed, but let my spear fly true when it's time.

All too quickly, I felt our destination nearby. I sensed an exit —though there wasn't any light to indicate an opening. Was it dark in Rome? I had no idea of the time difference.

Xin slipped around us on silent wolf feet, even though he hadn't shifted. *:There's a door. Press here, alpha.:*

Rik lifted his foot and shoved the door so hard that it crashed against something and swung back toward us. Xin caught the door before it could slam into me. Rocks tumbled outside, as if we'd broken through a wall or foundation.

Sunlight flooded the chamber. Wincing, I covered my eyes. Xin exited the passageway, and we waited just inside the door as he made a quick investigation of the area.

I could hear cars and city noise all around us, but surely we weren't going to step out into a busy, public place. Marne

Ceresa didn't strike me as the kind of queen who'd like everyday humans knowing about our kind and gossiping about her, though maybe she was already publicly known as the vampire queen of Rome.

:All clear, alpha. We're inside a small walled park shielded by trees. There are humans nearby, but outside the walls.:

Still, Rik waited, allowing the rest of my Blood to squeeze past us and out the door.

His heart thudded beneath my ear, calm and steady. *:Would you prefer to exit on your feet?:*

:I wish I could listen to your heartbeat the entire time.: I blew out a sigh. *:No, I don't mind. Carry me as long as it makes sense.:*

:To the moon and back, my queen.:

As he stepped outside, I stretched out my senses. I felt the ancient trees whispering with excitement. They recognized me, even here. Had my grove somehow talked to them? Across oceans and thousands of miles?

But I had my answer when a large crow swept down and landed on the ground before us. She bobbed her head and chirped rapidly, then leaped into the air and flew away.

:She said welcome to Rome, my queen,: Nevarre said. *:She's going to fetch the rest of her flock in case you need them. They've been watching all over the city, waiting to see where you arrived.:*

:They don't report to Marne?:

:Evidently not. She has her own spies,: Xin replied. *:There are three cars waiting at the gate.:*

Aloud, I said, "Does anyone know where we are?"

"Son of a bitch," Guillaume said, shaking his head. "Look at the door. Well, what's left of it."

Rik turned around so I could see. We'd come out of an old rock wall with two weird white statues on either side of a now-empty doorway.

"Fucking garden gnomes?" Ezra muttered. "Gives me the fucking creeps."

I couldn't argue with that at all.

"Not gnomes," Gina whispered hoarsely. "They represent Bes, an Egyptian god known as a protector of households."

Now that was a coincidence that I found difficult to brush off.

"This was known as the Porta Alchemica," Guillaume said. "Also, the Magic Portal. It was built in the sixteen hundreds, I believe. Supposedly it was carved with a secret formula for how to concoct gold from basic ingredients. The statues were taken from a temple not far from here."

"Dedicated to Isis?" I asked.

"I believe so, but the details are foggy."

"Rik, set me down a moment. I want to see the statues up close."

He stepped closer and carefully lowered me to my feet, while Daire and Nevarre grabbed the train of my gown and kept it untangled. I bent down, studying the short statues. They were rather grotesque, like gargoyles, only with short beards and dwarf-like features.

I straightened and studied what remained of the carvings. There was a white symbol above the doorway with letters around it. "Is that Latin? Mehen, can you read it?"

My dragon joined me and blew out a disgusted sigh. "*The center is in the triangle of the center.*' That makes a whole hell of a lot of sense. Oh, now that's interesting." He pointed to a lower sentence. "*There are three marvels: God and man, mother and virgin, triune and one.*'"

My eyes widened. "It actually says Triune?"

He nodded. "It certainly does."

"The time," Gina reminded me softly.

I curled my arm around Rik's biceps. "Let's get to the cars. I don't know how long of a ride we have yet."

As Xin had indicated, there were three vehicles waiting on us, long, dark Mercedes with tinted glass. The drivers waited at the rear doors, dressed in black pants and shirts with dark shades and hats to hide their faces. All they needed was a white collar around their throats and they could pass for priests. For all I knew, maybe they did secretly work for the Pope too. Was he descended from an Aima goddess?

:Not to my knowledge,: Mehen replied. *:The Church generally frowns on such a thing as drinking blood, which I've always thought ironic given the rituals they hold so dear, not to mention women in power.:*

Wordlessly, my Blood split up evenly among the other two cars, while Rik, Gina, and I got into the middle car. As we pulled away from the park, I noticed a scruffy-looking orange cat sitting on the outer wall, watching us intently.

Traffic was light. I thought we were making good time to wherever we were headed, but Gina kept checking her watch. Rome was a sprawling city that seemed to go on and on, ruins mixed in with modern and medieval-looking architecture at the same time. When we finally pulled over beside a large marble statue, Gina breathed out a tiny sigh of relief. "Five minutes," she whispered as Rik got out of the car and then reached back for me.

I took his hand, but he didn't draw me out of the car immediately. Daire stepped closer and gathered the train up in his arms. Once the billowing yards of fabric were under control, Rik squeezed my fingers in warning and then helped me out of the car. I stood beside him, head high, as Daire adjusted the train and Guillaume assisted Gina out on the other side.

The marble statue was a woman draped in fabric with one breast exposed. She carried a sheaf of wheat in one arm. I hadn't ever associated Marne Ceresa with an agricultural goddess. Another cat sat at the foot of the statue, this one black and white. Cats were evidently her spies in this city.

:Ceres is also a fertility goddess,: Guillaume said. *:Which I'm sure*

has been difficult for House Ceresa given their queen's inability to sire heirs.:

   :Marne doesn't have any daughters?:

   :Not a one. She did have several less powerful sisters, but none of them conceived queens either and I don't think any of them still live. House Ceresa will die out with her.:

Despite my difficulties with the queen, the idea of her ancient house dying out saddened me. Something about what he said resonated in my head. Sisters. That was important. *:How many sisters, do you know?:*

   :There were three Ceresa sisters from what I remember.:

The chime resonated again like a high, clear bell. *:Carys. Carys!:*

   :What?: she finally answered.

   :Does three sisters mean anything to you?:

   :Three sisters...: Her bond picked up the resonance I'd heard and magnified it. *:Maybe. Yes! Let me find it.:*

In the bond, I saw her racing from stack to stack to stack of books.

There were a lot of stacks. I had no idea how she'd organized them, but I had to hope she could find it in time.

With Gina on my left, Rik on my right, and the rest of my Blood lined up behind me, I stepped closer to the statue. The hairs on my arms tingled as we neared it, warning of Marne's blood circle.

A familiar woman stood waiting for us, but it took me a moment to place her. She looked like a porcelain doll with a pretty rose-bud mouth and large blue eyes. Even her hair was coiled into fat ringlets around her face, though she wore a modern dress. She'd been in the tower—one of Keisha Skye's former siblings. The envoy to House Ceresa, though I couldn't remember her name.

   :Daniella Thalassa,: Daire added helpfully.

"House Isador answers the Triune's summons," Gina said.

"Her Majesty, Shara Isador, last daughter of Isis, She who is all that has been and is and shall be, comes before Her Majesty Marne Ceresa as ordered."

"Your Majesty." The woman curtseyed. Not too low, but enough to be courteous. "House Ceresa welcomes House Isador to Rome."

"Thank you, Daniella."

"Your Blood are welcome to enter with you, but please be aware that Her Majesty's blood circle prevents you from accessing your power." She smiled, her manner friendly and not nasty, despite her words. "All of you."

The sound of grinding rocks filled my head. :*That means we won't be able to shift to defend you if need be.*:

:*That's not surprising.*: I tried to reassure us both, but my stomach quivered with dread anyway. The idea of stepping into Marne Ceresa's nest was already alarming. Knowing that I couldn't access my power...

And my Blood couldn't shift...

We'd be defenseless.

Gina leaned closer and whispered, "One minute."

I didn't have to be told that we'd probably all die if we weren't inside that fucking circle before time ran out. So what choice did I have?

"The circle is already coded by Her Majesty to allow House Isador to pass," Daniella said as she stepped aside, gesturing for us to pass through.

I stepped forward into the queen of Rome's nest.

GUILLAUME

My life was nothing. Shara must live. I wouldn't allow a single doubt to cloud my vision or affect my blade.

Though if House Isador died today...

I couldn't hope to meet the same fate. After dying so many times only to come back... I didn't believe that Coatlicue would truly allow me to die with my queen. It was a peace that I didn't deserve.

I'd be trapped here. With *her*.

We Blood followed our queen anywhere, even into the bowels of hell. The blood circle closed around us, and for a moment, sheer panic thundered through my mind. My hell horse was gone. I didn't feel the stallion's fierce courage or the drumming of his hooves in my blood.

At least we still had our bonds, though they magnified my unease as my brethren felt the same initial rush of panic at our beasts' loss. Mehen especially took it hard, understandably so. He'd been trapped as Leviathan for thousands of years. Losing the dragon was like losing the majority of his soul.

He clenched his jaws, a muscle ticking in his cheek. His green eyes blazed with malice and he snarled and frothed like a mad dog until Shara soothed him. She offered her left hand and the man plastered himself against her side, squishing her against Rik's bulk.

:*I'm still here,*: she whispered in our bonds. :*She can't take you away from me.*:

"This way, Your Majesty," Daniella said, leading the way down a wide cobblestone path. "This road used to be part of the Appian Way. We still receive our water from the Aqua Virgo built during Emperor Augustus's reign."

"Amazing," Shara replied. "Has Her Majesty's family lived here for a long time?"

"I wouldn't know," Daniella answered with a polite shrug. "I've only been here a few hundred years. House Ceresa has certainly held this nest for at least four or five times that long."

She chatted as she led us up the ancient Roman road to the villa. White marble columns framed an immense wrought-iron gate, also decorated in sheaves of wheat. The gates stood open, though my knight's eyes saw a history of defenses built into the two-story building. A heavy portcullis hung above, ready to drop at a moment's notice, and a beautiful cutout design on the second story's balcony wasn't merely decorative. Archers had once been stationed there, ready to pick off any intruder. Maybe some vats of hot oil too. The Romans had certainly been inventive.

My warrior senses knew there were many eyes watching us. Skilled eyes noting our weapons, planning who'd they attack and eliminate first. I couldn't see the other queen's Blood, but she was rumored to have at least one hundred sworn to her.

The grand entrance lead to a paved plaza, with two-story wings forming a rectangle around the gardens. Fountains tinkled among a mix of olive and lemon trees. The air seemed warmer and thicker, reminiscent of a beautiful late-summer afternoon in Tuscany.

A small white cafe table with two wrought-iron chairs sat beside a circular pool lined in dark blue or black tiles. It was oddly dark despite the bright sunlight and blue sky above.

Marne Ceresa sat in one of the chairs, reading a book and stroking a large white Persian cat on her lap. No one else waited in the plaza. No Blood, consiliari, or even a servant as we approached.

Another cat sat on the edge of the pool, staring intently at the water. A flash of gold and white swirled close to the surface but then darted back below. As we neared, I could see the thick vegetation in the water, explaining why it had initially appeared so dark. Large koi swam in the water, taunting the intrigued cat with tantalizing glimpses of their sleek fins.

Marne Ceresa set the book aside and lifted her gaze to my queen. She didn't rise or say a word in welcome. She wouldn't.

This was her nest. Her summons. She'd make sure we all knew our place, though her appearance was carefully understated. She didn't wear her crown or even a gorgeous gown, though her white silk caftan studded with glittering diamonds spoke of privilege and wealth.

We still knew she was the fucking queen of Rome.

Despite the nerves fluttering in her bond like frantic butterflies, Shara appeared perfectly calm and at ease. She stood easily, her arms tucked around Rik's and Mehen's arms, and though they were both much larger than her, it was clear to anyone who looked that they deferred to her.

We all did. She could bend us in half and drop us to our knees with the smallest lifting of her pinkie finger.

It was a test, one of several Marne Ceresa had set up to judge the worth and might of our queen long before we'd even arrived at her nest.

Shara tipped her head politely, but kept her gaze firmly locked on the other queen. Refusing to bend knee or curtsey, if that's what the Triune queen had expected.

A small smile curved Marne's lips. "Welcome to Rome, child."

So polite—and yet derogatory at the same time. A smile to cut like a knife.

"Thank you for the invitation, Your Majesty."

Another equally polite jab from my queen. This wasn't an invitation—but a summons from the highest Aima court in the world.

"Do sit." Marne swept her graceful hand toward the other chair opposite her. "Daniella, escort Shara's Blood to the kitchen for refreshments."

"No, thank you." Rik's voice crashed and rolled like an

avalanche as he escorted Shara to the chair and took up position at her back. "Your Majesty."

We positioned ourselves in an arc behind them both, shoulder to shoulder, though we faced away—ready to guard her from any direction, other than the queen directly opposite her. We could do nothing to stop her attack if it came to open warfare.

"As you wish," Marne replied. "I hope you'll join me for tea, Shara."

Gina stood to Shara's right, a pad and pen in her hand. "Would you like for me to keep the formal record of this conversation for the Triune record, Your Majesty?"

With a dismissive shrug, Marne picked up the teapot. "If you feel it's necessary."

Suspicion raged in Rik's bond. As Marne poured the tea, he fought the urge to leap across the table and knock the cup away from our queen. Poison. Tainted blood. The queen's own blood, as she'd tried to entrap Shara before in Kansas City. Who knew what foul treachery the queen might have in store for ours?

Outwardly unperturbed, Shara accepted the cup. Though I couldn't see her with my eyes, her bond gave us access to everything she saw. She watched Marne carefully, waiting until the other queen sipped first. Her hand trembled slightly.

Not because she'd been afraid of poison.

Nerves. Shara wasn't intimidated by this queen's power... but by her social standing.

She'd never sat and dined with a queen of this caliber before. She swallowed a small sip and set the cup back down in the saucer slightly too hard, with an inelegant clank that made her wince.

Servants dressed in spotless white livery crossed the plaza to set soup bowls in front of the queens. Shara glanced down at the endless array of silverware before her with a surge of panic.

:Take the furthest spoon on the right.: I quickly said. *:It's by the teacup.:*

She picked up the spoon. *:Thanks. Is it rude if I don't eat with her?:*

:Yes,: I replied, at the same time that Mehen growled, *:Fuck her. Do what you want.:*

:Does that green shit look appetizing to you?: Daire asked in the bond. *:It looks like someone blew their nose in the bowl.:*

More at ease, though now she was fighting not to laugh out loud, Shara dipped her spoon into the soup and risked a small bite. *:It's cold.:*

:Fucking nasty gazpacho,: Ezra muttered. *:Tastes like slimy slick cucumbers.:*

:It's not bad. I think it has some avocado in it.:

"Tell me about yourself, Shara," Marne said. "Beyond the obvious. I know your house and your goddess, but not how you came to be."

"I was raised in Kansas City, Missouri," Shara began cautiously. Truth only, as she'd decreed, but she also didn't want to give too much away to the Triune queen before she knew why we'd been summoned to court. "My aunt raised me, but I didn't know she was my aunt until only a few months ago."

"I remember Selena Isador. Not because of her power, which was unremarkable. No, she claimed to have fallen in love with a human and asked permission to leave her nest and house behind. It's so strange that this love story's timing occurred shortly before you must have been conceived."

Shara took another bite of the soup before responding. "His name was Alan Dalton. He helped raise me until his death."

"Remarkable."

Through her bond, I felt Shara look up at the other queen's face, trying to judge her sincerity and read between the lines.

"So you were raised as a human? You truly didn't know what you are?"

Shara set the spoon down and went back to her tea. "I had no idea until right before Christmas."

Marne tsked softly. "Oh, my. That must have been so shocking for you."

"It was." Shara smiled sweetly and sipped her tea without offering any additional information.

"Before her demise, Keisha Skye contacted me about you."

Shara widened her eyes, feigning surprise. "Oh?"

Shortly after calling her first several Blood, Shara had dreamed of a conversation between Keisha and Marne. The dream had proven to be real, not just prophetic. She had overheard the entire conversation without either queen knowing she'd been there.

"She claimed that you had a very unique parentage."

Marne waited, possibly trying to bait Shara into revealing that she'd overheard that conversation. Or perhaps she just wanted to see if Shara would admit the truth of her secret birth herself.

Shara wasn't falling for any such trap, but merely gazed back at the queen over her cup.

Sweat trickled down my back. The air weighed heavier, the heat quickly growing uncomfortable. What had seemed like a pleasant summer day had become the miserable, baking afternoon heat of a desert.

While two formidable queens sat staring at each other over cups of tea in the deadliest game of all.

"I don't know that I quite believed her. Not after what she'd done to conceive her own unfortunate child." Marne lifted her hand and the servants quickly returned to clear away the first course. "Just because she sold her soul to the god of light, that certainly didn't mean your true mother did the same with the god of monsters."

25

SHARA

I waited in silence while the servants switched out the dishes. This course was a lovely salad with mixed greens, mandarin orange slices, and something red that bled all over the plate. Chopped beets? Maybe? But it had a meaty-looking texture. Raw meat. On a salad?

I was a badass vampire queen. I craved blood. Just thinking about tearing into Rik's throat made me drench my panties and my fangs throbbed.

But I didn't crave blood that wasn't mine. And for goddess's sake, what kind of meat was it? Beef? Human? A hapless queen who'd pissed Marne off? Who the fuck knew?

She wanted me off balance. She wanted me to leap to Esetta's defense and retort that nothing my mother had done was anything like the torture and depravity that Keisha had committed.

She hadn't conceived her daughter when she fucked Ra, but not for lack of trying. I'd seen his massive baseball-bat-sized dick and that was not a sexual act I even wanted to try and picture. He'd used Keisha and lied to her when he couldn't impregnate her.

He'd told her that torturing her alpha would give her the daughter she craved. Unfortunately, he'd been right—and Tanza's soul had been corrupted by that horrible act. She'd been possessed by something demonic and evil.

I wasn't going to argue that I wasn't monstrous.

Because I was.

I could shift into a cobra queen and had poisoned—and ultimately killed—my alpha. Though I'd been able to resurrect him.

I'd drained Keisha Skye to death, literally absorbing her power into my own like she was nothing. A cup of water to the ocean that roared inside me.

I'd chopped Guillaume's head off in Heliopolis.

Of course, I was monstrous.

But I wasn't demonic or evil.

Nothing I could say would convince Marne otherwise. Watching her face, though, I realized that I didn't have to convince her of anything.

Better than anyone, she knew what I was.

And she hated me for it.

She hated me—because she hadn't been able to have an heir. Not just an heir to her house and power, but an heir to the Triune. Whatever Guillaume saw when he looked at me that had convinced him I would be called to the Triune… Marne saw it too.

That was the sole reason I was here, regardless of what she might claim.

"Don't you like steak tartare?" Marne asked.

I deliberately leaned back in my chair, dropping my head back slightly so I could feel Rik behind me. He immediately dropped his hands to my shoulders. "No, thank you. I'm not that hungry, I'm afraid."

She gave me a tight smile, her eyes narrowed slightly as she watched our interaction. "Very well. Violet, go ahead, dearest."

The white Persian hopped up onto the table from her lap

and settled down to devour the raw pile of meat on top of the salad.

"I'm familiar with your true mother's history, though..." She frowned, her jaws tensing a moment before she shrugged. "I can't say her name. I suppose that was part of her grand scheme to ensure you never swore allegiance to the Triune. Which is why I've summoned you to Rome."

Gina stepped closer to the table and laid a heavy-looking envelope on the table between us. "I beg your pardon, Your Majesty, but her mother made sure she was sworn to the Triunes at birth, as customary for newborn queens."

Triunes—plural? Because if I had to swear to one... Why not swear me to all? It sounded like something my politically-savvy mother would have done.

Esetta had gone to great lengths to ensure my freedom. If she'd been forced to swear me to the Triune when I was still an infant, I could totally see her swearing me to *all* of them so that I still had options.

"Oh?" Marne arched a brow but didn't move to pick up the paper. "How convenient. A piece of paper can be easily forged, especially when it was never lodged formally to the Triune consiliari at the time of her super-secret birth."

"It was sealed with the blood of two other witnesses," Gina replied.

Marne waved her hand dismissively.

"Both queens," Gina continued. "Or so I was told."

Now that interested Marne. Eyes narrowed she leaned forward, snatched up the envelope, and broke the wax seal. "Her sister won't convince me. Who else did she embroil in this mockery?"

Now I was just as curious. Another queen had known of my birth this entire time and acted as a witness? But who?

Marne pulled out a single sheet of parchment. As she read, her fingers convulsed on the paper, until she finally crinkled it up into a ball. She gave me a tight smile, though her eyes blazed with fury. "Of course. I should have known."

She threw the wad into the pond beside our table.

I hoped my mouth wasn't hanging open with surprise. I'd been so afraid to meet the famous queen of Rome. Not just because of her immense power and formidable reputation, but because of her age and position in the Triune court. Older than I could imagine, more experienced in the world and life in general, she made me feel like a stupid, gauche teenager with knobby knees and a bad complexion. She'd been alive longer than I could even comprehend. How did one prepare for a mental war, when the years of my life were the size of a gnat compared to hers?

Yet one of the most powerful queens in the world had just had a minor temper tantrum and thrown an important legal document.

Into a fucking koi pond.

Gina stared at her, too, a stunned look on her face. "I have copies—"

Marne slammed her hand down on the table, rattling the cutlery. "But of course you do."

Bewildered, I looked from her to Gina. "Who else signed it?"

A harsh sound escaped Marne's mouth, drawing my attention back to her. "You don't even know. That's rich. Your own consiliarius has lied to you from the beginning."

Gina whirled to me, her eyes round with horror. "Never. I didn't know, Shara. I still don't know. It was done by your mother and given to me to hold, but I never knew who signed it. Only that it would be needed when you were summoned to court. I swear it on your blood that you gave me—I have no idea who else was involved."

A strange sound buzzed in my ears. Almost like a high-pitched drone or hum. :*Do you hear that?*:

:*Hear what?*: Rik asked.

The sound grew louder. Shriller. It was so fucking annoying that I wanted to clamp my hands over my ears.

But if Marne was doing it... I didn't want her to know it bothered me.

I tightened my jaws, determined not to ask her what that horrid sound was.

"No matter." Marne picked up her napkin and snapped it sharply before smoothing it out in her lap. "I've already taken steps to neutralize her position. Though I must admit, Shara, that your dearly departed mother certainly played the game well. She almost had me."

That fucking sound. My ears ached with the incessant hum. I squeezed my hands together in my lap, digging my nails into my skin just enough to cause a little pain without drawing blood. That might be considered a weapon here.

"Let's get down to business, shall we?"

I blinked rapidly, forcing my eyes to focus on Marne rather than look around for that fucking noise.

Here it comes. This is her final move. This is where I either win the game or lose it all.

"I've been told that you love your Blood. If you want to keep them alive..." She smiled as her cat came back to rub against her, purring loudly. "Then you'll accept one of my Blood into yours. Or I'll kill them all and leave you no other choice than to accept a Blood of my choosing."

26

RIK

No. Fucking. Way.

I tightened my grip on Shara's shoulders as if I could physically hold her back from making such a terrible decision.

:*Is it so terrible?*: Daire asked. :*If we all walk away... Politically, it's the smart thing to do.*:

I knew he spoke sense.

But I still didn't fucking like it.

This was the kind of decision a Triune-level queen had to make. She would have to take Blood from other queens to form alliances, often with queens she didn't even like, in order to protect us all. A sibling like Mayte was well and good for a minor queen, but a Triune queen would have hundreds of Maytes at her beck and call.

And she still wouldn't have enough power to keep Marne Ceresa from devouring her house.

It was a simple numbers game. Marne had been alive for hundreds of years and had used those years wisely to make her power base as intimidating as possible. Shara had made some great connections, but she hadn't had a lifetime to gain the same allies.

She'd had months. Literally.

While she'd done a fantastic job of aligning House Isador with some firepower, we didn't hold a candle to House Ceresa and never would.

:Oh?: Shara's bond felt tight, like a violin string drawn so tightly that it sang. *:You don't think I can take her on?:*

:Of course you could,: I softened my grip on her shoulders and used my low, tender rumble to ease some of the strain in her mind. *:But you wouldn't want to pay the cost. It's a dangerous gamble and we might all die in such a war. Could you count it a victory if you lost even one of us to defeat her?:*

"Before you decide, you should know that I've taken steps to ensure all of your Blood will die at my command."

Shara pushed slowly to her feet, her shoulders trembling beneath my hands. "What? How?"

Marne lifted her cup and sipped her tea casually. As if she hadn't just threatened to murder us all. "Archers. On the second story balcony."

"Son of a bitch," Guillaume muttered.

Marne smiled brightly at him, as if only just now remembering that the great Guillaume de Payne was in her presence. "Oh, don't worry, sir knight. I've got special plans for you too."

Ideas exploded in my mind one by one... only to die as certainly as we would. I couldn't shift. None of us could.

Shara couldn't access her power.

So yeah. Archers could strike us down and she'd be forced to watch us bleed out. Unable to heal us. Unable to resurrect us, if Marne kept our bodies inside her circle.

And she fucking would. Because she was a fucking bitch like that.

Some fucking alpha I was. I couldn't do anything to help my queen. Nothing at all, but stand here and fucking die.

Shara pulled away from me and paced back and forth beside the table. Every once in a while, she reached up unconsciously toward her ears as if trying to block out a sound or voice.

I focused harder on her bond, pushing away my own dread. I searched her body, looking for any attack or foreign element that would be causing her pain or interfering with her magic, but I couldn't sense anything.

:Xin, do you smell or hear anything strange?:

:Nothing, alpha.:

:I don't hear it,: Itztli said in our bond. *:But I feel it. There's a vibration inside her.:*

:Like the dragon sonar?: Mehen asked. *:Maybe Tiamat is fucking with her.:*

:Shut up, all of you,: Shara retorted. *:Or goddess help me, I'll shut down your bonds. I can't fucking think with this noise!:*

"You hesitate," Marne said, sadly shaking her head. "I guess I need to teach you a lesson."

"No!"

Too late. I felt the heavy thud in my left shoulder before I heard the whooshing sound of an arrow slicing through the air. I grunted at the impact, but a single arrow wouldn't incapacitate me, even if it was a heavy six-foot-long spear rather than an arrow.

It was merely a warning.

"Rik!" Shara started to rush toward me, but I jerked my hands up to stop her. Well, my right arm cooperated. My left hung limply at my side.

"I'm fine, my queen. Tend to your business." Silently in our bond, I said, *:The last thing we need is a stray arrow hitting you. Keep your distance, from all of us.:*

Her eyes flashed with rage, her magic lighting her blood up like a bonfire. *:I will do anything to protect you.:*

:I know, my queen. I love you more than life itself. I trust you implicitly. Do whatever you need to do. Without question, it'll be the right thing. Your goddess has always guided your heart.:

:Take her fucking offer. It's the only thing to do,: Guillaume ground out. *:As surely as you chopped my head off in Heliopolis to win, you must accept one of her Blood. It's the only way out of this mess and she knows it.:*

"I made an oath," Shara finally said aloud, slowly turning to face Marne. "I swore to only take Blood that I love."

Marne laughed, a sound of pure delight. She even clapped her hands with mirth. "Oh, Shara, dear. You are so very, very young. I love it. I do. Such sweet devotion to your handsome Blood, but so incredibly naive of you."

My queen's gaze dropped to the ground. Pink darkened her cheeks. She suddenly looked like a shy, awkward young human. "I was a virgin when Rik found me. I thought…"

Marne nodded sympathetically. "Taking a Blood can be a marvelous experience, but that doesn't mean it's love. Any Blood worth his salt knows how to make you feel just as good as any of these that you've already taken. I've taken hundreds of Blood over the years, and let me tell you, with complete sincerity, that eventually, the wonderful feeling you have with a new Blood fades."

I wanted to wring her fucking neck with my bare hands. Just to start. Then I'd let Nevarre peck out her eyes while Itztli showed us how the Flayed One could strip the skin off a body and make it dance.

"It costs you very little to accept one of mine in exchange for all of your lives."

"And then you'll have a spy in my nest and in my bed," Shara said bitterly.

"True." Marne sat back in her chair, calmly stroking her cat. "But surely you can understand my position. You weren't raised in a nest. You have no surviving house to guide your way. You're a wild cannon that might misfire at the most inopportune time. This way, I can help you."

Shara snorted. "I don't fucking need your help."

"You must have decided you needed something from me. Why did you uncover my mirror if you didn't need my assistance in some way?"

She stared out at the water intently. So intently, I don't think she heard the other queen, until Marne called her name. Again.

Turning slowly, Shara faced me. Her shoulders drooped, and I knew the decision she'd made. What choice did she have?

I'd dreamed that we could go on as before. That we could still love her with the same depth and joy that we'd known. But she was a queen.

A fucking powerful queen.

Who needed to rise to the next level, no matter the cost. We would lose everything if she refused to make this compromise.

"I'll accept one Blood from inside your house." She swallowed hard and nodded. "I guess you're right. In the end, one Blood is very much like the others."

Goddess. Hearing those words come out of her mouth hurt more than the fucking spear in my shoulder. I'd rather let the cobra queen pump me with venom and liquify my body again than hear her say such a thing.

"Perfect. I'm so glad we could come to a reasonable arrangement. You may have your choice of any of my Blood, child, except my alpha, of course. He's relatively new and it takes so very long to break them in the way I like."

Staring at me, Shara ground her teeth together, her bond still singing with that strange, tight sensation. Like she was on the verge of breaking. "As I said, I'll take one from your house. Who else witnessed my birth?"

"Oh, well, I suppose it doesn't hurt anything to tell you now that we've come to an agreement. Undina Ketea signed as a witness. Your mother had you sworn to both courts."

:Skolos Triune queen,: Daire said in our bonds. *:Descended from the sea goddess, Keto.:*

:My mother really was a fucking genius. Hang on, Rik. I'll be back in a minute.:

I had no idea what she meant.

But suddenly, a tentacle as thick as my thigh wrapped around her ankle and yanked her into the pool.

27

SHARA

Water closed over my head. Thanks to Isis's heavy crown, I would have sunk like a stone even without the tentacle around my ankle.

The pond had no true bottom. Marne had disguised the pool as a simple koi pond, but I passed through foot after foot of water and vegetation. It had to be large to house a sea creature sporting such a massive tentacle.

Hopefully, I wouldn't pass out before he dragged me to him. Yes, he. I was sure he was an Aima king, though I didn't know why Marne had him locked up. I wasn't even sure that a lack of oxygen would even affect me. So far, I felt fine. I didn't need to breathe. Yet.

The shrill, high-pitched noise softened as I neared his prison. It was more like music rather than an annoying, painful sound, though it wasn't like any music I'd ever heard before. Sunlight barely flickered through the mossy fronds of plants dancing in the water. Just enough to illuminate the creature trapped inside a cave. The entrance was gated with iron bars as thick as my body, too close together for him to squeeze out more than his tentacles.

Giant tentacles curled around him and stretched out into the water. Too many for a normal octopus. It was hard to make out his shape inside the dark hole, but he had two glowing eyes that cut through the murk, and his tentacles gleamed with bright blue-green bioluminescence. From what I could see, he had a giant mouth lined with swords. Certainly large enough to swallow me whole.

For a moment, yeah, I was afraid that he'd eat me. But that fear passed as I neared him. He could have dragged me into the water as soon as I'd neared the pool. He could have ripped me limb from limb or bashed my head against the side of the pool. Instead, he drew me steadily but gently down to him. He'd waited, somehow sensing the perfect moment to drag me under.

Besides, I'd seen a hint of his existence in my grotto, which told me all I needed to know about his purpose.

He was inside Marne's house. He satisfied the compromise I'd asked for.

But he wasn't *her* Blood.

He was mine.

I could see him glowing blue-green in the tapestry of my mind, answering my desperate call for a way out of Marne's terrible bargain.

Because it was terrible, for me at least. I loved my Blood and always would. If I had to start taking Blood I didn't even care about just to keep my power and win a Triune seat, then fuck it all to hell and back again.

I wouldn't do it.

He pressed his giant head against the bars and the singing stopped. He gave me such a mournful, desperate look. I didn't need a bond with him to know what he was saying.

Get me the fuck out of here.

I grasped one of the ancient bars and gave it an experimental tug. It was still solid despite its age and as slippery as an eel with all that moss. Besides, he could have ripped them out with his tentacles if it was possible.

His glowing eyes moved down to the bottom right-hand corner of his cage, his tentacle shifting me in that direction. I used my hands, walking my way over to a black hole in the side of the rock.

Goddess. I didn't like unknown, dark holes only big enough for my hand to slip inside. If a sea snake bit me, Rik would have to swim down and drag me back out. Though I didn't think Marne would bother healing me.

Braced for something nasty to swim over my fingers, I stuck my hand gingerly into the hole, carefully feeling around for a lever to grab. Something tickled my fingers. Moss, I told myself. It was only moss. Not a creepy crawly.

I had my arm in the hole midway up to my shoulder before I found what I was looking for. There was a depression in the bottom of the hole, but the lever or switch that had been inside was long gone.

Frustrated, I pulled my hand out and scanned the ground. I needed a—

Oh, fuck me sideways. I had it. I had exactly what I needed.

I fumbled for the edge of my cape, searching for my knife that Rik had dropped into the secret pocket. My fingers were being stupid and ignoring what my brain told them to do.

My vision was getting darker, and my chest ached.

:Hurry,: Rik whispered in my head. *:Even a badass vampire queen needs to breathe eventually.:*

At his touch on the bond, my mind flashed to the scene above. Pulling off the act of the century, my Blood paced furiously along the edge of the pool, searching the water. Even though they felt me alive and unharmed, working to free the trapped creature at the bottom. Rik had them well in hand, though Ezra and Mehen were having a grand time yelling at each other while they threw punches and wrestled around on the ground.

Why they were fighting each other... I had no idea. But it made for an effective distraction.

Finally, I managed to slip the slim pocketknife out. Unsure how long I needed it to be to trigger the mechanism, I flipped it open to add the blade's length to my makeshift lever. I gripped it firmly, willing my numb fingers to hold on as I pushed my hand back down into the hole.

As if made for the slot at the bottom, my knife slid into place. Gears groaned. Metal screamed, echoing oddly in the water. The bars were moving.

I didn't try to swim for the surface but allowed the sea creature to pull me close against his body. He wasn't slimy at all. Though now my hands glowed too in the thickening darkness.

I wasn't afraid. I did my best work in the darkness.

My mother's voice floated through the dark stillness. *Look.*

I opened my eyes. I was still underwater, but the fronds in the koi pond had been replaced by slick rocks and roots. The water was deliciously hot, and my soul sang with joy. I recognized this place.

My grotto, but deeper than it had ever been.

Silver flickered, drawing my attention to a shadowed hole at the base of my heart tree. A place where the roots had opened up into a cave. I wasn't afraid as I floated closer. I was destined to be here. I was born for this.

A pearly silver glow brightened the chamber. For a moment, I saw Esetta's face, so like mine. Her smile of pride made my heart swell and ache with longing. My mother. I wished I had known her.

I hovered closer to the shining object. It was small. Maybe a foot tall and slightly rounded. A statue, I thought. But I couldn't make out the details.

Something pulled me back. Dragging me under, hauling me through water and vegetation. Toward the sun. Life. My Blood.

Yes. It was time.

Esetta's voice carried through the water to me. *You were sworn to all three Triunes—so you could choose.*

An image filled my head. I stared up at my mother's face. Two others stood on either side of her. A sharp prick on my heel made me wail, but she soothed me. Her whispers rocking me to sleep.

By her blood, Shara Isador is sworn to the Triune. By her blood, Shara Isador is sworn to Skolos. By her blood, Shara Isador is sworn to Triskeles. By her blood, last daughter of Isis, Great One, She who is and was and always will be, Shara Isador will choose her path with all the love in her heart.

Choose, daughter of mine, and know that I will always love you.

28

SHARA

Before I opened my eyes, I heard Ezra grumbling.

"Now we've got land, air, *and* sea covered. But fuck me sideways, is he uuuuuug-ley."

The sound of a fist landing on a hard body made me sit up. Mehen growled, "What makes you think we're ever going to have a battle at sea, you stinking pile of fur?"

Something was wrong with my neck. My head was ridiculously heavy and twisted around funny. It took way too much effort to hold my head upright.

I didn't realize the heavy crown had slid down, tangled in my hair, until Rik pulled it free and set it in my lap.

Naturally, he had me tight against his body, his one good arm wrapped around me. He'd been worried about me first, despite the spear still embedded in his shoulder. I turned in his arms and eyed the spearhead that protruded from the front of his body by a foot. They'd skewered him good. Fucking bastards.

"Can someone break the shaft and pull it out?"

Itztli immediately grabbed the tail-end and Tlacel the front. He held it steady while his brother cracked the thick shaft in half like it was a piece of kindling. Rik didn't even groan as Tlacel pulled the splintered wood out of his shoulder.

I drew Rik's head down to my throat and he had his fangs in me before Marne could stop him.

"You can't access your power," she retorted. "You can't heal him."

Calmly, I looked up at her, letting her see the flat, dead look in my eyes that promised I was beyond pissed. I was ready to hand out retribution all around. "You never said I couldn't feed, or that my Blood couldn't feed."

"Your blood is a weapon," she gritted out. "All queens' blood is dangerous. How dare you utilize such a weapon inside my nest?"

I shrugged. "You should have been more specific in whatever spell you laid on your circle. I won't use my power against you, but goddess help me if I'll sit by and allow my alpha to suffer when a few swallows of my blood will heal him."

"Besides, you did tell her to take a Blood, Your Majesty," Gina said in her most business-like voice. "She can only comply if she *feeds* said Blood. So this isn't expressly forbidden by the constraints you laid upon House Isador before we entered your nest."

A tentacle slithered closer, reminding me of his presence. He didn't touch me, but I knew what he wanted. What he needed.

Rik lifted his head, allowing my blood to drip down my throat. I stared up at the kraken's giant shape, amazed and yeah, a little repulsed, but he was also fascinating. His head was a weird arched hump at the end of an oblong body. His mouth and head were outlined in smaller tentacles, almost like a living, Medusa-style beard or mane. A spiny ridge lined his back, and thicker, longer tentacles sprouted from his base.

In broad daylight, he was a dark purple-gray with pearly soft lavender suckers on his tentacles.

Hesitantly, he reached out one of those tentacles, watching

my reaction as it lightly tickled my arm. He'd already touched me with them, and I hadn't run screaming, but evidently, he was worried about how I'd react now that I saw him fully.

"Duuuude." Drawing the word out, Daire shook his head and laughed. "She freed your miserable ass from the bottom of a fucking koi pond. I think she's gonna be fine with what you look like."

"Feed, my Blood. I want to see you and know your name."

The tentacle slipped around my throat, pressing suckers to my skin to vacuum up the blood. It wasn't completely unpleasant, though having multiple little mouths working on me at the same time was—

Daire snickered and opened his mouth.

Guillaume cuffed him in the back of the head before he could say something entirely inappropriate. I wouldn't mind if we were alone, but I didn't care to make jokes with sexual innuendo in front of the queen of Rome.

More confident, the kraken slid closer, curling another tentacle around my leg beneath the ruined silk of my gown. Ugh. After my trip through the pond, my gorgeous dress was streaked with baby-poop brown, and I might have a piece of moss or something slick very near my unmentionables.

Ah. No. That was just another of the kraken's tentacles tickling my thigh.

As most of my Blood when they'd first come to me, he wanted simple touch as much as he wanted my blood. Though so many tentacles touching me at once was interesting, to say the least.

I arched a brow at Marne. "I've done as you asked. I've taken a Blood."

She laughed and waved a hand at us dismissively. "He's not *my* Blood, so he doesn't count."

I smiled. "Gina?"

She flipped back several pages in her notebook and read

back our conversation. "Shara Isador said, 'I'll accept one Blood *from inside your house.*' Marne Ceresa replied, 'Perfect. I'm so glad we could come to a reasonable arrangement.'"

"I know what I said," Marne retorted. "I specifically said one of *my* Blood."

"In your first statement, yes. But that statement was modified by Shara, which you then accepted. Triune Articles Section 101.88.13 specifies that a compromising agreement is made between two queens when the queen requesting the concession indicates that an agreement has been successful and accepts the consenting queen's alternative offer. Shall I read the entire section again, Your Majesty? Or do you remember saying that a reasonable agreement had been reached?"

Marne stared at me, her face as still and cold as the marble statue we'd seen at the edge of her nest.

For the first time since entering Rome, I seriously thought she might try to kill me. She glared at me like an offensive creature who'd just tracked filth all over her perfectly spotless house.

I nestled back against Rik's chest. My new Blood slowly shifted to his human form. Shoulder-length black hair and neatly trimmed beard. Blue-green eyes the same color as his beast's bioluminescence. And as fine a physique as any of my Blood, bare and naked as a jaybird after shifting, though he did have some interesting-looking tattoos on his arms that I wanted to investigate further.

Oh, and of course, he was very, very happy to see me.

Without looking away from her face, I slid my right arm around the new Blood's neck. "What's your name, my Blood, and how long has she kept you there in that cave?"

"Okeanos Ketea, my queen." His voice was surprisingly melodic, much like his kraken song, though less shrill and desperate now that I had found and freed him. "I've been imprisoned by Her Majesty Marne Ceresa for one hundred years."

"That's why Undina agreed to act as witness to my birth," I whispered, nodding to myself. "She must have made a bargain with my mother to win your freedom."

"Undina is my mother, the High Queen of the Skolos Triune. She was forced to surrender me to Rome, but I don't know why."

I searched Marne's face, trying to read the millions of secrets in her eyes. How many other hostages did she have stashed around her nest or the world? "Why would a Skolos queen make such a bargain with the queen of Rome?"

Marne made a low sound of disgust, though I detected a glint in her eye. Amusement, perhaps. Or...

Maybe a tiny spark of...

Dare I say respect?

Goddess, it was about fucking time.

"He's a fucking king." Mehen's dragon roughened his voice. "In most courts, that's plenty to earn you a death sentence."

In the bond, I grasped Leviathan's scaly snout in my hands and pressed a kiss to his forehead. "Not in my court."

"Enough," Marne said, her voice as sharp as a whip. "Rise. All of you. So I can deal with you once and for all."

I held my hand up and Tlacel assisted me to my feet. I grabbed the crown before I dropped it, but I didn't try to put it back on my head. Not until I could fix the tangled mess of my hair. He stood strategically in front of Okeanos, blocking the other queen's view, though he remained plastered against my side. Rik enfolded me in his arms before him. Itztli pressed close on my other side.

Not to be left out, Daire dropped down low in front of me and entwined himself around my legs like the giant cat he was.

The rest of my Blood gathered close, but behind me.

I was their queen. I would deal with this threat and there was nothing they could do to protect me.

Marne Ceresa didn't show fangs. That would have been too gauche for the queen of Rome.

No, all she had to do to call down her power was *will* her blood to well up.

She lifted her right hand, index finger pointed up, and a single drop of blood dotted her fingertip. One. Measly. Drop.

Power surged in her so suddenly that my wet hair whipped into my face. The soggy material of my dress whooshed and slapped against me like a flag in straight-line winds.

Instinctively, I reached for my power. Urgency strummed in me. My throat squeezed in a fist of fear.

I hadn't come all this way to die.

I hadn't just freed Okeanos or healed Rik to watch them die.

My blood still dripped down my neck. It would be so easy...

Just in time, I caught myself. No power. I had agreed to those conditions when I'd stepped into her nest. I'd repeated the words myself. I wouldn't use my power against her.

I had been powerless before. I'd been poor, lost, and terrified. Yet I'd still fought back the only way I knew how. I'd stayed one step ahead of the monsters hunting me for years.

This monster might wear a pretty smile and control one of the most ancient cities in the world, but she was still a monster.

But not as big a monster as me.

I'm Shara fucking Isador.

Daughter of the god of monsters.

Last daughter of Isis, She who is and was and always will be.

Marne Ceresa would find me a slimy, poisonous bite to swallow, and I hoped to goddess she choked on me.

Standing in surging winds that whipped and howled around me, I swiped my hair out of my face and stared back at her. Chin up. Shoulders squared. Eyes blazing with fury. Determination. Love.

Love was my weapon. I loved my Blood. Fully, deeply, and without reservation. If we were to die today, so be it.

We would die together. I had bargained with the Mother of the Gods Herself to ensure no one would be left behind to suffer such grief.

"Did you think you could come into my house and disrespect me without paying the consequences?" Her words swirled in the wind, tearing at my clothes. "No illusion lasts forever, Shara. Especially the illusion of love."

That was it, I finally realized. My existence didn't piss her off. She was furious because I still believed in love.

For me, love wasn't an illusion at all, and that infuriated her. Because she'd seen the ugly side of that coin at some point in her life. She wanted to shatter my belief in that illusion by forcing me to take a Blood that I didn't love.

That I would never love.

And give herself a spy at the same time.

:I have it!: Carys crowed in my head. *:Il Pentamerone. It's a collection of Italian fairy tales, and one of them is called "The Three Sisters." It's about—:*

:I don't have fucking time for this.: Through the bond, I seized her head in both hands and...

Drank.

I pulled on her knowledge, swallow after swallow of the book she'd found. The story of a young, pretty, but common girl named Nella, who'd loved a prince, and the two jealous sisters who betrayed them. Her prince was dying, so she went on a quest to save him.

But when she came to heal him...he didn't recognize her.

He couldn't see through her illusion.

Which shattered her completely.

I released Carys, and she stumbled backwards in shock. Hopefully I hadn't damaged her or wiped her memories. I didn't have time to check on her.

Marne's idyllic summer day darkened. Thick black clouds blanketed the sky. Her howling winds bit at my skin. Locusts pummeled me with hard shells. Scratchy legs on my skin. Jaws clamping down. Tearing. The noise of their wings filled my head, a drumming, pounding drone meant to drive me insane.

Of course, the goddess of the harvest would know all about the scourge of a locust horde.

I gritted my teeth, fighting down my instinctual need to fight. To seize my power and strike back. That was what she wanted.

She wanted a reason to obliterate me and my entire house. All I had to do was break the conditions she'd set when I stepped into her nest, and she'd be perfectly within her legal rights to do whatever she wanted with us.

I made myself stand there. And take it. I'd take whatever she threw at me and smile while she did it.

I focused on her. Her golden hair perfectly coiled around her head. Her beautiful, ancient Italian villa. A queen who wore diamonds and silk to tea and fed fancy dishes to her cat on fine china. Wealthy and powerful beyond measure.

But she'd welcomed me to her house alone.

No Blood at her back. No friends. Not even her consiliarius. Byrnes didn't even live on the same continent.

Thinking of him made me remember Kevin's memory. Marne Ceresa, the queen of Rome, doing a simple household chore. *"Don't ever forget where you came from."*

I couldn't possibly fathom the long years of her life. I was too young, and she'd lived here for hundreds of years, in a villa that still used a fucking Roman aqueduct. For all I knew, she'd been alive when it'd first been built.

While I hadn't even been raised in a proper nest.

No wonder she'd pitied me and found my upbringing so shocking.

As shocking as a naïve slip of a girl who still believed in love.

The girl from the story. Nella. Marne. *Marnella.*

The high, sweet ringing of the goddess's bell cut through the droning locusts.

"Marnella! Don't ever forget where you came from!"

The howling locust horde dissolved as suddenly as she'd called them. I staggered a little, still caught up between my Blood.

My gown. It'd been soggy and disgusting after my trip through the pond. The silk hopelessly ruined.

Now, it was dry. The white, diaphanous silk was pristine.

My hair. Dry and controlled in a thick braid. After being whipped by a hurricane.

I jerked my gaze up to Marne's face, not surprised to see she now wore a formal golden gown heavily studded with diamonds and pearls. Was the gown only an illusion? Or had her idyllic tea party been the illusion? I would probably never know for sure.

"I haven't heard that name in centuries." Her formidable gaze raked over me, looking for the ace tucked up my sleeve. Or perhaps she was looking for the invisible wires or hidden compartment. Some illusion that hid my true identity. Because a twenty-two-year-old queen would never get the best of her. "How did you know?"

I smiled brightly. "I love it when my Blood read to me."

Speaking of… :*Carys?*:

:*What now?*: She retorted. :*Want to suck another book out of my brain?*:

I had to laugh. She was fine and back to her crusty self. :*Thank you.*:

"Well. I suppose your illusion still holds, Shara." Marne's lips curved slightly, but it wasn't a smile of joy or hope or even mockery. It was too brittle and didn't reach her eyes at all. "If you continue to remember where you came from, then perhaps it will last longer than mine."

I didn't try to tell her that my love wasn't an illusion at all. She wouldn't understand.

Rik pulled the crown from my grip and set it on my head, shifting it until it sat just right. "It's time for your formal presentation to House Ceresa, Your Majesty."

"Goddess help us." She smiled, and this time I believed the wry twist of her lips. "My court will never be the same."

29

SHARA

I squeezed Gina's hand, fighting to control my nerves. I'd done this several times before, but never on this grand of a scale.

Dressed in white livery with gold buttons and trim, the man at the door called my alpha's name in a loud voice. "Her Majesty's alpha, Alrik Hyrrokkin Isador."

Rik winked at me over his shoulder and then strode down the red carpet that lined the presentation hall.

Hall. Ha. What a joke. This was a fucking palace.

White marble pillars lined the walkway. The walls were all paneled in dark, rich wood draped in heavy red velvet. I hadn't even gotten to the throne yet, which from here, looked like it was going to rival the glory of the sun god's ornate seat.

:It's a gaudy hunk of garbage,: Daire said, making me giggle. :It must be very uncomfortable. If she offers you a seat, you should definitely sit on Rik instead. He'll be softer.:

Whispers and gasps drifted through the massive doors as Marne's subjects took in my alpha's appearance. She'd offered to have a new suit scrounged up for him when she'd sent her servants for some clothes for Okeanos, but Rik had refused.

The seams of his tuxedo pants still held—barely. His shirt was torn and bloody. He wore that stain proudly, and the onlookers definitely knew what it meant.

My Blood and I had tangled with the queen of Rome. But we were still here, still alive, and now, she was formally announcing our presence to her court.

I'd won.

Against all odds, I had stood firm against Marne Ceresa and won a reprieve. At least for now.

"Ma'am," the man whispered. "It's time."

Gina squeezed my hand and then stepped over to the door for her announcement. Marne had insisted that each of us be presented separately. Her court, her rules. Even though the thought of having to walk down that red carpet with thousands of people staring at me almost made me run for the koi pond again.

"Her Majesty's First Consiliarius, Gina Isador."

Oh goddess. It was my turn now. My palms were clammy, my stomach rolled like I was a seasick tourist, and my heart pounded so hard I almost missed my own announcement.

"Her Majesty Shara Isador, daughter of Isis, She who is and was and always will be." The man slammed a staff down on the marble so hard that the sound crashed through the court. "House Isador comes before Her Majesty Marne Ceresa, daughter of Ceres, High Queen of the Triune and queen of Rome, the cradle of civilization. Come forward, all petitioners, and be satiated by the goddess of the harvest."

:Fuuuuuck.: Ezra's bear growled in the bond. :There's going to be satiating? Sign me up for that shit. But not from her.:

Guillaume cuffed the burly man in the head, the same as he'd done Daire earlier. :If you don't shut the fuck up, I'm going to stuff your mouth with one of the new Blood's tentacles.:

And so I found myself smiling, even laughing softly, as I walked down the red carpet. Hundreds of people stared at me, not thousands. It was still nerve wracking, but all I had to do was look at my waiting Blood, not the onlookers or the intimidating palace decorations. Certainly not the powerful, deadly queen sitting on the gaudy piece-of-garbage throne.

As I neared my Blood, a weight grew in my stomach. A heaviness, like I'd shifted into Leviathan and gulped down that gold throne and the queen sitting on it.

The weight grew with every step, crushing my organs. Making it difficult to breathe.

"Shara?" Rik whispered, reach for me.

But I turned aside. No. The other way. I whirled around. Yes. The weight tugged on me, deep inside. Insisting that I come.

Immediately.

"I'm so sorry," I managed to gasp out. It was surely rude to turn my back on the waiting queen and her entire court to just walk away, but I couldn't. Not. Go.

It was like a giant fist had seized my intestines and inexorably pulled me inch by inch toward... Something.

I rushed out of the presentation hall, clutching my stomach. Holding myself together. I shoved open a door and stared down a dark hallway. Doors were on the left and right, leading to goddess only knew where. I'd never been here before.

So what was I looking for? The fuck if I knew.

The pull dragged me down the hallway. I tried to turn back. Tried to find Rik. My Blood. But the pull slammed me against the wall. Coils tightened inside me, slicing through me. I couldn't escape. I couldn't go back.

Was this some last-minute trick on Marne's part? A boobytrap? Make me think I'd won, let my guard down, and then wham, hit me with this... this...

I couldn't even think of an appropriate word.

URGENT. COME.

I couldn't stop.

I stumbled through another door and started to fall, but

hands caught me. Rik. Supporting my elbow, he didn't try to stop or question me. I was practically running now, blood roaring in my ears.

DOWN.

I fell to my knees, patting the ground. I couldn't see. I didn't even realize we'd wandered outside.

"What is it?" Rik asked. "What do you need?"

"Down." I panted, swiping through the dirt. Leaves. Grass. Rocks. Big rocks. Stacked or... no. Tumbled. Like a ruin. I ran my hands over them blindly, seeking. A ring. A switch. Something.

"Here." Marne said softly, her hand closing over mine. She guided my fingers over to the right and up.

I felt the faint impression in the rock, the perfect smooth place for my fingers. A hidden sharp spike that stabbed my thumb.

Like the legacy box. It needed my blood to open.

Rocks ground together, a low rumble of something large. I blinked frantically, trying to see. It was so dark. I hadn't realized so much time had passed since...

I'd completely lost track of time. I had no idea where I was. Only that I needed to go down.

I could barely make out stone steps revealed as the ground folded aside, carrying the ruins and boulders away.

Rik took my arm, steadying me as we went down. The steps were so old they had started to crumble. But I could see a little better. As we went down, it got lighter. It didn't make sense.

Waves crashed overhead, slamming against rocks. We were underneath the ocean. I could smell the salt. We hadn't walked that long, so we must have crossed through another portal.

The stone steps ended at the mouth of a low, dark cave. The ceiling height was barely tall enough for me. Rik dropped to his hands and knees, crawling beside me, my hand on his shoulder.

Thankfully it was only a few steps, and the cave widened to a soaring chamber.

Instead of rough-hewn rock, the walls glittered like the inside of a geode. The air was charged with the energy of a giant crystal generator.

In the center of the chamber, a slender pedestal held a dark, aged statue of a full-figured woman with a large, rounded stomach.

"Great Mother," Guillaume whispered.

At his words, the rest of my Blood, still on their knees, leaned forward to press their foreheads to the ground. Mehen actually stretched out on his belly, prostrate before the goddess.

I started to drop to my knees too, but Marne pulled me up, locking arms with me. "We're daughters of Her daughters. You already made your offering to Her."

My blood, on the stone to reveal the stairs. Immense pressure still weighed inside me, making my ears throb. I still felt the incessant force tugging me toward the statue, but it wasn't painful, now that I'd responded to Her call.

The *Triune's* call. The very call I'd dreaded.

"This is one of three Triunes," Marne continued, her voice reverent. "Each court was given a symbol of the Great Mother imbued with Her power. The Skolos Triune has their symbol much like ours, though I believe it has a few other unique features indicative of their line. There was also a third…"

"Triskeles," I whispered the word I'd heard in the vision.

Marne nodded. "Another Great Mother statue, though slightly different. We lost Her many centuries ago when Desideria Modron began her campaign against the other courts."

"She wiped them out first," Guillaume whispered, his voice raw with a thousand regrets.

My Templar knight had been her executioner. He must have killed many queens at her direction.

:Hundreds of lives met their end on my sword.: His hell horse whined a miserable whicker of grief that broke my heart. *:Goddess forgive me.:*

"Since the dawn of time, three Aima queens would come together here, around our Triune, and conduct the Mother's will in the world. Until Desideria Modron wasn't content with her title as High Queen of our Triune. She wanted to be the Highest of them all. The Supreme. We didn't even have such a title, but she was determined to create it."

Pausing, Marne released my arm and walked a slow circle around the statue so it was between us. Not halfway around the circle—but one third. I glanced to my right and saw a slightly darker spot on the floor where the Dauphine would stand, if she was here.

"Naturally, the other queens objected strenuously to Desideria's plans. If the Great Mother had intended for us to be ruled by one queen, then She wouldn't have given us a Triune of Triunes. Suspicious of Desideria's intentions, Jeanne Dauphine withdrew from the world, refusing to sit at the Mother's court, though she also refused to relinquish her seat so another queen could fulfill her duties.

"As a result, our power and status weakened. We lost one court entirely, and Skolos withdrew to the furthest reaches of their realms, determined to preserve their bloodlines despite Desideria's reckless disregard for the Mother's blood that flowed in the courts she decimated. We lost the ability to sire new queens, and courts were failing left and right. Our days were numbered.

"And then Desideria mysteriously died." Marne smiled, a slow, deadly curve of her lips that made chills slither down my spine. "When a Triune queen summons another queen to her court, a record of that visit is submitted to our shared records. So I knew that House Isador had paid a visit to House Modron as summoned. I had no proof of any foul doings. Indeed, for all intents and purposes, I found that Desideria had simply gone mad, driven insane by her insatiable lust for power. House Isador had left weeks before without incident.

"And yet..." Marne strode back toward Guillaume and paused over him, where he still knelt. "How, exactly, did Desideria, arguably the most powerful queen alive, die? How was it that her own executioner managed to survive the extermination of her entire nest?"

Staring straight ahead, my Templar knight didn't move a muscle. He'd endured untold torture at his former queen's hands, and countless years in a French prison before that. I didn't think anything would ever scare or break him.

:Losing you would break me into a thousand pieces, my queen.:

I swallowed the lump in my throat. *:And so would I if anything happened to my beloved knight.:*

"Conjecture. Suspicion. That's all I had to go on. House Isador had long been rumored to be much more powerful than they publicly displayed, and though they'd never tried for the Triune before, maybe their queen had decided to play the game after all. She was rumored to have a queen cobra in her arsenal of gifts, with a venom so vile that even the High Queen of the Triune would not be able to heal herself."

Marne trailed a single fingertip around Guillaume's neck. She couldn't see the scar beneath his suit coat and shirt, but she knew his history. "You were rumored to be dead, but I searched for you anyway. You were the key, Guillaume de Payne. Only you would have been able to execute everyone in that nest, and only the headless knight would have been able to walk away. Am I close?"

"Close enough," he replied evenly.

"As soon as word reached me of Desideria's death, I began a new game. Someone had made a play for the now-empty Triune seat. The moves were careful, thoughtful, and seemingly insignificant. But taken together, with that single visit to House

Modron, I knew what it must mean. House Isador wanted a seat at the table. But they had no queen powerful enough to even think about it. Yet."

She cupped Guillaume's cheek, and my jealousy reared its ugly head. I didn't like her touching my Blood. Not one bit.

Even knowing that she only did it to bait me, I still didn't like it. But if G could endure her touch… Then I could endure watching it.

"My game was ever so much more interesting now," Marne continued, still stroking his cheek. "Assuming House Isador was not only successful in breeding, which alone would be a magnificent feat, but also managed to sire a queen powerful enough to take a seat on the Triune… Surely impossible. Yet the impossible had been done with Desideria's death.

"So I had to ask myself which Triune did Isador want? Your mother was widely known for her love of monsters. I watched and gleaned information from sources all over the globe. How would she do it? How would she conceive you? Her alpha…"

Marne paused and gave a pitying look at Llewellyn. "As much as she loved you, gryphon, you weren't able to sire her heir. So she had to go elsewhere. When I read that Mount Vesuvius had an unusual moderate eruption at Halloween in 1994, I knew who she'd gone to. With a father like Typhon, perhaps the new Isador queen would be more interested in taking a Skolos seat." She hummed softly, her brow creased as if deep in thought. "But the Skolos court was full and had been full for over a thousand years. Whatever could I do to open a seat up, without openly killing a queen as Desideria had done?"

"My mother," Okeanos ground out. "That was the bargain you made."

"Indeed. I captured the mighty king kraken, the only one of his kind. I promised Undina that I would take excellent care of you. You would live, no matter how much you tried to escape me. As long as she stepped down from her seat if and when the time came."

My head ached. This was some crazy long-game shit that I couldn't even wrap my mind around. It was like cutting off your hand hundreds of years before you could even think about picking up the sword in the first place. "But... Okeanos said he'd been imprisoned a hundred years. I'm only twenty-two."

She shrugged. "Blackmailing the Skolos queen was only one contingency of many alternatives. Once I knew Typhon was your father, I could eliminate the others. I had the lure to free the seat. Of course, I had no idea he would end up being your Blood. Even I can't see or plan for *everything*."

I couldn't even. The fucking arrogance and complete disregard for life.

She'd locked a man up for a hundred years... Just. In. Case.

What kind of fucking game was that? Who else had suffered or died for her *contingencies*?

"That was a fine, fine game your mother played, Shara. I mean it, sincerely." Marne clapped her hands several times, a mockery of applause. "Maybe Undina told her that I'd taken her powerful king kraken as hostage. Or maybe your mother had actually seen my possible move long before there was a need to call on someone trustworthy enough in Skolos to keep her secrets. Either way, you were born, and we began to play the game in earnest."

My life had been a fucking nightmare of a chess game before I'd even been born. Ironically, I didn't give a fuck about the game. I didn't want the Triune seat that so many queens had been willing to murder and kidnap innocent pawns in order to win.

And yeah, rape and torture, if I added Ra to that list. He'd wanted a queen of his own, surely to get his bloodline on the Triune and corrupt the very courts the Great Mother had created.

"The next move is yours, Shara." Marne stepped closer, a smile still playing on her lips as if she was inviting me back to tea. "You've been called to the Triune, but as your dear mother foresaw, you don't have to choose *this* Triune."

In my head, I heard her replace *this* with *my.*

This Triune would always be hers.

Though the Dauphine might have something to say about that.

Goddess above, I couldn't imagine being the voice of reason between a woman willing to kidnap and hold a man for ransom for a hundred years just in case she needed to blackmail his mother, and a woman willing to resurrect her adversary's poor dead mother and send her as a fucking zombie with a message to mentally torment her.

Though I knew very little about the Skolos Triune, I certainly didn't want to force another woman to step down just to save her son. Though if it'd been my son that Marne had imprisoned…

Rome would have been wiped off the fucking map by now.

The vision I'd seen at the bottom of the koi pond filled my mind.

A chamber, so very like this one, beneath my heart tree. Was it really the third Triune statue? The one we'd lost?

My magic hummed with certainty.

The choice was mine. As my mother had intended from the beginning. As Isis had intended.

I closed my eyes, and I felt the softest touch on my cheek. I smelled something sweet, like sugar cookies hot out of the oven, and heard the gentle tinkling chimes in my head. My mother, Esetta.

She'd made the ultimate sacrifice for me.

She'd died. So I could be free. Free to choose my path. Free to decide which Triune court I wished to rule.

Fly, oh dark wings. Run, oh silent feet. Rise.

The words Esetta had left for me in the room where she'd delivered me in complete darkness. Safe from Ra's corruption. Safe from the Triune queens' games.

"Lo, Father of Monsters, look down from Heaven and see what we have wrought," I whispered, opening my eyes. Tears slipped down my cheeks and I felt her ghostly hand brush them away.

I stepped closer to the Great Mother and dropped to my knees. Her features were soft and vague, but Her eyes saw straight into my soul. She knew my decision, and I felt only abounding love as I kissed Her rounded stomach. "Blood flows from the Mother through the Great One to the Daughter of Chaos. I have heard Your call, Great Mother, and I choose to take the Triskeles Triune."

Marne laughed. "You can't take what doesn't exist, Shara. Triskeles is gone. Lost to the sands of time."

I stood and backed away, deliberately shifting my path until I gently collided into Rik's solid bulk. He wrapped his arms around me. This mighty warrior, my invincible alpha, on his knees, waiting for me to make my choice.

Loving me whatever I decided to do.

:*Always,*: he rumbled in my head.

"There are two very important things you should know about me, Marne." For the first time, I used her given name without her title. Her eyes narrowed, her mouth flattening slightly, as if she'd bitten into a bitter lemon. "What this queen takes, she loves, and what she loves, she keeps for all time. I am taking the Triskeles Triune. I will love and guard it with every drop of the Great One's blood in my veins. It won't ever be lost again."

"And the second thing?"

"Could you delay recording House Isador's visit to House Ceresa in the official Triune record for a few days?"

For the first time, her mask slipped.

The mighty chess grandmaster, possibly the most powerful queen in the world, though I was sure I could hold my own if we had to trade blows, was suddenly lost.

She had no idea what the next move was.

She had played to win the board, but I had simply walked away from the table. It made no sense to her. Either you played to win, or you died. You didn't walk away. You never gave up.

I didn't either. But she was playing chess, and I was playing hearts. *For* hearts.

She didn't believe I should love my Blood. She considered it a weakness. Something to use against me, forcing me into checkmate.

This was *my* fucking game, and I was playing to win.

Not for myself. Not for status. Not for a bigger crown or a tackier golden throne or even more power. Because I had plenty of power, thank you very much.

I played my own game for one purpose only.

To protect the ones I loved with my very life.

"Why... would I do that?" She asked slowly.

"Because I know where Jeanne Dauphine is hiding. I know *how* she hides. And if you don't let her know that I've been here, then you'll be able to..." I shrugged, letting my lips quirk suggestively. "Do whatever you feel like you need to do. She's been neglecting her duty for how many years now?"

Marne's mouth fell open with shock. I'd rendered the High Queen of the Triune speechless.

It was so comical that I laughed. I couldn't help it.

I laughed until I sagged against Rik and only his arms held me up.

She frowned. Her cheeks reddened, either with fury or embarrassment or both. But as I kept giggling, her lips finally twitched toward a smile.

A genuine smile. From one queen to another with utmost admiration and respect.

"That's why you used the mirror. That's why you finally reached out to me. What the fuck did she do to you that made you decide that I was the lesser evil?"

I started walking back toward the surface, my hand steady on Rik's back as he ducked beneath the low ceiling. "She fucked with someone I love."

30

OKEANOS

In a daze, I followed the queen who'd freed me. To the grand Roman presentation temple. To the secret lair of the Great Mother. Through a hidden door that ended in a tree, in a land so foreign to me that it might as well have been Mars.

Yes, I would have followed her there too. To the ends of the universe. I would find a way.

There was so much I didn't yet understand about my new queen, but one thing was abundantly clear to me.

This queen played for love.

And that was a game I wanted to win.

Never in my long, lonely existence had I been loved. My mother had loved me—distantly. It was one thing to love her son, but an entirely different situation when said son turned into a hideous monster. She had shielded me from hurt, from the outsiders who'd want to hurt me. So she said.

But while lying imprisoned at the bottom of Marne Ceresa's pond, I had made an important realization.

If my mother had truly loved me, she would have fought for me.

Undina was the High Queen of Skolos. Descended from

Keto, the goddess of the most dangerous seas, she could have swallowed Rome with a furious tsunami, bombarded House Ceresa with hurricane winds, and leveled the ancient city unless and until I was freed.

Yet she'd chosen to do nothing. Nothing at all.

I didn't hate my mother. I couldn't blame her in the slightest. At least locked away in Marne Ceresa's prison, I couldn't harm or terrify anyone. I was "safe."

Even if I wasn't free.

This was freedom. Walking on two legs, breathing in cold air, feeling the dance of moonlight and starlight on my skin.

The blessed touch of another body against mine, who didn't draw away in horror.

My queen even had a pool of water nearby, though judging from the steam, it was hotter than I'd like. I would adjust. Let her boil me until I turned red and my skin flaked off. I didn't care.

As long as she smiled at me again. I didn't dare even think of touching her again. My true appearance was too repulsive. Too abhorrent. Too—

"Okeanos."

Even my name on her lips rang like a siren's call in my head. I dropped to my knees at her feet.

Goddess below. The tender acceptance in her eyes undid me. I crashed like a ship on the treacherous rocks of the Aegean. I pressed my wet cheeks to her bare feet and wrapped my hands around her ankles. "My queen."

"Huh." One of her other Blood laughed. "The new guy has a foot fetish."

Her blood caught fire inside me. She whipped her head around to glare at the man, and he immediately dropped to the ground as well, mimicking my posture.

"Forgive me, my queen. I only meant to lighten the mood."

"Usually I love your jokes, Daire. But I won't have anyone

ridiculed for their need, let alone their pain. He's weeping out of sheer relief that I didn't turn him away because of what he thinks is his grotesque appearance."

I squeezed my eyes shut, shame rocking me to my core. "It's not what I *think*, my queen. I *know* that I'm grotesque."

"Hmmm." Her low hum smoothed some of the sharp edges shredding my soul. "Let's complete the bond first, and then I'll decide the best way to address this issue."

"You'll be more comfortable in bed." The big alpha's voice crashed and rolled like thunder.

And then I realized what he said.

Surely. Not.

I couldn't.

I didn't dare.

"True." Her fingers danced over the top of my head and along my cheek. Settling beneath my chin, she tipped my face up to hers and gently pulled me upright on my knees before her. "But I have work to complete here, and I don't want to make him wait until I'm finished."

I opened my mouth. Shut it. I didn't know what to say.

Her lips curved in a knowing smile that made sweat bead on my forehead. "Are you more comfortable in water than on land?"

Was it a trick question? My name meant ocean in Greek. I was a king kraken. I'd lived underwater most of my life.

She nodded. "Very well. I could use a good soak. Nevarre."

Another of her Blood with long black hair stepped closer and started helping her remove the beautiful royal gown. First the magnificent crown of Isis. The train. An outer skirt.

Goddess. Help me.

The inner skirt.

Leaving my queen's nude body shining in the moonlight.

I couldn't not look at her. Even though her beauty hurt me. It hurt because I knew how this story would end. The kraken devoured the princess—or the hero slaughtered the monster. Hopefully her alpha would make it a quick, clean death.

"The rocks are slippery. Help me step down into the grotto."

I honestly thought she was talking to him rather than me, but her eyes never left mine. She lifted her hand, offering her fingers.

To me.

Trembling, I closed my hand around hers. I could certainly help my queen navigate moss-slicked rocks. I backed into the water. Sweat instantly broke out on every inch of my skin. The borrowed clothes clung to me, soaking in even more heat and trapping it against my body.

I was on fire. Boiled and baked to a crisp.

But what a fucking way to go.

She sat on a low partially-submerged rock ledge and gently pulled her fingers free. I didn't say anything as she began unbuttoning my shirt. It was a relief to get the material off my body. It'd take time before my skin adjusted to being out of the water, let alone covered by tight, constricting clothes.

"How did I miss these before?" She touched the silver piercings in my nipples. Flicked them with her fingers.

And I thought I would die. Literally. I could not breathe. Darkness filled my vision.

She jerked my pants open. Relief. Too tight.

Everything inside me uncoiled. The kraken surged toward the surface of my mind. Tentacles unfurling. Mouth gaping wide to devour its prey.

Stop! I screamed internally. *Flee!*

I'd never been able to control the monster. No king could.

:*But I can,*: she whispered in my mind.

Her blood flowed through me, a dark, winding subterranean river. Something silver flashed in the murk. Dancing with joy. Tinkling a melody that only I could hear.

The kraken dove into that dark underground river, chasing the promise of silver tails.

Back inside the inner depths. Hidden in the basement of my mind.

I thought she would lock him there. That was what queens did to monsters. They were imprisoned where they couldn't hurt anyone.

"I won't allow you to hurt anyone," she murmured against my lips. "But I refuse to imprison you. You will always swim free with me, Okeanos."

I clenched my jaws, afraid if I tried to answer her that I would sob again.

She draped her arms around my neck and gently tugged me closer. "Will you feed me?"

I swallowed hard. Nodded. I wanted nothing more, even if I expired on the spot.

Until she continued. "Will you fuck me?"

I squeezed my eyes shut. Desperately afraid.

"Why are you afraid?"

Her mouth brushed my throat and my blood tried to turn my body into a giant fountain, eager to explode into her mouth and give her the power my queen required. Her thighs closed around my hips, drawing me closer. A siren, calling the ship toward rocky cliffs and treacherous straits.

I would go. Anywhere that she called.

More importantly, I would go *away*. When I couldn't hide the repulsive creature I was. When I couldn't bear the horror in her eyes.

"Ah." She lifted her head and stared deeply into my eyes. "I've seen you, Okeanos. I fed your beast. I wasn't repulsed, but you wouldn't know that, because you didn't have my bond yet. You couldn't feel my emotions. It was strange at first, but I don't mind. I'll feed you again. Anytime. Gladly. Man or kraken. I don't fucking care."

"Did you mean it?" My voice rasped, a raw agonizing thing of misery, but I had to know. "What you said to her before. Did you mean it?"

Her head tipped slightly, her eyes shining in the moonlight. "What this queen takes, she loves, and what she loves, she keeps for all time."

Each word hammered inside me, blow by blow laying waste to the desperate dam that I'd built over the years to contain the monster.

I couldn't ask the question written on my heart. I had no right.

But her blood flowed through my veins. She read my heart effortlessly, and her smile broke the last vestige holding me back. "Yes. You're mine, Okeanos. I took you from Marne, and I'm keeping you for all time. Unless… you'd rather go free? Because I would rather see you free and happy, than here with me and miserable."

I surged inside her, unable to deny her anything.

My queen. At last. My queen.

She tightened her thighs around me and dipped her head. Not to my throat, but to the silver bar in my nipple. She licked and tugged, driving me mad. Surely that is why I grunted so viciously with every thrust. Why I tried to bash myself to death on her shore. Why I bellowed like the raging winds of a hurricane when she sank her fangs into my throat.

I poured into her. Every look of horror. Every scream of fear. Every cringe of dread. Every drop of shame. She took it all and sorted through the wreckage to find me.

To shelter me. Through the darkest storm.

SHARA

I was Shara fucking Isador. Last daughter of Isis.

A badass vampire queen, with twelve equally badass vampire knights at my beck and call.

Though only the newest Blood's come was currently smeared on my thighs, I intended to work my way through all of them by daybreak.

I hungered. Not just for sex, though yeah, I wanted to fuck them all, as many as I could get into my bed at once.

I yearned for their touch. Their blood. Their bodies pressed against mine.

Even if one of them had tentacles or scales or fur.

Bring it the fuck on.

Lifting my head from Okeanos's throat, I licked the blood from my lips. He tasted salty, like the ocean. Different, but good. A fitting appetizer for the rest of my coming feast.

I left him dazed on the rock ledge, his legs still submerged. His body *needed* the water. Without a pool to at least swim in occasionally, he would wither and eventually die.

Luckily, the goddesses had foreseen his need and already blessed me with exactly what he—what I—needed.

Something rustled in the grass up above the grotto, though it wasn't big enough to concern any of my Blood. A small, dark shape rose on the upper boulder, making sure I could see her. Penelope. She was back, and...

Another rat crouched beside her, slightly larger. No, two. Three.

:*Mates,*: she squeaked in my head.

Laughing softly, I shook my head. Maybe the nest would be overflowing with rats and crows by next year. Not that I would mind in the slightest.

I drifted into the middle of the pool and met Rik's gaze. "I'll be back in a few minutes."

His eyes narrowed, his jaws working as if he was chewing boulders into gravel. He never liked it when I needed to go somewhere alone. "As you wish, my queen. Though if you don't return in five minutes, I'm coming in after you."

"Promise?"

"You fucking know it."

I didn't take a deep breath or close my eyes. I didn't need to, especially now that I had access to Okeanos's aquatic skills. I willed my body to grow heavier, and I sank beneath the surface of the water.

I could see Rik and the rest of my Blood hovering along the edge of my grotto, their concerned gazes locked on me. Even Okeanos was upright. He started to slide in after me, but Rik dropped a hand on his shoulder, holding him in place.

This was my destiny. I had to see it unfold for myself.

I punctured my wrist with the tip of my nail, just enough to allow my blood to seep into the water. I felt the answering pulse in my magic. Power shimmered inside me, lighting up the dark, murky water. I glowed blue-green, as if I'd absorbed the kraken's bioluminescence.

I swam beneath the heart tree's roots to the dark opening, just as I'd seen in the vision. My skin tingled as I passed through the cave. A portal, I was sure, to a place not in this world.

A place untouched by humankind.

The Great Mother's secret lair.

Light flickered through the dark water, guiding the way. I surged upward effortlessly, as comfortable in the water as I had been in the air with my dark wings. I soared out of the sparkling pool and landed on my bare feet, dripping water on shining white sand.

Tall palm trees arched above the small pool. A midnight sky sparkled with diamonds. In the distance, I could see the shining tip of Isis's pyramid with a crescent moon hanging low, almost pierced by its cap.

Slowly, I turned, scanning the horizon. The rest of the landscape was wrapped in darkness. Uncharted territory, and off limits, at least for now.

I turned my attention back to the small oasis, only it had changed. The palm trees had closed over my head and turned into a cave.

A round table sat beneath a circular skylight so moonlight could illuminate the short, rounded statue standing in the center of the table.

She was darker than the one I'd seen in Rome, Her skin a gleaming polished ebony. White symbols were carved in Her rounded stomach. A triple spiral.

Triskeles.

I stepped closer to the table and laid my hand on the back of the nearest chair. It shifted and flowed beneath my hand, its back rising into the familiar outline of Isis's horned crown.

This was *my* chair at the Triskeles Triune.

I didn't take my seat. Not yet. Not until the Triune was complete.

Two chairs waited for the Triskeles to call forth their queens. I walked around the table to the second chair and rested my hand on it.

I saw her. The future queen who would take this chair. She was a child, at least in the vision. Hiding, I thought. Under a bed. Terrified, her hand clamped over her mouth to stifle her screams.

Shuddering, I lifted my hand from the chair. *Goddess, please protect her. Bring her safely to Your loving arms here at the Triskeles.* I looked at the other chair, but didn't touch it. *Keep them both safe. Wherever they are.*

Rik tugged impatiently on my bond. My time was up. Before

I left, I held my wrist over the Great Mother's statue and allowed a few drops of my blood to drip onto Her.

Love welled in my heart. Boundless, overwhelming love. My gift. My greatest strength.

My enemies would try to use my love against me, but I knew the truth now.

Nothing could defeat the might of this queen's love.

As I swam back through the pool, my mother's words rang in my head. *Blood of Isis. Upon this House She builds Her future.*

With a swoosh, I surged up out of the water like a dolphin, and Rik caught me, gathering me into his arms so he could carry me to bed.

As he always would.

The End
(For now.)

AUTHOR'S NOTE

Last books are fucking hard, guys.

I wanted this book to be Shara's crowning achievement. It needed to fulfill all of your expectations. Make you laugh. Cry. Turn you on. Make you think.

Of course, she also needed to make you scream with rage and then sag with joyous relief as she dealt with the mighty Triune queens.

And won.

Naturally. Was there ever any question that Shara fucking Isador would win this battle? I think not.

So what's next for Shara and her Blood? Is this really the last book?

Yes.

Oh sure, she wants to have daughters someday, and there may be little stories that come up. I'd like to write some short prequels for each of her Blood, letting them tell you what they were doing when they first heard her call.

But this is the last book in her epic adventure as I know it.

Yeah. Me too.

That's partially why this book took longer than I expected. I didn't want to let her go, either.

Shara has taken her Triskeles. There are two seats open, and the Great Mother needs those seats filled.

Their Vampire Queen is not over. We need them now more than ever.

Shara, though, deserves a break. She has earned the midnight walks through her grove. The puppy-pile cuddles with her Blood in a massive bed that doesn't devour the king of the depths. And yes, epic, endless fucking. She has twelve Blood now, who all want her love.

So while Shara swims in her grotto and nurtures her nest and her Blood with her love, let other queens take up the story for a while. Shara will still be here. If and when these queens need her help, she will be the first to stride into battle—or simply stand at their backs and lend them her strength and love.

Trust me, when Shara's ready to have her daughters, she'll have more to say! But for now, I'm letting this twenty-two-year-old vampire queen simply enjoy her Blood and all she's wrought.

Since Queen Takes Triune took me so long to write, I am delayed with Queen Takes Avalon, the continuation to Gwen's story, Queen Takes Camelot (still available for a limited time in Captivated). It's coming, as soon as I get a few short anthology pieces caught up for their deadlines.

I will also be writing Queen Takes Darkness, the story of the wolf king's sister, for an anthology. Watch for more details in May.

I haven't settled on titles for the other spinoff queens yet. But they will come once the details firm up in my head. All I know at this point is that the little girl's name, who's hiding under the bed, is Karmen.

What else is coming? Let's see... I'm going to rework an old story, Beautiful Death, for an upcoming anthology, Seduced by Myths. Isabella Thanatos was always supposed to have more than one lover, but as I wrote in the Triune post, I failed to give her the story I had intended. I need to rectify that mistake.

I'm also excited to re-release Lady Wyre's series, A Jane Austen Space Opera. Originally published 2015-2016 by Samhain Publishing before they went out of business, these books will be coming in the next few months. Ladies in space, with an assassin and a former lawman at her side! I never finished Lady Wyre's story and am excited to get back to her next book. It's at least a ménage, but Lady Wyre wouldn't be opposed to taking more men under her wing. I already have **four** finished stories in this series... So you'll get quite a lot of new reading material with this one!

I also have a super crazy and fun RAPTOR SHIFTER REVERSE HAREM story. Yes. Dinosaurs. I know. It sounds stupid. I wrote the first book as a joke a couple of years ago (before Queen Takes Knights), but I absolutely loved it. I have the covers. I just need to sit down and write the next two stories. I would love to have these out this summer, but we'll see how things go.

I also have a trilogy of covers to continue Crimson Black's story. Conjured Shadows was in the What Goes Bump in the Night anthology (now delisted).

Beyond that, I am open. Waiting for the Call that tells me which story needs to be told the most. I'm sure there will be some surprises.

I have covers, guys.

So. Many. Fucking. Covers.

Epic covers.

Just waiting to be used.

Dark contemporary, dark fantasy, more paranormal... You name it, I have it, and I want to write it. I'd love to know what you want to see next too, so shoot me an email or join the Triune and tell me there.

I hope you stick with me for the next journey.

Long live House Isador!

Printed in Great Britain
by Amazon

78568898R00180